CW01483601

THE GIRL FROM BERCHTESGADEN

BY ALISTAIR BIRCH AND KIM RIGBY

The Girl from Berchtesgaden © 2024 by Alistair Birch and Kim Rigby. All rights reserved.
No part of this book may be reproduced in any form or by any electronic or mechanical means, including information storage and retrieval systems, without permission in writing from the authors. The only exception is by a reviewer who may quote brief excerpts in a review.
This book is a work of fiction. Names, characters, places and incidents either are products of the authors' imagination or are used fictitiously. Any resemblance to actual persons, living or dead, events or locales is entirely coincidental.
Alistair Birch & Kim Rigby

This book is dedicated to Archie George Afford.

He was brave throughout the toughest days, faced everything with a cheeky smile, and was loved by everyone who knew him. Archie was the most precious son and adored little brother.

His favourite thing to do was play and dance with his big brother all day long. His smile and laugh were infectious, and he would light up any room. We miss him every single day.
Archie the Brave.
Forever 2

THE GIRL FROM BERCHTESGADEN

'He alone, who owns the youth, gains the future.'
Adolf Hitler 1935

PART ONE

1

AUTUMN 1931, *BERCHTESGADEN*

Dieter loved the morning. Perhaps that was too broad. He really loved the morning when he could see the sun rising across the Bavarian Alps to the tune of the dawn chorus. Today, he'd risen later, but that didn't matter. The rain had fallen during the night, leaving a glorious sheen across the grass and leaves. Locating a large tuft, he settled down to watch the river. Before the damp grass could seep into his threadbare trousers, he pulled the back of his shirt down to create a makeshift barrier. Settled, he spied ahead to monitor a heron perched upon a rock. The bird balanced majestically as Dieter looked on, entranced.

The animal reinforced Dieter's love of the natural world. It also reminded him of the importance of solitude. He knew if he moved closer, he'd scare the bird away, though not as quickly as a crowd would cause the bird to take flight. The only sounds came from the river as it flowed a meandering path off into the distance. Perfect.

After half an hour, a numbness seeped in, and Dieter stood and stretched. The heron was long gone, though spying three swans and a kingfisher maintained his buoyant mood. If the rules which governed his life allowed, then he would have stayed for the entire day, though he knew he had jobs to do. Reluctantly, he set off along the path, which curved off into the distance. He had a long walk, but that didn't matter. Stepping carefully around potholes and weeds, he almost danced along the path. So great was his mood. At one point, his step caused a loud squelch as mud threatened to suck the shoe from his foot, but it didn't matter, and he continued alone. As he approached the next bend, his nostril twitched. Something felt wrong. Dieter marched on, keen to push past the alien smell, but then he stopped. An enormous pile of rubbish lay off to the side, half wrapped in an acrid smoulder. Dieter couldn't identify most of the charred items, though none belonged within his paradise. The vandals had set light to the pile and, with wooden furniture at the core; the stack had burnt well. It wasn't just household junk he spied. Further along the bank, Dieter could see a cart and beyond there, he saw the boys.

Sorrow and disgust paused as his eyes narrowed to watch them approach. Seeing four of them, Dieter felt an uncertain knot in his stomach. A flicker of recognition sat tantalisingly out of reach. Did he know one boy? Maybe, he wasn't sure, but the others appeared strangers.

He could see where they'd come from. Ahead, perhaps a hundred yards, lay a ramp which cut upwards onto the road.

As they came closer, Dieter tried to assess who the strangers were. Playful laughter sounded across the gap, and they too stopped in shock when they saw the smoking pyre.

'That's a shame. Look what someone's done. It's awful.'

The tallest boy had spoken, though his friends all agreed. Hearing this, Dieter felt slightly reassured. At least they shared his values.

Bravely, he spoke up. 'You're right. The river is so beautiful. It's really sad someone dumped all this rubbish.'

The boys stopped. Dieter watched as each boy appraised him, and for a moment, he thought he'd misread the situation.

'Yes, it is wrong. My name's Stefan,' he said, offering a hand. 'The others here are Otto, Klaus, and Walter.'

'My name is Dieter,' he responded, while accepting the shake.

For a few minutes, the group discussed the rubbish, and if there was anything they could do. They couldn't touch half of the mess for fear of getting burnt or, at the very least, covered in filthy ash, but the cart offered one method of removal at least.

Within half an hour, Dieter felt elated. True, most of the rubbish remained, but together they'd wheeled several large pieces closer to the road. The group had gelled with a common goal of clearing some mess. Within minutes, Dieter's reticence had melted away as everyone mucked in. Now a new, smaller pile sat at the bottom of the ramp. Not a significant improvement, but further away from the river, and Dieter was sure a few items were salvageable.

Stefan tipped the last trolley load before cheering. 'You did a great job, Dieter. I don't think we'd have bothered if you hadn't come up with the idea.'

Dieter beamed. He wasn't used to praise, though this time it felt justified.

'Hey. Do you mind if we try something?' Otto asked.

The group whirled around and watched as he pulled the trolley up the ramp leading to the road.

'You're not doing what I think you are?' Stefan joked.

'Just get up here and help me, will you? It'll be fun.'

Dieter followed as everyone climbed the slope, keen to be included and equally intrigued to see what the boy planned.

'Right, this is my dry run,' Otto instructed, as everyone looked on.

The penny dropped as Dieter saw Otto's intent, and after their exertion, he had no objection to some fun. They lined the cart up and directed it off at an angle down the ramp. The tiny wheels made a racket, and the wooden cage picked up speed quickly, but as soon as it hit the bottom, the soft earth acted as a natural brake. Gleefully, Otto ran down to retrieve the trolley.

'Right, now we've seen it work, we're going to do it properly. Just stay with me when I go down, will you?'

It took some doing, but with Dieter's help, Otto climbed into the cart and the group pushed him off. Everyone struggled to keep up as they shot off down towards the dusty bottom, but seconds later Otto drew to a halt with a yelp which sent birds to flight. Dieter couldn't believe what he'd witnessed, though it seemed safe enough and Otto seemed keen to have another go. The group helped him up and, as though they were old friends sledging in the snow; they set about loading their next passenger.

Stefan went next. His run was less successful owing to his height, though he still made it to the bottom unscathed. By the time Walter and Klaus had taken their turns, Dieter was ready. He'd done nothing like this in his life, but suddenly the excitement took over and he had to try. Klaus and Otto helped him into the trolley while Stefan and Walter held the vehicle tight to prevent them from running away before they were ready.

From inside the cart, Dieter looked down. Suddenly, the ramp looked a lot steeper, and he wondered how the others had managed the run without showing fear. Too late, he had committed. He closed his eyes, desperate to hide his own emotions, which threatened to spill outward. He could feel himself shaking, though he hoped as soon as the trolley began moving he'd be all right. The group encircled him now as Dieter thought about his situation. A weird thought struck. He was in a trolley, ready to hurtle down a steep slope, while surrounded by a group of strangers. It was absurd. That wasn't right. Why would he agree?

A shunt came from one side, and he opened his eyes. Now he knew something was wrong. They had changed the angle of the trolley and now they were pushing. Dieter screamed as he registered their plan. He wasn't trundling down towards the safety of a bit of dirt. They had other ideas. All four boys were shoving hard, and the momentum forced Dieter down. Suddenly, he knew he'd made a terrible mistake.

He could barely hear their cries of delight above the screeching wheels which bounced along the stone slope. If he could, he'd have heard shouts of 'drown the filthy Jew,' echo across the water. Everything was a blur as he moved fast, too fast. Surely the ramp had to end soon and then they'd let him off?

Dieter felt a terrible bump which jarred his spine, but the nightmare didn't end. He was sure his head must bleed, as he felt his scalp strike repeatedly against the frame. And then silence. Just for the briefest moment, before the splash. Everything went haywire as Dieter dived headfirst into the river. Before he could react, the cart landed upon him, trapping him like a lobster pot. The icy water stung, and the impact chased valuable air from his lungs. Down he sank until he felt silt and rocks below. And there he settled, bewildered, trapped, broken.

Dieter couldn't work out how long it took him to climb out of the river. When he finally made it to the bank, the boys had vanished. Shivering, he pulled at the long grass until finally he found purchase and the strength to pull himself out. He felt battered, and as his fingers tracked the jagged edge of a cut etched into his cheek; he knew things would never be the same.

2

AUTUMN 1931, *BERCHTESGADEN*

Ingrid smiled as she crept away from the house, hoping her delicate footfall wouldn't disturb her parents. It took half a minute before she walked normally. Then, confident her parents couldn't see her, she allowed her lungs to suck in a deep sigh. At last, freedom. Ingrid picked up her pace, heading along *Bahnhofstraße* towards the footbridge where she would meet her friend.

In her arms, she clutched her precious artwork. Usually, she drew all the natural things around her, but today she had something special in mind. Today she would draw her best friend, Gerda. Friends since childhood, Gerda's scientific mind was the perfect counterbalance to Ingrid's artistic ability. The pair were inseparable, and the *Berchtesgaden* townsfolk had become accustomed to seeing the two girls together. One blonde head and one dark huddled together as the girls shared a secret. Today, Ingrid would create a masterpiece. She knew she could. It would become her birthday gift to Gerda. The idea gave her goosebumps of pleasure. All she needed now was the kindness of Mother Nature, and, of course, her friend.

She needn't have worried. As she rounded the bend, she spotted two girls by the bridge. She recognised the slender build and sleek blonde bob cut of her friend Gerda. The other girl was new. She was tall, much taller than Ingrid, with a long blonde plait that fell halfway down her back. Gerda hadn't mentioned bringing someone else along, and Ingrid bristled at the thought of sharing her friend with a stranger.

'Hi, Gerda. Who is this?' Ingrid asked as she reached the girls.

A beaming grin echoed back as her friend replied. 'This is Christa. Her family recently moved here, and she doesn't know anyone. I hope you don't mind, but I thought with it being such a nice day, she could come along.'

Ingrid did mind, but she offered a contrite acceptance all the same. 'Hi, Christa, I'm Ingrid and as you've already discovered, Gerda is my best friend.'

'Hey. Play nice.'

Ingrid felt her face burn as she flustered. Why was she suddenly in the wrong? Before she could respond, a new, softer voice broke the ice.

'It's OK. I'm sorry. I shouldn't have come. This is your time together and I don't belong.'

The new girl turned to walk away before Gerda gripped her arm, forcing her to stay.

Ingrid bowed her head. 'No, I'm the one who was in the wrong. You caught me out a little, but I am sorry I didn't welcome you properly. If Gerda likes you then, why shouldn't I. Can we start again?'

Gerda's grip relaxed and although her eyes flashed a warning, it seemed the crisis had passed.

'What were you both talking about before I arrived?' Ingrid asked as she tried to regain the initiative.

Gerda looked about to reply when something caught her eye and she nudged Ingrid to look along the riverbank.

'Isn't that Dieter? He looks half drowned.'

Ingrid's jaw dropped in agreement. Ahead, she could see her brother stumbling along the bank in a wretched state. Taking the lead, she dumped her bundle and sprinted ahead of the others.

'Dieter. What happened? Are you all right?'

The figure looked, and for a moment, only empty eyes greeted the girls. Then came the recognition at seeing Ingrid, followed by something else, embarrassment maybe as Gerda and Christa arrived.

'I'm OK. I just need to be left alone, and please say nothing. Promise?'

The request was impassioned, and Ingrid's head immediately bobbed in compliance.

'Of course, but you need to go somewhere and dry off. You must be freezing. Then, maybe when you are ready, you'll tell me what happened.'

Dieter patted a wet arm across Ingrid's hand before retreating further along the bank. She didn't know where he was heading, but for now, at least he was close by within the town, and that would have to be safe enough. Still, the sight ate into her to see his lumbering form.

'Who was that? He'd be quite nice if he wasn't sopping wet.'

This time Gerda rallied to Ingrid's defence.

'That, dear Christa, is Dieter, Ingrid's brother. And whatever happened to him this morning is none of our business until he decides it is.'

The strength of Gerda's defence surprised even Ingrid, but her friend was right. Something had happened which would stay secret until Dieter was ready to share. Before she could ponder any deeper meaning, the wind kicked up and Christa shrieked.

'Your papers.'

Lain down upon the bridge unguarded, Ingrid's artwork fluttered. Ingrid looked on in horror. She knew she'd recklessly discarded them when they ran down to Dieter. Christa was first to react, her long legs setting off at a sprint while the others struggled for breath behind. Within seconds, a swirling eddy formed, leaving Ingrid fearful she'd lose everything as her artwork whirled tantalisingly close to the edge. Almost in slow motion, Christa dived at the floating pile. Her athletic body disappeared into the mass and then they heard a harsh grunt as their new friend landed hard.

By the time Ingrid and Gerda caught up, most of the papers had either settled safely to the floor while Christa gripped others tightly. Looking down, Ingrid felt a pang of guilt as she spied the bloody graze across Christa's knee and immediately, she set about helping the girl back up.

Mud stained some, but most of the bundle appeared to be intact. 'Wow. Thank you. You don't know how much these papers mean to me,' she stammered.

'That's OK,' Christa replied. 'Does this mean we're friends now?'

With Gerda gripping them both in a hug, Ingrid's reply came easily.

'Yes, I think we're going to be great friends.'

3

SPRING 1932, *BERCHTESGADEN*

'Hurry, will you? He'll be here soon, and I won't tolerate any tardiness.'

The stern voice came from Helmut Weiss, who stood admiring his reflection in a full-length mirror. Alone, within his bedroom, his critical eyes scanned the reflection before hovering over his new insignia. The four icons marking him out as his newly gained rank of *Sturmbahnführer*. After dispatching a stray hair with alacrity, he turned. Confident in his own appearance, he needed to make sure the boy, Stefan, wouldn't let him down. Helmut turned abruptly before marching out of the room and down to the ground floor.

'Stefan.' he bellowed.

'Here, Papa. There's no need to shout. I won't let you down. I know how important today is for you.'

Helmut's eyes followed the sound until the dazzling sun forced him to shield his eyes. After blinking a few times, he inspected his son, waving an arm to direct the boy to turn around. The tan Hitler Youth uniform looked immaculate.

'It will do,' he offered.

Before he could critique the boy any further, their chauffeur stole his attention. The driver exited the car, pulled open the passenger door, before snapping his right hand upward in a *Sieg Heil*. Helmut returned the salute with enough gusto to cause a jab of pain in his shoulder, but he didn't care. This was his moment.

Alongside, Stefan echoed the movement, causing Helmut to gleam as brightly as the car's bodywork.

Helmut climbed in and then looked amused as Stefan attempted to access the car from the same side. With neighbours looking on, there was no way he would cede, and he waved the boy away dismissively. Impatience grew as Helmut waited for Stefan to drag himself to the opposite side of the car. His son's movement took barely seconds, but when Stefan tugged fruitlessly at the door handle, his patience snapped. He immediately directed his ire toward the driver, despite inwardly dismissing his son as the fool.

'What's the matter with you, man? Can't you see the door's stuck? Get it open, will you?' he roared.

The driver hopped as though scalded and scampered around to release the door, which opened with ease.

'I'm sorry, *Herr* Weiss,' he stammered.

'You'll address me as *Herr Sturmbahnführer* from now on. Now get us moving, or I'll have you out on the street before the day is over.'

The man paled and with the briefest of nods; he returned to the driver's seat and a moment later they drove off toward the parade ground.

****

Stefan noted the chauffeur's discomfort with interest. True, he felt foolish that he couldn't work a stupid door handle, but that moment had passed, and with the driver bearing the brunt, Stefan felt empowered. The sweet lavender scent of Edelweiss reflected both his surname and his mood, and he knew the best was still to come. Klaus, Otto, and Walter would be there, but today they would have to look up to him even more than usual.

As they journeyed down the road, Stefan exalted his newly found status as he studied the growing crowd along the streets. He itched to stand and offer a Nazi salute, keen to identify anyone who would defy the gesture, but with his father sat firmly alongside, he kept his posture low. Still, despite his slouch, he kept his eyes alert for any signs of insurrection. Ordinarily, he wouldn't expect *Berchtesgaden* to be a hotbed of aggression towards the Nazi Party, but today, with their special visitor, he couldn't afford to take any chances.

Halfway to their destination, he saw Otto. Clearly running late, his friend lumbered down the road, his tan shirt flapping away at the waist, while dark stains marked the boy's underarms. Stefan recoiled in disgust. *The other two better not let me down.* Before his father could catch sight of his flailing friend, he pointed at the largest mass which had gathered to the east of their destination. The group stood too far away for identification, but something in his gut told him they meant trouble.

'Who are they?' he queried.

An arm waved dismissively. They were merely ants; it seemed to show, who could offer no potential threat, although Stefan noted his father's left hand rested upon his pistol holster. The Mercedes swept down the street towards the group, leaving the gatherers behind. Within seconds, a furore of cheers erupted. Ahead stood a parade stretching out across the sporting fields with Klaus and Walter taking the head and Stefan exhaled a slow, deliberate breath. While a few lined up looked like they hadn't bothered, his friends at least appeared they'd made the effort. Stefan committed the faces of the shabbiest to memory, while pointing them out to his father, who agreed immediately.

Knowing his father would deal with the scruffy boys swelled his ego and as he exited the car, he sped across the ground with only one thing on his mind. 'You three. Why are you all dressed like tramps?' With his father's authority behind him, Stefan knew an opportunity when he saw one and seeing three boys wither before him only fuelled his mood. 'Look at you, you're cowering. It's pathetic.' A cough sounded and Stefan turned to see his father patting a glove into his hand. His heart leaped, causing Stefan to assess his father's mood. He had to get this right. Studying his father's thin lips offered no clues, but he had to do something, otherwise he'd look like an idiot.

Deciding upon aggression, he turned back to see the scruffs. Two of the youths had wisely stepped back, and that sealed the fate of the closest. Stefan swung his arm behind his back. He wasn't sure whether to punch or slap, but before he could accomplish either, someone grabbed his wrist, holding it firm. The leaping heartbeat returned. Only one person would have dared stop him from hitting the other youth. To test his theory, he tried to pull, but the grip held him tight, confirming his fear. *Damn it, Papa. Why do you always want to embarrass me like this?* Feeling like a scolded child, he turned slowly to face his father, fully expecting a stern rebuke. He knew the three unkempt boys would slink away, and the thought produced a silent scream that exploded inside his head. His inner fury meant he baulked at any eye contact with his father. Instead, he wanted to look anywhere else, and this error meant he didn't see the other man until it was too late.

The grip relented, leaving a red mark across his wrist. Stefan left his hand hanging in the air until the absurdly placed limb registered and he meekly lowered his arm. Internally, Stefan had directed his ire towards his father for the stupid interruption, but as he registered the newcomer, a tingle danced across his back while his jaw held slack. This time Stefan cursed inwardly. The one person he wanted to see was standing before him, while he'd played the fool in a needless display of aggression. And worse was to come as Stefan detected wide grins from both his father and the other. Were they mocking or congratulating? Not knowing infuriated Stefan, but he had to salvage something before the situation disintegrated any further. Straightening up, he clicked his heels together and followed with a sharp upward salute. 'It is a pleasure to meet you, sir. I'm truly sorry you had to see this, but some boys here showed disrespect towards you with their slovenly appearance.'

Stefan stepped back and spun, fully expecting the three to have vanished, but they remained. The boys still looked a mess, though each had exploited the interruption to tuck shirts and push their hair back into some normality.

'Baldur, my son is just like me. He won't stand for youth members who cut corners. How should we punish the three slackers?' Stefan spun once more, keen to hear from their leader.

Baldur von Schirach paused in thought while Stefan looked on in anticipation. *Come on, you lead the Hitler Youth, for god's sake. Make an example of them*, Stefan's mind screamed. Instead, Von Schirach studied Stefan, further fuelling his sour mood. A flurry of thoughts bounced within Stefan's head, most of them suggesting he could do a better job of leadership, when Von Schirach spoke to settle.

'Do you think striking them down is the answer?'

Naturally Stefan did, but what was the answer that Von Schirach wanted to hear? Going against his initial action, Stefan offered a moderated reply.

'Perhaps I was hasty and striking them for their failure, too harsh a response, though the Hitler Youth means everything to me and as one of the senior boys here, it falls to me to uphold the standards.' He wasn't senior, but he banked that Von Schirach, with the entire Hitler Youth to manage, wouldn't know that and with his father's support so close, his natural confidence won out.

'Bravo, you sound like I did at your age. Impetuous, sometimes angry, but in the end fair. So, now you've decided not to beat them. What do you suggest?'

Stefan beamed. Maybe Von Schirach was worth listening to after all. Allowing his eyes to sweep the vast field, he decided. 'With your permission, as there are three delinquents, I'd like them to run three circuits of the field and then, once they report back to us, we can send them home for the day, as I'm sure they'll be too sweaty for an inspection. It will keep them fitter and serve as a reminder to maintain our polished standards.'

Mountains surrounded their town, with Klinger Eck showing in the distance. Although several miles away, it meant the run he'd recommended held one steep path to the east. Three laps would challenge everyone there.

'Good. I agree with your assessment and since you chose the punishment, it is only fair you instruct the three you singled out to carry out your task.'

Von Schirach emphasised – your – in his response, which suited Stefan who wanted to be seen as the authority, but just before he could deliver the punishment, Otto lumbered onto the field to sour the moment. His friend looked ten times worse than the three he'd singled out. It pained Stefan to admit it, but in order to save face, he'd need to dispense a harsher punishment to his friend.

'You,' he shouted, showing the three boys. 'With the authority given to me by *Herr* Von Schirach, you will all complete three laps of the training ground while we watch on. Go.' Once they'd set off, he turned to address Otto. 'I'm very disappointed in you, Otto. You knew how important today is for all of us, yet you stayed in bed, feeding your face with your mother's pastries. You are in a worse state than those running in the distance, so your punishment must reflect that.' Stefan saw his friend's piggy eyes pleaded, but in front of his father and Von Schirach, he would show no mercy. 'You must complete five loops of the ground.' Otto appeared stunned.

With a hundred Hitler Youth boys looking on, Stefan walked up to his friend and firmly shoved him in the back until Otto lumbered after the three who'd almost disappeared from sight.

4

SUMMER 1932, *BERCHTESGADEN*

The weather felt mild and despite a recent heatwave, Ingrid felt a comfort which had been rare for some time. Escaping from the family home to see Gerda and Christa had become a regular activity which hadn't gone unnoticed, but for once, her mother hadn't interfered.

Ingrid picked up her pace, keen to arrive at the meeting early. Just one more turn. Approaching the corner, the familiar lilt of Christa and Gerda sounded, followed by giggles. Ingrid slid to a halt, intrigued to learn what her friends were talking about.

'I knew you liked him. It shows, you know.'

'What about you? I've seen you staring at that other boy. Have you found out his name yet?'

'He's called Walter, and he's dreamy, but it won't work between us.'

'Why not?'

'He's always hanging around with the other boys. We've only spoken once, but I feel he's interested in someone else.'

After further unintelligible whispers and laughter, Ingrid decided she wanted in on the conversation.

'Hey, you two, what are you talking about?'

The laughter stopped, and both Christa and Gerda flushed before regaining their composure. It was Christa who spoke.

'Just boys. Is there anyone you have your eye on?'

Ingrid squirmed. She hated to have questions turned back upon her.

'No,' she replied flatly. 'Though I'm interested to hear who you were chatting about just now.'

While Gerda remained quiet, Christa accepted the invitation with glee.

'Why shouldn't you know? I've found a boy I really like. He's called Walter, but I'm struggling to get to know him, and in a second piece of news, Gerda has her eye on someone too.'

Ingrid's eyes flicked left and immediately she saw a look of panic cross Gerda's face. Within a heartbeat, curiosity, empathy, and fear jostled for position within Ingrid's psyche. Aiming for somewhere in the middle, Ingrid wrapped a comforting arm around Gerda's shoulders before asking, which had bounced to the forefront of her mind.

'You don't need to tell me if it makes you uncomfortable, but we're friends and I care about you. Who is your mystery boyfriend?'

Gerda pulled away. 'He's not my boyfriend. I just like him, that's all.'

'Who?'

'Dieter.'

Now Ingrid understood. The idea of Gerda and Dieter seemed ludicrous at first, but after a few seconds of contemplation, she settled on the idea. Not that bad. There was only a year between the pair, and Dieter wasn't too awful for a boy.

Before her grip on Gerda's shoulders could become awkward, Ingrid relaxed and, after taking a step back, she faced her friend.

'We could become family.' Ingrid chuckled, immediately followed by a gasp from Gerda and a snort from Christa. 'I'm glad you like Dieter. Do you know if he likes you?'

The comments broke the tension, and all three girls leant in for an embracing hug.

5

WINTER 1932, *BERCHTESGADEN*

'Why must you always make a mess in the house?' *Frau* Stiepermann cried.

Ingrid turned away from her mother, a shadow masking her scowl.

'It isn't a mess. They're my drawings', she challenged, before retreating along the hall.

'Ingrid. Don't talk to your mother that way. Your drawings are beautiful, but you can't behave like that. We all share this space. Now go back and tell her you're sorry.'

The voice came from Gerhard Stiepermann and Ingrid immediately felt a pang of guilt at her father's reasonable tone.

'Sorry, Papa. I will go now.'

As she turned back toward the kitchen to mumble her apology, she felt her father's reassuring hand on her shoulder.

'Good girl. It's good you like to draw, but now you must gather up your sketches, or there'll be no dinner for you.'

Doing as she'd been told, Ingrid picked up the delicate papers with their chalk and coal etchings, taking care of their transport, before carrying the bundle upstairs. Despite a recent warm spell, the first floor felt cold as always, so she placed her artwork on the landing and settled her bottom upon the top step. The landing wasn't comfortable, though the other rooms offered a musty smell which clung to her and here at least a small amount of air could circulate. She knew they were luckier than many of their neighbours. Only a few days earlier, she'd visited Gerda, and both had lain upon bare floorboards while staring at stars through a gaping hole in the roof. The teenage pair formed a sweet union as they pointed at the night sky while discussing the mysteries of what lay beyond. Ingrid cast her artistic mind back to those conversations. Practically her twin, Gerda understood her and while Ingrid brought creativity, Gerda seemed to resonate scientific curiosity and intelligence. Together, with new friend Christa, who offered empathy to every situation, they made a formidable team. She hoped after dinner her parents would allow her to walk into the *Marktplatz* to see her friends.

'No. It can't be true.'

Her mother's shrill voice broke into her thoughts, and Ingrid leant forward to hear her parents' conversation. The voices quietened, forcing Ingrid to risk the creaky steps as she shuffled downwards.

'You were at the market. Surely you must know more than me.' Silence. 'Well, I heard a group vandalised *Herr* Huber's store. From what I hear, he woke and tried to fight them off, only to be beaten within an inch of his life.'

'I know this is terrible, but Gerhard, you're an architect, not a shopkeeper. Surely this won't affect us.'

From her hidden vantage on the stairs, she sensed her father's impatience as he let out a grunt.

'How can you say that? Of course, it affects us. We've known *Herr* Huber for years. Have you forgotten *Frau* Huber babysat a few times when the children were young? We can't turn our backs on them.'

'I know darling, and I didn't mean we should abandon our friends, but surely this is a one-off act of thievery.'

'Thieves? They may have killed him, he's in such a bad way. Don't you see what is happening around us? Listen to me Freda, people are turning away from us, from our community. We're Jews and for no reason I can understand, we are on an ever-growing hate list. We've already seen how little work is coming through and it will only get worse. And this thing, with the shop, it won't be the last time, just you wait.'

'Oh, Gerhard. Is it really that bad? Do you think the children will come to harm?'

Ingrid stiffened as silence greeted the question. Finally, her father responded.

'Yes. I think we're all in danger. I don't think we should stay in Germany.'

After an electric jolt that ran the length of her spine, tears formed in Ingrid's eyes. What did it mean? Surely, they wouldn't stop her from seeing Gerda and Christa at school. This news was devastating. Straining her ears, Ingrid listened, desperate to learn more. An eerie silence settled beneath her and she pictured her parents comforting one another, but then her father spoke again.

'You know I'm right. This is just the beginning. They can't stay in school, not with the new pro-Nazi teachers they've just hired, and if things worsen, we may need to leave the country.'

'I...don't know, there must be a better way. Where would we go?'

Ingrid's body tensed as she waited for an answer.

'England, or perhaps the United States.'

Ingrid pressed a hand over her mouth to stifle her outcry. She did not know who these people were, the ones who'd destroyed *Frau* Huber's shop, but she could immediately see the consequences, and moving schools was just the start.

Suddenly, the mildew on the bedroom walls wasn't such a problem, after all.

6

WINTER 1932, *BERCHTESGADEN*

Frau Stiepermann succumbed to her daughter's continued pleas. 'Enough, Ingrid. You may see your friends, but be back in time for supper. We must be careful.'

Her mother's warning played in Ingrid's mind as she crossed the river and made her way up the steep hill towards town. Surely, the attack on *Herr* Huber's store was an isolated incident? She didn't want to consider the repercussions. She didn't want to connect that attack with the recent treatment Dieter had received at the hands of the local boys.

The girl was content in *Berchtesgaden*. There was a hint of something more with a boy. She'd kept that quiet. Not even Gerda and Christa were aware. It was special, something she tucked away inside, something she could bring out in the darker moments that were becoming all too frequent.

Ingrid reached the *Franziskaner* church and turned right along *Maximilianstrasse*, toward Gerda's house. Like Christa, Gerda lived above the *Marktplatz*, although Gerda's house was not as grand as the Schneider house on *Doktorberg*. It didn't matter. Ingrid and Gerda had spent countless hours together in the small and cheerful house tucked away behind the *Königliches Schloss*, building memories, building their friendship.

Each summer, Ingrid took delight in the window boxes that adorned the Muller family house. *Frau* Muller insisted on doing things differently, planting white geraniums instead of the traditional red, and interspersing the white with violet petunias in a nod to the traditional white and blue Bavarian colours.

Another two minutes uphill, and Ingrid reached Gerda's house, slightly out of breath. She heard laughter coming from her friend's bedroom and she bounded up the stairs, eager to be a part of the merriment. Ingrid reached the doorway and froze, her mouth open in disbelief.

Gerda and Christa turned, their cheeks flushed with excitement. 'Come look, Ingrid.' They dragged her into the room. 'We received our League of German Maidens uniform today.'

They'd lain two dark blue skirts out on the bed, with two crisp white, short-sleeved blouses above. Kerchief-style neckties completed the look, with leather barrettes to hold the scarves in place. Ingrid's eyes darted between the uniforms and her delirious friends. 'I...I didn't know you'd joined,' she stuttered.

'Oh yes, Christa and I joined up together,' Gerda said.

A sudden stab of envy hit Ingrid. *I'm not a part of this. I never can be.*

'It will be wonderful, Ingrid,' Gerda continued, oblivious to Ingrid's discomfort. 'They've given us an entire program of events. We'll learn about farming, domestic work and physical exercises.'

Exercises? Ingrid stared at her petite friend. Since when had Gerda ever been interested in physical exercise? 'But what of your plans to study science at Frankfurt University, Gerda?'

Gerda's pale face flushed. 'There'll be time for that, I'm sure. This is more important now.'

'That's right. We'll attend all the major celebrations and parades in Munich and Nuremberg,' Christa spoke up. 'You'll have to grow your hair longer, Gerda.' She eyed her friend's short blonde bob. 'It will look so much nicer in braids.'

While her two friends laughed and hugged, Ingrid shivered.

7

WINTER 1932, *BERCHTESGADEN*

The girls met a week later, at 4 p.m. after school on Friday. Now that Dieter and Ingrid were at a separate school, Ingrid missed seeing her friends and was grateful for the catch-up. The girls could chat freely, share some gossip, and have a giggle, before slipping back into the maturity required of them as teenaged daughters.

Ingrid glanced at her wristwatch as she arrived at Gerda's house. Five minutes to four, perfect timing. After greeting Gerda's mother at the door, she heard Christa's voice carrying down the stairs, and an ugly emotion flared in her stomach. *I never get the chance to talk with Gerda alone anymore*, she lamented. However, she brightened considerably when she heard the girls discussing the upcoming holidays.

'Hi, Gerda. Hi, Christa,' she said, entering the room. 'What's the plan for this holiday weekend? Perhaps we can all do something together.'

Christa frowned, and Gerda's face was suspiciously blank.

'Oh, we can't do that, Ingrid,' Christa said, a patronising tone creeping into her voice. 'Gerda and I are attending the League of German Maidens camp. We'll be working on the land near Bad Reichenhall. Everyone has to do it in their first year. Hitler Youth do the same thing.'

'Do they?' Ingrid said, her voice stony.

'Oh, yes.' Christa prattled on, oblivious to Ingrid's annoyance. 'It's a prerequisite before we do any advanced studies. We learn to

23

be more responsible. It certainly helps in circumstances like we experienced in school today, doesn't it, Gerda?'

Gerda nodded half-heartedly and muttered something unintelligible.

Ingrid's eyes darted between the pair. 'What happened at school today?'

'It's been a long time coming.' Christa hedged. 'And to be honest, he deserved it. How did he think he'd get away with it?'

'Who?' Ingrid's impatience was growing.

'*Herr* Huber,' Gerda finally spoke up. 'They have dismissed him as head teacher.'

Ingrid's hands flew to her mouth. 'Good gracious. What did he do?'

'The silly old fool refused to display the swastika in the classroom. And he didn't return the *sieg heil*, either. It's quite clear he's unfit for the job. He can't keep up with the times.'

****

Her head reeling, Ingrid left Gerda's house. She hurried towards the marketplace, head down as she contemplated this latest news. Christa was right: in some regards, *Herr* Huber's dismissal came as no surprise. He was a gruff, older man, with old-fashioned values and little time for the social standing of his student's parents. His job was to teach the children of *Berchtesgaden*, not to pander to their parents and their new-found political allegiance.

It convinced Ingrid that this had something to do with Stefan Weiss, although Christa had steered away from the topic. *She wouldn't dare to say a word*, Ingrid thought. The girl had made remarkable inroads in her short time in the village, befriending most of the girls in their class and quite a few of the boys, too. *Boys that I'd pay to stay away from, including the arrogant Stefan Weiss and his band of Hitler Youth thugs.*

Christa's choice of friends was a side issue. It was the girl's reaction to *Herr* Huber's dismissal that bothered Ingrid. There had been no sympathy for the head teacher rather, Christa detailed his downfall with excruciating detail, gloating over his humiliation and even laughing when she described the tears on the old man's cheeks. And worse, Ingrid had detected the faint creep of a smile on Gerda's face as Christa told the story. *Oh, Gerda. Where is your compassion? This man has taught us since we were children.*

Dieter's bullying, the violence against *Herr* Huber, and then his cruel dismissal from the school. *When will this end?* Ingrid thought as she reached the fountain. *And who can we trust?*

A figure darted around the corner and bumped into her. '*Entschuldigung,*' a male voice muttered. There was a pause, then the young man looked down at her in shocked surprise. 'Ingrid. It's you.'

Ingrid caught her breath. 'Walter. It's good to see you.'

The tall boy took her by the arm, drawing her away from the major thoroughfare. 'It's been too long since I've seen you, particularly now we're not in the same school.' His blue eyes were dark with emotion, and he sounded genuinely upset.

'I know,' she replied. 'I've only just found out about *Herr* Huber.'

Walter frowned. 'That's Stefan for you. He got rid of him. I think he's been harbouring a long-term grudge. But look,' he took her hand, 'I don't want to talk about that. Come and see me again, please. I've missed you, *mein schatzi.*'

Ingrid's heart fluttered at his affectionate words. She knew it was wrong for a girl of her age to meet with a boy unchaperoned. If her parents found out, they'd punish her soundly. Despite her fear, she bit down on her lips and nodded, her eyes shining. 'I can come tomorrow if you're home.'

Walter's face lit up with a smile. 'I'd like that very much. Until tomorrow, sweet Ingrid.'

8

WINTER 1932, *BERCHTESGADEN*

'Ingrid, you'll not be attending school today,' *Frau* Stiepermann announced at breakfast. '*Herr* Huber is still struggling after the attack and *Frau* Huber needs help in her shop.'

Ingrid did not acknowledge her mother. Head down, she toyed with the small piece of pumpernickel on her plate.

'Did you hear a word I said?'

The girl raised her head, and *Frau* Stiepermann drew in a sharp breath. 'Liebchen, what's the matter? Why are you crying?'

'Nothing's the matter, Mama. Nothing.' Ingrid wiped angrily at the telltale tears. How could she explain to her mother? 'I'll finish up here and go to *Frau* Huber.'

She took her plate to the sink and washed it. Her mother had caught her in a rare moment of vulnerability, and she vowed it would never happen again.

Ingrid's mind strayed to the events of two weeks ago, and she pushed the thoughts away. *No. I can't look at it.* After weeks of surreptitious flirting, she'd visited Walter and opened her heart to him, and it had ended in disaster. *Worse than a disaster*, Ingrid corrected herself. What happened was both perverted and terrifying, thanks to Stefan Weiss and his hideous sense of entitlement. And Walter had crumbled to Stefan's will with barely a whimper.

Ingrid decided she hated all the members of Stefan's Hitler Youth gang. The group had progressed far beyond the mantle of

26

schoolyard bullies. They'd humiliated Dieter on one occasion, and now Stefan had done something unspeakable to her. She would not tell, she couldn't. She could only pray that in a month's time, her body was unaffected. The alternative sent shudders rippling through her.

****

Later that afternoon, three youths approached the Konditorei in the marketplace. The two boys and girl were in high spirits. School had finished for the day, and the trio were laughing at a private joke as they passed the Huber store.

Ingrid watched the group, hidden safely inside, behind the repaired shopfront. Stefan, Christa…and Walter. Her heart leapt in her chest and then sank. Whatever love she'd felt for the boy was gone. Walter did not care for her, that much was clear. He'd valued his reputation above all else. He was weak, and Ingrid needed powerful people around her, not weaklings.

Christa had also made her intentions clear in the last week: Walter was the grand prize, and she would do anything to win him over. Ingrid watched the tall blonde girl touch Walter's arm, her pale blue eyes awash with adoration. The boy saw Christa's look, and he blushed, averting his gaze.

Before the three could enter the pastry shop, a stout figure came into view, blocking their entry.

'Move out of the way, woman.' Stefan blustered at *Frau* Huber. 'You know who we are. We're here to spend our money. Don't make us wait.'

Frau Huber placed her hands on her hips. 'Yes, I know who you are, Stefan Weiss. You're not as clean as your name suggests, are you? My favourite memory is of you aged seven, wetting your pants in front of the school, when my husband outed you for stealing. I bet your father doesn't know about that, does he?'

Stefan's cheeks burnt with humiliation, but *Frau* Huber was only getting started. The shopkeeper's wife was three steps above the youths, and she fully used the height advantage, glaring down at the trio. 'I imagine you've been waiting all this time to seek revenge, haven't you? But what you did was unforgivable. My husband did not deserve the treatment he received at your hands, Stefan Weiss. It was *you* and your slippery words to the *Gruppenführer* that resulted in his dismissal from the school.'

Stefan drew himself up. 'How dare you. My father will hear about—'

'I'm not finished,' *Frau* Huber interrupted, her voice steely. 'I don't care *who* you are, or who your father is, Stefan Weiss. And you two' – she turned to Christa and Walter – 'what are you doing hanging around with Stefan? He's the last person I would choose as a friend.'

The old woman had worked herself into a state, her face flushed with anger. 'After twenty years of faithful service, you've guaranteed my Franz will never work again. For that reason, the three of you – and yes, Klaus and Otto as well, Stefan – are no longer welcome here in the Konditorei. Do we understand each other?'

Stefan's face turned pale. 'You can't do that.'

He moved forward, intent on mounting the stairs, but *Frau* Huber barred his way, her arms folded across her chest. 'You and your gang are not welcome here. Take your custom elsewhere.'

Stefan swore at *Frau* Huber, and for a moment, it looked as if he would strike the old woman. Walter and Christa intervened; their faces red with embarrassment. 'Stop it.' Christa pleaded, clutching Stefan's arm. 'Don't make a scene.'

With Walter's help, Christa pulled Stefan away from the shop and into the central thoroughfare. *Frau* Huber witnessed their retreat, her eyes glowering. She stepped across the threshold, placed a *closed* sign on the door, and withdrew.

'A scene?' Stefan yelled after the woman. 'I'll make that witch regret crossing me. She's a sympathiser, for sure. I'll make her pay.' He swung around and the sight of the rejuvenated Huber store only further enraged him. Ingrid ducked out of sight beneath the window, her heart pounding. Had he seen her?

Outside, Stefan was still ranting. 'I'll make them pay, those dirty Jews: Huber, Stiepermann, all of you.'

Ingrid flinched at the sound of her family name, but before she could process Stefan's comment, a rock flew through the front window, shattering the glass and raining fragments down on her.

9

WINTER 1932, *BERCHTESGADEN*

Dieter punched his hands together in frustration. He'd heard mutterings within the family, but nobody would tell him what was going on. He also didn't like the cold, and today, few would venture outside as a dusting of snow shrouded the streets. It appeared the freeze had lasted months, though the temperatures had only dropped earlier that week. In boredom, he threw a wooden dog, which skidded across the floor before slamming into the wall with a dull thud. It was a child's toy, and he looked at the object with disgust.

Months earlier, his parents removed him and his sister from school with no explanation. At first, he thought the action a blessing, though Ingrid seemed distraught. The mood didn't last and now instead what he felt was a cloying anxiety he couldn't shake off. There had been a replacement school of sorts, though the rickety community house run by Rabbi Braunshardt seemed an eternity away from any education he could use. Everything seemed geared towards ancient texts and scriptures, certainly nothing of value in the modern world. The rabbi wasn't too bad, but more often than he'd like, the formidable *Frau* Vogt took class. The woman somehow made her voice carry across a noisy classroom, despite her petite frame. Everyone became silent when she spoke.

He saw that even his older sister, Ingrid, suffered the same fate. For her, it was possibly worse since their parents had dictated new rules stating the children should only use paper for writing from now on. Ingrid bore the withdrawal of her art supplies with better grace than he could, but then she'd always been the pragmatic one. Often, when the weather allowed, she'd steal charcoal from the grate and disappear to find a wall somewhere. Her simple distraction wouldn't work for him. He needed two things: natural solitude, or some mechanical object he could tinker with. The wooden dog lay on its side, offering no remediation to his plight. Instead, the object, minus one snapped leg, reminded him both of the prison his home had become, and the unfairness with which all adults now treated him as the youngest child.

Despite a gnawing hunger which should have kept him at home to await dinner, Dieter set out into the cold winter air. Taking care to avoid any icy potholes, he walked along *Bergwerkstraße* toward the river. Few others walked the streets, though Dieter waved at *Herr* Friedrich before the shopkeeper disappeared back inside to the warmth. That suited Dieter as he preferred solitude, heading towards his favourite hideaway, a derelict barn on the outside of town. As he walked, he could feel icy stabs within his chest as the cold air hit his lungs, but he paid no heed and soon he arrived. Climbing a battered ladder, he took himself up to the hayloft and from there, he could watch the natural world in peace. He smiled from up on his perch. The blanket he'd stolen from home was still there, tucked in a shadowy corner. He pulled the threads across his shoulders and, once wrapped, he adopted his favoured watchful pose. Ahead, the river ran slowly as ice threatened to stem the flow. Patting his pockets, Dieter cursed at finding them empty. He'd planned on snatching a crust or two. The birds would have to go hungry today.

As he settled, he shielded his eye from the low-lying sun, when something caught his eye. Shocked, he ducked into the shadows. It couldn't be, could it? With his heart thumping in his chest, he chanced a second glance. He recognised the boys and panic flooded his being. For a second, he froze, but then one looked his way, and he dived back into the darkness. Had they seen him? He could hear their voices, louder now, and he shrank back, pulling the blanket shield ever tighter. The freezing temperature of the morning reminded him of the brutal cold when they threw him in the river and left him to drown, and now those fears returned with a vicious inner force.

Dieter cowered under the blanket, convinced they would find him and equally certain they'd throw him into the river a second time. Only today, with lethal ice shards covering the water, he knew he wouldn't resurface. He didn't much like his life, but the thought of being cast into a watery grave was too much to bear. Questions ate into his brain as he thought about how cruel nature could be. Was he a mouse about to be eaten by a swooping owl? And if so, why? What had he done to be cast in the role of prey? They were boys, just like him. What gave them the right to wield such power and control over his life? And then he remembered. They weren't like him at all. They were Jew haters.

The voices were quieter now, and finding new resolve, Dieter chanced another look. The four boys had moved off and now stood facing away from the barn. An unfamiliar emotion stirred. This time, he felt anger. How dare they reduce him to a cowering mess, just by their presence? Gripping a stout beam, Dieter hauled himself up in order to study the group properly. His eyes narrowed as he spied the boys. Wrestling back some self-control, he suppressed the urge to lean out fully across the void to secure a better view. Instead, Dieter tracked a cluster of footprints which disappeared across the snow-covered track and there they were, Klaus, Otto, Walter, and last, the tall and overbearing Stefan. Dieter's fists shook as his tight grip turned them white. He hated them all for what they'd done, but his ire held a special place for Stefan.

The boys followed a low-lying wall until they located an object Stefan had chosen. The teen stooped down to grab a pipe, which he waved above his head in some demonstration of control. Next, he whirled about and brought the metal down hard on an oil drum. A dull boom echoed out across the field, followed by another. And then he cheered, repeated in sycophantic fashion by the others. Each boy took a turn, and as they continued their meaningless violence, Dieter looked on from his loft. While one teen pounded out a dreadful tune, the others paced around jackal-like until the circle was complete. Dieter viewed them from deep within his hideaway. Each gang member wore a similar brown jacket against the cold, but one thing stood out. They all wore a red and white diamond attached to their sleeve and in the middle lay the darkest of symbols, a swastika.

Dieter shuddered as he recognised the emblem and, despite the bile at the back of his throat, his fear returned. He knew these boys were members of the Hitler Youth movement and with this knowledge, his hatred intensified. They were the thugs who'd thrown him into the river, and their families were the ones who'd forced their removal from school. Evidently bored, the pounding stopped, and Dieter focused again. This time, Stefan passed the pipe to Walter before gesturing to the drum. It was clear what he wanted. After a couple of grunts which carried across the valley, they hefted the drum onto its side, before kicking the metal canister, which rapidly picked up speed. When the splash finally came, each boy roared with laughter before they set off as a group across the field. A cheer erupted. The sound carried clearly to Dieter's perch, and again, he ducked down. A second splash sounded, but this time, an angry voice followed the action. Dieter couldn't resist another stolen glance.

'Walter, you idiot. You threw away my pole. I only meant you to hold it while we rolled the drum into the water and then I wanted it back.'

Walter sank back submissively as Dieter continued his reconnaissance with interest. From his vantage, it looked like Stefan was shaping to hit the other boy. A balled fist wavered before Klaus calmed the situation by returning with another metal pole, which he offered to their leader.

'Thank you, Klaus. See, Walter, someone around here knows their place. Come on. It's time we left.'

Dieter expected no less from Stefan, though the rebuttal showed new insights into the group. They were gone now and, with clear ground ahead, he climbed down from the loft. Wanting more answers, Dieter performed a crouching run to the low wall.

Against his better judgement, he wanted to find where they all lived.

10

NOVEMBER 1932, *BERCHTESGADEN*

Dieter's breath blew out in plumes, and he clasped both hands across his mouth to stem the steamy escape. Ahead, he could hear the four boys. As expected, their conversation ranged across the cold weather and the fun they'd had rolling the drum into the river, any indiscretion from Walter apparently forgotten. Behind the wall, Dieter held his position in silence.

Slowly, the group moved off, and Dieter cursed. It looked likely they were heading towards the parade ground rather than one or more of their homes. Dieter wanted to know more about Stefan but heading to the parade ground would do him no good as up there, he'd only find more of their kind. He held the station while pondering if he should continue to trail the group.

Before he could decide, something shoved him hard, causing Dieter to tumble onto the icy ground. He landed hard with knees and palms bearing the impact as pain shot across his body. This time, nothing could prevent his cry of angst.

'Stefan, come quickly. Look at the dirty creature I've just found. He's a filthy Jew spy. This nasty boy was listening to us from behind the wall.'

The call had come from sycophant Klaus and lain prone on the icy ground. Dieter knew he was in trouble. Had Dieter been thinking clearly, he'd have scrambled up and fled. Instead, he froze, which gave the gang the upper hand. Now he sat, staring through bleary eyes, surrounded. They circled him in slow, deliberate movements. Stefan still held the metal pole, which he wielded with menace, and Dieter cringed. He'd seen the dents they'd inflicted on a sturdy metal drum. Was he going to be next?

Slap. Stefan patted the bar into his palm before repeating the process. The intimidation worked, and Dieter changed tack. 'I'm sorry I was watching you. I just wanted to see where you were going. You must see, I meant no harm.'

'Why is that, Jew boy? Did you think you could be part of what we are?' Stefan asked in disgust. 'You are nothing. You'll be nothing. Not you, not now, never.'

'I...I...' Dieter stammered before lapsing into silence.

The bar continued to slap against Stefan's hand in slow, deliberate movement which matched the circling. Dieter craned his neck, wondering just how far the boy would go, fearing the worst, before snapping his head around to keep Stefan in view. The taunting continued. A tiny part of Dieter's brain considered the rationale that last time when they'd dumped him in the river, it was further away. Here at least, near the parade ground, someone would come if they tore into him, causing him to cry out. Unless, of course, they smashed his head in first. The thought added another tremble to his already freezing body. 'What do you want with me?' he finally asked, showing bravado he didn't really feel.

As though he'd read Dieter's mind, Stefan swung his body about in a rapid movement, intended to scare. The others drew closer, and Dieter feared the worst.

'Halt. What is the meaning of this?'

Dieter's eyes, clamped shut in fear, suddenly snapped open. Towering over the boys stood a man. Immediately, Dieter's heart sank as he looked between the smaller figures and took in a black uniform. He didn't know who the stranger was, but it could only mean more trouble.

The boys seemed equally shocked as Dieter watched Stefan slip the pipe behind his back and pass the object to Klaus, who quietly propped it up against a wall.

'Oh, it's you, Papa. We found this boy cowering in the cold and weren't sure what to do.'

'Well, you'd better help him up.' The man grunted as he shoved the other boys to one side. Confusion flitted across Dieter's brain. Were they going to help him up? Had he heard right? Was this Stefan's father? Before he could plan any kind of response, he felt hands reaching down, each finding a careless grip upon skin and jacket before hauling him back to standing. Once Dieter was upright again, the boys stepped back, formed an orderly line followed by the salute which Dieter despised.

'You're Gerhard Stiepermann's boy, aren't you?'

Dieter couldn't hide his surprise, though responded with a simple nod.

The man paced as he continued his inspection. Suddenly, he wheeled about in the same manner Stefan had earlier. 'You three. Go up to the lodge beside the parade ground. I'll see you there in a minute.'

Klaus, Otto, and Walter kicked off as though stung, leaving Stefan, his father, and Dieter. Dieter's shivers returned. 'You'd best be off home before your parents worry. And…if you have any sense, you won't come around here again.'

Stefan looked aghast at his father's decision, while Dieter felt elated. Immediately he set off at pace, back towards the barn and from there back to home.

****

As soon as Dieter had disappeared out of earshot, *Herr* Wiess turned to his son. The officer's eyes were burning. 'I don't mind you beating the boy. After all, he is an *untermenschen*, but don't do it on our doorstep. Here, take this and go after him,' he said, reaching for the metal bar which Stefan had tried to hide. 'Don't kill him, but make sure he never comes near us again. Oh…and Stefan, you mustn't let anyone see you.'

****

Dieter couldn't believe it. The man, no Stefan's father, no less, had let him go, unscathed. It made little sense, but as he picked up

37

speed down the path, he let his shoulders sag as the tension he'd held found a release. What was he thinking? True, he hadn't identified where they lived, but did that really matter? Not really, he accepted. As he rounded the end of the wall, he cast a glance. Seeing an empty path, and no pursuer, he allowed a sigh. He'd expected Stefan or the others to seek him out, but there was no one chasing.

Feeling secure, he reverted to a plod as he moved back towards the barn. He'd stowed the blanket on the floor within the high loft, and he couldn't return home without it. Climbing the ladder back to his former vantage point, he found the threadbare lump, but as he reached down to seize it, his blood ran cold once more. He spied a figure hurtling down the path, wielding the metal bar. Dieter knew at once the figure was Stefan. Dieter's brain went into a frenzy as he tried to calculate whether he could climb down in time to escape. The answer was no. With every passing second, Stefan crossed the ground in a measured charge, aiming squarely for the barn. Deciding defence was his best strategy, Dieter looked around, vainly searching for anything he could wield as a club. Beyond dust, straw, and the blanket he already held, there was nothing.

'Jew boy. I know you're in here. Now that I've got you alone, where nobody can hear us, I'm going to teach you. Do you know what I'm going to teach you, boy? It's about time you learnt why I am superior to you in every way.' Silence. 'Are you going to stay up there, hiding like a pathetic coward, or will you come down and fight me like a man?'

Dieter's insides squirmed. There wouldn't be anything fair if they fought on level ground. At least atop the ladder, he held some slight advantage.

'I'm not dirty, like you say. There is nothing wrong with me, or my family,' he replied, though it was impossible to hide the tremor from his voice.

'Oh, but you are. You're a filthy Jew and if you don't come down soon, I'll get bored and make you frightened. How about I burn the barn down? That would clean you forever,' his aggressor chuckled.

Dieter gulped. *Would he?* He considered the threat. On the surface, it seemed unlikely, but that was only because Stefan would find it difficult to set the barn alight given the icy weather. Stefan had shown malice more than once. The uncertain tremor crept through his bones once more. He would watch and wait and if Stefan lit a flame, then that would force Dieter to flee. As he sat, Dieter sought the best vantage point. He needed to know if Stefan meant to climb up the ladder, but equally, Dieter had to check if reinforcements were on their way. He'd given up hope anyone would come to his rescue. No saviour would pass their isolated spot, but there was the possibility Walter, Otto, and Klaus could return. The standoff continued, though Dieter could sense Stefan's growing impatience. Every few seconds, a dull clang sounded out as the pipe connected with a wooden upright.

'I thought as much. Stupid Jew, you're nothing but a coward.'

Dieter gripped the top of the ladder as anger threatened to overrule his head. He pushed backward, sinking to the floor, acutely aware that something needed to give. And then he heard it. The creak. The same creak he'd caused when his weight had pressed down on the first rung of the ladder. Stefan was climbing to get him. Fighting his first instinct to back away into the corner, he peered over the edge. As expected, Stefan's mop of blonde hair was only a couple of feet away. The boy looked up, and their eyes met with a fusion of hatred and fear from which Dieter found difficult to pull away. Dieter's hesitancy would cost him as Stefan's left elbow reached over the top, allowing him to pull himself upward. In his right hand, Stefan brandished the bar.

Dieter kicked out feebly, but the action did little to quell the impending attack. Stefan was almost level now, with just one leg hanging back on the top rung, and he swung his weapon in anger. It connected with Dieter's wrist, exploding in a torrent of pain. Shrieking in terror, Dieter drew back as wide eyes sought an escape which could not come. Now, all he could manage was to adopt a foetal position while he accepted his fate. He tucked his hand under the blanket, knowing it offered no protection as the tears streamed.

A new scream erupted as Dieter fought through the waves of pain, trying desperately to orientate himself. Had a scream come from Stefan? Slowly and fearful the assault would continue, he shuffled to the edge. Below stood Ingrid wielding a pitchfork. Her eyes showed only lethal focus. At her feet lay Stefan. She must have pulled him down from below.

The heap, which had been Stefan, groaned before slowly getting to his feet, his weapon lost in the fall. Blood trickled from his scalp, but otherwise he appeared to have come through the drop unscathed. Ingrid jabbed the pitchfork forward, just enough to nick Stefan on the side. He immediately howled before leaping to the barn exit. From there, he ran in a lumbering fashion before turning and swearing in hatred at the pair. Dieter knew she'd bettered him and he was glad, but he also knew this was just the start.

11

Ingrid girded herself as her foot landed on the step, which would take them back into the family home. Behind her stood the cowed figure of Dieter. During the hurried walk back from the barn, she'd use the time to think and although it would be a desperate betrayal to hide the truth, she knew they'd have to lie. After the smashed shop window, she knew, no good could ever come of a Jewish family pointing the blame upon the Nazis. With her heart beating wildly, she called out. 'Mama, come quickly. It's Dieter. He's had a fall.'

Their mother flew out of the kitchen with eyes wide. 'Oh, Dieter, my boy. Come in, quickly. Let me see.' The teens moved forward and once inside the hallway, Ingrid pressed herself into the wall to allow her mother to appraise Dieter properly. She knew what would happen, but still her mother's scream caused Ingrid to jump. As the blanket slid to the floor, the pair looked on in horror. Dieter whimpered softly as his right hand supported the left, which sat limp at an unnatural angle. There was something very wrong with Dieter's wrist. After a moment of shocked silence, their mother rallied, pulling Dieter into the kitchen so he could rest his arm on the table. Despite being as gentle as she could, Dieter let out a cry of anguish.

'Ingrid. We need the doctor. Go get him, and hurry, while I try to make your brother comfortable.'

41

Ingrid turned and ran. Doctor Brandt lived almost a mile away, up the hill and above the village, and she soon felt her chest heaving as she gasped for air. A stitch dug into her side, but nothing would cause her to slow. With houses flashing past, Ingrid found herself at the Brandt's house ten minutes later. Immediately, she let rip, pounding her knuckles against the door.

'All right. Hold up, I'm coming.'

A bolt slid and as the door drew back, Ingrid pushed forward, causing the woman behind to cry out in dismay. 'Oh, *Großmutti* Brandt. I'm sorry for rushing, but we need the doctor to come quickly. It's Dieter, he fell, and he's broken his arm. He's in a lot of pain.'

The woman's features melted, and despite the intrusion, she turned to call. 'It's all right, mother. I'll tend to the girl. It's Ingrid, isn't it? Tell me, child, what happened?'

On any other day Ingrid would have bristled at being called child, but not today. Taking a second to gather her breath, she repeated the information.

As Doctor Brandt peddled furiously, Ingrid trotted at a slower pace down the hill. She felt torn. She wanted to make sure Dieter would be OK, but equally, she wasn't ready for all the questions which would come. Still, one thing brought a smile, the revolting Stefan. Seeing him turn from aggressor to retreating coward was one small win. She knew a scared face when she saw one. Soon, she spotted the doctor's bicycle leaning against their wall and she knew she'd need to offer an explanation. As expected, while the doctor tended to her brother, Ingrid walked into an icy stare from her mother. The gesture to follow to the garden left no room for the manoeuvre.

'Close the door. Tell me what happened.'

Once they were outside, Ingrid complied, silencing the doctor's muttering from within the house. While facing down Stefan, she'd felt fearless, but now her fingers fidgeted in anguish. 'I'm not sure,' she stammered. 'I'd seen Dieter playing down at the barn by the river, but wasn't watching,' she said before recovering. 'Gerda was expecting me, but then I heard a cry. It wasn't any animal, and I was sure the sound came from the barn. Then there was silence, and I wasn't sure what I'd heard. But since I'd lost sight of Dieter, I went to look. I found him crumpled on the floor. I think he fell from the hayloft and landed badly.'

'Hmph. Well, I can see your brother's broken his wrist. I think it will be too severe for Doctor Brandt to set, but I'll wait to see what he says before we decide what to do. I will, of course, ask Dieter what happened, and I want you to leave him alone until I've asked him, but thank you for looking after your brother.'

Ingrid paused. Was that it? Where was the full inquisition? She pursed her lips together in silent expectation, while her mother's gaze lingered. Her mother always knew what was going on, and she could feel her insides squirm. She wanted to ask to be excused but couldn't bring herself to ask. Instead, she waited. Eventually, a call came from within the house, and her mother moved off to see what the doctor wanted. Ingrid shut her eyes and exhaled. For now, at least, any wrath from her mother had passed. With the back door ajar, Ingrid could instead turn her attention to the conversation between the doctor and her mother. Everything sounded muffled and so, reluctant to go back inside, Ingrid moved off to sit on a solitary bench at the furthest end of the garden. Once rested, her thoughts turned to Stefan. One prevailing thought stuck. Ingrid knew she could have rammed the pitchfork into Stefan's gut, and not for the first time, she wondered whether her hesitation would have consequences.

12

DECEMBER 1932, *BERCHTESGADEN*

Newly promoted head teacher, Monika Vogt peeled back the curtains and stared at the mountains beyond. To her left, in the near distance, stood the parade ground, and the middle-aged woman wrinkled her nose in disgust. Off to the right, the view was much more satisfactory, as she gazed towards the towering Bavarian Alps, which had been her home all her life.

A mantel clock chimed, drawing her away from the vista. There was enough time before the start of school to dash off a letter to her brother, who lived in Stuttgart. After some local success as an artist, Martin made the move to the larger, more culturally progressive town. His career had flourished, and while Monika missed her brother, she was proud of his success.

Their mother had always encouraged the pair to be creative. *To forge an alternative path is the hallmark of courage and independent thought*, she often told them. Monika and Martin had done their best to live up to their mother's mantra. Martin became an artist specialising in cubism, while Monika followed her dream of becoming a teacher, where she could encourage a new generation of children to think for themselves.

Over the course of the last year, it had become apparent to Monika that this freedom of thought and expression was now frowned upon. Dangerous, even. And in the small village of *Berchtesgaden*, it was unwise to make too much noise. The meteoric rise of ultra-conservative Adolf Hitler had surprised many within intellectual circles. Some of Hitler's grand plans for the country could ameliorate their damaged pride and help rebuild the economy after some truly dreadful years, *Frau* Vogt conceded. But his desire to streamline all the children into the national bodies of Hitler Youth and the League of German Maidens was worrying. Worse, his attitude towards the Jews was horrifying. Thankfully, Monika's brother shared her view, as the pair had learnt under Jewish teacher *Herr* Bergenstein before the outbreak of the Great War in 1914. Bergenstein had died in the war, and *Frau* Vogt had picked up the slack, tutoring her children while war raged around them.

Monika recalled her last meeting with Martin, when they both voiced their growing concern for their work and the future of Germany.

'Are you aware that Hitler dislikes cubism, sister?' Martin rolled his eyes.

'He prefers the classics,' Monika said. 'I've heard he's a painter himself. I imagine his work is quite conservative.'

Martin snorted. 'More than likely. I'll be an outcast in six months. Thankfully, I've made some big sales. The Russians are fond of cubism, and not afraid to spend a ruble or two. With fat pockets, I intend to find another pursuit while I'm ahead.'

'I trust your earnings are far away from Germany?'

Her brother nodded. 'Naturally. I have money and contacts in England, contacts I can trust. But we are German, Monika. We can weather this storm. I'm concerned about my Jewish colleagues, however. I sense life will become increasingly difficult for them.'

'My thoughts as well,' Monika agreed. 'I have already noticed some parents removing their children from school, and against my better judgement, I joined the Nazi teachers' association back in April. It was that, or face dismissal. I've already heard rumours about our Jewish teaching colleagues. If Hitler decides they are no longer worthy of their position, we will face teaching shortages. Twelve per cent of all professors in Germany are Jewish, I believe.'

Martin paused, his hand stroking his manicured beard. 'Perhaps that's his plan, Monika. Remove the unworthy and replace them with those loyal to him. Change the curriculum to reflect the Nazi ethos.'

Monika shuddered. 'Perish the thought. Surely there's something we can do about this.'

Martin nodded. 'I believe there is. Perhaps *Herr* Hitler does not deserve the brilliance of our Jewish colleagues. Perhaps they should leave to safer realms. What do you say, sister?'

'I've not forgotten *Herr* Bergenstein. We owe it to his memory to help where we can.'

'I agree. Let me contact my English friends. It would be wise to stay ahead of events.'

Downstairs, the school bell rang out. The letter to her brother would have to wait. Monika was eager to share her news. Two days ago, a family had approached her about leaving *Berchtesgaden*. During the brief time she'd taught the children, a girl called Ingrid and her younger brother Dieter, she'd judged both were bright and well-mannered. She refused to witness the breaking of their spirit, and she hoped Martin could facilitate their exodus. Gathering up her books, she vowed to write to her brother after school finished for the day.

13

JANUARY 1933, BAVARIA

They left *Berchtesgaden* early; the train pulling away from the station as the sun kissed the peaks of the Jenner and Watzman massifs. The mountains wrapped around *Berchtesgaden*, providing comfort when there was little to cling onto, but the mountains could not protect the Stiepermanns from the growing tide of Nazism. Now the family divisions formed: *Frau* Stiepermann staying behind to support the frail *Ōma*, while *Herr* Stiepermann, Ingrid, and Dieter were embarking on a journey to find a safer home in England.

Or at least that was the way Ingrid's father sold the idea to her. 'We have one chance at this,' he said as the train wound its way into the hills. Besides the Stiepermanns, the carriage was empty, and the family could speak freely. 'You've seen the violence against the other Jews. Look at what happened to the Hubers. Poor Franz Huber, dismissed from school on the say-so of Stefan Weiss.'

Don't mention his name, Ingrid thought, her face reddening in anger. *I despise that boy and everything he represents.*

'We've already drawn the ire of the Weiss family ourselves, haven't we, Dieter?' *Herr* Stiepermann couldn't help looking at his son's hand.

Ingrid squirmed at her father's knack at unearthing the truth. She thought their story where Dieter had simply fallen would hold water. Yet once again, he'd worked everything out. Deciding to let it go, Ingrid tried to change tack. 'But how long before we can be a family again, Papa?'

'As long as it takes, Ingrid. We have to be brave, all of us. There's a shadow falling over Germany, and it's best we get in front of it.'

It wasn't the answer Ingrid wanted, but it was clear her father knew more than she. They'd all felt the sense of quickening, a growing anxiety that they were running out of time. They'd all witnessed the growing fervour for Adolf Hitler and his new policies. It was no longer safe to be a Jew in Germany. They could not simply stand by and watch the Nazis take their liberties from them.

Just because I agree with Papa's decision doesn't mean I have to like it, Ingrid thought. She tried not to think of last night's tearful farewells with her mother and grandmother. *Frau* Stiepermann, kindness exemplified, had suggested Ingrid still had time to say goodbye to Gerda and Christa. Thankfully, she'd missed her daughter's wooden resistance to the idea. It hurt to leave without saying goodbye to Gerda, but Ingrid would be content to never see Christa again.

Christa's elation at *Herr* Huber's dismissal had been a horrifying revelation. Her undisguised glee had mortified Ingrid, further emphasising the gulf between the two girls. Gerda had been notably quiet, but egged on by Christa, had finally expressed her approval too. It was this capitulation that upset Ingrid the most. Her childhood friend, the gentle Gerda, now wearing a BDM uniform and espousing the benefits of strenuous exercise and being a good wife. What of her brilliant mind, her plans to enter the previously male-dominated world of science?

A tear escaped and rolled down Ingrid's face. She quickly brushed it away before her father noticed and arranged her face into a smile. 'How about breakfast?' she said. 'Mama packed us pumpernickel and beef liverwurst, and there's a flask of tea as well. We'll finish in time to change trains at *Freilassing*.'

****

48

After the smaller, regional train stations, Munich *Hauptbahnhof* was a bustling metropolis. The platform was a mass of people: chic women in tailored suits with hats tilted jauntily over their curls, men in suits, long coats and hats, and a smattering of men in uniform. Ingrid's eyes veered away from the uniforms, instantly mistrusting them. She glanced at Dieter and saw an unusual wariness on his face. 'We don't have to get off here, do we?' he asked.

'Not unless you need to stretch your legs, or use a decent-sized toilet,' their father said. 'In my case, I need both. Why don't the two of you stay here, and I'll be back in a few minutes.' He stood up and patted his pockets. After a moment's hesitation, he pulled something out and handed it to Ingrid. 'These are yours and Dieter's tickets. Put them in your pocket. I'll need mine to re-board the train. Won't be long.' He waved over his shoulder as he left the carriage, and a moment later, Ingrid saw him threading his way through the crowd, his dark head strangely bare amidst the milling people. However, his face had lost some of its worry, and there was a spring in his step as he entered the building.

With her father out of sight, Ingrid turned to Dieter. 'Are you hungry? I think there's some food left in the bag Mama packed.' Head down, she rummaged through the bag on the floor. 'Some of father's papers, a book, spare handkerchiefs...Oh, what luck,' she said after a moment. 'Mama packed some onion bread rolls. She must have snuck these in while I wasn't looking.'

Ingrid drew the food out of the bag, but Dieter suddenly dropped to the carriage floor beside her, his face ashen. 'Stay down,' he barked, his voice hoarse. 'I just saw Stefan and a group of SA soldiers. They're right outside on the platform, talking to Papa.'

'Stefan Weiss? From *Berchtesgaden*? What's he doing here in Munich?'

'I don't know,' Dieter whispered, 'but I'll bet he's up to no good.'

49

Stefan's intentions became obvious when he called out in a loud voice, '*Herr* Stiepermann. I am detaining you under the order of *Sturmbahnführer* Weiss on suspicion of…'

Ingrid risked a peep out the train window. Her father had his back to the train. He stood, talking to the group of men, his arms splayed wide in a defensive gesture. Ingrid willed him to turn around. *Look at us, please,* she thought, her heart accelerating. *Face us and tell us that everything is going to be all right.*

But her father continued to face the other way, answering the SA guards' questions, and she finally realised what he was doing. 'He's protecting us,' she whispered, ducking back down beside Dieter.

Dieter nodded and placed a finger to his lips. 'Let's see what we can hear.'

'Are you travelling alone, *Herr* Stiepermann?' The children heard the clipped voice of one of the SA guards.

'I am.'

'That's not true,' Stefan's voice interjected. 'We heard he was travelling with his children.'

'This is a business trip,' *Herr* Stiepermann said evenly. 'I would never take my children on a business trip. Search me if you must, you will only find my ticket on me.'

A sharp whistle blew, and Ingrid risked another quick look. The station master approached the group of men, the whistle swinging from his fingers on a lanyard. 'Will you gentlemen be boarding?' he enquired. 'The train is about to leave.'

'He's not a gentleman,' Stefan sneered, pointing at Stiepermann. 'He's a *Jew*, a second-class citizen, and he's coming with us. We must make him answer to my father, *Sturmbahnführer* Weiss.'

'I'm sure this is just a mistake,' *Herr* Stiepermann said. 'But I'll happily come along and clear up the misunderstanding.'

The final whistle blew, and the train shuddered forward. Ingrid couldn't help herself; she raised her head above the window for one last glimpse of her father. He'd turned to face the train, his shoulders slumped, his face pale and devoid of expression. *Oh,*

Papa. A deep pain lodged in Ingrid's heart. She longed for this to be a mistake, for the train to stop, so that her father could re-board and continue their journey. Frozen in place, Ingrid locked eyes with Stefan as the train pulled away from the platform. His mouth gaped open, and his astonishment quickly turned to rage. He yelled and gesticulated wildly to the stationmaster, but it was too late. The train gathered speed as the guards took *Herr* Stiepermann by the arms and led him away. Ingrid and Dieter held onto each other, an unspoken question in their eyes.

What are we going to do now?

14

JANUARY 1933, SOUTHERN GERMANY

Ingrid watched the German countryside flash past the train window, her mind elsewhere. The scenery had opened up as they left the Bavarian Alps behind, and rolling black forests replaced the steep mountainous country the children were familiar with. After Munich, they'd passed one tiny village after another, each punctuated by the steeple of a church. It was still Germany, the country the Stiepermanns had called home, but now everything had changed.

A sliver of anxiety worked its way inside Ingrid as she reviewed the events that transpired at Munich *Hauptbahnhof*. She could still see her father being led away, a forlorn figure between the uniformed SA men.

Stefan's interception on the platform had caught everyone by surprise. Ingrid remembered the bravado on his face, and she immediately knew why the boy had travelled to Munich. This was an outright act of revenge for the pitchfork incident. And while *Herr* Stiepermann had saved his children from arrest, his own fate was less clear. *I'm sure this is just a mistake.* It was a lie, and Ingrid knew better. The SA had made an example of *Herr* Stiepermann, publicly humiliating him by detaining him at the station. That alone sent shivers through her. Would she and Dieter see their father again? Or would he be just one more Jew who disappeared at the hands of Hitler's SA?

There were no answers to Ingrid's incessant questions, so she turned her thoughts to another dilemma. Who informed Stefan of their whereabouts? Only one other person outside the Stiepermann family was aware of their movements, and it broke Ingrid's heart to consider the implications.

Not Gerda. She's my friend, and she cares for Dieter. How could she?

She was not the only person to betray Ingrid, and as the train rolled through the German countryside, Ingrid's hatred for Stefan rose as a buried memory bubbled to the surface.

****

Ingrid smoothed the curls framing her face and glanced at her reflection in the mirror. She was pale with nerves, and she pinched her cheeks to brighten their colour. In the absence of lipstick, she'd pressed a raspberry onto a saucer and then rubbed the bruised fruit across her lips. The stain accentuated their soft curves without being too obvious. It would have to do. She hoped it wouldn't be long before Walter's lips pressed against hers, tasting the raspberry, tasting her. She blushed at the thought, washed her hands, and left the bathroom.

Ōma passed her in the narrow hallway. 'You look beautiful today, Ingrid.' The old woman paused and peered more closely at her granddaughter. 'Are you off somewhere special, Liebling?'

The colour rose in Ingrid's cheeks again. 'Oh, no, *Ōma*. I'm just going to Gerda's house.'

The old woman's eyebrows rose. 'Forgive me. For a moment, I thought a young man might have been involved.' She noted shrewdly.

Ingrid feigned innocence. 'I'll be home for supper, *Ōma*.'

She left the house and walked the short distance to the footbridge that crossed the Ramsauer Ache. Now she faced the steep incline that led up into the village. As she climbed the hill, she could see the twin peaks of Watzmann off in the distance, remarkably clear in the late afternoon light. It would be a beautiful day tomorrow, and Ingrid hummed to herself as she took a shortcut through the small *friedhof* next to the village. Unlike Gerda and Christa, Ingrid loved the cemetery nestled beside the *Franziskanerkirche*. While the village had lost many of their menfolk in the Great War, relatives tended the graves daily with flowers, and it was love and reverence that Ingrid felt, not loss.

Her thoughts returned to Walter and the secret they shared. She had always entranced him, even when they were young children. Back then, it had been appropriate to visit his house. They went to the same school, and everyone knew Walter's parents. Walter's father was the *burgermeister*-in-waiting, the deputy mayor, a jolly man with a rounded face and bright blue eyes, and he welcomed all children into the Gorst house. Gerda and Ingrid visited often, partaking of the beautiful strudels and gingerbread Walter's mother made. The children played, talked, and occasionally Ingrid sketched amusing caricatures of their teachers that provoked delighted laughter from her friends.

Walter had enjoyed Ingrid's presence in the house, clearly preferring her soft voice and shy smile over Gerda's matter-of-fact nature, and it was around that time that Gerda's visits waned. As the children grew into teenagers, Ingrid saw the boy with fresh eyes: his golden-blond hair, engaging blue eyes beneath dark brows, and a tall and strong body. Likewise, Ingrid blossomed into the early stages of womanhood, and she felt Walter's eyes on her more and more often. Ingrid left Walter's house one afternoon, but moments later, the boy caught her up in the laneway. He was out of breath and stammering, his bottled-up feelings tumbling out as he professed his love for her. She was beautiful. She was so different from all the other girls. He realised they were only fifteen, but he wanted her, and one day he hoped he could be with her. He kissed her tenderly on the cheek, and Ingrid reeled at his closeness, his strength and vulnerability.

Their clandestine meetings continued for some months. A stolen kiss when they were alone, a steamy embrace in the darkness when the family retired to the parlour to listen to the wireless. But today, Walter had planned something special. Mr and Mrs Gorst were attending a meeting at the town hall. They would be alone for the first time, and Ingrid's heart fluttered in anticipation.

She reached the fountain in the *Marktplatz* and turned left, her head down, not wishing to bump into anyone she knew and suffer delays with idle chatter. *Oh, no. There's Frau Huber. Don't let her see me, don't let her see me.* She liked the former head teacher's wife, but the woman was long-winded, and would delay her with questions about her mother and Ōma. Thankfully, *Frau* Huber found another victim and Ingrid hurried on past the Konditorei. She passed Bier Adam tavern and ducked into the laneway that led up the hill to the larger houses on *Doktorberg*. She tapped on the door and waited. Walter answered immediately. He must have been waiting, Ingrid realised. His eyes darted left and right, scanning the street for witnesses, before beckoning her inside.

His eyes were dark with desire as he pushed her up against the door, his powerful arms around her waist, his lips crushed against hers. 'Oh, God, Ingrid. How I've waited for this moment.'

He dotted kisses down her throat, and her body arched against his. 'Oh, Walter.' Her mouth parted, their tongues met, and the heat of desire radiated through her body. She didn't know what was going to happen, but she no longer cared. She was in love with Walter, and she wanted to share this moment with him.

Walter took her by the hand and led her upstairs. He sat beside her on the bed, his hands gently exploring her body as they continued to kiss. They were both oblivious to the front door opening and the furtive footfalls on the stairs.

'Well, well,' Stefan said as he burst into Walter's room. 'What have we here? Are you consorting with a dirty Jew, Walter? What will our *Gruppenführer* have to say about this?'

Walter and Ingrid broke apart. Ingrid's racing heart now beat with fear. She had never liked Stefan, and she hated the influence he had over Walter. Would he really resort to telling the Hitler Youth *Gruppenführer*?

'Of course, there is an alternative.' Stefan sidled further into the room. He ran a finger down Ingrid's throat and onto her chest, cupping his hand under her breast. Walter cried out in protest, and

Ingrid shuddered away from the other boy's touch. 'The whore wants it. Can't you tell?' Stefan licked his lips and undid his belt. 'I'll tell you what. I won't say a word about you hanging about with *Jude*, and none of us will say a word about what's going to happen now. Is that clear? Try to stop me, and the whole of *Berchtesgaden* will hear about you, Walter Gorst.'

Stefan pushed Walter away and roughly threw Ingrid back on the bed. Lifting her skirt, he removed her panties, then squashed himself down on top of her. Stefan pushed into her, and Ingrid cried out in pain. As the older boy grunted and thrust above her, she waited for the moment Walter would pull Stefan off her, when he would hold her in his arms and comfort her, but the rescue never came. She opened her eyes and saw that Walter's tears mirrored her own as he stood powerless in the room, witnessing the rape of the girl he loved.

****

With some effort, Ingrid dragged her thoughts away from the horrific memory. She gazed across the carriage at her brother. He'd grown so much in the past year, she realised with a shock. His body was filling out, while his face had lost the plump innocence of childhood. *Or perhaps Stefan and his gang put paid to any innocence he had*, she thought, as her eyes drifted down to Dieter's disfigured hand.

Both of them had experienced betrayal and disappointment in *Berchtesgaden* from completely unexpected sources. This train trip was to mark a change of direction, a step towards the future. *But it's already in tatters*, her mind clamoured. *They took Papa. Will they send more guards to escort us from the train in Stuttgart, or will they allow us to go on?*

Ingrid pushed the panicked thoughts aside. She caught Dieter's eye and forced herself to smile. 'We'll be in Stuttgart soon.'

Dieter snorted. 'What does it matter? We might escape, but we left everyone we love behind. And worst of all, I opened my mouth to someone I thought I could trust, and she betrayed me.'

'Who, Gerda?'

He shifted uncomfortably on the bench. 'All I wanted to do was say goodbye. I passed her on my way home from the village. She said she was going to visit Christa. I told her we were going to Stuttgart. I said nothing else, I promise.' His eyes were bright with unshed tears.

Christa. Anger and jealousy flared in Ingrid's belly. *Gerda told Christa, and Christa bleated to either Walter or Stefan.* As physically strong as Christa was, she was as weak as all the others, giving up any piece of information to ingratiate herself upon Stefan or charm Walter.

Ingrid reached across the carriage and clasped her brother's arm. 'It's not your fault. Whoever we thought Gerda was, she's not that person any longer.'

The realisation hit Ingrid, and her face crumpled into tears. She cried for Gerda, a childhood friend lost to the Nazi propaganda machine. And she cried for their father, cruelly snatched away just when they'd dared to hope. 'We can't do a thing about this here in Germany, Dieter.' She sobbed. 'We've become the enemy, and if we don't get away now, they'll kill us all.'

'Not if you and I have anything to say about it.' Dieter vowed. 'I'm going to settle the score with Stefan.'

Ingrid produced a handkerchief and blotted her face. 'I hate him too,' she said, blowing her nose. 'But we're just two children fleeing our homeland. Who would want to help us?'

'Don't forget, we're meeting *Herr* Vogt in Stuttgart. He'll think of something, I know it,' Dieter said. 'He'll help us, and in time we can repay the favour. You'll see, Ingrid. Just you wait.' He lifted his jaw, his eyes dark with anger.

Ingrid stared at him, surprised at her brother's new-found resolve. 'We'll do it together.' She squeezed Dieter's hand.

15

JANUARY 1933, *BERCHTESGADEN*

Freda Stiepermann paced the kitchen in a worthless waste of energy.

'Yes, I know, Mama. But what if they're caught, or worse, someone hurt them? Ingrid and Dieter only know this town.'

'You can't talk like that. They only left a few hours ago and it will be weeks before we know they are safe, but they will make it to England. Nobody knew they were travelling today, let alone the route they've taken. With thousands of people travelling, they'll soon become lost in the crowd. Come on, you're making me uncomfortable. Walk with me. Some winter air will do us good.'

As they walked, the sun shone brightly to lift their mood. Hildegard couldn't manage long walks any longer, so the pair settled for a bench near the *Franziskaner* church where they could rest, knowing they could walk down a gentle slope back to home. The scene before them played out as it had a thousand times before, with shoppers wandering about their business. Although she knew it to be an illusion, the sight calmed her frayed nerves and, leaning in, she wrapped a comforting arm around her mother. Within a few minutes, her mother's head dropped into slumber, forcing Freda to adjust her position to offer support. Although uncomfortable, the blanket of sunshine allowed Freda to let her own eyes drop.

'What are you doing here?'

Freda's eyes blinked furiously, and it took several seconds before she recognised the owner of the voice, Christa. Freda's face hardened. 'Why shouldn't I be here? We live here.'

'But I thought you'd all taken the train,' Christa stammered before backing away and turning to run.

Freda's hand flew to her mouth in anguish as the realisation hit.

If Christa knows, then Stefan does, too.

16

JANUARY 1933, ESSLINGEN

'Dieter, stop daydreaming,' Ingrid commanded. 'We're getting close to Stuttgart and I'm worried Stefan called ahead to the SA to stop us. I'm sure he'll figure out we need to change trains there.'

Dieter rubbed both eyes before replying. 'How much further do you think we have to travel?'

'To Stuttgart, and then onto Heilbronn. Beyond that, I'm not sure, but I heard the conductor mention Esslingen, and that's close. Maybe we should get off there and wait a day before we move on again.'

Before they could plan, the carriage shuddered, and the train slowed. Nudging her brother, the siblings studied the platform in desperation. They saw uniforms waiting, but that wasn't unusual. But were they SA thugs ordered in by Stefan? 'Come on, Dieter, there aren't many. Let's see if we can get off now and pass through to wait them out.'

Moving to the front carriages offered their best hope, better that than the rear, where they would have to walk the length of the platform. Despite slowing, it seemed a painful age while they waited for the train to stop, and Ingrid felt her breathing quicken. Her hand felt slick against the door handle until Dieter reached over to offer reassurance. 'I'm with you. We'll do this together.'

That's what we said when Papa was with us, Ingrid thought miserably. The pause while they wrestled with the door handle helped as several other passengers had already fought their way onto the platform, so, using them as a screen, Ingrid and Dieter followed boldly. The only sign they did not belong came from Ingrid, whose eyes danced left and right in full expectation of imminent arrest.

'Come on,' Dieter offered, gripping her hand in comfort. A little further along the platform, the small crowd thinned out as they shuffled through an entrance marked *ticket office*. If someone stood inside to arrest them, then they would not escape. With each step sounding like a death knell in Ingrid's ears, her pace slowed, though Dieter's grip remained firm to drag her along.

'I can't,' she begged, but Dieter's pull was insistent. Accepting people would look if she struggled too hard, Ingrid dipped her head and followed her brother into the shadowy interior. Eight strides later, the pair exited into a blast of wintry sunshine. They chose a brisk pace, away from the station. The next five minutes comprised a tense trot, regular pauses while they looked behind or changed direction, and finally, with a deep expulsion of breath, Ingrid halted. 'I think we're safe.'

'I agree, but I do not know where we are. Do you?'

She looked about and had to agree. The town of Esslingen seemed bigger than *Berchtesgaden* and with no mountains as landmarks, she became nervous. Were they lost? No, worse, they were alone with no clue who they could trust. They hadn't planned upon this and now, as they slumped against a wall, the enormity of their situation hit home. So far on their journey, Dieter's strength held Ingrid together, but even he appeared beaten.

No, her mind countered. If they both flagged, then things would only become worse.

'Here, drink this,' Ingrid said as she passed the flask of tea. He drank half before handing it back.

'It's a little cold, but better than nothing.'

She agreed, and despite quenching their thirst, the empty canister meant they'd need a refill before too long. As the light faded, another worry hit. Where would they sleep that night?

'Come on, dear brother. We need water and a place to rest before we get back to the station tomorrow and with dusk coming soon, that means we have to get moving.' This time it was Ingrid's turn to grip her brother's arm and haul him up to standing. He seemed reluctant to move. His reticence caused her to snap.

'What are you waiting for? We can't stay here. It's warm now but give it an hour and these streets will become icy. And we're going to need something to replace the tea we drank.' Ingrid took charge, pulling her brother along a narrow road that took them up a steep path. Although she suspected they were heading away from the station, she hoped the extra height would offer a suitable route.

'There,' she said triumphantly, while jabbing one finger towards the river which snaked through the town. She couldn't believe they'd been so stupid. In their hurry they'd forgotten the railway ran alongside the river, but now as she traced its route, she saw the station in the distance. It wasn't much more than a mile away, and the realisation meant she could retrace their steps with a reasonable confidence. The downhill journey took less than twenty minutes and upon seeing the river, she ordered her brother to refill the flask, knowing if they came upon a better water source, they could pour what they had away. Now that they knew they could return to the station, the pair scoped out a place to sleep.

'Come on,' Ingrid said. 'There are plenty of trees on the opposite bank. Maybe we can find shelter where we can stay out of sight.'

A few minutes later, they'd crossed over the nearest bridge and disappeared into the shadows.

****

Although dry, Ingrid and Dieter endured one of the longest, coldest, and most miserable nights of their lives. Every movement sent pinpricks of pain across the breadth of Ingrid's back. Turning onto one side did little to help, other than it made it easier to hug Dieter and hold on to a semblance of warmth. They woke at first light with hunger pangs gnawing where the distant memory of liverwurst taunted the pair with vengeance. Today, they faced two daunting challenges: securing breakfast and boarding the first train to Stuttgart. Both brought trepidation, but if they were to continue north to Heilbronn without empty bellies, then they had to try.

Despite looking like urchins, they recrossed the bridge and began looking cautiously around for any scraps of food, knowing they stood out should they meet any early risers. In reality, the quiet scene helped them, and they swept into the silent station to read the timetable. After confirming the time against the station clock, they knew they had three hours to remain hidden, get food, and then board the train they needed. As they walked along an empty street, Ingrid wondered how they would feel if they discovered scroungers back in *Berchtesgaden*, sympathetically she thought, but not everyone would show charity like them. 'Make sure nobody sees us,' she cautioned before remembering they'd spent most of the night discussing their strategy for the morning. There was one problem with bedding down in the woods, she realised. As the previous evening's light faded, so did any chance they could scout somewhere to eat for their breakfast, and now they were at the mercy of guesswork. With sunrise came an urgency as they walked beyond one warehouse after another. They had to find food before they boarded the train for the next hop on their journey.

'Damn,' Dieter cursed when they stumbled upon an empty warehouse with bales of straw stacked in the corner.

'I know, but it's too late to worry about a bed now. We've got food to find.'

For half an hour they followed the line of the river, content they held a bearing back to the station, but their hearts sank as the buildings slowly petered out. In the distance, they could see a few farms, which could offer plenty of risk for little reward.

'Come on, Dieter, we're going there,' she said while pointing at the nearest homestead.

'Why? Come on, there's more chance of us finding food in the town.'

'Yes, I know, but if the farmer is kind, then we can eat and get warm while we wait safely for our train, and if they refuse us, then we can run away before they raise the alarm.' Seeing Dieter weigh up the logic and nod, they set off.

The pair were well used to walking in the countryside and they covered the distance within a few minutes as the clean air invigorated their souls. They were filthy, an unusual sight at that hour, but farms were one place where early risers were commonplace. They approached the dwelling, but the crumbling walls and a rickety fence caused their optimism to fade. Had they come this far only to return empty-handed? As if in answer, the smell of freshly baked bread wafted toward them on the morning breeze. Moments later, a woman appeared in the doorway. Her mouth parted in surprise, and she looked ready to call for help, then thought better of it. The woman held the pair's gaze, a vague question in her eyes.

Ingrid knew their future hung in the balance. Deciding upon a bold but friendly approach, she spoke up, breaking the deadlock.

'Good morning. I'm sorry to bother you so early. I promise we mean you no harm. We're just hungry and we smelt the bread.'

'Well, you'd best come in then, but be quick, before my husband sees.'

'Thank you, madam,' they both replied as they trouped into the kitchen where the warmth and aroma made the pair weak at the knees.

Five minutes later, and true to her word, the lady ushered them both back the way they'd come with a gift of food. Inside their satchel, two large hunks of bread and a smaller round of cheese. The pair remained unnoticed on the return journey until they found the urban sprawl of Esslingen, though they knew others would surface soon. They still had plenty of time to wait, but with hungry stomachs, they settled in to wait on a step with an obvious line of sight to a clock tower.

'Come on,' Ingrid commanded. 'It's time to go. Our train leaves in a few minutes and we need to get onboard unseen.' Her voice trembled as she spoke, and she knew Dieter's fear mirrored hers, but they had no other choice. They couldn't return home to *Berchtesgaden*. They had to make their father's arrest count for something. A deep plume of smoke spiralled into the sky as they sped down the lane back to the station. Feeling confident after their food, they knew they'd timed their approach to perfection, but still the nagging demons persisted. Before entering the ticket office, the pair walked a carefree arc, testing the water to see whether any uniforms waited inside. 'Now,' Ingrid urged when she saw the path was clear. As if to confirm her instruction, a whistle sounded as the train entered the station. They ran through unopposed and readied themselves to board. Dieter yanked on the handle before the train rested, but it didn't matter. They had tickets, and they were onboard. For five agonising minutes, they waited as passengers came and went. With each second clicking through on the station clock, their tension rose to crippling levels, but then a whistle sounded, a flag waved, and they were on their way once more.

For that morning, one question sat upon their lips. Would Stefan's SA guards greet them when they arrived in Stuttgart?

17

JANUARY 1933, STUTTGART

For the second day running, Martin Vogt paced nervously along the platform at Stuttgart, and, with each passing minute, the knot formed by twisting his goatee tightened. With the pleas of his sister Monika ringing in his ears, he stamped his feet before moving off to complete another circuit.

The station clock chimed a dull announcement just as Martin walked past a tiny sheet pinned to a post, which offered a timetable. With soldiers further along the platform, he ducked down to examine the document for the fourth time that morning. As expected, he learnt nothing new, and once the soldiers moved away; he returned to his vigil further along, away from their presence. At last, he heard a new train approaching. Would his passengers arrive this time? He knew his constant presence over the last two days would set tongues wagging. The previous day, he'd kept himself busy by setting up an easel to capture the mood of all the travellers. He created three pieces of art which would have value to the right buyer, but standing, observing, even as an artist held risks. It got him noticed.

Today, he'd dispensed with the previous flamboyant outfit, opting instead for a dull grey suit, flat worker's cap. He also slouched in the hope others would view him as insignificant. That, too, held risks as appearing weak singled you out to those in power. Despite the dangers, he knew his behaviour was necessary, if he were to stand any chance of carrying out his sister's wishes.

Now, as the air bit cold and seeped into his bones, he yearned to return home to his studio. Wrapping his thumbs deep within each armpit, he resisted until, finally, the approaching train steamed into the station. Martin checked the platform and the stationary carriages for activity, and once clear, he shuffled forward with head bowed. A few commuters had come and gone, and as far as he could tell, the soldiers remained some distance away, but he could see no sign of the Stiepermanns. He cursed inwardly as yet another train seemed devoid of the people he'd sought. Had he missed them already, and were they already en route to the border with Holland or Luxembourg? Martin doubted it. Monika would have spoken with the father, Gerhard. But the mystery of their location remained. He sighed while considering his options. His first choice would be to wait two hours for the next train and then wait again should that prove fruitless. Then again, the meagre warmth of his studio had to be better than here out exposed in the cold. He could get home within fifteen minutes and back again before the next train arrived. The prospect of shelter away from the station pulled him along towards the ticket office, but as he closed the gap, the soldiers returned, sending a tremor across his spine. He tried to convince himself that his fears were unfounded, only they weren't. The group of uniformed figures had swollen, each checking papers of all nearby. While Martin dithered, a cry echoed across the open space. An old man showed resistance when called to identify himself, and the soldiers rushed him, engulfing him in an instant.

Martin turned away, sadly knowing that to get involved could easily bring a beating for himself. The old gent would have to fend for himself. Before he could question his decision, Martin gripped the nearest handle and hauled himself into a deserted carriage, where he sat as inconspicuously as he could manage, though fingers fidgeted while he waited to see what would happen next. He expected the soldiers to come and then, if he complied and quietly accepted their authority, then maybe they would accept his story that he was merely travelling to help a friend with their building restoration. His hands, soft from years of delicate painting, were at odds with his story, but now was not the time to come up with something better. Instead, he waited and for a while, all thoughts of the Stiepermanns disappeared.

It took a while before he looked up to examine the world outside the train. As his eyes sought answers along the platform, he felt sweat. Damp and lingering across the base of his spine, and with it came a sense of shame. The old man had vanished, and in his place, the soldiers chattered like ants who'd just delivered a prize to their queen. The change in their manner surprised Martin until he remembered they were merely the blunt tools used by others in the military. And then he saw them. Outside of the station, beyond a lichen covered picket fence, stood a trio of black uniforms. A wheezy cough hit his chest, causing him to duck down. *Damn, what now?*

A whistle blew, tearing his eyes away, and then, after the briefest of flag waves from the signalman, the train lurched forward, taking him away from the SS officers.

****

Ingrid had seen them all. The soldiers, the old man, struck down upon the ground before they kicked him unconscious and carried him away. And last of all, she'd seen the black uniforms as three officers at the perimeter. Each held an animated conversation while pointing towards the others in uniform. After their uncomfortable night, she'd watched Dieter's eyes drop, leaving her to hold vigil alone. Typical. Didn't he realise her exhaustion, too?

With the train at a standstill, Ingrid used the time to assess her options. Assuming the siblings could open a carriage door opposite, then some scrub land offered slight hope, but as she pictured herself rousing her brother and making a sprint for it, a crippling fear gripped. If the soldiers saw them running away, they'd open fire. *How far can a bullet fly? What if they hit us?*

A sickly sensation threatened to erupt, forcing her to gag back the sensation. As she lurched, she slammed into her brother, who almost fell from his seat.

'Hey.'

'Hush, be quiet.'

After a brief grumble, Dieter's tone softened, and he allowed Ingrid to point out the soldiers waiting nearby. Together, they held hands, each fully expecting an imminent arrest. Despite the freezing temperatures, their interlocked palms were damp with sweat until Ingrid pulled her fingers away. The carriage jerked and suddenly they were moving again. The juddering increased, and Ingrid tore her gaze away from the platform. Dieter's face looked white as together they wondered if they could escape unscathed. Ingrid felt her breath quicken as an undercurrent of panic held ready to explode. *Why's the train going so slowly?*

An agony of waiting finally ended when the locomotive dragged them beyond the sidings and out of the station. She exhaled deeply once the soldiers had disappeared from view.

'That felt too close. Do you think the guards saw us? And if they did, were they looking for us?'

Ingrid's question remained unanswered, though she guessed her brother shared her fears. She tried to settle, if only for his benefit, but the doubts persisted and then she saw someone watching them both, and the tremor returned.

Trying to act discretely, Ingrid nudged Dieter. Her eyes flashed alarm and within a second, he'd read her concern. She leant in close. 'That man, the one at the opposite end of the carriage. I'm sure he was watching us.' Her brother leant into the aisle and stared. His obvious movement prompted a stifled scream as she yanked his arm back. He looked baleful. 'Well, since you made it obvious, is he watching us?'

'I don't know. He could be, but if he was, he wasn't watching when I looked. Do you think he's with the secret police, then?'

Ingrid shuddered at the idea. How would she know whether the stranger operated as some kind of spy? But then, how long was Stefan and his father's reach? She stole another glance. He appeared distinguished, though that meant nothing. If he was some kind of agent, then he'd hardly advertise the fact.

For the next couple of miles, a bizarre standoff held. The man sat still while Ingrid and Dieter cowered. They were travelling too fast to jump from the train, though Ingrid considered leaping at the first river crossing they should encounter. She motioned the idea before Dieter shut it down. And then she remembered the day Stefan and his cronies had launched her poor brother into the river. No, diving off a bridge at speed wasn't an option.

They plotted with heads together for a few miles, and when Ingrid looked up, her blood froze.

'It is you, isn't it? I wasn't sure, but Monika described you both. It's just you're alone. Where is your father?'

'Who are you?' Ingrid blustered, trying to make sense of the newcomers' introduction.

'Of course. How rude of me. My name is Martin Vogt. My sister, who taught you both, asked me to help you and your father escape across the border. Please, you must tell me, where is he?'

While Dieter remained silent, Ingrid marshalled her thoughts. All the talk of spies left her unsettled. She'd known Miss Vogt's brother would help, and they were expecting him, but the mistrust borne of her own anxiety couldn't quite believe it. 'What is it you do, Mister Vogt?'

The man smiled. 'I paint the world and sell my art where I can. It has opened some doors for me and given I have contacts, and a conscience, I want to help you both. Now, you were going to tell me why you are travelling alone.'

Still uncertain whether this was some sort of trap, she stalled for time with a brief explanation of their journey.

'That explains why I met all those empty trains yesterday.' He beamed before a sombre smile returned. 'I'm sorry to hear they took Gerhard, though. This must be a terrible worry for you both.'

'Tell me about your sister.'

Although innocent enough, Ingrid's question sought to mine the man for information before she could embrace any kind of trust.

'Of course. Where are my manners? I am a stranger to you both and it is only natural you show reticence at my arrival, though you were expecting me, weren't you?'

Before she could block his movement, Dieter nodded. Martin Vogt merely smiled and continued. 'My sister is three years younger than me, aged forty-two. Her favourite colour is red, and she has an unusual snort, if you ever make her laugh. She is serious, dependable and' – lowering his voice to a whisper – 'she hates Nazis. On her left hand, you'll find an emerald ring, and she often wears an ivory brooch inlaid with a carving of a couple in love.'

Ingrid remembered the brooch, but the comment about hating Nazis stuck. Together with Dieter, their father had offered some information, so Martin Vogt's arrival wasn't wholly unexpected, but still. How did his sister secure the prestigious school head if she wasn't in league with them? It left Ingrid feeling overwhelmed.

'How did she secure her post in the school if she hates them so much?'

Vogt leant back and clasped his hands together. 'She has to pretend to follow their ideals. I know you can't believe this, but it is true. For her to fight for you and others like you, she has to stay in her post. What good is she to anyone if they realise she hates them as much as you do? Now, I understand you are both tired and scared. I hope you recognise my description of Monika and for now, at least, you'll consider me your friend and ally. We'll arrive in *Mannheim* before the hour is out and then you can go on your way, or if you prefer, we can journey on together across the border and onward to the coast. I'm sure with each passing mile, we'll move beyond your enemy's reach.'

At that, Vogt offered a flask of water, accompanied with ham and pickles which Dieter tucked in to with enthusiasm.

Ingrid wasn't ready to trust this man, not yet, but staying together seemed a better idea than her earlier ideas of leaping into the unknown. Unlike her brother, she nibbled mouselike at the food, as her focus remained upon their new companion. In between mouthfuls, she chose insightful questions, but no matter how hard she tried to trip Vogt up, his answers married smoothly, with everything she knew about his sister and their home.

'What have you brought with you?' she asked, trying a new tack.

'About time you asked.' He chuckled. He stretched both arms to one shoulder before undoing a buckle which released a long tube. Ingrid recognised the object and leant in, keen to see the contents which spilled out across a seat. His paintings were wonderful. Where Ingrid's art looked delicate, Vogt's style punched vibrance. Now she trusted him. No impostor could produce paintings of this quality.

'Thank you for showing us both. These are beautiful. You're a wonderful talent.'

'From what I've heard, you are quite the artist yourself, and you, Dieter, you're an engineering marvel.'

Ice finally broken; Ingrid cast her eyes outside. Another new town drew closer. 'Is this…?'

'Yes, we're arriving at *Mannheim*. See how we're following the Rhine on the left? We will need to get off this train for a while. Would you like me to go on ahead or do you think we'd stand a better chance as a group? After all, if they're still looking for you together, a trio may pass unnoticed.'

With the platform rushing towards them, Ingrid looked to Dieter for guidance, though as usual. He shrugged quietly. 'We'll stay together,' Ingrid announced firmly.

18

JANUARY 1933, *BERCHTESGADEN*

'Damn.' Stefan swore as he slammed the phone receiver back into the cradle. Otto and Klaus looked over, though they remained quiet. 'What are you both staring at? Can't you see they're getting away from us?'

The pair offered reddening faces and more silence, added to Stefan's ire. He turned away in disgust. It wasn't their fault, but as he studied a vast map of the country, he knew the chances of trapping Ingrid and Dieter were fading away. With each passing hour, the choices of route multiplied, leaving their father as the only remaining link. He'd been too soft with his questioning. He knew that now, and he wouldn't make that mistake again.

****

Gerhard Stiepermann cast a worried eye around the cattle truck they'd dumped him in. When they'd taken him away at Munich *Hauptbahnhof*, he'd feared the worst. The delightful sight of Stefan's outraged face as they'd watched Ingrid and Dieter steaming off into the distance had worn off and now only a hollow dread remained. His earlier bluster at saying this was merely a business trip had failed the moment Stefan saw his children in flight.

Now Stefan knew the truth, that they were fleeing, and there would be consequences.

The truck bounced violently across the pockmarked road, sending jolts of pain across his shoulder where rifle butts had rained down the previous day. That wasn't the only source of his agony. Not knowing whether Dieter and Ingrid were safe left a deeper wound. He hoped Martin Vogt would find them, but within the dim confines of the lorry, no answers would reach Gerhard's ears. Clasping his palms together, he mouthed a silent prayer for salvation. In almost a meditative state, he purged the swaying vehicle and its destination from his mind. He would know soon enough and there would be no sense in worrying about it until he had to. But there would be no escape from his fears. Stirring within his thoughts, he pondered Freda, his wife of almost twenty years and her mother, Hildegard. Equally vulnerable. Two more people he'd failed in his duty to protect. A tear meandered down his face, compounding his shame. Only here, alone in a darkened lorry, could he allow himself this moment of weakness.

As the journey continued, the inevitable thoughts of his own situation crept in. He'd been unconscious when they'd loaded him into the truck, and only the din coming from the engine, coupled with the brutal bouncing carriage, had brought his addled brain back to life. He had no recognition of how he came to be there. The only memories came from Stefan's rage as Gerhard refused to yield any information about his children, with each denial to cooperate marked with a violent beating. When he'd finally awoken, his entire body ached. Lain precariously across a wooden bench seat, he'd tried to sit up fully, before discovering a chain anchoring him to a stanchion. A metal cuff bit into his wrist, and he moved with more caution after that. Imprisoned just behind the cab presented another issue. The tightly fixed canvas tarpaulin completely obscured the view outside. There was nothing left to do except wait.

****

'It's all right, Mama,' Freda soothed. 'We have heard no news, and we won't if they've crossed the border out of the country.' Placing some water on to the stove, she fussed to keep her mind focussed squarely on the new life, caring solely for her mother. This was all part of the plan, that Gerhard, Dieter, and Ingrid should find sanctuary abroad while she cared for Ōma. It's what they'd agreed. Only now, here, alone, Freda felt the actual weight of isolation settle. A fleeting thought that they should have travelled too came and went. No. Ōma was too frail, and of course, a travelling family group would raise questions. It was better this way.

Freda rubbed her calloused palms above the stove to banish the cold, which never seemed to end. To her right sat Ōma, snug as always in the shawl they'd crocheted together the year before. Her mother yawned and closed her eyes once more, sending a pang of jealousy which Freda quelled by warming her hands with greater vigour. Somehow, she'd held her emotions in check on the journey home from meeting Christa. The previous day's meeting and the worries it brought went unnoticed by her mother, but not Freda. Tormenting demons plagued her thoughts, leaving no room for sleep. Despite crippling fatigue, Freda pushed on, chopping potatoes for the pot, while pondering whether visiting Gerda would offer any answers. Probably, she concluded, but then Christa and Gerda seemed inseparable and there was no way Freda could see the other spiteful girl.

With darkness falling, Freda stepped outside. She knew the risks, should she stumble into the wrong person, or if Ōma tipped from her chair while left alone, but she set off towards Ingrid's former friend, desperate to learn the other's fate. Wind bit her cheeks as she hurried through the shadows. Each gust swirled around, negating the shelter offered by the buildings. The chill left each street deserted and allowed rapid progress towards Nonntal. When she finally arrived, Freda took stock. She'd known Gerda Müller and her family for over a decade. Over the last year, however, any friendship had evaporated. Studying the house, a thought struck. Despite the wind and the day marching towards dusk, people should still be outside. Workers didn't down tools and shops certainly didn't close, not at this time, anyway. Caught between knocking and turning away, Freda jumped as a bell tolled.

More chimes rang out, and then she heard the voices. A muddled cacophony melded together, followed by a cheering crowd. It explained the empty streets at least. Everyone must have gone to the *Marktplatz*. This time, Freda slowed her pace and headed cautiously towards the uproar.

From the shadows, she looked on with creeping unease. Soldiers had hastily built a stage near the fountain and there, standing, waving, and postulating, above the crowd, stood Helmut Weiss, together with his vile son, Stefan.

'People of Germany. I stand here, together with you, upon this momentous day as we celebrate the dawning of a new era. Our country is proud and now, with Adolf Hitler as our new chancellor, we will be strong again. Heil Hitler.'

Freda choked back tears as friends, neighbours – a community she'd known her entire life – cheered.

19

January 1933, *MANNHEIM*

'How much further?'

There wasn't any trace of a whine in Dieter's question, though Ingrid couldn't help feeling frustrated. They had a long way to go yet. Despite being just a couple of days into their journey, it felt longer as fatigue took hold.

'Come on,' Martin offered. 'We can rest near the river and decide our next steps together.'

Ingrid's ears pricked. Before, when their father was with them, they had a plan, but what now?

'What do you have in mind?' she asked, directing the question to Martin.

He cupped both hands underneath his chin before answering. 'We have two choices. Either we stick to our original route and head north beyond Cologne or we skip west to *Saarbrücken*, which is our closest border crossing.'

She knew the outline of their original plan meant north and onward into Holland, but that was before the disastrous intervention. Ingrid pinched her eyes shut as images of Stefan flooded her brain. She knew her nemesis would do anything in his power to extract their route, though equally, she knew their father would resist. Biting down on her cheek, she pushed the worrying thoughts aside.

Turning to Dieter, she ran a hand through his tousled hair, searching for inspiration, but as usual, her brother offered no direction. She wanted to thump him each time he cast the mantle of responsibility upon her shoulders, but as always, he remained quiet, forcing her to lead. Speed versus a measured escape along a route known to Martin, or the third choice, return to *Berchtesgaden*, hoping to reunite with their parents. The draw homeward was strong, but she knew that route was closed to them. Conflict tore into her as she considered heading west. Nobody knew that route, and the idea they could make it out of the country later that day held enormous appeal. But where would that leave them? None of them spoke French beyond a few words, and Martin had no contacts. That decided it. They would head north and pray that their father didn't reveal their true path.

****

Three days later, the anxiety that Stefan would catch-up with them lessened, but new unknowns swept in to fill the void, eating away at Ingrid. She was sick of the train now. The noise, the buffeting, Dieter's sorrowful stare. Martin had come good, at least. He'd found them bed and board each time they'd needed a sanctuary, and she was grateful each host sheltered them with minimum fuss. Despite this good fortune, a feeling of dread remained. She couldn't help herself. Whenever they stepped out into any public space, her furtive glances saw threat everywhere. Whenever she could, Ingrid clutched her brother's hand, more for her benefit than his, and today she pinched his fingers even tighter.

'Are you sure this will work?' Ingrid fretted. 'After all, you are used to crossing the border on business, but what about us?'

Martin slowed his stride, twisting his goatee as he considered. 'I think we have to cross the border together. If Stefan alerted them, then they'll look for you both as a pair. Passing across to Holland as a threesome will be safer. I'm carrying some of your artwork with me too, so if they ask, then I'll reveal we are all artists.'

'But I'm no artist. What if they ask to see some of my work?' Dieter pressed.

78

The inner churn returned at hearing her brother's valid question. She could see a red and white barrier in the distance, squashed between two buildings, each flanked by guards. *Why haven't we worked all this out? We're almost there.*

Despite slowing, Martin continued his onward march, and Ingrid found her unwilling body keeping pace. He offered a smile, as though that would solve all their problems. But beneath her thin coat, a layer of sweat formed as her mind worked frantically through every probable scenario. As usual, Dieter bowed his head in silence. She could make out the features of some guards now. Three looked barely older than her. Was that a good sign? The fourth guard reminded her of Klaus, and her whole body baulked in spasm. Before Martin could take another stride, she grabbed his elbow and pulled hard, jerking him to a halt. 'It's him…I know it is.'

'Who?' Martin asked.

She couldn't say. Something stuck in her throat as she tried to say Klaus's name, resulting in an unintelligible gurgle. Dieter looked on and his uncertain stare convinced Ingrid that one of their enemies blocked their path. She couldn't help herself as both feet wobbled backwards, her whole body desperate to distance them from the guards. Klaus's doppelgänger looked on, ready to call them to a halt, when another traveller walked up, waving papers, demanding his attention.

'Klaus and the others are hundreds of miles away, while we're just a few steps from freedom.' After days of lassitude, Dieter's words calmed, and Ingrid forced a smile. Following Martin's lead, they walked forward, trusting in their friend.

The wobbly steps continued and Martin, conceding defeat, accompanied the pair out of sight around the corner. 'What happened?' He punched the wall in frustration. 'I thought you two wanted to leave the country.'

It was Dieter who broke the tension. 'Back home in *Berchtesgaden*, there were boys, dangerous nazis who threatened us both, and that guard, the one closest. I think he was one of them.'

Ingrid exhaled. There, Dieter had expressed her fears and Martin nodded in understanding. 'Well, if we can't cross here, there may be another way, but it could be dangerous.'

'Please, can we just go? If we stay, they're too close. They will find us and take us back,' Ingrid implored.

****

From the outskirts of Venlo, they abandoned the border crossing and struck north for almost fifty miles, riding on farm carts and delivery trucks whenever they were able. Each mile took them further away from Martin's network, but seeing their fear, he accepted the alternative route with few complaints. These less-travelled paths were slow and cold but brought a new-found belief that they could break free. Everyone was a stranger and that held risks, but most rural areas embraced the travellers. One thing held their favour, Nazi sympathisers flew the swastika, a clear marker for them to avoid.

With bags weighing heavily, they waited until dusk before skirting the small town of Kleve. Ahead lay open fields and Martin could see peril written across the teen's faces as they crossed the exposed area. 'Come on,' Martin commanded as he dragged the pair along a hedgerow. In the fading light, he could just make out the dark shape of a copse and then, beyond, he hoped, would be the river. They entered the thicket in silence. Icy tendrils nipped at their bodies and Martin knew if he felt the cold, the others were suffering, too. But after they'd abandoned the official crossing, this was the only way he could think of to break out of Germany. 'Shush,' he urged, as Dieter's boots snapped several twigs. The group waited, huddling together, their plumes of breath heavy in the biting air. Once Martin was sure they were alone, they pushed on, keeping to the shadows while remaining at the outer edge of the woodland, and five minutes later he spied the telltale glint of water.

'Is that...'

'The Rhine? Yes, and on the far bank where you see the lights' – he pointed – 'is Holland.'

Ingrid's hands flew to her mouth, and Martin fully understood her trepidation. The Rhine stretched out into the distance, its width ten times that of the *Berchtesgadner Ache*. Dieter looked on in solemn silence. Even Martin felt conflicted at the sight. He sighed inwardly, knowing that days earlier, when they'd baulked at his preferred crossing, he'd offered this as an alternative. Despite this, he unpacked his backpack and began making a raft. While Ingrid and Dieter carried food and water, Martin's load was more practical. With oilskins, rope, and a large knife, he set about his work, coaxing Dieter's engineering brain to the task.

It took them three hours, and by the time they'd built the raft, Martin could barely feel his fingers. Gripping their punt would not be easy, but the distant lights drove him on. Half an hour, that's all they needed. The raft wobbled precariously as he climbed on and with thoughts that he'd never paint again haunting him; he ushered the others aboard and pushed off from the bank.

The sound of slopping waves came as a welcome relief, but as they eased into midstream, Martin looked down and spied the white faces of his passengers. Ingrid shook but remained calm, while Dieter's eyes were wide in fright. He cursed inwardly. He should have waited and tried another land crossing, but it was too late now, and he dug the punt deeper to steer them back on course. In the freezing gloom, he'd lost track of how long they'd been in the water, but it felt like an eternity. And then he saw something which sent an icy shiver through his bones.

A shout rang out, clear in the silent evening. One voice, then many, calling, ordering from the German bank. Lights followed, lancing out across the water, catching them in the view. While Ingrid clutched her brother, Martin dug the punt in deeper and pushed as hard as he could. They moved, but only sideways, making them barely closer to the Dutch side. The shouting from the patrol continued, but with a hundred metres of water separating the groups, an uneasy standoff settled.

They can't reach us.

The thought drove Martin on as he shoved the full-length of the punt into the water, inching them across the Rhine. 'Come on, paddle!' he shouted, spurring Ingrid and Dieter on. And then, just as his hopes rose, a gunshot sliced the night apart. Wild and high, followed immediately by the sound of a motor in the distance. As the lights danced across the shore, he knew they were seconds away from disaster. More shots sounded, and Martin knew they were sitting ducks on the slow-moving raft. There was only one option.

'Ingrid. Take this bag, as it's the most likely to float. I need you to take your brother and jump, and swim to the shore.'

He saw the conflict in her eyes, and her loyalty warmed his heart. But with a militia following and firing at will plus a boat on the way, splitting up was their only chance. 'You must.' He took her by the arms. 'I know this is frightening, but if you stay on the raft, they'll catch us all. I'll lure them away while you both slip quietly into the water. Look, we're closer now. The lights aren't far and once you reach the beach, they won't dare to take you. Just promise me that one day, when it is safe to come back, you'll find my sister Monika and tell her this story.'

Her lips pressed together in fear, Ingrid nodded mutely. She pulled the bag and her brother into the water with scarcely a splash. Seconds later, the raft moved clear, and Martin dug the punt in hard. Only this time, he pushed along with the flow to draw the attackers away.

20

January 1933, Holland

Ingrid woke to the feeling of pain. For one numb minute, she didn't know where she was, then she remembered and wept. Her sobs woke Dieter, though he remained quiet as usual. One fact was unclear. Both Ingrid and Dieter were each in their own bed, shrouded in warm blankets.

'Good, you're awake. Mind you explain why you swam across the Rhine last night before beaching upon my doorstep?'

Ingrid blinked back the tears, as her shocked mind tried to appraise the newcomer. She registered an old woman, but the talk of the Rhine set her eyes streaming once more.

'Oh, hush, my *lieve*. There's no hurry. You're safe here, so rest up with your friend and I'll make you both a drink.'

A few minutes later, Ingrid regained her composure, and true to her word, the woman returned, carrying two steaming mugs of tea. Aware of Dieter's reluctance to engage in conversation, Ingrid took charge. 'Thank you,' she said, wrapping her hands around the hot mug. 'I'm sorry, we've been rude. I am Ingrid and this is my brother, Dieter.'

Kind eyes reflected. 'So, Ingrid and Dieter, my name is Anika and I'm the one who answered the door when you collapsed against it last night. Do you want to tell me what brings you to Lobith?'

'Where?'

'Lobith,' the woman repeated. I assume you crossed from Germany last night.'

The place name meant nothing. Tight-lipped, Ingrid nodded. As her head slipped back upon the warm softness of the pillow, a spike of anguish ran through her and she jerked upright once more. 'Martin!' she shrieked. 'What happened to Martin?'

Anika's brow furrowed. 'Martin who? I'm sorry, child, but I saw nobody else last night. Was he with you on the river?' With head bowed, the woman scuttled past Ingrid to draw back the blinds. Sunlight flooded the room, and with the glare came the realisation that they were both unclothed.

The stranger was unfazed and even slipped a chuckle.

'Don't worry about your clothes. They are drying downstairs and you can have them back soon, but for now we need to find your friend.'

This time, Ingrid bound the blanket around her body before rising from the bed. On any other day, the sight of the slow-moving Rhine would have brought joy, especially as they'd escaped the Nazi persecution, but Ingrid's shoulders dropped on seeing the empty river. She knew Martin wouldn't be there, and the dark woods on the opposite bank reinforced her inner emptiness.

****

Anika attended them for three more days. She didn't pester for answers, she merely continued her everyday life while accommodating her two visitors. With dry clothes returned, they'd tentatively explored the perimeter of her house. But Lobith was just another village on the Rhine, and their arrival created barely a ripple. Ingrid's insides churned. They had lost their father to Stefan's clutches, and now Martin was gone as well. There could be no going back. But while hopes had dwindled, they had achieved something. The oilskin bag had survived. Led by Anika, they'd found it snagged downstream on the second day. The parcel contained valuable spare clothes. However, Ingrid's stony mood persisted as she retrieved the Reichsmark banknotes, which dissolved to her touch. As though reading her mind, Anika's first action upon returning to her home was to decant a pile of guilders into her hand, before silencing her protests. Ingrid did not know their worth, but the knowledge that they'd found another ally buoyed her mood.

'I can take you as far as Arnhem, but then you'll need to find your own way from there. There are good links to the coast and the money I've given you should get you that far, at least.'

'Thank you, Anika,' both siblings chimed. 'You've been so kind,' Ingrid added. 'How will we ever repay you?' Although gone in an instant, a flicker of sadness crossed Anika's eyes, and Ingrid sensed an untold story. The tearing sensation she'd become so accustomed to returned. She didn't know whether Dieter sensed people's moods like she did, but there was a sorrow behind their host's eyes and it pained Ingrid that they had to leave. After all, they'd escaped Germany. Wouldn't it be sensible to remain close so they could return when the troubles had passed? Deep inside, Ingrid knew that was a fool's errand, and the Nazi rise would only strengthen until its overwhelming force crushed the opposition. She wished these bitter pills would lessen, but in the meantime, it meant summoning courage and travelling on for a greater chance of safety.

After breakfast, they set off and for the first time in their journey, Ingrid didn't feel the need to look over her shoulder. She remained vigilant, but as they passed through villages and gradually saw more people, her mood mellowed. People smiled and waved. Many knew Anika, which helped, and together, with no swastika flags flying, they entered a different world. They arrived at *Arnhem Centraal* railway station and their buoyant mood held. Their fear of discovery, fuelled by the expectation of armed soldiers, was just that: fears. Once they'd purchased tickets to Rotterdam, Ingrid choked back her gratitude as Anika waved to them from the platform. They were safe, but once more alone.

21

JANUARY 1933, *DACHAU*

When they released Gerhard from the lorry, he cast his weary eyes across an alien landscape. Barring occasional toilet breaks, he estimated they'd kept him chained to the running boards for over a week. Each day took him further away from Freda, Hildegard, and his children. He wasn't sure which separation cut deepest, but now as he stared out at fences topped with intricately woven barbed wire, he knew he was in trouble.

There were twelve other travelling companions in the lorry. All strangers loaded at different points in their stop-start journey. He wasn't aware of the other men's circumstances. One man had tried to strike up a conversation, only to be shut down with a brutal rifle butt to the guts. His fellow prisoner lurched in agony before the chains halted his slide and with at least one armed guard stationed throughout their journey, everyone observed a mute subservience. At last, the lorry drew to a halt, and the guards allowed the captives to exit their transport. Gerhard stepped down, gripping a metal step on unsteady legs. The step was wet, and he ran a palm across the metal before wiping his fingers across his lips, savouring the drops of moisture. The act didn't sate his thirst, but with cracked lips and an arid tongue, the moisture was welcome.

Keeping in pairs, the men crossed a ditch, and Gerhard's ears detected a disturbing hum from the wires stretched around the perimeter. Glancing to his left, his companion caught his gaze and nodded in resignation. Further afield, lines of huts stretched into the distance, some complete while others were just a wooden framework. The base was not yet operational, but it held an ominous air.

'Good. Now that you've arrived, look around, but I warn you: don't rest for too long.' Following this ominous introduction, the soldier in an SS uniform splayed his arms wide before indicating towards the builders working at the far end of the compound, a cruel grin on his face. 'We've brought you here for your own protection, but as you can see, your colleagues haven't yet finished building your accommodation. While this oversight is regrettable, it means you won't have a roof over your heads until you've finished building.' A murmur echoed through the ranks before the soldier held up a gloved hand. 'And, before any of you get ideas that while this establishment isn't fully functional, you can leave. We will guard you – for your own protection, of course,' he added, his eyes narrowed with cold humour.

It was late afternoon; they hadn't eaten since a pathetic gruel, served hours earlier, and with the morning frost persisting, Gerhard's body sagged. Heads down, the men shuffled forlornly towards their fate.

22

January 1933, Rotterdam

Ingrid clutched her brother's hand as they looked out over the Rotterdam docks. Everywhere north of the *Nieuwe Mass* was busy, and she imagined the opposite bank was just the same. It had taken the pair almost a day to march through the city, navigating along the river, weaving between trucks being loaded and emptied. By the time they saw the twin stacks of the TS Vienna belching smoke in the distance, both were exhausted.

By the looks of things, the ship was steaming into port. Perfect. Fingers crossed they could secure a berth. Feeling hopeful, the pair surged forward, until something caught Dieter's keen engineering eye. The ship had docked, and an army of workers scurried about, working cranes and winches, as passengers descended the gangplank. Nobody bade the pair any heed, and the hubbub left Ingrid feeling insignificant. For a few minutes, the siblings sat and watched. The people and systems were efficient as both passengers and cargo spilled from the ship.

Despite their need for rest, Ingrid roused herself. Sitting still wouldn't serve them. 'Come on, Dieter. It's too cold to stay here. We need a meal and shelter, or to find someone who knows about the ships.'

They found such a person in a rickety harbour office twenty minutes later. Climbing some wooden stairs, they rapped nervously upon the harbour master's door. 'You two want to cross on the Vienna, do you?' Ingrid saw mirth behind the man's wide blue eyes, and she sensed he was mocking them. Dieter's elbow nudged her rib, further fuelling her angst.

'Can we travel or not?' She didn't mean to sound abrupt, but her own fatigue and something in the way he smirked triggered.

The man's features hardened. 'No. Not if you come in here, raising your voice. Anyway, the ship you've got your eye on won't depart until tomorrow and even then, there's a fare to pay.'

Ingrid felt a second dig in her midriff. 'I'm…we're sorry. We didn't mean to presume. It's just we're desperate to cross over to England.'

'Desperate, are you?' The habour master ran gnarled fingers across the white of his beard, his eyes alert to an opportunity. 'It'll cost you. What can you pay?'

Ingrid drew the purse and displayed its contents. The man snatched the purse and emptied it across his desk. He counted, then let out a guffaw. He pushed the purse back to her. 'I'm sorry, but that won't get you beyond *Noorderpier*.'

The sour taste returned to Ingrid's throat, and she stumbled backward before Dieter held her in check. *That's it, then. We can't go.* Her mind reeled at the prospect before she turned and, seeing her brother equally deflated, she rallied. 'How much then?' she challenged.

The man shrugged. 'It depends.'

Infuriated, Ingrid held her tongue, waiting for him to explain. While a clock ticked noisily, she fidgeted before remembering a note Anika had given them a day earlier. She pulled it out and passed it over.

It wasn't a long letter, but he took his time and two minutes passed before he returned the document. Splaying his hands, he spoke. 'So, you have a sponsor who says I should help you? This makes matters worse.'

Pushing her brother to one side, Ingrid squared her shoulders. 'What do you mean?'

'Well, look at you both. Practically vagabonds, with barely any money, and if this letter is to be believed, you've no identity papers.'

Ingrid and Dieter remained silent.

'Listen. It's getting dark. You can't stay here and you'll freeze if you stay on the dock overnight. I hear a lot of sob stories, but I'm going to take a chance on you both. That's if I can believe what this woman wrote about you. Head back down the steps and ask to speak to one of my mail runners. He's called Jan Visser. Easy to find as he's got the biggest smile in all the city, plus he's around your age. Tell him you've spoken with me and he'll guide you to my home. Don't worry,' he said, offering his hands in reassurance. 'My wife is there. She'll look after you both. With luck, she's made some *Erwtensoep* for supper.'

With no idea what fate awaited them, Ingrid looked at her brother's exhausted face and turned to go. As she pulled the door open, an icy blast hit. With the light fading, she led Dieter into the gloom.

****

'There you go,' Elsje Visser offered as she decanted two steaming bowls of stew.

Learning that Jan was the son of the harbour master had caught them off guard, but once processed and introductions made, their surprise turned to relief. Even Dieter managed a rare smile. With thick curtains drawn, they all relaxed.

The door banged as Dirk, the harbour master, arrived home. In the warm glow of the room, his character took on a new, kinder light, triggering fond childhood memories within Ingrid's mind.

23

FEBRUARY 1933, ROTTERDAM

'You're not cutting my hair.'

Ingrid stormed to the window. Both hands gripped the curtains, threatening to rip them from the rail. Her protest was futile, but how many more concessions would she need to make before they'd find safety? Dieter had it easy. She'd already seen how the Vissers had kitted her brother out. When Jan and Dieter stood shoulder to shoulder, the way Elsje had styled them, you'd have thought they were brothers.

Now, as Ingrid slouched upon a seat, Elsje would need to work her wiles to make her fit the same mould.

'There. I knew I could do it. Here, look,' the woman said while passing a hand mirror.

Ingrid gasped. The dark hair, which minutes earlier had rested at the base of her spine, was gone. She'd grown her locks for years and now she felt lost as a stranger stared back at her. There was nothing to be done, not now the scissors had done their work. Accepting needs must, she gestured to Elsje to finish the makeover.

After a filling meal, they left for the docks at dusk, with Jan leading the way. Only Elsje remained at the home. Although it sounded simple, the plan was fraught with risks, but after a week spent protected by the Vissers, it was time to move on.

The first time they'd arrived at the dockyard, they were weary, confused, and threadbare. This time, multiple woollen layers kept the chill at bay, but dressed as a boy, left Ingrid vulnerable and self-conscious.

In the dim light, the procession marched onwards until the TS Vienna loomed into view. Two gangplanks linked the ship to the dock. The closest was empty, but further along, Ingrid saw a hive of activity as people hurried back and forth, carrying sacks and other cargo.

'Right, you know what to do,' Dirk Visser said in a reassured tone once they were closer to the workers.

Both Ingrid and Dieter dipped their heads and reached for a sack each. With a cloth cap and shouldered hessian sack each, they followed Jan onto the ship while the harbour master remained on shore.

Within half an hour, the workers had loaded the last of the mail sacks and departed the ship, leaving two stowaways tucked inside.

****

'Dieter,' Ingrid whispered once a monotonous drone sounded, and they knew the engines had fired. Her brother's reassuring fingers interlocked with hers in the pitch-black store. They rested, using the sacks as a makeshift bed, aware they had most of the night before landfall. But sleep wouldn't come, and before long, the pitching of the ship combined with the oppressive closeness of the hold left both siblings retching as they hit the rough water of the North Sea.

Hours later, a crack of blue light appeared through the porthole. 'Get your head down,' Ingrid demanded, before lapsing to silence. They waited for people to come, fully expecting capture, but beyond the gentle lapping of waves outside, nobody arrived. Even the noise of the engines had lapsed. The open doorway sat tantalisingly close and when no sounds came, she ushered her brother forward. Just as when they'd entered the ship, both tipped their caps down while wrapping a sack across one shoulder. She'd memorised the layout when they'd boarded, but a night laid churning in the darkness left her uncertain. They could see the sky at least and down to the left, aged ropes wound down to the dock where someone had secured the moorings. Was this England? People were coming. Footsteps behind them, paired with alien voices, left the siblings feeling frightfully exposed. Waiting meant certain capture and questions they weren't ready to answer, so with Ingrid adopting her usual lead, they stepped along the port side. As before, in Rotterdam, two gangplanks bridged the gap to shore and with passenger activity on the furthest forward, they took their chances on the rear. With every downward step, the wooden bridge shook alarmingly, and it took all their courage to keep moving through the frosty morning air. The only thing standing in their favour was the early start. From their higher vantage point, Ingrid chanced a glance. Two orange flares showed briefly before lapsing back into shadow. It was enough. Ingrid turned away from the smokers, leading Dieter into the shadowy confines of a large shed where casual onlookers would not see their plumes of breath.

Before they could venture further, Ingrid collated everything she'd learnt since they left the mail hold on the Vienna. 'Did you recognise any of the words the men said before we left the ship?'

Dieter shook his head in frustration. 'Come on. We can't stay here. It'll be light soon and they will find us.'

They stumbled to the furthest end of the storehouse and from there, out into the open. An orange glow in the east signalled sunrise, and with seconds to spare, they scrambled out across a layer of scrub land. Tall grasses, blown by a harsh North Sea wind, whipped their ankles as they ran, but soon they were clear and finding a dip in the land, they paused for breath. To the left, they saw a hotel and a signpost with the name Parkeston and Ingrid felt her body falter. *What is Parkeston? I thought we were docking in Harwich.* Her brain felt wired with awful possibilities. Held in a darkened hold, the ship could have gone anywhere. Had the Vissers in Rotterdam betrayed them? Turning about, she cast her eyes back to where they'd come. Despite the low-lying sun which forced Ingrid to shield her eyes, the TS Vienna remained. That meant something. After all, she'd seen posters back in Rotterdam, explaining the route. Twin lines sparkled ahead, and she realised they'd crossed a railway in their haste to get away.

While she deliberated their next move, she checked the sack she'd brought from the ship before nudging Dieter to do the same.

'Good.' She smiled once she'd checked hers. Dieter's eyes dropped, and she knew immediately something was wrong. When he remained silent, she pushed him aside. 'Dieter!' she shouted in dismay. Instead of clothes and food like hers, Dieter's sack contained letters and parcels. Despite her anger, she drew her brother close. 'It's OK. The ship was dark. Here, we still have some clothes and food. Come on, it's too cold to stay here. Look, they're firing an engine. If we can climb aboard a wagon before they depart, we could be in London in a few hours.'

She did not know where the railway line would take them, but with Dieter's help, they climbed aboard a deserted boxcar. Thirty minutes later, the carriage jolted, and they were on their way, travelling into the unknown.

24

FEBRUARY 1933, YIEWSLEY

'Come on, Smiler,' the man said as he ran a rough palm across the workhorse's forelock before bringing his hand back to stroke the equine's ears. The horse shook his head playfully before snorting a reply through both nostrils. 'Glad you agree.' He chuckled.

After one last pat, he returned to sit in the wagon, where he surveyed the road ahead. Seeing it empty, he released the brake and, following a gentle shake of the reins, Smiler pulled them both forward without complaint. Immediately, a judder travelled the length of the man's spine. He was used to the vibration and keeping his mouth closed stopped his teeth from rattling. Today he had more reason for the button lip. It was exceptionally cold, and he had no desire to suck in more icy air than was absolutely necessary. There would be a brief respite, as he had plenty of houses to visit before his round was complete, and then he could return home to settle in front of the fire.

'Morning, Roy.' A woman's voice carried across a nearby field, and the man identified as Roy whistled. He pulled gently on the reins and Smiler drew to a halt.

'Morning, Maggie, how's your Frank doing these days?'

The woman dragged herself forward with balled up fists planted deep into her apron. 'Oh, you know, Roy. My lazy bugger doesn't do a lot.'

'Come on, Mags, he fought for you, me, and the King. Saw more action than most, even more than me. He's not lazy, he's just...damaged.'

'He's more than damaged.' She chuckled in reply. It was a conversation they'd had many times before. 'Get on with you, he's had years to get over what happened,' she continued, 'but where is he now? Asleep in the front room like always, while you, you're out here freezing your mitts off? I don't suppose you'd fancy a swap and come live with me, would you?'

This time, it was Roy's turn to chuckle. 'I couldn't ever leave my Florrie, you know that and well, I'm not sure she'd want your Frank either,' he ceded. 'Well, much as I'd love to stay here all day, someone's got to take the deliveries around and that job looks like it's fallen to me. What'll you be needing today?'

Roy climbed down as Maggie disappeared behind a hedge on her way to the garden gate. He quickly stretched, wincing at the lumbago, which pained him during any cold snap. She reappeared, and he immediately straightened.

Maggie's order rarely changed. He handed over two glass milk bottles before waiting for Maggie to turn away. He knew the bottles would be icy to the touch and she wouldn't linger. True to his expectation, the woman scuttled off in search of warmth and Roy continued along his way. The rest of his round was more of the same. Young Alan Foster popped up, telling Roy and anyone who'd listen about his big plans to open a shop which would sell everything to anyone. Pie in the sky ideas which didn't fit in with rural Yiewsley on the northern edge of London. With small clusters of cottages interspersed with fields, such a place wouldn't work. Still, harebrained or not, at least the lad wanted to do something with his life, even if he'd fail. As the cart wobbled along the road, Roy allowed himself a rare moment of reflection. For most of the year, he loved his job. His deliveries were hard work and on icy days as these, they could be unpleasant and detrimental to his physical health, but he wouldn't swap it, even if it was for the warmth behind a counter. The crisp air was part of it. So too was Smiler, who drew the cart even though some called him a nag.

People relied upon Roy and seeing their gratitude as he brought milk and other provisions straight into their homes filled his soul. And then there was Florrie. He'd known her almost all his life, even before the great war. There had been no place in his heart for anyone else.

A clump of mud hardened from cold, jolted the cart harder than usual, causing a few bottles to clink loudly. Roy sighed. Ahead stood his least favourite obstacle, the bridge over the railway and then, where it narrowed, the Grand Union Canal. In summer, the bridge became a snarled bottleneck and a frequent source of argument as rivals, reluctant to queue, forced their way forward in fruitless attempts to pass. Now that the winter had come, a new challenge presented. Smiler slowed as the horse and driver shared the same trepidation. The horse always found the sounds of shunting railway trucks alien and today was no different, though it was the narrow pinch crossing the canal which would be the issue. More than once, the horse had struggled for traction and the cart had teetered all too close to the edge. The load was heavy, especially given the bulk of the deliveries were still to be made. They drew to a halt so he could assess the path.

'Could be tricky today,' he murmured. Leaving the wooden slat which had tortured his backside for the previous few hours, Roy stepped down. With no time to waste, he set about gathering up gravel and dirt which lay strewn along the railway side. Using an old sack he carried for the purpose, he worked quickly until he'd completed his mission. Next, he dragged the detritus to the path ahead, especially where it became steepest. Twice he nearly lost his balance, but soon grit, gravel and other debris coated the road. Using his boots in a rhythmic stomp, he compacted the mixture until, finally satisfied, he returned to the cart. Smiler was unsettled, and Roy knew the horse wouldn't enjoy being stood idle in the cold. 'Come on, my old darling, let's get this over with.'

They crept forward and Roy sucked in his cheeks as the horse strained to pull the load. It was the same every day. As they nudged up the slope, he could feel his knuckles grip tighter until his hands shook in rhythm to the wagon's movement. The wheels were slipping, and he knew Smiler was another day older, but deep down he knew they'd make it to the top, where he'd expertly steer them both around the bend and back down the other side. He let out a breath as they made it, but Roy knew they couldn't continue on this way. He couldn't bear the thought of putting his horse out to pasture, but like him and the cart, that time was approaching.

The rest of the round was a simple affair. Further north, more houses had sprung up and their stops became more frequent, along with the conversations. Chatting happily, he showed good grace considering his fingers and toes had turned numb. Thoughts of seeing Florrie encroached. That always warmed him as much as the prospect of a fire. Still, it was good to take time out spent in chatter, even in these days of frost.

As the day wore on, the aches intensified, but they were nearly done. Their cottage lay just ahead, but before he could call it a day, Smiler and the empty cart had to be returned to the depot. Only then, once Smiler was untethered and settled with a well-earned bag of oats, could Roy walk home. The urge to drop in at home was strong. It wouldn't be the first time he'd called in before finishing his work, but not today. With one last glance towards their house, his eyes knitted together as he detected the outline of three figures in the window. One was Florrie, of that he was he was certain, but the others were unfamiliar to him. In an air of puzzlement, Roy nudged the tired horse forward.

****

Florrie Nash considered the pair standing in her lounge carefully as two sets of eyes studied her intently. She detected a range of emotions, fear and uncertainty flashed across her visitors' faces. Well, that would never do. 'Come on, you two, sit yourselves down.' Seeing confusion, she jabbed a wrinkled finger towards the threadbare sofa until the boy and girl complied. Once seated, Florrie continued speaking, though this time she slowed her words deliberately in the hope something would get through. With more silence greeting her, she slapped both hands on her hips in exasperation before returning to the kitchen. Behind her, she caught one word. *Danke*. Florrie knew the word, though having a pair of German teenagers in their house added another layer of mystery.

While she planned what to say to Roy, she busied herself. Taking a small mallet down from a hook, she whacked a pipe twice before returning the mallet to its spot. A gurgle of water flowed into a kettle, which she quickly transferred to the stove. The fire was burning, so she knew a hot drink of tea would be available, though whether her intruders would accept the beverage was uncertain.

It had been an odd morning. Florrie noted with a chuckle. Of all the buildings the teens could have hidden away in, the pair had chosen the shed at the bottom of the garden. If the girl hadn't sneezed when Florrie had stepped out for the loo, they'd have gone unnoticed. But, before she could empty her bladder, curiosity took hold, and she'd opened the rickety wooden door to find them cowering. Both Florrie and the two children seemed as shocked as one another. On any other day Florrie may have assumed the worst, that these were merely scoundrels on the take, but a lot can happen in those first few seconds when meeting someone new and this rare encounter struck her innocently enough. Maternal instincts triggered, Florrie thought about what she'd say to Roy. He'd be home soon, hopeful of three things: warmth, sustenance, and solitude. Well, maybe four things if you added the affectionate hug and pat on her backside he offered as part of his daily routine. She could help with warmth and a hot drink, but the evening meal wouldn't be the best. Tonight, they were having a meagre stew that had been on the hob for hours. She knew it would be tasty enough, but it would be a stretch to dish out four bowls instead of two.

Well, tired and cold or not, Roy would have to share. With the light fading rapidly, she couldn't countenance putting the children out on the street. Not tonight. Decision made, Florrie motioned gently for the pair to follow her into the house. Halfway along the path, she turned, amused, as two pairs of eyes stared out from within the murk of the shed.

'Come on, you two, or I'll leave you there to freeze.'

The girl moved cautiously into the open, closely followed by the boy, who loomed over her. They stood at the far end of the garden, watchful. Florrie shrugged in response before moving off into the house. While the water boiled, she dug out a tray which she filled with cups and saucers before filling a small creamer jug which she placed upon the table 'Come on, don't go blocking the doorway,' she called in vain, before setting everything down. Realising she'd missed something, Florrie dug around in a drawer, searching for the strainer, when a cough sounded, and she spun around.

'Are you going to hurt us?' the girl queried in faltering English.

Florrie's heart melted. Her instincts had been right. 'Whatever makes you think I'm going to hurt you, dearie?' she asked. Blank faces looked back. She tried a simpler tack. 'No, dear. You are safe here. I won't ask today, but maybe soon, once you're both warm and rested, you can tell me why you've been hiding out in my shed.'

At that point, she knew she'd made a commitment. That meant talking Roy around, but for now, until she came up with something better, they'd take them in.

25

AUTUMN 1933, *BERCHTESGADEN*

Freda rubbed both eyes before returning to the task at hand. With just two in the house, the pile of laundry took little effort, but despite this, deep lines etched across her face and hands. She rubbed her face a second time, but it was no use. Nothing chased the fatigue away. A pang of jealousy hit upon hearing her mother's languid snoring from the bedroom above, before she chastised herself and returned to air their wet clothes.

Outside, rain poured down with enough ferocity to rattle the shutters, despite the hooks holding them in place. Using a battered old clothes horse for support, Freda draped the final skirt across a rung and leant towards the window. She stared through the grey haze as droplets fought a hectic downward race. Downward. Exactly her mood since the others had left, but while the rain would ease in a day or two, her mental descent seemed destined to continue. Sensing a tear forming, she shook her head and forced her weary body to the door. Without a fire, the clothes wouldn't dry and their meagre log store lay beneath a tin awning at the furthest end of the garden. The wood would likely be wet, but there was no alternative. She pulled the door open. Her body bucked against the gale and before she'd even made it off the porch, her clothes were as wet as those inside. Necessity forced her down the path.

Retrieving the logs seemed to take an age. Twice she dropped her load and twice she battled with the inner demons, which told her to forget the wood and retreat indoors. By the time she tugged the door back open, Freda flopped inside, her energy spent. She collapsed on the floor, a crumpled mess with sodden clothes shrouding her foetal form. The tears were gone, replaced by streaks of rain and mud as her eyes pinched shut to stem the shakes wracking her body. The effort was futile. She was cold, aching, and wet to the bone. She rested her head on the floor.

****

'Freda.'

The voice was distant, yet familiar. Freda opened one eye, then the other.

'Good. You're awake. Here, drink this.'

A hand cupped underneath her neck and pulled her forward, followed by a honeyed liquid which dripped into her mouth. A warm sensation filled her throat, raising almost to a burn, before spreading within her insides.

'You're a sorry sight. What were you thinking, going out in this weather? If the boy hadn't come and woken me, I don't know what would have happened.'

Slowly, the cobwebs fell away and Freda recognised her mother. Normally subdued, especially since the others left, the caring maternal touch was a welcome relief. Freda tried to sit up, but her mother was having nothing of it.

'No. Silly child.' she scolded. Rough hands pushed her back to the floor, tugging a pillow back under her head. Admonished, Freda accepted the instruction. She waited, wondering what was to come. Had she really blacked out? She couldn't be sure. Something had changed, though. Warmth flooded the room as the fire burnt brightly to work its healing magic. Looking down the length of her body, she could see a pile of blankets added to the heat. She reached down. Her clothes were dry. Somehow, her mother had changed her. It had been almost forty years since that had last happened, and the thought made her blush. She closed her eyes.

When Freda awoke, the fuzziness had eased, though her back ached, courtesy of the stone floor and only a thin rug as a barrier. She looked up, catching her mother's warm brown eyes. Eager to avoid another telling off, she eased herself up onto one elbow.

'How long have I been here?'

'I found you yesterday morning, so a little over a day. You should have said something.'

Freda paused in reply. Maybe her mother was right. Something had to give. Hildegard smiled and offered a drink, which Freda accepted greedily. After the warmth of the blankets and fire, the icy water came as a welcome relief. She sat up properly and as the blanket dropped, a cry caught in her throat. She was wearing her husband's pyjamas. Sadness, swift and brutal, returned and this time she couldn't stem the tears.

'Hush now, Liebling,' her mother soothed. 'I know you miss him, but most of your other clothes were wet through or wouldn't offer you the warmth you needed. Here, look at this.'

Freda blinked furiously, wiping the tears on her sleeve. Her mother waved a document before her.

'What is it?'

'It is what you need right now. It's news. At long last, we know what happened to them.'

Freda's breathing quickened as she unfolded the paper. Trembling fingers gripped tight as she recognised her daughter's handwriting.

Our Dearest Mama and Ōma,

I write to you with a mix of great excitement and deepest sadness. With help from our mutual friend, we escaped the country and now live to the north of London. We won't say who aided our journey, for fear of reprisals, but if this letter arrives, then it is because of their kindness and courage.

Our journey faltered early on when Stefan came to the station to take Papa away. We know nothing of what happened and can only pray he returned to you safely. It tore into our hearts as we hid on the train. Papa did everything to protect us. And then, to our horror, Stefan saw us as the train departed. We wept when we left Papa to an unknown fate. Both of us knew we had to keep going, leaving our beautiful mountain home behind. We hid, fearful of capture, before our mutual friend found us and gave us the means to leave the country.

I can't believe how many months have passed since we escaped. It took time, but we've found sanctuary with a childless couple who've taken us in. They're called Roy and Florrie, and you'd love them. Roy delivers milk to the local homes while Florrie tends their home. She's a wonderful woman who protected us during the dark times when we felt utterly alone in this strange land. Roy is kind too, but is afraid of showing it, although once Florrie accepted us, he did too. Our English has progressed since you taught us those few faltering words all those years ago, though switching language serves as a brutal reminder of just how much we miss you all.

Dieter is well. A little quiet, but then he always was. He helps Roy on his daily round and fixes things around the house, which helps. You won't believe the things he's repaired. Their sink used to make a dreadful noise, Florrie thought, a ghost haunted from behind the U-bend. That's all sorted now, though.

The early days after our arrival were the worst. Odd looks and people talking behind our backs as soon as we'd spoken. Some didn't even hide their disdain, which affected Dieter the worst, but with help from Florrie and Roy, we've settled, and I think most neighbours have accepted us.

Things are so different here. Not the industry. Dirt is dirt, and poor people struggle just as we do, but the people talk freely with no trace of fear. It's not fair that you all had to stay behind. I know if you could, you'd follow in a heartbeat. Starting again with nothing isn't so bad when you're lucky to find good people. One day, we will be together again. In fact, I dreamt we were the other night. Dancing through the fields. Do you remember Papa telling Dieter off when he wouldn't stop kicking the Edelweiss? He sulked all the way home but then, just when we thought his mood would spoil the whole day, he made you both beautiful bouquets to say sorry.

For now, that's all we can do for each other. Offer hope where there was none and choose happy memories to chase away the horrors within our homeland. We are safe and well and building a new life together, but we will never forget you. You are in our thoughts every day.

Dieter sends his love. He wasn't ever one for writing, but you know he misses you every bit as I do. I'll write again soon, but please keep this letter safe and reply soon if you're able. Being away pains us so much and I know you share this ache.

At least you know we are safe beyond the reach of the fanatics.

Forever love,

Ingrid and Dieter

26

SPRING 1934, YIEWSLEY

Roy found it strange to have Ingrid and Dieter accompany him on his daily rounds, but somehow the newcomers had settled into a routine, and he had to admit the pair were a worthwhile addition. He didn't have any issue with the Jews. Heck, they didn't even look Jewish. Not to him, at least. Just ordinary German refugees in need of shelter.

Christmas 1933 had come and gone and with it, any suggestion of their German visitors leaving evaporated. With the months passing, so came the thaw and with it, every day seemed brighter. With no children of their own, Roy's mood brightened. 'Come on, lad, you know what to do.'

Although ungainly, Dieter dropped to the ground and walked forward to help guide Smiler across the canal bridge. The horse liked Dieter and that stamp of approval, along with Florrie's, was, for now, enough. That morning, Dieter's task was minor, but leading the horse while Roy guided from above made a big difference.

Both Germans had been an instant hit as most friends and neighbours alike warmed to the new arrivals with their endearing language which faltered at every sentence. The only ones who offered any opposition were a clique of teenagers, though with none living immediately close, this wasn't a problem and neither newcomer had so far sought their own age group. Another bonus was their help meant they finished the round early every day. He still returned to the depot at the same time every day, otherwise the owners would just increase the size of his round, but late afternoons had fallen into a happy rest time where even Smiler took an extra break.

There were other things too which had caught both Roy and Florrie off guard. He still hadn't figured out how, but Dieter had tinkered with the water and now the taps worked perfectly, and it had been weeks since anyone had used the mallet. Ingrid, too, had brightened the place. Beautiful drawings showing floral arrangements had become a new and welcome addition to the home.

Despite all this, however, Roy questioned the longevity of the arrangement. It worked, he couldn't deny that, but they weren't family though they'd all settled as though they were. 'Woah,' he called, drawing the cart to a stop. Quickly, he dropped and tipped his cap toward an approaching newcomer.

'Evening, Mister Haynes. Unusual to see you out and about. Is everything all right at the depot?'

The man walked stiffly along the track using a cane for support until he came near enough that his tobacco breath carried. 'Just walking the rounds, Mister Nash. Making sure everyone is doing their jobs properly.'

Roy stiffened. 'I...hope you don't mean I'm doing something wrong, do you?'

His boss remained uncomfortably close. 'I wouldn't say that exactly. Who are these two who are helping you do your work? There are rumours circulating, mister Nash.' Roy took his cap off and scratched his brow before replying. His mind whirled. *Rumours? What on earth was Haynes talking about?*

'Sorry, Mister Haynes, you caught me off guard there. Have I done something wrong?' he repeated.

'No, not you exactly, but tell me about him.' Haynes pointed to Dieter with his cane.

It was clear his boss was taking issue with Ingrid and Dieter, though Roy couldn't fathom why. He tried a softening tack. 'That one there. He's Dieter. We've left his older sister Ingrid at home this morning. It's true they've come along on my rounds some days, but they're doing no harm. In fact, I'd say sales are up since they came to stay with us.'

'But they're Germans and, if I've heard right, filthy Jews to boot. Don't you remember anything? Christ, man, you fought just like I did. We can't have their sort running the show. We won the bloody war and they're the enemy. Don't you remember?' With every word spoken, Haynes's face grew a darker shade of red. Next, he poked one finger animatedly towards Dieter.

In response, Roy calmly raised both palms in surrender.

'Don't you try to push me.'

He hadn't touched the man, and Roy immediately saw the thin ice laid out before him. His mind frantically sought some way in which he could pacify the one person who held Roy's livelihood in the balance. Stepping back was the obvious choice, but the cart prevented that escape. It was no good. In one swift move, Haynes raised his cane, determined to strike Roy down. He cringed. He didn't mean to, but his arms flew up in a defensive posture, ready to block the strike, which was sure to come.

****

Earlier, Ingrid studied Roy's face from the doorstep. Today, as with every other day since their arrival, she questioned how long their stay could continue. Her landlord's features gave nothing away as he patted down Smiler's mane before climbing into the cart. Soon he tapped the reins across the horse's back, and they moved off as usual. Roy wasn't one for talking, not to her, at least. Florrie was the primary source of conversation and that helped anchor their stay with the couple. Each evening Florrie dug deeper into their Germanic upbringing, often asking questions far too personal for Ingrid to answer. It was a game Florrie played; Ingrid was sure. She often caught a glint in Florrie's eyes, followed by a cheeky smile. And Florrie never pressed for an answer should Ingrid fall silent. Reassured by her at least, she still felt she needed to work her magic with Roy.

Today she would make a start. With Roy heading off on his round, and with Dieter trotting alongside, Ingrid stepped back in the house. The morning passed swiftly and with afternoon, so came hunger. This time, however, Ingrid wanted to do something which would make her guardians happy.

'*Tante* Florrie, please can I bake today? I have a few pennies saved from helping *Onkel* Roy, so I can go to the dairy to buy butter and I know you already have a little flour.'

'So, what'll you be making for us then?'

'Have you tried *lebkuchen*? They're German biscuits.'

The happy gleam which Ingrid hoped to see flashed across Florrie's face. They weren't any blood relation, but within days of arrival, their adoptive guardians insisted on aunt and uncle titles. Florrie gave a nod of approval and within a minute Ingrid had snatched up her small satchel and skipped brightly out of the house. Once she'd secured the latch on the garden gate, Ingrid rushed into the sunshine. Looking to her left, she saw her brother standing by the cart in the distance. That way looked as good as any. She turned and ran, her long legs taking great strides across the track. Ingrid intended to run on past, offering a wave as she ran, but everything changed in an instant. She didn't know who the man was, but one thing was clear: his intent. 'Nein.' she roared as she barrelled into him, sending them both reeling in the dust. For a moment, everything went haywire. Ingrid's heart pounded in her chest as she rolled clear. In an instant, Ingrid spun into a crouch, ready to launch. The man lay groaning in the dirt, all fight temporarily gone.

Now a crippling uncertainty grabbed her. She'd felt a rush before when dealing with Stefan, but then the boy had fled. This time, she'd defeated a stranger. She knew Roy and Dieter were staring. *Had she done the right thing? What would happen now?*

While she pondered those two questions, Roy approached, shielding her from the stranger. His response caught her off guard. 'What the hell do you think you're doing?' Before she could respond, Roy turned his back and helped the stranger to his feet.

'I'm sorry, sir. Maybe you're right, maybe they shouldn't be here. They won't come out on my rounds again.'

Once standing, the man dusted himself down before nervously looking beyond Roy towards Ingrid. She could feel a wave of hatred directed at her. Her head dipped in disgrace.

'Don't come to the depot again, Nash. You no longer have a job working for me.'

As the man stalked off, Ingrid bit her lip as shame gripped her. *What had she done?*

By nightfall, she knew, or at least she thought she did. Once the man had gone, they finished the round in absolute silence, though today Roy lingered at the cottage rather than returning to the depot. Only Smiler seemed worthy of conversation. 'Well, looks like they're going to break-up our partnership, old thing. I'm sure going to miss you.' Then, as he stared off into space, he commanded Ingrid and Dieter to get inside. 'Tell Florrie I'll be in later once I've sorted the horse.'

Ingrid squirmed as she led Dieter inside. She knew this meant trouble, and yet she still believed in her actions.

'Whatever has happened?' Florrie asked in surprise. Dieter stood mute, allowing Ingrid to take the lead. As she spoke, coming closer to the awful moment when she'd thrown Roy's boss to the ground, she felt herself sink. Finally, the words were out, and Florrie let out an audible gasp. *Was it true? Had she cost Roy his job and if so, what would become of them?*

Dieter broke his silence. 'He said we were the enemy, that we were filthy Jews. Then he went to hit *Onkel* Roy and…We aren't filthy, are we?'

'No dear, you're not, and that Clifford Haynes had no right to behave the way he did, but it leaves us with an awful problem. He's the sort who won't back down now that he's sacked your uncle.'

'But he did nothing wrong,' Ingrid protested.

'That won't matter. Mister Haynes was a nasty piece of work ever since I've known the man.'

Again, Ingrid squirmed as she felt tears prick her eyes. *Was the situation hopeless?*

She'd never set foot inside the depot, always staying beyond the perimeter, until Roy and Smiler arrived, but today she would have to fix things. Before courage could leave her, Ingrid accepted her fate. '*Tante* Florrie, I know this looks hopeless, but I made this mess. I'll talk to the man. I'm sure he will calm down and see reason.'

'Don't be daft, girl. If he lost his rag with Roy over you and your brother, you'll only make things worse.'

'Worse. *Tante*, how can I make things worse? I've already cost your husband his job. Maybe if I apologise and offer to work for free, then I can get *Onkel* his job back. Don't you see? I have to try.'

And before she lost her nerve, Ingrid dashed out, desperate to see whether she could smooth things over. Ten minutes later, she could feel her bravado wavering. People were looking at her. They all knew what had happened. Now the conviction that she could undo her assault seemed fruitless, as everyone she met took on a new and threatening persona. Her only relief came that she hadn't seen Roy when she ran to his workplace. She did not know where he had gone to, but he wasn't the person she needed to see.

Finally, she reached the red brick entrance, where she caught her breath. Ahead stood a wide-open yard, which led to a vast stable block. To her right, she eyed some sort of processing plant and to her left lay the offices. Pushing down the urge to vomit, she stepped out into the open. As she walked, questions flooded her brain. *Was this like Germany, where a lorry would drive down to collect upstarts and usurpers? Would there be an outcry as she appeared, or if they learnt she was a Jew?*

Before they'd left Germany, she'd grown to expect the worst, and it felt both strange and scary that after softening to the English way, things were turning bad again. Perhaps she'd got things wrong. Maybe, wherever men were in the world, cruelty would lie close at hand. She hoped there were exceptions. If Dieter or Roy ever changed to become oppressors, it would be too much to bear.

She eyed a dull sign which read – *Office*. She still had time to turn away. Maybe she could fix things by finding the owner. After all, Haynes was just the manager. She didn't think he held outright power, though she knew she could be wrong.

'Ahem. Can I help you with something, young lady?' The shrill voice startled her with the pleasantry.

Taking in the woman before her, Ingrid responded with as much confidence as she could muster. 'Yes, I need some help if you could be as kind.' She had learnt this was the deferential way people spoke, and she hoped she'd intoned the question correctly. Before she could check herself further, she continued. 'I'm here to see Mister Haynes.'

'I see. You're not from around here, are you?' The woman chuckled. 'Do you have an appointment as he doesn't like to be disturbed?'

'I'm sorry, no. You see there was an accident and I've come to his office to apologise for my awful behaviour.'

The older woman tilted her head in surprise and Ingrid felt sure she'd love some juicy gossip. 'An accident, you say. What kind of accident? He won't be happy if you've damaged our property.'

It seemed the woman wouldn't allow Ingrid access until she'd offered an explanation, so, sucking in her courage, she spoke. 'Earlier I knocked into your manager, and he fell to the ground. I was running, you see.'

An undisguised smirk traversed the woman's lips. Then, in hushed tones, she whispered, 'Good on you. Stupid old sod deserves to get knocked on his arse, if you ask me. Don't say I said it, but well done.' Ingrid's hand shot to her mouth in surprise. Here, at least, she'd found an ally. 'Come on then. Don't stand there dallying, there's a waiting room upstairs. Ignore Dolly who does the typing. She's cut from the same cloth as Mister Haynes, so you'd best stay quiet.'

Ingrid looked past her new friend and up the stairs, which seemed to go on forever. Clutching a wooden rail for support, she began her ascent. Each step felt heavy as her gallows mindset came back to taunt. Nearing the top, the heavy click, click – click sound drummed into her ears. Fully expecting a monster, Ingrid found the top step and looked at the petite woman causing all the noise.

'Hello,' Ingrid offered meekly.

The woman looked down disdainfully down her spectacles at the intruder. 'Well?' she boomed in a voice that belied her size.

'I…wanted to talk with Mister Haynes. I'm afraid I knocked him down, and I came to say sorry.'

'So, you're the Jew, are you? I doubt he will want to see you, but you'd best wait over there while I ask.'

Ingrid sat as instructed. As she perched nervously, she studied the room, fully aware her fingers were fidgeting uncontrollably. The typist had already unsettled her. *What did it matter if she was Jewish?* Of course, she knew from their escape from the Nazis, others would share the same horrific values. She slowed her breathing. This wouldn't be easy.

A loud ticking had replaced the noise made by the typist. Seconds clicked into minutes, all the while, Ingrid's fidgeting intensified. It would be teatime soon. The thought caused her stomach to lurch. How had her day, which started out with the promise of baked *lebkuchen*, turned so sour? Another minute ticked agonisingly by, followed by twenty more. Ingrid spent the time considering her options. She knew only one thing mattered; she had to do everything she could to get Roy his job back.

'He'll see you now.'

Ingrid gulped before standing and walking into the manager's den. As soon as she'd appeared inside, the secretary retreated, shutting the door, sealing her in. Ingrid looked at Mister Haynes in trepidation. Two empty chairs stood in front of the desk, but Ingrid knew they were out of bounds unless the manager allowed her to sit. Instead, she waited patiently, while trying to calm her nerves, which threatened to overwhelm at any moment.

'What's your name, girl?'

'Ingrid, sir. I'm so sorry I knocked into you earlier. Are you hurt at all?'

Haynes looked conflicted in choosing his answer. 'Don't be silly, girl. They make us Brits from sterner stuff. It'll take more than a Jew girl to cause me any pain.'

The jibe stung, but Ingrid imagined worse was to come. She waited patiently. She'd already apologised. *What else did he want?* Deciding to take the initiative, Ingrid pushed on. 'It wasn't Mister Nash's fault, what happened. He shouldn't lose his job over something I did.' The man placed both elbows on the desk before resting his chin on interlinked fingers. Clearly, he was weighing up the situation. Maybe he would be reasonable after all.

'You're wrong. Nash was wrong, too. You and that brother of yours live with him, don't you? If that's true, then Nash is guilty of harbouring you both.'

So that was it. Roy would lose his job because of her. In a last-ditch attempt, Ingrid changed tack. 'I really am sorry I knocked you down. Please, Mister Haynes. Is there anything I can do to make you change your mind?'

Haynes lifted his chin and leant back before stretching both arms behind his head, his enjoyment obvious. She could see him studying her, and the inspection made her skin crawl. The manager made no attempt at discretion, his appraisal predatory. Ingrid's body shook as she guessed his intention. *No, surely not.* The torturous wait for an answer continued. As she watched Haynes reclined form, her revulsion intensified. It started when she saw the man's skeletal fingers, which played as though he was already massaging something or someone within his mind. Next, she saw pockets of brown rash which coated a chin any cockerel would be proud of. Overall, the man appeared feeble. It was no surprise she'd skittled him with her charge. Seeing the rash along the manager's neckline triggered. She wasn't dirty; *he was.* Anger suffused her before Ingrid reminded herself why she'd come. For the second time that day, she bowed her head in submission.

'Good. It's about time you learnt your place. Maybe we can come to some arrangement.'

Ingrid's heart sank. With his lascivious glance, there was no mistaking his intention. She'd have to do whatever disgusting task he asked. And then it hit her. Haynes held her on a hook, and he would force Ingrid to submit until the man became bored. Then, should that time ever come, Roy Nash would lose his job for good.

And in that moment, Ingrid did the only thing she could. She screamed.

It took just five seconds for the secretary to burst into the office. Within half a minute, four other members of staff had rushed up the stairs to see what the fuss was about. During that time, Haynes had fallen from his chair and now lay scrabbling around upon the floor. His posture suited Ingrid, and she pressed home her advantage. With a new group assembled, she launched.

'That man,' she said while pointing at Haynes, 'he touched my leg and tried to grope me. He said he wanted all of me, otherwise he'd give Roy Nash the sack.'

Nobody moved into the office, and Haynes remained stranded on the floor. The assembled group looked torn. The first voice to speak came from the secretary. 'How dare you accuse Mister Haynes of such debauchery? He is a man of great standing in this company, and he would never sully his hands on a pathetic Jewish girl.' Immediately, the mood changed.

'Oi, Dolly. I know this girl, and she isn't one to lie. Now from where I'm standing, we have old man Clifford, who has, let's say, a reputation, caught sprawling while an innocent girl stands by, terrified of his advances. What say you?' he asked, turning to his co-workers, who all nodded in agreement.

'You can't talk to Mister Haynes like that.' the secretary squealed.

'I can, I am, and I will. And I want you to reinstate Mister Nash within the hour, or you'll have more than us walking out. Isn't that right, lads?' Again, support was forthcoming, and soon more workers had scampered up the stairs to find out what the fuss was about.

Finally, Haynes gathered himself up and stood. He was flustered but wasn't about to cave just yet.

'I don't know what you're talking about, Doug, but you can't threaten me.'

'Look sonny,' Doug replied. 'You're the office manager here. I get it, and I'm the foreman. And I'm betting I know who has the ear of the old man and support on the ground. Now stop your jabbering. Let the girl go and then get Roy Nash back on the payroll. Do I make myself clear?'

Haynes sank, defeated, before waving the crowd out of his office. As she left, Ingrid suppressed a smile. She wasn't sure who Doug was, though clearly, he held enough sway to offer some protection.

'Thank you,' she offered meekly as she descended the stairs to head for home.

Inside, her stomach had unknotted and instead, an air of jubilation took hold. She knew she'd made an enemy, but with Roy's job secured, maybe she could cap the day off with the *lebkuchen* after all.

27

SEPTEMBER 1934, YIEWSLEY

Ingrid stared down at the letter before carefully folding the paper and placing it on her bedside table. A mixture of emotions traversed her thoughts. On the one hand, she felt elated to hear news at last from her mother, but as she'd read down beyond the first few lines, her mood soured. When they'd seized her father at the station, she'd expected a minor punishment before sending him home, but this was much worse. She had never been to *Dachau*, but no matter how many times she read the word 'camp', the images she considered filled her with a creeping unease.

Her mother's letter continued, sharing nightmarish stories where other citizens from *Berchtesgaden* had woken up to discover friends and neighbours had gone. The Nazi response was simply they'd take them somewhere safe – *for their own protection* – but it fooled nobody. Anyone undesirable or brave enough to show any kind of opposition to the Nazi machine had vanished. Ingrid sat upright, the iron springs within her bed creaking ominously. It seemed the entire structure would collapse if she dared adjust her position. Once settled, the bed returned to its silent state as Ingrid resumed her thoughts.

Mama said that she and Ōma Hildegard were both well. That offered some comfort, at least. As she sat alone in her thoughts, Ingrid wondered how much to share with Dieter. How would he react to the news? Not well, she surmised. Deciding she'd wait a while before sharing, Ingrid grabbed the letter and tucked it beneath her mattress, while telling herself this was an act of protection.

In the months since the altercation with Haynes, a subtle change had occurred in the household. Roy's grouchy but kind demeanour had hardened. She thought she understood why, although the reason seemed absurd. Somehow, Roy had lost face, having a girl sort out his mess with the attempted sacking. She knew she'd done nothing of the sort, though she had been lucky. For many nights after, Ingrid woke in a startled panic, fearful that the odious manager was lurking nearby. Still, for all of Roy's toughness, everything balanced out with Florrie's vibrant and often excitable demeanour. Today Ingrid was baking strudel. She knew the sweet pastry would help bring the family together.

With rain threatening, Ingrid scampered down to the shed where Florrie had caught them over a year earlier, before making Yiewsley their makeshift stay. Now, instead of refugees, crates lay filled with autumnal fruit. She chose pears, dropping a few into her apron, ready for the walk back into the house. Soon, a delicious aroma filled the kitchen.

'Thank you, dear. I expect my Roy will still be grumpy, but mark my words, he'll come back for seconds if they're offered. And, with cooking like this, he'll want you here for another few years yet.'

Ingrid stopped. *Tante* Florrie's comment brought cheer, but it also forced her to collect her thoughts. Somehow, this corner of England had become their home. Yet, how could it be without her parents or grandmother?

'Are you OK? You look upset.'

'Oh, *Tante*. I'm truly grateful, and Dieter is too, but what about everyone we left behind? I got a letter today. It's been so long since we received any news, but things sound so terrible back in Germany.'

Florrie's face creased. 'It's OK child, you can always talk to me. I may not understand what's going on, but I believe you and if this letter worries you, then I'm worried too. Do you want to tell me what it said? It's all right if you want to keep it private.'

Ingrid thought for a moment before deciding to share with Florrie. Then she waited, allowing her aunt to consider the contents.

'Have you told Dieter?'

'I should really, but he is so withdrawn. I don't want to make matters worse.'

'Well, I'll keep your secret about this letter, but I think you should tell him. After all, the boy is probably out of his mind with worry. At least getting some news from home, tells him that your mother and grandma are alive at least.'

'I'll think about it, but can I keep quiet? Just for now, until we hear more from *Berchtesgaden*.'

'Of course, child. This can stay between us both, but please think about what I've said. It isn't good to keep things from Dieter. Now, since you've made such a delicious looking strudel, we'd best clear away. I love your cooking, but you don't half make a mess. Come on, you get all the peelings off to the compost heap, while I wipe down.'

Outside, the light had faded, though Ingrid knew the path. As she approached, her nose crimped in disgust as the aroma of rotten vegetables hit. Despite the length of their stay, this was one place she couldn't get used to. They had rotten piles in Germany, of course, but the crisp mountain air always purified any stench. She smiled wistfully. She couldn't remember the last time she'd climbed up somewhere high to settle and admire the view. The daydream persisted until a cough broke the silence.

'Dieter? *Tante* Florrie?'

There was no answer as Ingrid squinted into the gloom. The only light source came from the house, but that was too far away to help. With no reply, Ingrid softened her breathing so she could listen. Someone was in the garden with her, she was certain. Standing stock still, she wondered whether her mind was playing tricks. The longer she held her ground, the faster the blood pumped through her veins. All she could hear now was the rhythmic pounding as her heart increased its pace. As the seconds ticked by in silence, Ingrid chastised herself, but then another cough sounded, and her knees weakened. While she wavered, she heard the faint scrape of metal on wood coming from the vicinity of the shed. Whoever they were, they'd abandoned any attempt at concealment. Yet still they hadn't announced themselves. Now, the fear gripped. Great waves ran across both shoulders before traversing the length of Ingrid's body. With eyes wide, she gripped both fists together, mashing the pear peelings and newspaper, before forcing herself a single second to wrestle back some composure. Now she knew roughly where they were. She strained her eyes towards the structure, while stepping backwards towards the house.

As her brain went into overdrive, she wondered whether screaming would help like before. *No. I can't let Florrie come to harm.* Still, Ingrid had to get back to the house. There, at least she'd have light and a door to slam. The backward steps continued with excruciating slowness, as her eyes refused to veer away from the shed. Finally, she detected a soft glow as light from the kitchen shone through. No unfamiliar noises reached her, but the taunts rang in her ears. She paused. Ingrid knew all she had to do was turn around and take a few steps to safety, but that would mean looking away. Silent seconds ticked by until at last, with some conviction that nobody would charge down the path. She turned.

'Hello dearie,' a guttural voice sounded behind her.

As Ingrid spun about, an enormous fist arched towards her face. The impact caught her squarely above her left ear, though the punch barely registered before blackness took hold.

****

'Ingrid.'

The voice, which sounded distant yet familiar, pushed through a haze within her head. Ingrid flicked both eyes open before a wave of pain caused her to pinch them shut again. The voice sounded again, followed by gentle hands which slipped under her neck and waist. She could feel a floating sensation. *Was she dead?*

'Oh, my lord. What's happened? Here, Roy, bring her inside and take her straight upstairs. I'll follow with a lamp. Dieter, gather up a towel and some water and bring it to your sister's room, will you?'

Ingrid groaned, though her eyes remained resolutely shut. She didn't want to experience that pain again. Not yet, at least. The floating sensation remained for a few seconds until several loud creaks echoed across the room. She knew where she was. The sound of her bedsprings was unmistakable. Convinced she was in her own room, Ingrid ventured another peek. The pain came again, though this time it had lost its harsh edge. Several blinks later, and she could focus.

'*Onkel* Roy,' she whispered.

'Aye. Now, little lady, it looks like you've taken a fall.'

'A fall? You, you're being daft. Someone attacked her.'

'All right. I was just coming to that, now hush will you while I ask.' Ingrid sounded out each word she'd heard, to make sure she took everything in. She guessed the other person, standing in the shadows, was Florrie, but they'd returned to silence, allowing Roy to continue.

'Do you want to tell me why we found you face down in my vegetable patch with a face as bruised as a rotten potato?'

Ingrid's brain fought against the throbbing pain. *What had happened?* And then she remembered. Someone had spooked her by lurking in the darkness by the shed. But that wasn't the worst. There had to be two assailants, maybe more. She'd only snatched a glimpse of one before the punch landed. Knowing Roy wouldn't ease until she'd answered, Ingrid offered everything she could.

'There were men in the garden. At least I think there were. I heard someone up by the shed. Watching, coughing, taunting. I...I couldn't see down there, but I heard them.' She composed herself before continuing. 'I asked them to come out, *Onkel*, but nobody appeared, just the sounds continued. It felt odd, so I backed away. I know I could have called out, but with only *Tante* Florrie here, I couldn't.'

As she gathered herself, a softer voice broke into the conversation. 'It's all right, Ingrid. We can see you're shaken up by this. Right, Roy, go out with Dieter and check the garden. Do it properly mind. I'll care for Ingrid while you're gone.'

'Humph, I want to know what happened.'

'I know you do, you great lump and I'll find out and tell you, I promise, but if there is someone out there, I'd like you to see.' With her husband dismissed, Florrie took charge. 'Don't worry about Roy. You know he's rough around the edges and a little direct, but he means well. When you're ready, and only when you're, I'd like you to tell me everything else which happened tonight.'

Ingrid relaxed a little. The pain still bit, but Florrie always calmed most situations. 'There isn't much more to say, really. I'm sure there had to be two or more. The shed disappeared into the gloom while I was walking backwards. I refused to take my eyes off the building while the scraping and coughing sounds carried across the garden.' She paused. Ingrid knew what she had to say but bringing those words out into the open meant she had to remember her attacker again.

Florrie's sixth sense triggered as she wrapped one hand around Ingrid's palm. 'This can wait. Shall I get your brother to make a pot of tea?'

Ingrid chuckled. *What was it with the English, their resolute belief that a nice cup of tea would fix everything?* She nodded. Despite the pain, she decided the drink would help. While her aunt disappeared downstairs to place a kettle on the hob, Ingrid steeled herself for the conversation to come.

'Thank you, *Tante*. I'm ready now,' Ingrid said before resting the empty teacup on her nightstand. 'Earlier, when I said something had frightened me, I thought, just for a few seconds, that everything would be all right. I walked backwards, knowing each step brought me closer to our house. But then, just as I sensed I was back and safe, I turned, and a hideous giant thumped me.'

'Oh, my lord. What an awful thing to happen, right here on our doorstep.' Florrie's grip tightened before relaxing again. 'I'm sorry. The last thing you need is me crushing your poor hand after some ruffian took to hitting you so hard. Your poor head must hurt something proper. I don't have steak to put on it, but we'll come up with something to help you, I'm sure.'

Before the questions could continue, Roy returned to the bedroom. Ingrid sat up, but before she could talk, Florrie intervened. 'Come on then. What did you find out there?'

'Nothing. I tell you, if someone was in our garden, they're long gone by now.'

'Someone. Don't be a buffoon. There's a gang out there and one of them tried to take Ingrid's head off.'

Before the situation could bubble over, Ingrid raised her voice. The action hurt, but for a second at least, both Roy and Florrie stopped their bickering. 'There was one hiding by the shed and a second man, who leaped out at me just as I turned to come into the house. It all happened quickly, so I know little. All I can say is the man who knocked me down was big. Huge. I couldn't see his face as had a scarf wrapped around, but I'd remember his eyes if I ever saw them again. Dark, like coal, we'd put on a snowman.'

Ingrid closed her eyes as exhaustion set in. She wanted to stay awake. She wanted to help Roy and the others by taking burning torches outside to scour the area. But no sooner had the thought appeared, sleep with its cathartic properties swept over her.

28

SEPTEMBER 1934, *BERCHTESGADEN*

Stefan looked at his approaching father with growing unease. *What does he want this time?* Despite himself, he flattened the pockets across the front of his tunic before running a hand across his waist. As always, his uniform looked immaculate. The move was unnecessary, but he lacked the desire to fuel another harsh critique.

'What are you doing standing there?'

'Nothing, Papa. Just enjoying the sun.' Stefan cringed as soon as the words tumbled out.

'I didn't raise a layabout. You should get out, like I do. Leadership, that's what this country needs.'

He'd heard the diatribe throughout his youth. The words stung, more so as his father lacked the insight to see the pain he caused. He'd led. The others in the Hitler Youth looked up to him. Didn't they? It irritated him to think of such things. He led some, but others, older boys mainly, were forging greater paths, as his father felt pained to show. Next would come the other bone of contention. Though fortune smiled before his father could nitpick any further.

'Christa,' Stefan called as the girl marched into view.

'May I?' he asked his father, before stepping off the porch. Stefan lacked the bravery to up and leave without permission, but knowing his father's expectation, helped. He moved forward and gripped the girl's hand before she could refuse. Her hand felt soft and warm and immediately, she squeezed back in acceptance.

Stefan pulled her to one side before whispering in her ear. She nodded and together they set off up the hill. A minute later, they'd moved beyond Helmut Weiss's stern gaze.

'Thank you for saving me. My father, he gets...'

Before he could finish, Christa leant forward to plant a kiss. Her move was completely unexpected, and his eyes went wide while her soft mouth sought his. For a second, he accepted her advance before pulling away. He'd only kissed a girl once before, though he'd boasted other encounters. But this felt different. If they hadn't walked away from his father, he'd have persisted, if only to quell the usual accusatory glare. Now, as he pulled back, he saw confusion, swiftly replaced by anger.

Christa's fingers broke the hold, and she stormed away. Stefan looked on, uncertain if he should follow and somehow retrieve the situation. He knew he felt little for the girl, though a relationship held advantages, if only to keep his father at bay. But Christa would never struggle like Ingrid had, and that could prove a problem.

29

SEPTEMBER 1934, YIEWSLEY

Haynes fidgeted as he waited for the news. Pubs weren't his thing and as the other patrons milled about, he couldn't help allowing his lips to curl inward, forming a sneer.

Idiot workers are too dense to see they're beneath me, he thought. While he waited, the office manager nursed a pint of bitter, reluctant to pay for a second drink. Unaccustomed to beer, his cheeks puckered inwards in response to the sour taste. He'd have to accept it. Everyone drank the same here, and he needed to remain discrete.

Without thinking, his left hand picked at a scab along his neckline. Once done, he flicked the dried skin towards the neighbouring table, chuckling as it landed squarely in someone's drink. He smirked as the tiny crust sank into the frothy head, nobody the wiser.

'Where are they?' he muttered to himself. A mantel clock behind the bar chimed, emphasising Haynes's prolonged wait. With every passing minute, Haynes chastised himself. Why on earth had he agreed to meet in such a dive? There were a hundred better places, and they shouldn't call the shots. The room muggy as more men wandered into the bar. Old men, young men, workers all greased and covered in grime. None were the trio he was expecting. It was too much. Although he wanted news, they were obviously a no show. Gathering his cane, Haynes headed for the door.

Once outside, he stepped away from the door and allowed himself a minute to study the street. The pub had smelt of sweat and hops, and outside was just the same. Red brick tenements lined off in four directions, all covered with a blackened tar. To the south lay the river. On any other evening Haynes wouldn't head that way, but tonight he marched towards the water, clipping his cane against any bystander who came too close.

'There you are.' He blustered to a trio of men huddled by a warehouse. 'What's the big idea, keeping me waiting? I sat in that rat infested bar for almost an hour.' The biggest of the three men moved forward, leaving Haynes to crane his neck upwards. 'Well?'

'All right, gov. We had another job. A man's got to earn a crust. We're here now, aren't we?'

Haynes sighed before capitulating. 'I suppose so,' he muttered before directing the group to an alley where they could talk in private. Once the four hid in the shadows, he returned to his questioning. 'Did you get her as planned?'

'Yeah, we jumped her. Just like you asked. We had our fun with her. Jack and Cyril gave her a fright from the back of her garden while I looked on. The silly bint thought she was safe until she turned around and met my fist. You should have seen her face.'

'Did she see you then?'

'Nah. I put her lights out before she could get a look and anyway, I had my scarf and hood up.'

'Aye, and the lights were behind you, Sid. No way she'd recognise you,' the one called Cyril chipped in.

Haynes mulled over the update. He'd have preferred it if the thugs had taken the Jew girl to the river before dumping her in a sack. No. Running one hand across his chin, a new, lewd idea formed. They could have brought the cow to him for his pleasure first. Then the riverbed would call. Quietly, Haynes allowed his hand to run down his front as he ignored the others. After all, he could see their faces, but nothing else in the shadow. Before becoming too aroused, Sid tapped him across the shoulder, breaking the spell.

'Come on, gov. We did just as you said. Now where's the money?'

A fleeting thought flashed across Haynes's mind as he considered paying half the agreed price until he could verify the girl's condition. 'Stupid,' he muttered to himself before dismissing the idea.

'Eh?'

'Sorry, nothing. Here, put your hands out and I'll pay you.'

'Good. Cause now you're keeping us waiting.'

Haynes glowered at the implied threat. 'You needn't worry. Here's your cash,' he said, digging into his pocket to extract the purse he'd prepared earlier.

Haynes felt a bump as the three thugs jostled about, eager to check their money. Satisfied, they turned to go with nothing more than a cursory grunt, leaving Haynes alone. His hand dropped once more, though the urge had gone. Feeling mixed emotions, he turned to go, hopeful at least the beating dished out to the Jew girl would serve as a warning.

30

SEPTEMBER 1934, YIEWSLEY

Ingrid groaned as light flooded into her bedroom. Someone had drawn the gossamer curtain to one side. She couldn't ever remember feeling this rough. Her fingers reached for the sore spot on the side of her head before retracting in pain. She knew she had to rest. The fatigue wracking her body offered little option, yet downstairs someone was shouting. Clutching a pillow across her face helped until curiosity got the better of her. *Euch, what now?* Ingrid strained her ears. Whoever had raised their voice returned to silence. She was glad; her head and neck hurt from straining towards the door. Closing her eyes, she sucked in great lungfuls of air as she willed the headache away. It didn't work and to compound her misery, the raised voices returned. Somewhere downstairs, a heated argument raged.

As she continued in her attempts to eavesdrop, Ingrid wondered who was instigating the noise. In all the time they'd stayed, she couldn't recall an angry exchange. This was a peaceful home and whatever was going on, Ingrid was determined to keep it that way. Getting out of bed meant a laboured shuffle, which left Ingrid breathless and steadying herself on the door handle. She waited – out of necessity more than stealth – before creeping onto the landing. Here, at least, she could overhear more of the shouted conversation below.

There was some kind of three-way battle going on between Dieter, Roy, and Florrie. As the words became clearer, Ingrid forced a painful smile. Dieter, it seemed, wanted to go out and scour the area until he found and punished her attackers. She knew his gesture was futile, but it warmed her still. Eager to learn more, Ingrid opened the door a crack. The hinges creaked like most of the house, but nobody heard her movement. She pressed on, finally choosing to sit on the top step where she could easily listen.

From her vantage, Ingrid heard the fight leave her brother until only sobbing remained. It left her wondering how Roy and Florrie were handling the situation. Would they tell him to keep a stiff upper lip? She wasn't sure what the phrase meant, like many British idioms, but the quiet below gave her hope that their guardians were offering support. Ingrid moved to join the family, carefully descending the stairs. The sight which greeted her warmed her heart. Florrie held her brother, allowing him to work through his emotional state. Ingrid couldn't remember the last time she'd seen her brother cry so unashamedly. Even after Stefan broke his wrist, there had been barely a whimper. Now, even Roy seemed to be caught with moisture in his eye, though he'd settled awkwardly against the sideboard, hands thrust deep in his pockets. Maybe he wasn't the sort to hug.

Shrugging off the pain, Ingrid gripped Dieter in a fierce embrace. 'Thank you, brother dear. I heard your calls to go after them. It's OK. I know you feel your own pain at seeing me hurt. We are together. A pair. I was the same when they attacked you. I understand, and in time you'll come to learn what I've learnt.'

Dieter turned his head. 'What do you mean?'

'I'm sure you know the world isn't fair. Not to us, fleeing our homeland. Not to Roy when he almost lost his job because of me.' Ingrid saw Roy flinch, but she pressed on. 'There are some battles we cannot win and some we shouldn't even attempt to fight, but that doesn't mean we shouldn't fight. Tonight, you showed you have spirit. It's a part of who you are, and I never want you to lose that spark, but we must pick our battles.'

Ingrid gripped her head as the pain returned.

'All right, Ingrid.' Roy launched himself off the sideboard to support her. 'All this talk of battles sounds great, but it's back to bed for you.' He scooped her under the arms and steered her out of the room. As Roy carried her up the stairs, the floating sensation returned, but this time Ingrid didn't mind. This time, she knew she was safe.

****

By the time Ingrid awoke, the room had returned to darkness. She yawned before carefully touching her head. The lump remained tender, though the pain had dulled. Instead, a new sensation gripped her hunger. She couldn't fathom what the time was, so, fearful of waking the house, Ingrid stepped from her room and quietly descended the stairs. The flickering light of dying embers lit up the final few steps. The room was empty. For a moment, an irrational fear came over Ingrid as she glanced at the door leading out to the garden. Biting down on her lip, she crept forward. Shadows leapt across the room, but Ingrid looked only at the door. *Good. It's bolted.*

'Don't you worry, I locked up earlier.'

Ingrid gasped. She spun around to find Florrie standing behind her.

'I've seen to it the house is secure. We won't have any unwelcome guests here tonight. Now, why don't you take a seat and tell me how you're feeling?'

Ingrid settled in a chair while Florrie fussed about making them a drink. While she perched, she marvelled at her aunt's skill in moving silently about the house, when every step could cause a resounding creak. '*Danke, Tante.* I'm feeling a lot better. How long did I sleep for? I'm starving.'

'You're starving?' Florrie chuckled. 'It's no wonder. You slept all yesterday and right through until…oh, I don't know what the time is. But it's blooming late, I know that much. We'd best be quiet, or Roy will get the hump, but I made some biscuits earlier. I think your baking is rubbing off on me. I made those, whatever you call those things.'

Now it was Ingrid's time to giggle. 'They are *lebkuchen*, as you well know, *Tante*.'

'Aye, well, maybe I'm just used to the English names.' Florrie set a plate down, and Ingrid tucked in. After she'd wolfed down three giant biscuits, Ingrid slowed her chewing.

'Anyway, as I was saying,' Florrie continued, clearly picking up that Ingrid had missed the last minute of conversation. 'Roy and I were thinking about, you know…what happened in the garden.'

Suddenly, at the mention of the attack, the sweet pastries lost their appeal, and Ingrid placed the fourth biscuit back down on the plate. *Where was this leading?* As though reading her mind, a gentle hand patted down on hers. 'What am I thinking? You've had this awful thing happen and here I am dredging it up again. I'm sorry dear, maybe we'll talk about this again when you're feeling stronger.'

'No,' Ingrid answered sharply, before softening her tone. 'No,' she repeated. Seeking reassurance, Ingrid cast an eye back to the bolt which secured the back door. 'If you and *Onkel* Roy are talking about me, I want to know.'

Her aunt patted her hand lightly before withdrawing to take a seat alongside. 'All right. If you say so. Anyway, as I started telling you, we were both talking.' Ingrid fidgeted with impatience. It was clear her aunt was reluctant to voice her fears. The movement went unnoticed as Florrie sighed, a hand touching her throat. 'We're worried about what happened, and no matter how strong you think you are, those thugs were stronger than you, stronger than us.'

Her aunt had a point. If there had been two or more, then they could have done anything they liked to her and nothing would have stopped them. 'Yes, *Tante*. I know,' Ingrid replied, her shoulders lifting in a faint shrug.

'Well, yes, dear. And that's our point. If this attack is anything to go by, then you aren't safe here.'

Ingrid gasped as her aunt's words hit her. 'Are…' Ingrid choked back a sob, 'are you asking me and my brother to leave?'

Florrie's hands flew to her face. 'Oh, my lord, no child. You are family to us, and we'd never ask you to leave.'

The response left Ingrid confused. *They don't want us to leave. What then?* She studied her aunt's expression, hunting for clues. Eventually, her aunt continued. 'Of course we want you here. We were just thinking of ways in which we could make you safer. Just for now, until things become better.'

After the recent attack and how her own country had descended toward anarchy, it seemed better was an unlikely option, but she drew her focus back to the conversation. 'Roy says you'll love him.'

Ingrid shook her head in confusion, then gripped it as the pain returned. 'Sorry...love who, exactly?'

'Blimey, must I keep repeating myself? Archie. Like I just told you, though by the looks of things, the bump on your noggin sent your brain foggy.'

Noggin? Archie? 'Sorry, *Tante*. Please, can you go over that again?'

Sigh. 'We've known Archie Afford for years. He's a grand lad. Strong as an ox and a happier young man I'm yet to meet. He's around your age and we think he'd make a good friend to you,' she said with a twinkle in her eye. 'And Dieter, of course,' she added as a hurried afterthought.

Ingrid considered her aunt's suggestion. On the one hand, she had no friends her own age. Would it hurt if she made some friends here in England? But Archie was a boy. The very idea terrified her as images of Walter and Stefan tore through her mind. She couldn't help it. Her throat closed, leaving Ingrid short of breath. *Nooo*, her mind screamed. Her head dipped until it rested upon the table, and then the tears flowed. The throbbing pain along the side of her skull felt like the gentle brush of a feather compared with the anguish erupting within.

By morning, Florrie knew everything.

31

OCTOBER 1934, YIEWSLEY

Despite all Florrie's reassurances, Ingrid felt uncomfortable. The logic offered by her aunt was sound and, if Roy and Florrie trusted this Archie character, then that should be good enough for her. But it wasn't. How could it be, after the trauma of her experiences back in Germany? She tried to reconcile herself that this was England, and he'd be different, but still the doubts plagued her. Looking at their suggestion from all angles always returned her to the same conclusion. Boys would be boys, irrespective of the country. Dieter was the exception, she hoped. She knew her brother held passion. He'd displayed as much when he'd learnt of her assault. There was more to his character, she knew. Underneath her brother's skin lay a sparkling intellect whenever he could find any mechanical object to tinker with. It would come as no surprise if one day he came down to breakfast with a new, mechanised hand to replace the useless one which he normally cradled away from enquiring eyes.

Although the voice in Ingrid's head told her she wouldn't trust this new boy, she'd finally agreed to meet him, just to get some peace. 'Dieter should be here, not me on my own,' her mind teased, though she knew from the shine in Florrie's eyes that her aunt saw something in this new boy which she couldn't yet understand.

'Come on, Ingrid. I've already told Archie all about you. He hasn't stopped jabbering since I mentioned your name.'

Ingrid's face pinched. '*Onkel*. I said I'd meet him to keep you and *Tante* Florrie happy, but I know nothing of the boy. But you…'

she said, raising her voice a note. 'You've told him all kinds of tales about me and Dieter. What have you said?'

Her uncle smiled warmly. 'Don't you go worrying. Archie knows me and he knows Florrie and we are both saying he's a good kid. And as for you, we've only told him the truth.'

Ingrid buckled. Roy wasn't about to go into any detail, so she'd just have to find out for herself. Walking like a condemned prisoner, she followed her uncle towards the railway. Crossing the canal, a trip she'd made a hundred times, Ingrid became an emotional mess. To any onlooker, she appeared composed, yet still her insides churned. Lately, she felt vulnerable. *England was safe. Wasn't it?* Roy walked a few yards ahead while she dallied behind. Now and then he would turn and pause. With just a simple nod of the head, she quickened her pace, just long enough to draw close, and then as he set off again, her staid plod returned. Her uncle did not hide his amusement at witnessing her discomfort. Finally, as they crossed the tracks, Ingrid took the first look at Archie Afford.

The boy she expected to meet wasn't there. Instead, stood a handsome giant. Thick arms wrapped around a huge sack of coal before hefting the load with ease onto a cart which stood nearby. Then, before she could utter a word, he stepped forward to offer a grimy hand and a smile which stemmed from ear to ear.

'All roit there?'

'Good to see you, Archie. Here's young Ingrid, the lass I spoke about. Now, you look after her for me, will you? I've got to stop by the fish market, so I'll be gone a while, so you two can get better acquainted.'

Wait, what? Roit. What does that even mean? No. You can't! Ingrid's mind screamed, though no words came. Instead, she just stared while her mouth dropped open in an involuntary yaw. The newcomer's mouth widened in an enormous grin, and then from nowhere, Archie let out a howl of laughter. Ingrid looked to Roy for guidance, but her uncle had already turned and begun his march toward the market. Now she understood how a baby bird must feel when its parent pushed its offspring out of the nest. Her mind went into freefall.

It must have shown as Archie's laughter stopped abruptly. Suddenly, the man before her became solemn.

'I'm sorry for laughing. That weren't right. It's just when I saw your face.'

The comment riled her. The Nazi boys had judged her and now, standing here in England, where she was safe, a boy, no worse, a stranger, was laughing at the sight of her face. *What's wrong with how I look? Why did he laugh?*

Ingrid balled both hands, ready to swing a punch. And there it was again, that wide, cheeky smile staring back at her. *Argh. How can he insult me and then stand there with that grin?* Without thinking, she let rip. Ingrid swung her right fist as hard as she could towards Archie's chin. The arcing punch missed and immediately Ingrid found her body wheeling out of control.

'Whoa. Hold on there,' Archie said as both arms wrapped around Ingrid, halting her fall. The move seemed effortless and once he'd steadied her, his grip slackened, becoming gentle. Ingrid's emotions went into turmoil. Nobody had ever held her this tenderly, not since Walter. Her anger faded, leaving confusion to fill the void. Feeling foolish, Ingrid stepped back. Looking down, her dismayed eyes caught black streaks covering her dress. The smudges around her hips weren't Archie's fault. What had she been thinking? Her head dipped, and she cast a sideways glance. As she searched for an exit from the awkward meeting, Ingrid's mind rewound to play the scene back. Moving past the laughter which triggered her anger, Ingrid sounded out Archie's words in her head. His voice sounded unfamiliar compared to Roy, Florrie, and the other Londoners. Each sentence ended with an endearing twang. Now it was Ingrid's time to laugh. The titter, which formed, spiralled outward until it became a huge belly laugh. Ingrid doubled over, her sides hurting. She couldn't remember the last time she'd laughed like this, but the release was long overdue. When Ingrid finally stood to catch a breath, one look at Archie's stunned expression set her off again.

'I'm so sorry,' she offered when her laughter finally ran its course. 'Can we start again? Hello, my name is--'

'I know who you are. You're Ingrid and I'm Archie,' he replied simply.

This time, she accepted his offered hand. Ingrid looked down. Her fingers looked tiny against his. Yet after both their outbursts, her discomfort had vanished. She even allowed her hand to linger for a few seconds longer than needed. Archie was strong. That much was clear, though Ingrid felt charmed by his underlying gentleness, and she smiled as a flutter ran across her stomach. Maybe the glint in Florrie's eyes meant something after all.

****

Ingrid pressed her fingers down the side of her pinafore before admiring herself in the mirror. She'd grown taller over the last year. She'd almost certainly overtaken her mother in height. The realisation triggered a moment of sad reflection. A little voice pricked inside, telling her she had no right to see any beauty within herself with the world in the state it was. She turned away, choosing to focus on the outside view instead. Beyond the shed at the end of the garden sat a field where tall grasses blew with the wind. The shifting pasture resonated with her mood, but she lifted her jaw and straightened up. *I'm the best I can be today,* she thought, eyeing herself in the mirror. She turned away and stepped onto the landing.

'Are you going off to see him again?' Dieter stood against the doorframe of his room.

Ingrid bristled. 'What do you mean, *again*?'

'You know what I mean. You're off seeing *him* again.' Dieter failed to keep the petulance from his voice.

For once, her brother's outburst left her speechless. How dare he dictate her friendships? She stormed downstairs and out of the house. Without checking whether she'd shut the door, Ingrid burst along the path. Seconds later, her long legs had taken her to the back of the garden. As the shed flashed by, any thoughts of a hidden assailant vanished. Instead, her focus was on the gate ahead. With grim determination, she sped up and at the last moment, she hurdled the gate in a graceful vault. Then she ran. The grasses whipped her legs as she crossed the meadow, but Ingrid didn't care.

Using Dieter's words as fuel, her pace quickened until her sides hurt. Finally, with the meadow far behind, Ingrid came to a halt, clutching a wooden fence for support. Despite the great heaves coming from her chest, Ingrid dug her nails into the moss-covered post until her breathing steadied. A tear formed, which she wiped away in disgust, leaving a dark smear above her nose. As she lowered her hands back to the fence, Ingrid blew out both cheeks. This wasn't her. She didn't argue with her brother, then turn and run away. Seeing her gnarled green fingertips only added to her angst, and she felt another tear fall, immediately followed by another.

'Ingrid. Is that you?'

A jolt of horror swept through her brain as she recognised the lilting tones that could only have come from Archie. *He can't see me like this.* In response, she buried her streaming nose deeper into her palms in the vain hope he would go away. Silence engulfed the scene, persisting to add another layer of awkwardness. If her lungs would have allowed, Ingrid would have run again, but she knew she couldn't. Not now. Instead, she did the only brave thing she could. She looked up. Archie's wide smile greeted her, melting her anxiety, and immediately Ingrid forgot how messy she looked.

'Oh, Archie. What are you doing here?' she asked, hoped to distract him from her state.

'Well, I'm supposed to be at work really, but I saw the way you took off across the field like a scalded cat and I had to come and see.'

He'd seen her and chosen her wellbeing over incurring the wrath of the coal merchant. A warmth spread across Ingrid's cheeks. Suddenly tongue-tied, she looked about, eager to divert his attention while she gauged their location. In the distance, she could see the canal dissect the landscape. With that landmark found, she traced her eyes to the right until familiar buildings appeared in the distance. Patting her eyes dry, she made a quick decision.

'Come on,' she called. 'I'd feel terrible if you got into trouble because of me.' Before Archie could query her action, Ingrid skipped off towards the coal merchant as though she didn't have a care in the world. Yet inside, all she felt was an exciting turmoil. As she glided across the field, Archie caught up. If her friend seemed worried or unsure, she couldn't read it with her casual glance.

'I remember Roy said you were Jewish. What's that like?'

The question caught her off guard and she quickened her pace to give her time to plan her answer. With Archie's greater stride, the move didn't work, triggering a familiar frustration, as her temporary escape met with Archie's wide smile. Accepting defeat, she slowed, though she still wanted to get Archie back to work, so couldn't let-up entirely. Given they would keep each other company for the next few minutes, Ingrid considered the question properly. As she did, a sense of shame settled across her shoulders. *She was Jewish and proud, wasn't she? Yet, where was that pride in her religion now?* Archie's question had been innocent enough, but somehow, all Ingrid's thoughts focused on her family back in Germany. When she'd fled the country with Dieter, they'd seen it as an escape, only now their escape seemed like some kind of betrayal. As she worked through her muddled thoughts, Ingrid looked up. They were closer to the coal merchant now as the blackened building sat starkly against the green field where they walked.

'Erm...' Ingrid stuttered. 'I'll tell you about it. Just not today. Look, I've made you late for work. You mustn't get into trouble over me, so go now. Please.'

This time, a frown formed across Archie's brow. Nodding curtly, he turned away. Ingrid dropped her gaze. She couldn't work out why the morning had gone badly. *Stupid brother, stupid Archie, stupid religion*, her mind mocked. She waited until Archie had rejoined his workmates before taking her muddled thoughts back along the path. One thought was clear. Ingrid – and Dieter, if she could persuade him – needed to contact the Jewish community in London.

32

WINTER 1934, MUNICH

Stefan studied the platform as rain tumbled across the tracks, creating little crowns before the water finally settled. In the distance, a train rumbled forward, ready to disgorge the passenger he needed to see. As he waited, mixed memories surfaced. It had been two years since he'd last visited Munich *Hauptbahnhof*. Then he'd suffered the indignity of Ingrid and Dieter's escape, only offset when he'd arrested their father. The sour taste lingered. A loud whistle stirred him from his thoughts. Now, instead, he looked on with amusement as dark smoke engulfed a couple who'd lingered upon the footbridge.

Stupid fools, he thought as the rain beat down, soaking anyone who hadn't sought shelter. Safely dry, behind the platform, Stefan straightened before looking down at his uniform. Everything looked smart. It had to be. He knew today could become the start of something new, and if this meeting went well, then maybe, for now at least, this would sate his hunger.

He'd felt sublime during the journey to the *Hauptbahnhof*. When his father suggested the idea, he couldn't believe it. But it had happened. Stefan, alone and in control while their chauffeur drove the way. Watching the pathetic Jews working to patch the roads while a thunderstorm raged, caused absolute delight. As they passed the wretched figures, his mind conjured up the Stiepermann family. The daydream faded as their car motored past, though a bitter resolve remained. The dark emotion steeled him as the miles swept by until finally his driver delivered him to the station.

'Come on, you idiot. Can't you see it's raining? I mustn't get wet. Hurry.' Stefan commanded before the car had come to a stop. His driver hurried out into the torrential rain before returning seconds later with an umbrella which threatened to implode against the storm. Stefan would have liked to walk tall and proud into the station, but even he could see it wouldn't be possible. What would be the point, anyway? Commuters scurried about, heads down. None were offering him a second glance. He shrugged off his driver with a firm instruction to stay with the car before marching forward. Then came the ninety-minute wait. Despite berating his driver's slow reactions when they'd arrived, Stefan couldn't risk missing this meeting. But even he found his toes freezing up as the train finally arrived. A riot of passengers disembarked and then, as the crowd thinned, Stefan felt a chill. Had he met the wrong train? His mind spun. Instantly, an accusing thought flew into his head. *It's my driver's fault. He's delivered me to the wrong train. How could he? I'll see to it he never drives me or my family again.* Bile rose in his throat as he sought an explanation. Despite a shaking fury which had erupted from nowhere, Stefan waited. What difference would a few more seconds make? To calm himself, he counted down the carriages, one, two…eight. And then he realised. Nobody had exited the last carriage. *Could that be them?* Surely not. That carriage lay beyond the shelter of the platform roof. They wouldn't let anyone as important as this get wet.

Stefan stamped his feet in frustration. Even with his umbrella, he wouldn't venture out into the storm. It felt a fool's errand. While he dithered in confusion, a new whistle sounded, and the train lurched forward. Slowly, each empty carriage paraded before him, and Stefan turned in disgust. During the previous hour, boredom had set in, leaving him to count every brick on the wall. The screen echoed an emptiness and his body sagged. He didn't hear the train's momentum slow as the last carriage pulled fully into the station.

'Stefan. What are you doing, staring at the wall?'

Stefan heard the familiar twang of irritation and he spun around. Instantly his eyes locked onto those of his father, triggering a chill which sped along his spine. 'Papa. What...Why?' he stammered.

The questions died upon his lips as a flurry of guards exited onto the platform. Each quickly formed a guard of honour with two precise lines. Once assembled, a further figure stepped out onto the platform and Stefan gasped. The newcomer was immaculate and with his blond hair trimmed short across the sides, Stefan recognised the man: Viktor Lutze, the head of the Sturmabteilung. This was who Stefan needed to see. He could hardly believe it.

As Stefan waited for Lutze to walk forward, he felt his feet solidify and a panicked voice squeaked within his head. *I shouldn't be here. Not now, not with Papa standing by.* He could feel his father's breath blowing condensed plumes across his neck. As the tiny hairs behind his head bristled, Stefan gripped his collar to stem the cloying sensation.

'Viktor, please come here. Let me introduce my son.'

The surreal sound of Helmut Weiss's voice echoed across the platform as Lutze marched forward and offered a disarming smile. Stefan tried to meet the man's enquiring stare with one of his own, though as heat rose to his cheeks, he couldn't match the appraisal. He lowered his head before a fierce slap between his shoulder blades snapped him back to attention.

'You old rogue, Helmut. He's just like you. I'm sure he will be just the person I'm looking for.'

'Of course. He's my boy. Didn't I tell you he'd make the ideal candidate?'

Stefan's brain spun. He'd come to the station for one reason, a private meeting with Lutze and yet his papa had taken over, leaving him in a muddle. It irked, but now was not the time to quarrel with his father.

'It's good to meet you, sir,' he offered, showing confidence he didn't feel.

142

'Ah, you have a voice. Excellent. Do you know why we've asked you here today? Come, walk with me.'

Before he could answer, Lutze wrapped an arm around Stefan's shoulders and, like an old friend, led him away. 'Here, sit, watch with me a while,' Lutze said as he directed Stefan to a bench.

Stefan sat and looked about at the passing commuters while Lutze sat alongside. He'd already studied the travellers for over an hour, but this time, under Lutze's scrutiny, he observed with fresh eyes. Most visitors to the station ambled about, interested only in timetables and when they could leave. A few hopped excitedly about as weary travellers disembarked. Some looked at his father and the assembled guards with fear in their eyes, while others offered only pride.

'What are we looking for?' Stefan asked.

'Do you remember my predecessor?'

Stefan knew. 'Ernst Röhm,' he muttered.

Lutze nodded. 'And do you know anything about him?'

The question threw Stefan. *What's he after?*

Before he could plan an answer, Lutze took control of the conversation. 'When I asked you to look about the station with me, I wanted to see whether you see all the undesirables that I see. I mentioned Röhm for a reason. He had certain…preferences.'

The word hung. *What preferences?* Stefan wondered.

'The *Führer* has his own reasons which we won't question, but he turned a blind eye to certain behaviours exhibited by my predecessor. I am not Röhm,' Lutze finished firmly.

Stefan struggled to put the pieces together, and then he saw it. Across on the opposite platform, lurking within the shadows, stood two porters. If his eyes hadn't been scanning, he'd have missed it, but as he squinted, something in their behaviour triggered. He could only see part of their bodies, but what he saw, told. One man was clearly stroking the arm of the other in what showed as a display of affection.

Lutze tracked Stefan's shocked stare and smiled. 'See?' he said with glee. 'I knew you'd understand.' Immediately, the officer signalled to his guard detail. Stefan looked on as four of the soldiers broke away and hustled over the bridge. Within seconds, they'd reached the platform opposite, where they sped up to reach the alcove. Stefan looked on in breathless excitement. Two soldiers approached, while the remaining pair held a perimeter with guns raised. Across the void, Stefan watched. His lips salivated as he sensed the porters' fear, but the soldiers gave them no chance. The two foremost soldiers hefted their rifles high and before anyone could protest, they swung the butts down in vicious sweeping blows. One porter collapsed into the shadows, while the other toppled forward, his body splayed across the platform. *'Verdammt homosexuell,'* shouted one guard, before kicking the prone form.

The guards stepped away and turned to face Lutze. Stefan looked on, his throat dry, as he processed everything he'd seen. 'An excellent demonstration, *Stabschef* Lutze. What will you do with them? Send them to *Dachau?'*

'Dachau. Hmm…We could, I suppose, but I'm sure you know how overpopulated the camp is.'

Lutze turned away and signalled to his personal guard on the opposite platform. The men dragged the two slumped porters to the platform edge, where they waited for the next train to approach. As the train swept into the station, Stefan realised their plan, but even he couldn't quite believe it. Once the smoke had cleared, both porters had vanished.

****

The return journey to *Berchtesgaden* was sombre. Despite a rare show of encouragement from his father, Stefan felt a mixture of emotions.

'Come on, boy,' his father goaded. 'Why aren't you thanking me? This is a great opportunity for you…for us. You must accept the offer, or you'll make me look bad.'

Stefan nodded, agreed with his father. Lutze had given him a massive promotion, one which any other eighteen-year-old would kill for. The problem was that he didn't feel ready. Bossing Klaus, Otto, and Walter about came naturally. It was even fun, but this time he would lead men. How would they respond to him barking orders? But even this responsibility wasn't the actual issue. Dishing out twisted abuse towards the Jews held appeal, as did punishing the vagrants and gypsies. All were scum in his eyes. No, there was one other issue, hidden deep within. One porter had regained consciousness in the moments before the guards pushed him and his friend to their deaths. They didn't deserve that, but Lutze had made his position clear. He'd tasked Stefan to lead a team to hunt all of Lutze's deviants down. Something deep inside him wrestled with the notion. He could do anything he wished with all who opposed, but there were some quarters of German society which he wanted left well alone.

33

SPRING 1935, LONDON

Ingrid swept into the kitchen, a huge smile across her face.

'You look happy,' observed her brother.

'I am,' she replied, offering no further detail.

Dieter rolled his eyes. 'Go on then. Tell me.'

'I will, just give me a minute.' She paused, amused that delaying her explanation left him infuriated. She waited still longer before sighing. 'Here,' she said, offering him a newspaper she'd hidden behind her back.

'What's this?'

She tutted and snatched it back. 'Here, look.' She jabbed her finger at the title.

'So? You've found a newspaper.'

'Ach. Are we even related? It's the Jewish Herald. I've been looking for a copy for weeks. Now I've found one, I've been reading the articles. It's such a relief to hear news, even though some bits are scary.'

'You're happy because the newspaper scares you. And you ask if we're related.' Dieter chuckled. 'All right, I'm listening. What is it about this newspaper that's got you excited? And where did you find it, anyway?'

'*Tante* Florrie got it for me. She's a treasure. I don't know who gave it to her.'

'You're rambling.'

'Sorry. Here it is,' she said, flicking through the pages. Pressing the paper flat across the table, she showed her brother the article which had caught her eye. It detailed a list of services at a synagogue on Philpot Street in Whitechapel.

Bursting her bubble, Dieter shrugged. 'And so?'

'And so I'm taking the train there...even if you don't want to come.'

Her brother's eyes lit up. 'Really? Of course I want to come.'

****

Ingrid pressed her nose against the train window, while Dieter settled himself into the seat opposite. When she finally withdrew, her brother wiped a smudge from her cheek. 'We can't have you looking messy where we're going.'

She nodded gratefully. As the train sped up, she returned her attention to the window. Although they'd only travelled a few miles from Yiewsley, everything looked different. Row upon row of terraced houses, each brick coated with blackened ash, raced by. Only the rattle as each carriage moved along the rails offered any familiarity. This really was a million miles from Bavaria. The carriage appeared the same though, and for a second, Ingrid's mind returned to the day when they'd hidden like cowards while Stefan had taken their father off for questioning.

'I know. I miss him too,' Dieter comforted as he read the situation.

Ingrid shrugged defensively. She refused to let her wandering mind sully her plans. 'I hope you'll help me find our next train,' she said, switching the subject.

Dieter's eyes widened in surprise. 'I thought you knew where we're going.'

She did, or at least she thought she did. Roy had explained the London trains, but once they'd left Yiewsley behind, her belief faltered. She'd enjoyed the walk to West Drayton station, Dieter trailing along behind. The weather was warm and everywhere she looked; she saw new life erupting in an array of shades. She loved the blossoms the most. They had a softness and innocence Ingrid desired in her own life.

Roy's instructions had been clear: From West Drayton, take the line all the way to Paddington. From there, after a short walk, they must take the Metropolitan line all the way to the end where the trains would halt at Aldgate station. From there, they had a short walk into Whitechapel and the address they sought. They'd caught the first train and arrived in a haze of excitement. But now, as more stations came and went, Ingrid wondered whether they were on the correct line. She knew other trains went elsewhere and cursed herself for not checking.

Dieter sensed the mood. 'Don't worry, Ingrid, we're on the right train. I checked before we boarded.' Her brother's words comforted, and she settled back to enjoy the journey. As the carriage rattled along the line, she turned to study her younger brother. Dieter had always been tall, but now he towered above her. His keen eyes took in everything around them, though while she studied the people, parks, and flowers, he examined the mechanics of the carriage. Right now, she tracked his eyes, which followed the line of a pull cord, designed to act as an emergency brake. She hoped they wouldn't need it.

Despite the constant bumping as their carriage clattered along the tracks, Ingrid wished she'd brought some paper, though even she couldn't etch one of her beautiful drawings before the landmarks flashed by. She'd have to settle for composing them from memory later, though she knew there were too many to recount. The volume of sights and sounds left her slightly giddy, and despite Dieter's earlier lethargy, she knew he felt the same. Only one niggle remained. *Will all Londoners hate the Jews?* Roy and Florrie reassured them, but still the thought wormed its way into her brain. The train entered a tunnel, and Ingrid shuddered, clamping both eyes shut.

'It's all right, Ingrid,' Dieter comforted. 'We've been through tunnels before.'

She knew he was right, though the tunnels in Germany lasted just a minute or two, and then they would burst free to look upon a panoramic vista once more. Here, she felt the blackness would never end. Now she felt every vibration as the train lumbered onward, travelling deeper into the void. A voice filled her head, a familiar, taunting voice. Travelling the length of the garden path and that horrid scraping noise, all designed to frighten her — 'Ingrid.'

She didn't respond. Opening her eyes would lead her back to that place, one where a monster would strike her down. Her hands balled into fists. She couldn't face another attack. The voice sounded again, this time with greater urgency. Her eyelids fluttered, allowing a sliver of light to enter. A firm hand gripped hers, and as she traced a finger across one palm, she recognised the unusual shape of Dieter's weakened hand. 'I...I'm sorry,' she wept. Her brother drew her into a hug, masking her from the other passengers.

'It's OK. I should have seen this coming. You didn't like the dark when we were little. Do you remember that time when *Ōma* Hildegard helped me carve pumpkins, and I snuck into your room to give you a fright?'

The childhood memory worked its magic to push her attackers from her mind, and she smiled. 'I remember. Mama was ever so cross, though if I remember correctly, she was angry with herself as she couldn't help laughing, despite how upset I felt. I forgave you, though.'

'And the next year, you carved the pumpkins into beautiful fairies, which shone like a protective ring around the room when we placed our candles inside. One day, my sister, we will make them again.'

Ingrid heartened at the thought. 'Where are we?' she asked, bringing them back to the present.

'We're just leaving Great Portland Street. It won't be long now.'

He was right. Five minutes later, the pair burst out of Aldgate station into a riot of sunshine. Away from the stifling interior of the carriage, Ingrid breathed in the sight. The street was full, but everyone was going about their business, and nobody gave any attention to Ingrid and her brother. Her mood brightened instantly.

'Come on, let's go this way,' she suggested, while playfully tugging her brother's arm. They turned left and followed Whitechapel High Street until Ingrid spied a right turn, leading them down Commercial Road. Ingrid and Dieter marvelled at the wide roads. Travelling through the suburbs, Ingrid had caught sight of grim, blackened buildings. Here, though, everything looked well kept. The sight filled her with pride. 'See, Dieter. The Nazis call us dirty Jews, yet everything I see before us is clean.' Hope mirrored in his eyes, which energised her as they continued along. As they moved further down the street, bright awnings dazzled, while cars wound their way around a stall holder who'd set up his wares in the middle of the street. 'Wow, Dieter, have you ever seen a street like this?'

Her brother shook his head and grinned, before pulling Ingrid away from an imminent collision with a porter loaded up with a crate of vegetables.

Ingrid grew uncertain as homes replaced stalls, and where the former dwellings had shone, these buildings reeked of neglect. Tiny urchins peered out from every doorstep. Innocent, enquiring faces that touched Ingrid's heart. *Surely that many children can't live in these tiny homes.*

Ingrid knew they would have to stop and ask a stranger for directions and the usual questions regarding acceptance bombarded her. She baulked at approaching the first few who walked nearby. Everyone looked so alien. With each opportunity passing, her anxiety grew until she spied a man with a kippah. 'Shalom,' she began. 'I wonder if you could guide us to the Philpot Street Synagogue?'

The man smiled kindly. 'Shalom. Of course, if you follow this road for two more streets, you'll see the turning on your left. The synagogue is about halfway along. You'll like the rabbi, he's a good man,' he added.

Buoyed by the positive instructions, Ingrid and Dieter arrived outside the synagogue a few minutes later. They'd seen a few impressive buildings in London, but they'd forced them to worship in a small wooden hut back in *Berchtesgaden*. There was no comparison. Two vertical columns stood tall, with a stone façade on each side. Atop, the solid gable echoed an ancient temple. A small crowd gathered outside, and, despite their sombre attire, Ingrid saw nothing but family. She stepped forward, only for Dieter to pull her back. 'Are you sure you want to go in?'

'Of course. We are strangers in their world, but we've come this far and I'm certain they will welcome us. Besides, the man who directed us said the rabbi is a good man.'

While they paused, a small girl emerged from the throng and scuttled towards them. 'You're new here, aren't you? Can I show you my puppet? she asked while waving the toy. 'Papa says it's Isaiah. What do you think?'

Both Ingrid and Dieter faltered as they regarded the pair of innocent brown eyes which stared unerringly back. 'Well, I think your papa is wise,' Ingrid finally replied. 'Which one is he?'

The girl offered a merry wave towards a man exiting the synagogue. 'Papa, we have visitors. Come and see.' And with that, she skipped away into the crowd.

The rabbi smiled self-consciously, torn between his obligation to regular worshipers and welcoming the newcomers, but after a moment's hesitation he threaded through the crowd towards them.

'You must forgive my daughter, Millie. She is so innocent, a trait we strive to protect during these troubling times. I am Rabbi Cohen. Welcome to our synagogue, though you'll have to excuse me as Shacharit is about to start.'

Ingrid beamed and once the rabbi had departed, she pulled Dieter towards the girl called Millie.

'Millie,' Ingrid called.

The child turned, shielding her eyes against the sun. 'Oh, hello. Did you see Papa?'

'Yes, we did, and he said that you're the most important person here, and that if we asked kindly, you would show us where to go so we could enjoy the service.'

Millie beamed. 'My papa says I'm the most important person here, often, but I don't think he is right.'

'Your father is wise in choosing you, but why do you think others are more important?' Ingrid queried as they walked inside.

'I've been reading the Torah and when Moses led us out of slavery, he saw everyone as important,' she proudly explained.

'Ahh. You are as clever as your father, Millie. Now, do we have time to see your puppet before the service begins?'

Millie grinned excitedly.

****

'See. That wasn't too bad, was it?'

'You were right.' Dieter agreed. 'I enjoyed it. Though I'm not sure I'd want to come every week, and not in the winter.'

'We can't afford to come every week.' Ingrid sighed. 'But this is a start. Did you see how many people came? I couldn't believe it. There were at least four times more than we'd see back home.'

'Hardly surprising. We are in London, after all.'

'Well, I plan on coming back as soon as I can. Millie is an absolute delight and I know I'll miss her as soon as we return to Yiewsley.' Ingrid saw the half smile on Dieter's face and knew he felt the same way.

While they stood outside the synagogue, Ingrid saw Dieter's body tense. Along the road, some men were pounding on the front door of a nearby house. Their angry cries sent shivers through her, but Ingrid forced herself to focus. The door showed signs of wear as tiny flecks of green paint fluttered to the floor with every thump. However, the door stood firm, increasing the men's ire. Ingrid realised they would have to walk past them if they were to follow their original route back to Aldgate, and she scanned the area for a suitable detour. She caught Rabbi Cohen's eye and beckoned him over.

'You're worried about what's happening? Watch a moment longer. You'll see.'

They didn't have long to wait. Soon, enough locals rallied to see off the angry visitors.

'What just happened? Who were they?' Ingrid stuttered.

The rabbi gave her a wry smile. 'The first men were bailiffs. Many here cannot pay the high rents.'

'But who came to scare them away?'

'They're the communists. There are plenty who live nearby. Here, and by the docks. And, like us Jews, they stick together.' He cleared his throat and lowered his voice. 'We live side by side, along with another community of Irish Catholics. You saw firsthand our vibrant mix of neighbours. They're good people, and we're lucky to share this piece of our world. Now if you'll excuse me, I have some homes to visit.' He turned to go but added a last word. 'I know today you've seen some unity and for that I'm glad, but, as I'm sure you're aware, there are those who visit these streets mean us harm. They prey on the young and elderly alike, daytime and night. I admire your courage in coming today, and little Millie loved the attention. You'll always be welcome here but stay together when next you visit. I bid you a safe journey, my children.'

Despite Cohen's praise, his last comments stuck, and Ingrid's fear resurfaced. She didn't like to see groups squaring off against each other, and she quickened her pace, forcing Dieter into a trot.

As soon as Aldgate's station hove into view, Ingrid steadied herself. This time, she knew what to expect, though the prospect of travelling through a dark tunnel dampened her mood. With Dieters' help, she readied herself. She would not buckle and allow the fear of darkness to win.

34

MID-SEPTEMBER 1935, *BERCHTESGADEN*

A sharp knock sounded at the front door, waking Hildegard and causing Freda to curse. 'Who is it calling this late?' she grumbled. The month had been cold and with little money for heating, aches were commonplace, though Freda rarely grumbled. It was the timing of the caller that bothered her.

'Yes?' she called testily, drawing back the bolt on the door. Stefan and three others loomed on the doorstep, all intimidating in their smart uniforms. She wrinkled her nose in disgust. 'Well?' she asked, unable to remove the sour note from her voice.

'Good, we didn't wake anyone. I'm glad,' Stefan said.

They had, but arguing the point would bring no reward. As the cold air flooded in, Freda's patience waned. 'May I ask why you are calling this late in the evening?'

Stefan clicked his heels together. 'Of course. I'm sure you know by now that the laws in our country have changed.'

She didn't, though the mention sent a chill across her back. 'No. Which laws?'

Stefan's face lit up. 'I'm sorry nobody has told you.' Freda could see a transparent lie when she saw one and steadied herself against the frame for what would come. 'They're called the Nuremberg race laws, a master stroke, if you ask me. As of yesterday, you and your mother no longer have German citizenship.'

Freda's mind danced skittishly in search of answers. *What does this new law mean? Nothing good if Stefan Weiss is delivering the news.* Though eager to close the conversation and the door from the howling wind, she feigned interest. 'We hadn't heard,' she responded, hating the tremor in her voice.

'Well, now that you're aware, you will naturally allow me and my men to inspect your house, as I am sure you are both good German subjects.'

She didn't understand, and the word *subjects* frightened her. Freda faltered, unsure what to do. Seeing his chance, Stefan shoved his way inside, the three others following close behind. 'Excellent,' he said. 'You'll find things are a lot easier when you comply.'

The threat was obvious, especially with Gerhard gone, and a feeling of helplessness swept over her.

'Who is it, dear?'

Freda heard her mother calling from the next room, which filled her with a sudden fear. These thugs did not distinguish between the young and older adults, the fit and the frail. Would they use their new-found powers against her mother?

'It's nothing, Mama,' she replied, quickly shutting the front door. There was nothing for it. She'd have to stifle her anger and show them around as quickly as she could, though being ordered about by mere boys left a bitter taste in her mouth. Before Freda could draw breath, she heard a cry emanating from their living room.

'Get away from me, you oaf.'

Freda barged in, knocking one boy out of the way. The youth glared menacingly but held his tongue as Stefan took the lead. Within the confines of the tiny room, both women held still. Even her mother realised the perilous situation they found themselves in. Freda trembled as the smell of sweat within the confined space cloyed at her throat. Turning her head to one side, away from the smell, she sensed Stefan's eyes as they bored into her skull. She felt repulsed by him, but worse, Stefan's observation caught her mood.

'You don't like us and yet here we are, showing you a kindness.'

Kindness, how can any of this be kind? The irony was breathtaking. She had no answer, so she sealed her lips and waited for an explanation.

'You don't see it, do you? You're nothing without us and knowing this, we came to share the wonderful news about these laws. This is good, isn't it? After all, with things changing, you wouldn't want to find yourself, or your mother, caught disobeying the law. Now, would you?' His eyes narrowed.

'Thank you.' She forced the words from her mouth. 'May I ask what these new laws mean for us, and others like us?'

Stefan's smile widened. 'Ah, some gratitude at last. All it takes are a few manners. Maybe you Jews aren't beyond salvation after all.' The teen smirked. 'I'm joking, of course. You will learn your place; you'll never rise to our level. We are the superior race.'

Freda lowered her head before casting an eye towards her mother, hoped she'd follow suit. For a second it looked as though Hildegard would lash out with her walking stick, but the older woman thought better of it and gripped the cane before her with both hands.

'Now, woman,' Stefan said, pointing at Hildegard, 'I want you to show me around all your rooms while your daughter keeps the other's company. You can do that, can't you?'

Freda's slight frame wobbled while her mind calculated which was the lesser evil: to stay with three baying teenagers alone, or to go upstairs with the conniving Stefan. For a second, she considered defiance, before Stefan's stare shut her down. She knew they couldn't win this battle, so she asked her mother to go with Stefan and to shout if she needed anything.

Watching Hildegard slowly climb the stairs was torture. Stefan jabbed at the woman from behind, though the old woman could go no faster. A fantasy image appeared where Hildegard mule kicked Stefan to send him falling fatally down the stairs, before dissolving into an empty dream. The pair disappeared to the landing, and Freda turned her attention to the three boys. She knew them all: Otto, the son of the baker from the furthest edge of *Berchtesgaden* whose girth reflected his family, Klaus, the sycophant, and finally handsome yet weak Walter. *How could Ingrid ever see anything in you?* Freda's eyes lingered and Walter shrank beneath her stare.

'What are you staring at?' Klaus demanded.

Freda bowed her head, realising she might intimidate Walter, but not the others. The four stood in an awkward standoff, with everyone unsure how to behave. The mantel clock's distinctive ticking filled the room. Freda found the normally southing sound jarring. What was Stefan doing upstairs with her mother? How much time had passed?

For a minute, nobody spoke, but Freda could see the boys' bravado building. Klaus cracked his knuckles loudly in a show of disinterest, before he and Otto sauntered toward the kitchen, leaving her alone with Walter. She waited until they were out of earshot before speaking. 'You don't need to be like them, you know.' Walter's face reddened, but he offered no reply. Freda shook her head and followed the other boys into the kitchen. Otto had discovered their remaining food, a tiny piece of mutton, and was stuffing pieces of it into his mouth. She despised his greed. Especially now the cupboards were bare. She caught the boy's eye, imploring him to stop, but there was no remorse on his face. He grabbed the last piece and shovelled it into his mouth, where he chewed noisily. Once finished, he burped loudly, showing off rotten teeth. *And they say we're inferior.*

It wasn't just Otto's greed that left her unsettled. Klaus stood appraising her, his eyes inspecting the curve of her waist. The inspection showed no subtlety, and she wondered how she'd respond if he closed the gap. A plethora of panicked thoughts rattled around Freda's mind as she realised taking any action would cause a ripple effect. Stefan was still upstairs with her mother, while Klaus's mocking eyes only added to her torment. Freda dropped her eyes, choosing to stare solemnly at the table instead. Behind Otto lay a carving knife, and she knew that if she had to, she'd use the weapon. But for now, she had to keep her wits and that meant lifting her stare to track the boys before they could launch any assault towards her. She focussed on Klaus, fearing him most threatening. She was wrong.

Otto reached in from the side, pinning both her arms. 'That's it, struggle, my little Jew whore,' he jeered as Freda resisted.

Pressed against the table, Freda had no option other than to wait for a release. While her mind worked feverishly for a way out, she relaxed her taut body. The move surprised Otto, and the thug slackened his own grip before twisting his face in front of Freda's. Her eyes flickered, but she refused to look away. A pink and white piglike face stared back and then it began. Greasy fingers touched her hips and lingered, as though Otto was unsure of where his hands should creep next. Freda closed her eyes while mentally remembering the knife only a few feet away. Otto had released her arms, but the boy was still in front of her. Her nose twitched as he exhaled, foul air in her face.

Otto pressed a finger across her lips before pushing against her teeth. 'You like that, don't you?' Otto chuckled. 'See, Klaus, the woman likes meat.'

Otto's finger withdrew, and Freda praised herself for blocking his attempt by clamping her jaw shut. She twisted her head away from him and closed her eyes. Someone spat and before she could calculate who, the finger returned, only this time the digit was slick with saliva.

'Come on, you Jew slut, swallow.'

Freda's lips wavered and for a second, she thought Otto would force his chubby finger into her mouth, no matter how much she struggled. *But they're boys. I mustn't let them intimidate me.* Despite those calming thoughts, she knew she would need to make a choice. To submit or to fight back. Before she could decide, Freda heard a scream from upstairs.

35

Ingrid walked across the field behind their home, with Archie following close by. Although flat, unlike Bavaria, this was a place she loved. Just a small, by London standards, patch of land where the greenery won out against the grime. In the distance stood the kissing tree. She didn't know why the locals had named it so, but within the first year of arriving in the country, several boys had tried their luck by summoning her. She'd rebuffed all their approaches. Maybe naming the tall bough was another one of Archie's cheeky tales. Ingrid smirked at the thought as Archie's huge strides threatened to speed past her. For the briefest of seconds, she wondered what it would feel like to share a kiss. *Don't be stupid, girl. He's my friend, and he isn't interested in me, anyway.*

Choosing to ignore her inner monologue, she let her left hand drop by her side, fingers stretched, inviting. Would he hold her hand and offer a signal of closeness to be? Her fingers flexed, but remained untouched, and the moment passed. Balling them back into a fist, she spun, causing Archie to bump into her.

'Oi, Ingrid. Why'd you stop so suddenly?'

Her lips pursed together as heat flooded her cheeks. 'I didn't stop. It was you, getting too close again,' she said, raising her voice to punch out the word, 'Again.'

'But...'

She turned away as irrational anger swelled. She knew she was ruining the day, but she couldn't stop herself. Before he could properly respond, she let rip. 'Just go, will you? Leave me alone. You're always thumping into me like I'm one of your coal sacks.' It wasn't true, but the words spewed forth all the same. Archie stood, bewilderment etched across his face, and then Ingrid did something shameful. Without thinking, she shoved him hard to force her message, before turning and marching away.

Stupid thoughts told her he'd understand. *Archie's going to come after me, hold me close and forgive me.* But he didn't, and by the time she reached the shade within the kissing tree, she saw just how wrong she'd been. Archie was nowhere to be seen.

36

MID-SEPTEMBER 1935, *BERCHTESGADEN*

Freda leapt forward, sweeping Otto out of the way. Even Klaus cowered as she stormed past, leaving both boys in her wake. Within four strides, she'd reached the stairs and climbed, her heart racing. If her mother lay injured by Stefan's hand, nothing would stop her from scratching his eyes out. Raising a battle cry, she flew into the bedroom. 'Mama.' Her mother lay slumped on the bed in tears, Stefan towering over her with an object in his hand.

Stefan stood ready to launch, one hand gripping the family menorah. Several of the branches twisted off at odd angles, and Freda immediately understood her mother's angst. Spurred on by the women's dismay, Stefan pulled at the candlestick until it snapped.

Freda balled her fists, ready to charge, when a mournful cry from her mother reeled her back in. She switched her gaze from Stefan's mocking stare to her mother, leaning in to comfort the older woman. 'Don't worry, Mama, we'll still celebrate Hanukkah.' The coiled lump which was her mother merely dug her head deeper into her embrace, and Freda spun her head back to Stefan.

'Are you happy now?' she said, disgusted. A flicker of shame appeared on Stefan's face, but as Klaus, Otto, and Walter appeared, any regret vanished as pompous aggression returned, and the shame transitioned to Walter.

It would do no good, Freda realised. They could and would make them suffer. All that mattered now was protecting her mother. Reaching for a blanket, she wrapped Hildegard in the shroud before standing to face Stefan.

'If you come with me, I'll give you what you want,' she said before brushing past the boys in the doorway and heading toward the stairs. She paused, waiting to confirm all four were following, before moving back down to the living room while her mother remained behind. The bottom step loomed, and Freda closed her eyes, knowing what was to come.

37

JANUARY 1936, LONDON

Clifford Haynes shifted impatiently as he scanned the stage. *It should be me up there,* he thought. He plunged forward, carelessly brushing an old woman to one side. Her plaintive cry went unheard as more people packed into the town hall. Haynes didn't care. If they barred the stage from him, then he'd still make sure he'd be front and centre when the debate started. Taking his preferred seat, he patted his bowler hat on his lap while he waited for everyone to arrive. As more people took to the audience, he cast his eyes along the line, first left and then right. *Riffraff,* he thought. Still, being surrounded by the great unwashed held one advantage. He would stand out, and that suited him.

As his eyes scanned, a familiar figure entered the room and Haynes snapping his face back towards the stage. Foreman Doug Plunkett from the dairy had just arrived. *What's that bloody man doing here?* He fumed. He bowed his head until more people filled the rows behind, providing a screen. With the room nearly full, the lights dimmed, and all eyes fell on the stage as the curtains drew back. Haynes saw a long table with eight chairs facing the audience. Although someone had muted the stage lighting, they'd taken extra care to place a spotlight on an imposing emblem on the wall behind. A dark blue circle, intersected by a vertical lightning bolt, shone out towards the assembly. Haynes nodded in approval. This was what he wanted to see.

Muted conversation rippled around the room as everyone waited. *Disrespectful dolts*, Haynes thought, despite the tardiness from the yet-to-appear speakers. He lacked authority to silence the group. His annoyance festered, and he hid his shaking fists beneath his hat. He sat quivering as an uncomfortable mixture of anger and anticipation fluttered in his belly.

An itch nestled along his neckline which he desperately wanted to scratch, but Haynes distracted himself by stretching to look into the wings. Finally, a man walked down the aisle and up some steps to address the crowd. It took several seconds before an acceptable hush settled, but then the compere reeled off a list of names. The speakers, six men and one token woman, went unnoticed by Haynes. *Where is he?* As if reading Haynes's thoughts, the compere revealed the last speaker to take centre stage, directly in front of Haynes.

'Ladies and gentlemen. Please be upstanding and show your appreciation for our lead speaker this evening...the chancellor of the Duchy of Lancaster himself, Sir Oswald Mosley.'

At last! Haynes beamed.

A palpable silence settled within the room as a tall man entered the room. Even the peasants knew who this was. Wearing a dark three-piece suit, Mosley stepped forward to take his space at the table. Everyone rushed to their feet. With his pristine appearance and sharply coiffured moustache, Haynes looked on with a respect bordering on adoration. Even though Mosley showed a slight limp, this man was everything Haynes hoped to be. He struggled to tear his eyes away from his icon, but when people finally sat down, Haynes reluctantly followed suit. As he settled, he couldn't help but notice two groups of Blackshirts waiting on either side of the stage. Their presence stressed the power of the man on stage.

Haynes watched as the debate began. An insignificant counsellor weighed in with a dreary speech, explaining how the community should rally to help everyone flee Hitler's tyranny. The man didn't get far before Mosley shut him down with a vicious stare. 'How dare you.' Mosley gave the man a withering stare. 'This country has endured the harshest of times. Have you forgotten the great depression? Our population has suffered. But they are *still* suffering. And you stand there before these hard-working Englishmen saying we should load their shoulders even more. I won't stand for it. Never. I will defend every man within this hall, and I say no to your pathetic suggestion. We must protect these sovereign lands. Our own people must come first. And if that means refusing sanctuary to these parasites, then we must.'

The rebuttal caused an uproar across the hall, with Haynes's cheers among the loudest. They soon drowned the few dissenters out. More speeches followed, but each continued along with a similar theme where Mosley won out. Once everyone upon the stage had spoken, Mosley stood to close the meeting, though even he struggled to stem the delighted uproar.

Haynes stood clapping, vehement in his approval. It took several minutes before the crowd thinned and noise levels dropped, but once the majority had disappeared into the night, Haynes cautiously looked about. *Is the damned foreman still here?* He scanned the room, interested to see whether the man had remained in the room. During the furore, Haynes had tuned the crowd out, but now he realised he'd missed an opportunity. Was Doug Plunkett a supporter, one where he could build bridges and find common ground, or had he sided with the Jew worshippers? He felt he knew the answer, but it would have been good to know for sure. Likewise, he wondered whether Plunkett had seen him sitting in the audience. Shrugging off the questions he had no answers for, Haynes stepped forward. The Blackshirts held station on both sides of the stage, blocking access to all but the invited. He wondered whether he should have worn black in a show of unity, before dismissing the idea. Haynes held no desire to become a Blackshirt. He wanted to lead them.

Haynes placed his bowler neatly atop his head, puffed out his chest and strode towards the nearest Blackshirt. He knew his arrival at the stairs would meet with resistance, however, his inner superiority rose to the surface. 'Would you excuse me? May I have a word with Sir Oswald?' Haynes felt sure that by using Mosley's first name, they'd admit him immediately, so the shove he received came as a surprise. 'Oi,' he squeaked.

The Blackshirt loomed over him, blotting out the stage, and a mild panic set in. 'S...sorry,' Haynes mumbled as he stumbled backwards. He loathed himself for capitulating so easily, but he had no comeback for the Blackshirt. He turned away when he heard a cough from above. Haynes removed his bowler, scratched his neck, and turned, fully expecting disappointment.

'I saw you approach the stage. I'm sorry my followers blocked you off. They didn't hurt you, did they?'

Haynes couldn't believe his eyes. The dominating Oswald Mosley was gone, replaced by a calm and compassionate individual. 'Sir Oswald. Thank you for addressing me. I just wanted to convey my utter appreciation for everything you and your followers are achieving.' He knew his voice babbled, but he couldn't help himself. His idol had sought him out. Mosley smiled and waved to the side. As the Blackshirts parted, Haynes felt his jaw drop. This was his chance. Using the bowler to cover his shaking hands, he marched forward, glaring at the guard who'd shoved him earlier. Euphoric glee ran through him. He climbed the first step, drew level with his aggressor, and stared him down. Despite the guard's impassive face, he bowed his head and moved out of the way. Satisfied, Haynes continued up the steps until he arrived on the stage. Although he wanted to bask, he knew that meeting Mosley was the priority, and he stepped forward.

'Thank you for allowing me to come up to talk with you, Sir Oswald. I am so pleased with the way you charmed the audience with your views.'

'I should thank you for listening to what I have to say. After all, not everyone agrees with our ideals.'

Haynes heard the word *our* and his cheeks flushed. He hoped the reduced lighting would mask any redness. 'Of course, I agree with your values. These people are overrunning our country, and it has to stop. In fact, that is why I wanted an audience with you tonight.' He paused. He'd practiced his pitch before coming and now was the time to deliver.

38

FEBRUARY 1936, TEGERNSEE

Walter drew a deep breath. The air around Tegernsee was bracing, fresh off the surrounding foothills, moisture-laden from the nearby lake. It was a beautiful location, with echoes of his hometown of *Berchtesgaden*. 'It reminds me a little of *Königsee*,' he whispered, a cloud of steam floating before his face. 'The dark hills beside the water, although Wallberg is not as steep as Watzmann,' he added, gazing towards the enormous mountain beyond the steeple of St Laurentius church.

The sun was dipping below the hills, and Walter turned to look at the castle behind him. Bright sunshine reflected off the windows, but he had the peculiar sensation that he was being watched.

'No one else needs to know about my past,' he muttered, his eyes dropping away. 'We are all strangers here. Beautiful strangers with only one thing on our minds: making children for the Fatherland.'

His thoughts returned to the events of the previous week. At a loose end after his transfer to Munich, Walter's *Obersturmführer* had called him into his office.

'Gorst. You have proof of Aryan blood, yes?'

Walter drew himself upright. 'Naturally. Our family's lineage traces back to the 1500s.'

'Good.' The officer nodded. 'I will amend your posting. We received a request for the purer SS to help in fathering children for the *Führer*.'

'I beg your pardon?'

The officer saw the look of confusion on Walter's face, and he grinned. 'It's true. Even I qualify, despite being married. But you, Gorst, with your movie star looks and pure blood, you are exactly what Himmler is looking for. Pack your things, you will leave for Tegernsee in the morning.'

Walter could hardly believe his luck. He'd endured months of drifting from meaningless position to meaningless position, the victim of Stefan's cruel vendetta. Ever since their humiliating run-in at *Berchtesgaden*, Stefan had been working away in the background, using at first his father's sway – and now his own – like a puppeteer, orchestrating one awful posting after another as a punishment for Walter's Jewish dalliance.

But now there was nothing to stop his latest assignment. Not even Stefan could refute Walter's Aryan purity. And what an assignment to be given. Living in the lap of luxury at Tegernsee, surrounded by physically and morally superior beings that would carry the Third Reich into the future.

Now Walter sat ensconced in the privacy of a small castle by the Tegernsee, his every need catered to. He had endured further tests to prove his Aryan birthright, where they'd even measured the length of his earlobes. Despite these impositions, he passed with flying colours, and they deemed him fit for service.

They instructed the SS men to mingle with the women at the castle and form a connection such that, when the time came, one (or two women, if they were fortunate.) would choose them to father their child.

Walter hurried indoors and changed into his dress uniform. He glanced at his reflection before leaving for the dining room. A tall, broad-shouldered man stared back, with high cheekbones and short golden-blond hair above strong blue eyes. Yes, he was Aryan. There was no doubt at all. And despite his initial attraction to the dark-haired, dark-eyed Ingrid, he dismissed that obsession as the foolishness of youth. Any desire he once felt lay squashed beneath his shiny black jackboot.

Thankfully, he couldn't deny the beauty of the other participants. Walter had met most of the young women over the course of the last three evenings, and tonight, the women would choose their partner. Walter felt a stirring in his loins as he made his way downstairs. He had his eye on two girls. Petra was tall, with a tanned face and icy blue eyes. She was a natural athlete; high-bosomed, with endless long legs. He imagined those legs wrapped around him as they made love, and his pulse quickened.

Hannah was shorter than Petra and curvy, with a pretty face, cornflower-blue eyes, and pouty lips. Walter saw himself kissing those lips, groaning her name as he gave into passion.

There was a press of people at the foot of the stairs, waiting to enter the dining room. Walter smelt a mixture of cigarettes and perfume, vices normally frowned upon by the hierarchy, but condoned here at the castle to foster a sense of freedom and abandonment.

Walter scanned the room, hopeful of catching sight of his preferred matches. That hope quickly faded as they ferried the men into one room, while ushering the women into another. Dinner was served, and then one by one, the men were called for their rendezvous.

There was a ripple of excitement in the room, and the men grinned nervously at each other. There was no jealousy. They were fully aware of the rules, that each girl could choose more than one partner, and this allayed the men's fears. There were a few whispers circulating that some new girls had arrived over the course of the last day, but Walter was unconcerned. His thoughts were on Petra and Hannah. He'd felt a connection to both girls, and he knew they felt the same…

'Gorst. *Komm.*'

Walter stepped forward, his heart thumping. He followed the staff member into the next room, wondering which of the girls had been victorious. Would it be Petra, with those legs that went on forever, or would it be the pretty and sweet Hannah? He faltered in confusion as another girl loomed into view, a girl from his past.

'I always wanted you, Walter, and now you're mine.'

Christa smiled at him, and as he shuddered, she tucked her arm in his and led him away.

39

AUGUST 1936, TEGERNSEE

Christa Schneider pulled the shutters apart before opening a rear window and leaning out to breathe the warm summer air. As expected, the neighbouring houses looked deserted, but she took her time to scan the area. Satisfied, she coughed up some phlegm before spitting across the garden. It didn't matter that her daily ritual lacked grace. In Christa's eyes, her actions embraced a new, coarser side of her character, though if one of her Nazi friends saw her, she'd say she was merely spewing away the bitter taste found by coalescing with the Jews. The thought caused a smirk. Most of the Hitler Youth would flounder as soon as she opened her mouth.

Things, for her at least, had changed. What a disappointment she'd unearthed by choosing Walter Gorst to father her child. The thought caused her to spit again, but once she'd dispelled the last of her saliva, new powerful thoughts stole in to fill her mind. She knew she'd acted rashly by dismissing Stefan Weiss two years earlier. After all, it was only one failed kiss. Recent news showed his rapid advancement within the Reich.

Once the baby arrived, duty done, she would seek him out so together they could rise.

40

AUGUST 1936, LONDON

'Millie, it's lovely to see you again. Look how you've grown.'

Millie bounced over, waving the puppet she carried everywhere. 'Thank you, miss Ingrid,' she said before skidding to a halt. Her eyes suddenly went as wide as saucers.

Ingrid knelt before reaching out. Placing a finger across her lips, she whispered. 'Yes, I know. He's big, isn't he? But don't worry, he's really friendly. This is my friend Archie.' She wrapped an arm around Millie's waist, causing a giggle as she hoisted the child upwards. 'There we go. Millie, meet Archie.'

Two innocent smiles met. One from the six-year-old Millie and one from Archie, an Oxfordshire man whose hard work hauling coal meant clean children, was an alien concept. He offered a giant paw which dwarfed Millie's tiny fingers.

Millie wriggled in Ingrid's arms, striking a painful thought. *Will I ever raise a beautiful daughter like Millie?* She felt a moment of bitterness as the memory of Stefan's attack reappeared, but Millie's giggles buried the memory.

'May I?' Archie asked as he offered to carry Millie. 'You look like you're struggling there.'

Ingrid feigned a cross face before asking if Millie would like a ride on the giant's shoulders. 'Yes, please. Just wait until Papa sees I'm taller than him.'

'Then we'd better go see him. Point the way.'

Archie plucked Millie as though she weighed the same as a feather and placed her across his broad shoulders, and then the three strode forward. A metal arch, topped with a light, greeted them, forcing Archie to duck slightly to pass.

'Papa. Come quickly. Look at me, I can touch the light.' she squealed.

Rabbi Cohen greeted them with a delighted expression. 'Look at you, my *mammele*. And who is this?'

Ingrid stepped out from behind Archie, passing Millie's dangling legs. 'Rabbi, you and your daughter are without a doubt the most cheerful people in London. You really are lovely, both of you. This is my friend Archie. He's my…chaperone.'

The rabbi shook Archie's free hand. 'You needn't worry today. As you can see, the streets are safe. So, what brings you to visit? You must know we haven't another service for hours.'

Ingrid knew. While north-west London had become her sanctuary and *Berchtesgaden* her home, Whitechapel bridged the divide. 'I like it here and wanted to visit. Dieter is working, so Archie offered to come as my escort.'

'Well, I welcome you both. Millie's smitten, and that's good enough for me. Why don't we all head to our home? Millie helped me make some strudel dough earlier. I'm sure she won't mind sharing.'

****

The afternoon flew, and it wasn't long before Rabbi Cohen and Archie were chatting like old friends. Ingrid spent most of her time playing with Millie. A picturesque backdrop of mountains would have made the day perfect.

41

OCTOBER 1936, LONDON

Haynes inspected his uniform closely. Every stitch aligned perfectly; every button gleamed. He looked immaculate. A smug expression formed as he examined his reflection. He loved doing this. Solitary time mentally reworking his meeting with Mosley. Glossing over the fact he'd fluffed his lines, Haynes basked. Mosley had listened to him, and that was enough. Though the real win was happening now. Haynes's elevation to the role of lieutenant. He wanted more, but this was a start. No more managing the insignificant staff at the dairy. This could lead to his place among the ruling elite. And then, he thought with relish, he could have any woman he wanted, every way he wanted.

He checked his watch, then smiled. Knowing he had plenty of time, Haynes returned to his bedroom, where his thoughts turned toward Ingrid Stiepermann. She wasn't his yet, but at least he could plan.

42

OCTOBER 1936, LONDON

It saddened Ingrid to watch how quiet her brother had become, but another emotion triggered as she thought about Dieter, and that was anger. She loved him, but his recent lassitude forced her to work harder to maintain Florrie and Roy's good grace. Looking down, Ingrid studied the cracks running across her palms. *Where had the gentle days gone where she could stare at a beautiful landscape while creating a stunning watercolour?* She knew, of course, just as she'd learnt from gossiping, stay-at-home parents and navvies down at the railway. Their homeland was in turmoil, and she couldn't feel safe, not even on the northern edge of London. Casting her morose thoughts to one side, Ingrid walked along the path which led her back home. Although late in the year, a bright autumn sun was warm on her shoulders and as she walked, Ingrid forgot about Dieter. Soon after, Ingrid arrived home. As she gripped the door handle, she heard someone shouting.

'Don't be a fool. You can't go there, it's too dangerous.'

'I can look after myself. I must help. They're my people.'

Arguments in the household were rare. Ingrid had often sucked back harsh words for fear Roy or Florrie would tell them to leave. Now, though, Dieter and Florrie's voices rattled through the window frames and out into the street. Yanking the door open, Ingrid caught Florrie's exasperated expression.

'You tell him, will you? He won't listen to me.' Florrie thrust a newspaper into Ingrid's hand and stormed into the garden.

Dieter was shaking and pale with rage. 'Are you OK?' Ingrid asked. 'What happened?'

Dieter pointed to the newspaper. 'You'd better read it.'

Following his lead, she examined the newspaper, and her frown deepened.

We urgently warn Jews to keep away from the route of the Blackshirt march and from their meetings. Jews who, however innocently, become involved in any disorders will be actively helping anti-Semitism and Jew-baiting. Unless you want to help the Jew baiters, keep away.

'When is this march? Where?' she asked before she'd read the entire piece.

'It's happening this Sunday and I'm going to stop them. I don't care what the stupid *Chronicle* or Florrie says.'

Ingrid's mind reeled. She knew why Florrie's stance had appeared both stubborn and harsh, but she couldn't disagree with Dieter when Millie and her father were in danger. She pulled him into a hug. 'You must go. Don't worry, I'll talk to Aunt Florrie. But I can't have you travelling to the East End alone. We're doing this together. And none of that nonsense about me being a girl. I'm your older sister and that means you're under my care. Besides, Archie will come too, and with those enormous fists, he'll batter every one of those bloody fascists.' Ingrid couldn't remember the last time she'd sworn, but the words energised her into action and, placing the newspaper down, she rushed upstairs and retrieved an item from her room.

'Aunt Florrie. I know you're upset and worried about Dieter,' Ingrid soothed. 'Here, sit with me in the sunshine. There's something I want you to see.' Ingrid took out the etching she'd drawn a few weeks earlier.

'Is that...?'

'Yes, this is Millie. You've heard me talk of her. She's precious. Do you see now why we need to be there? She's six years old. I know her papa will do his best to protect her, but what if he can't? You and Roy have shielded us these last few years. I don't know how we would have coped if you hadn't taken us in, but you did. You've protected us and loved us as though we're your own. I'm twenty years old, not a child anymore, and Dieter's an adult too.' Ingrid saw her aunt's eyes glisten, but she pushed on. 'We care about Millie and her father. We love them and my brother is right. He needs to be there for them, and I do, too.'

Florrie's face crumpled into tears, and she reached over to hug Ingrid. They stayed together until her aunt's tears subsided.

'We'd be heartbroken if anything happened to you or Dieter, Ingrid. I understand your position, but is there any way I can persuade you both to stay away? That's what the newspaper said.'

'*Tante*,' Ingrid said, reverting to German, which she only used when she wanted to appear stern. 'If we follow the newspaper, then we lose. Mosley and his fascists will march right through Stepney, unopposed. That's what happened in Germany. Ordinary, good people stood by. Some were afraid, while others wanted to believe the Nazis' lies. We must stop them, whatever the cost.'

Ingrid knew she'd won the argument. It pained her to go against her aunt's wishes, but along with her brother and any others who'd offer support, they would travel to the East End on Sunday.

****

Ingrid looked fearfully around the carriage. The journey always spooked her, but today they were heading straight into danger.

Sensing her nerves, Archie patted her hand. 'It'll be all right. Remember how we spoke about this yesterday? We may not like the communists, but their paper, the *Daily Worker*, shows us Mosley's route.'

'You may not like the communists, but I like all the ones I've met.'

'You should meet the ones in the rail yard.'

'Come on, you two, we all have to stick together today,' Dieter chipped in. 'Right, Archie, have you plenty of pennies?'

Ingrid watched as Archie patted his pocket. The pair had devised a plan, though Archie's face had soured once they'd laid everything out. While Ingrid and Dieter would travel to Philpot

Street to offer protection to the rabbi and Millie, Archie's job was to scout out the fascist marchers as they moved in from the west. The siblings knew people within the Jewish People's Council, so once Archie gained news, he could find a public telephone box and call ahead. Then, once everyone knew the battle landscape, they could act in Millie and Rabbi Cohen's best interests. Ingrid worried Archie would get too close to the fascists, though both she and her brother knew they couldn't travel west to meet the intruders without their emotions boiling over. They'd agreed on his route. Archie would continue west along Fenchurch Street until he could switch south down Mincing Lane in order to avoid being labelled as an East Ender.

A lump rose in Ingrid's throat as Archie disappeared along Aldgate High Street. Dieter gently tugged her arm, and they headed in the opposite direction. As they approached Gardiner's Corner, she looked up at the unusual clock tower which sat atop the clothing store, Gardiner and Company. It was 1.30 p.m. and already the crowd had swollen to a level they'd never seen before. Turning right along Commercial Road offered challenges. They watched on, keen to avoid the swirling mass of people ahead. Everyone appeared civil, some even jaunty, although Ingrid detected an underlying tension. While they waited to cross, a driver brought his tram along the road and an absurd flicker of fear crossed Ingrid's mind. Surely, they won't use tram cars to push through the crowd. Her fears were unfounded. The driver drew to a halt and, once stationary, he alighted from the tram, tipped his cap, and walked off. Soon, two more tram cars followed suit, effectively blocking the middle of the road. The fascists couldn't move them, even if they wanted to, and she found the sight heartening.

'Come on, we'll never get there if we don't push through. Hold my hand while we cross,' Dieter commanded.

179

43

OCTOBER 1936, LONDON

Clifford Haynes felt elated. He loved his uniform. It comprised a black military-cut jacket, dark grey breeches, jackboots, a black cap with a shiny peak capped off with a red and white armband. Within the confines of the depot, he'd always held back from any public expression of his views, but here, he felt like a king. Sweeping his eyes along the vast line of people which trailed west from the gardens above the Tower of London brought a surge of satisfaction. At last, he was with his own kind and there were thousands more lining up, pledging their support.

He'd even seen Mosley in the distance, though their leader was too far away for meaningful conversation. Bystanders watched in awe, many waving Union Jack Flags while others took up their own repetitive chants:

We're going to rid the Yids. We're going to rid the Yids. Come on with us, we're going to rid the Yids.

Blackshirts stood everywhere he looked, but as time marched on, Haynes grew unsettled. Mosley had disappeared from view. At his last sighting, Mosley was speaking with Lord Rothermere, the owner of the *Daily Mail*, and Sir Philip Game, the Commissioner of Police. Despite observing they had support from the establishment, seeing the trio triggered frustration. With thousands ready to march, he couldn't get close to stand with them. All the shiny uniforms in the world meant nothing if he couldn't rise to the top. Shaking his head, he pushed away the dampening thoughts. For now, it didn't matter. All three had vanished, leading Haynes to wonder why the march hadn't started. After the earlier chants and goose-stepping parades, the others who stood alongside in orderly parade lines clearly felt the same.

While they waited, Haynes reconciled his concerns. They may not be moving, but without question, this was a display of power. And this display filled him with a quiet certainty that the people he'd aligned with were an army. Even the on-duty police offered support with smart Hitler salutes of their own. That feeling alone meant he could stomach the wait.

44

OCTOBER 1936, LONDON

As Ingrid and Dieter passed further along Commercial Road, their awe grew. Everywhere, people were turning out in support. Some had chalked *No Pasarian* along the wall, while others opted for the English translation, *They Shall Not Pass*. There were too many for Ingrid to recognise, though she identified with many from their clothing and behaviour. The Jews were out on the streets, of that she was certain, but others, communists, dock workers, Irish Catholics, and more spilled out across the East End in an epic show of support.

'Look Dieter, we've passed the gateway into the East End and there are thousands standing between us and Mosley. There's no way they can break through. Millie will come to no harm today.'

As if to confirm Ingrid's growing confidence, she heard a message broadcast via loudspeaker to the crowd:

'Keep Mosley out of Stepney. Get down to Gardiners Corner now. Do your duty and stop him.'

Part of her wanted to go, but the notion was foolish, and she continued with Dieter as they fought against the onrush.

They made slow progress, and Ingrid knew they'd both receive a few bruises before the day was out, but they finally made it to their destination. Philpot Street stood ready, with medics and ambulances at the ready.

Millie leaped up from the steps and ran over. 'Ingrid.' she wailed happily.

Ingrid scooped the child up and swung her around at shoulder height to a chorus of delighted squeals. 'Where is your papa, little lady?' she asked as she settled Millie on the ground. The youngster twirled around in mock dizziness before running back inside.

Rabbi Cohen walked out to greet them. 'My saviours. Millie's cross with me because I won't let her play in the street today. It's lovely to see you, though I wonder why you've travelled here today, with everything that's going on.'

Dieter spoke up. 'Rabbi Cohen, we've received such kindness from you since we first visited. Your teachings mean the world, after we'd been away from our faith. Our time spent here is special – it's like we're back in Germany.'

'He's right,' Ingrid added. 'We love you, this place, and most of all, we love little Millie here. We had to come to see you're both safe.'

'Well, you're both unfailingly kind and your presence here means a lot to us. Now you're here. What are you planning to do? I hope you won't join the crowds I've heard about.'

Ingrid considered their plan. 'I want to wait here to see you're both safe while Dieter runs down to see the Jewish People's Council. They know him and we've sent Archie to spy on the fascists. Archie will telephone the council when he has news.'

The rabbi listened intently. 'What were the crowds like when you came through from Aldgate?'

'We've packed the area, especially around Gardiner's Corner,' Dieter spoke with enthusiasm. 'We saw police about, but our crowd heavily outweighed them.'

'And how was the mood?'

'Don't worry, Rabbi. While some looked tense, most of them were peaceful.'

The rabbi's face softened. 'When I first heard about the march, I feared the worst, and today I'm ashamed to admit I wanted to bolt the door to keep Millie safe. What kind of rabbi am I?'

'You're the best kind.' Ingrid reassured him. 'If I had a daughter as perfect as Millie, I'd do the same. You said you wanted to bolt the door. Have you changed your mind?'

Cohen's expression shifted. 'That's very astute of you. Before you brought this news to me, I did indeed want to hide away, but now, with you both here, I want to do what's right. And that means I should go see the People's Council. I know it's closer to the crowds, but from what you've told me, we have nothing to fear, and anyway, we all want to hear Archie's news as soon as it comes in.'

Five minutes later, once the rabbi had gathered a shawl for Millie and secured the synagogue, they began the walk south towards the Council.

45

OCTOBER 1936, LONDON

Archie looked on at the gathering of Blackshirts. Even though they were in the distance, his mouth went wide. There were thousands, too many to count.

But that wasn't all. Alongside the fascists, offering protection, stood hundreds of police. He couldn't believe it. *How could they? The fascists, with their vile philosophies, don't warrant safeguarding.*

He watched for a few minutes and then, once he'd concluded they were staying put, he sought a phone box.

Dieter needed to know how bad this looked.

46

OCTOBER 1936, LONDON

When they arrived at the council, the place was in an uproar and, for a moment, Rabbi Cohen faltered. Ingrid could see conflict written across his face and if they weren't waiting on the news from Archie, then she, too, would have turned back. Seeing his expression change, she offered to pull Millie to a corner where they could safely play, while Cohen and Dieter could find out if Archie had called.

Once they were away from the others, Ingrid looked down at Millie and saw her pale face with trembling lips.

'What's the matter?'

'I've lost Isaiah.' Millie cried.

Ingrid inwardly breathed a sigh of relief. On a day like this, losing a doll seemed a small price. She forced a smile. 'I know Isaiah isn't with you today, but I'm sure he's waiting for you safely at home.'

'He isn't. I carried him with me, but now he's gone.'

'Who gave you Isaiah?'

'Mama gave him to me when I was a baby.'

Now actual tears formed as Ingrid sensed the fragile path they'd wandered onto. She didn't know what had become of Millie's mother, though she feared the worst. With Dieter and Rabbi Cohen busy, she'd have to act as surrogate mother as best she could. She wrapped her arms around the small girl, and Millie burrowed her head into Ingrid's shoulder. They sat on the floor in a tender embrace, their world at a temporary standstill while chaos surrounded them.

'Ingrid.'

Dieter's voice dragged her from her reverie. Keeping Millie's face pressed against her chest, she turned to listen. Using her eyes to signal she wanted to keep any news from Millie's ears, she waited until her brother came close enough to whisper.

'Archie's called. He says there are thousands of them near the Tower of London,' Dieter said, careful to avoid naming who *they* were. Millie didn't stir, so he continued. 'There are just as many police with them, and they are supporting the marchers.'

Ingrid blew out her cheeks in surprise. Which way would they go? Each alternative offered the same risks. 'Has the march started yet?' she asked. 'Which way are they heading?'

Dieter offered an infuriating shrug and remained silent.

'Well?' Ingrid pressed, louder than she intended.

'Archie said that only the police were making any moves. He thinks someone's ordering them to clear a path, starting at Gardiner's Corner. That's all I know. I guess we'll have to wait until he calls in later. He wants to follow the police at a distance to see what happens. At least those trams are blocking the road.'

Ingrid mulled the information over. From memory, the trams blocked the road straight on, but what if the police turned right instead? Whichever way she looked at the situation, they were under threat. On the one hand, it sounded like many more people stood in opposition. A human wall, surely impassable, people who had rallied to block Mosley's thugs. Ordinary, law-abiding citizens. Would they stand in the way of an army of police officers? She wasn't sure, but if they stood strong against the law, a bloodbath could eventuate. Suddenly, the synagogue, tucked away on a quiet side street, seemed a much safer option. She realised they were almost certainly at risk if they stayed here. If the police and fascists broke through, losing a doll would be the least of their concerns.

A sense of anxiety overcame Ingrid. She was desperate to act, but nothing would be possible until Dieter and Millie's father returned. Archie wouldn't call again for a while and, with a heady buzz of activity all around, Ingrid continued to hug the child, almost for her own benefit.

The clock ticked on beyond 2 p.m. This was taking too long. *Can't they see this building isn't safe for a little girl?* Ingrid hoisted Millie onto her hip and walked through the crowd. They'd waited long enough. Now she needed Rabbi Cohen's permission to move them somewhere safer.

'There you are,' she exclaimed as she came across Dieter. 'I need to talk to you.'

Dieter looked away from the telephone with a guilty flush. 'Sorry, I wanted to hear any news from Archie before the others.'

She did too but brushed the thought aside. Other matters were more pressing. 'I'm worried. If the police force their way through, then Mosely's lot will rush to fill the gap, and I think they'll head here. We need Archie's updates, but I worry about her,' she said, nodding downwards at the girl asleep in her arms. 'She's too young to get caught up in this.'

'You're right.'

Relief flooded through Ingrid as she heard Rabbi Cohen's voice behind her. She spun to face him.

'I'd like to stay,' he said, regret on his face, 'but I couldn't bear it if anything happened to Millie. I think we should go outside and see what the crowds are like. We're close to Leman Street. We can figure out what is going on, then head back to Philpot Street. Ingrid, I'd be immensely grateful if you would mind Millie while I assess the situation with Dieter. I trust you and know she won't come to any harm.'

Crestfallen, Ingrid nodded. Inspecting Leman Street made sense, though it came with risk and she wished someone else could go.

They filed out into the street, with Cohen leading the way. The crowds here were fewer, allowing Ingrid to hold back while her brother and the rabbi walked on ahead. Draped across her shoulder, Millie clung on. By the time they'd reached the junction with Leman Street, Dieter and Cohen had disappeared into the crowd. Ingrid guessed they were in the middle of the street, talking to locals to assess the situation, but she couldn't see them.

Millie's weight was taking its toll, and she looked about, seeking a haven. Two tea chests sat outside a shop window. After testing to confirm they were sturdy, Ingrid climbed up and pulled Millie to stand alongside. Once elevated, they could see over the heads of the rally, and she set about finding the lost pair. While they stood, Millie's mood lifted. Used to always looking up from waist height, suddenly she stood atop a platform where she was taller. She giggled and pointed at all the different people in the crowd.

Ingrid's view sent a chill through her. To the north, hundreds of police had lined up. With batons raised and horses baying, the intention was obvious. *Surely the police won't charge. Not with the crowd acting peacefully.* Obviously, other closer to the cordon felt the same way, as some figures backed away to the safety of a side street.

Others appeared ready to fight. One hefty man, about Archie's build, dug into his pocket before waving a fist filled with tiny balls that glistened in the sunlight. She knew what they were. She'd played with them as a child back in *Berchtesgaden*. They were marbles. Her agile mind knew why the man carried them, and a new urgency rose. They had to find Dieter and Rabbi Cohen before time ran out and the powder keg blew. She scanned the crowd, desperate for a glimpse of the pair.

Millie spotted them first, calling *Papa* excitedly while pointing. Ingrid plotted the best route to reach them before realising they'd lose sight as soon as they stepped off the chests. 'Come on, Millie, wave with me and shout as loud as you can. We have to get their attention and bring them back to this side of the road.'

Steadying herself on the chests, Ingrid and Millie waved and called in the desperate hope Dieter or the rabbi would see them. But above the noise of the crowd, three loud whistle blasts froze Ingrid's heart. The police were about to charge.

They mustn't! The gigantic horses would trample anything in their path, and Dieter and Rabbi Cohen were stuck, helpless amid the crowd.

'PAPA.' Millie screamed. The little girl was terrified, and as Ingrid swept her eyes back towards their crates, a fresh horror surfaced. Millie's hand slipped from hers as the child scrambled down to save her father. There was no time to lament her failing. She had to follow even as the drumbeat of pounding hooves and the shrieks as the two sides clashed mere metres away. Jumping down, Ingrid shoved against the crowd, following the direction Millie had taken seconds earlier.

She met an immediate resistance. The crowd was moving further down Leman Street to avoid the police onslaught, and the gap where the little girl had been was gone. Deafening cries sounded around her, but Ingrid pushed on, using every ounce of her strength to carve her way through. Once in the middle of the road, she spun in a tight circle. They had to be close.

As Ingrid turned, two things happened simultaneously. To her right, she saw Dieter and the rabbi. Both were struggling but standing tall at least. Down to her left, Ingrid heard a shrill wail that could only have come from a child. Her brother and Rabbi Cohen would have to look after themselves. Nothing mattered now except saving Millie.

'Millie.' she yelled. It was no use. The crowd was in total disarray as the inevitable charge ripped through their ranks. Horses stood dangerously close, their riders wielding batons which whipped down with little regard to whose skull they cracked. The screams intensified, and the crowd pushed backwards. There was no room to move, and Ingrid realised Millie would be terrified, her tiny frame no defence against the press. To her side, a man sought safety by climbing onto the crates where, seconds earlier, they'd stood. An apparently sensible move, until the flight of backtracking protesters shoved the man through a baker's window, shards of glass peppering the poor man's back.

Ingrid forced herself to look down in search of Millie. Almost immediately, they shoved her back, and she tumbled forward.

Swirling bodies buffeted against her. Her footing gone, Ingrid was falling, and there was nothing she could do about it.

47

OCTOBER 1936, LONDON

Archie stepped out of the Hoop and Grapes pub; dismay etched across his face. As promised, he'd called the Jewish Council to send updates, only this time, nobody had answered. After waiting a couple of minutes, he rested the receiver on the cradle and looked outside. The scene was worse than he could have possibly imagined. Where earlier a peaceful rally ambled about, now people were fighting for their lives. Mounted police punched holes in the crowd before regrouping for another assault. As the horses retreated, police officers on foot charged forwards, meting out a similar punishment to pavement bystanders.

It made no sense. Mosley's thugs were lingering half a mile away, yet somehow someone had given the police a mandate to attack the innocents. There were too many in the crowd and a horrific, almost tidal ebb and flow formed as both sides rallied for supremacy. At the second mounted charge, the East Enders fought back, throwing marbles across the street while others threw a substance which formed black clouds before floating gently towards the ground. Archie watched as two horses skittered upon the glass orbs, sending their riders careering to the ground. Other horses reared in fear, their nostrils filled with pepper.

The charge halted and for a moment, Archie thought they'd quelled the threat, until busloads of police reinforcements arrived. Buoyed by their support, the horses spun for another thrust.

Helpless, Archie watched on. In the distance, he saw someone scramble onto a crate before being thrown through a shop window. The scene was becoming a rout, and he feared for Ingrid and Dieter's safety. His powerful body was no match for this crowd, and with the situation out of control, Archie wedged himself in a doorway, a witness to the battle.

48

OCTOBER 1936, LONDON

At the precise moment of the fall, Ingrid was terrified. The world spun in slow motion as she dropped, leaving only one thought in her head. Their sole purpose for coming to the rally would end in failure. She knew she wouldn't ever stand again, not once she hit the ground, and that final thought left her feeling wretched. Millie's eyes swam before her as her arms flailed in descent. Her head dipped lower. Suddenly, a sense of drowning enveloped as though someone had placed her into a coffin and now the bearers had set to lower her into her ultimate resting place.

One flailing arm caught upon something solid and Ingrid felt a jarring pain as her hand snagged. In desperation, she gripped with all her might, unaware she'd grasped onto a man's belt buckle. After an agonizing pull, the surprised docker pulled her upright. There was no time to offer thanks as Ingrid pushed backwards and, once free, spun about to resume her search.

Ingrid couldn't wait for the crowd to clear. She knew the police were readying another strike, one where many more injuries could occur. Millie would not survive unless Ingrid acted now. Taking a deep breath as though diving for pearls, she gripped two burly bystanders and ducked her head down once more. More people collided, boxing her ears, but Ingrid refused to buckle. She pushed forward, her head down, grasping people's arms to steady herself. The movement sapped her strength, but she'd not stop. She had to find Millie. With each surging wave of buffeting, her breath became shorter, until a constricting force gripped her chest.

And then she saw. A tiny scrap of red cloth appeared before the crowd surged, blocking her view once more. In a crowd full of browns and greys, the bright fabric stood out like a beacon. With renewed hope, Ingrid pushed towards the patch of colour.

Pushing against the throng was impossible, but with each rocking movement, Ingrid paused until the sway switched direction and, sensing a gap, she shoved forward. Each time, the pounding of elbows and shoulders robbed her of strength, but she knew if she was suffering, Millie was much worse. She caught another glimpse of red, nearer now. The sight energised Ingrid, and she clawed at men twice her size to reach the little girl. She knew time was running out, and then, as her hands reached for another burly man and missed, she snatched a flailing sleeve and heard the familiar, shrill cries of a girl in anguish. The sound was pure joy. Moments later, Ingrid reeled the girl in.

'Millie, it's me,' she shouted. She wrapped an arm around the girl and hauled her upwards. She needed to get them both to safety and then, once she'd removed Millie from harm, she could return to find the others. This time, with Millie shrouded in her arms, the movement seemed easier. Just standing erect helped, as the crowd moved in unity, away from the police. Each step weighed heavily, but Ingrid had no other choice, and they drifted further along Leman Street, away from Dieter and Rabbi Cohen.

As the throng crept away from their uniformed attackers, movement became easier, and Ingrid lifted her eyes to take stock. In the distance, the battle raged, with neither side gaining the upper hand. More and more police descended, disciplined groups thrusting into the bystanders with ferocious baton strikes. She knew that somewhere between her and the police, Dieter and the rabbi were fighting their own battles. Casting her eyes about in desperation, she realised they'd gone beyond the side street that led back to the Jewish Council. Cursing, she turned about and followed the fleeing crowd down to Cable Street.

49

OCTOBER 1936, LONDON

Archie stood, drawing a deep breath as he rose. The inhalation helped to dampen the morose thoughts plaguing him. There was no escaping the riot playing out before him. The police seemed to have taken the upper hand. For a while they'd struggled, as horses and riders alike fell, but only a few protestors carried weapons and little by little the uniformed officers, wielding their batons, carved a path along the road. As both sides moved further away, he turned, half expecting Mosley's soldiers to be upon them. Relief flooded through him as he saw they'd hardly moved. Knowing he couldn't help anyone battling along Leman Street, he left his safe space in the doorway, intent on spying on the fascists. He reached Aldgate station and ducked inside, where he could watch the Blackshirts unobserved. People crashed into him as they escaped, while others vied for the best viewing platform. At last, he found a pillar to shield him from other onlookers, where he could see the fascists up close.

The solid black line stretched further than he could see. He estimated their numbers to be far fewer than the Jews and dockers in the East End, but the equally smaller group of police had broken through to push halfway down Leman Street. Everything held in the balance. Deciding there was no benefit to waiting, Archie stepped out. He was just about to turn back towards Gardiner's Corner when a familiar face appeared. Strutting along the ranks was none other than Clifford Haynes. A tempest of rage swept through him, followed by an aching frustration that he couldn't challenge the man. Not now. Tearing his eyes away, he resumed his inspection of the police onslaught. The uniforms had moved further away, out of sight, so taking courage in both hands, he turned left and ran towards the carnage.

By the time he'd run back to the corner with Leman Street, his lungs ached, but he pushed on regardless. The street was in total disarray. Windows stood as gaping holes with smashed glass strewn around, while bloodied onlookers looked on. Others were so moved they buried their faces in their hands.

Knowing his friends were in danger, Archie smothered his instinct to help the fallen and pushed on. At any moment, the crowd could leave him trapped, but with a backward glance every few steps, he jogged down the street, dodging the injured, while searching for familiar faces. At one point, Archie skidded to a halt, his heart in his mouth. A figure on the ground wearing a blue jacket similar to the one Dieter had been wearing. Fearing the worst, Archie kneeled down and rolled the still figure over. It wasn't Dieter, but awful cuts slashed a crisscross pattern across the man's face. After checking the man could still breathe and knowing he couldn't stop for every casualty, Archie leapt up and continued on. Reinforcements hadn't arrived, but he could see police in the distance and they were nearing Cable Street. He stopped at the corner of Hooper Street, desperate to figure his next move. Turning off would take him away from the clashes up ahead, and, he thought, towards the Jewish People's Council. Filled with indecision, he hovered inside the side street.

50

OCTOBER 1936, LONDON

Ingrid ran headlong along Cable Street, Millie slumped across her shoulder. Frantic thoughts filled her mind. *Would they smell the breath of the police horses before too much further?* Her eyes narrowed, forcing her to focus. The sight ahead took her breath away, and she slowed to a halt.

The locals had built a gigantic barrier spanning the entire breadth of Cable Street. Assorted pieces of furniture stood stacked in a formidable lattice. As Ingrid studied, she could see all the pieces stood locked together in an intricate arrangement. The sight looked both bizarre and amazing. A dozen men lined the crest, each heavily armed with an array of items, ready to repel any attackers with a choreographed bombardment. Adjusting Millie to her other shoulder, Ingrid waved at the nearest man.

'Please, help us. They'll be here soon.'

The man wavered, uncertain how to help without dismantling the entire structure, when another shoved him to one side.

'Don't worry, love. Hang on there. We'll get you to safety.'

He disappeared and while they waited, Ingrid lowered Millie to the ground. She gripped Millie's head gently, forcing eye contact. 'We're almost there, Millie. These men will help us climb over the barrier and then I promise you, nobody will hurt you. I'll protect you.'

'What...about Papa?'

Her question tore into Ingrid. She wanted to run back and answer that question, but she had to get Millie to safety first. 'I'm sure they're both fine,' she reassured, despite her growing fear. 'Look, the man has come back, and he's brought a ladder. He's our friend. You can trust him.'

Ingrid waited for signs of understanding, but Millie looked understandably suspicious.

'Millie, you've been so brave today, but I need you to be brave one more time. Don't worry, I'll be here right with you.' The child looked confused until Ingrid nudged her towards the ladder. Millie looked up. Immediately, she backed away from the strangers, who reached down to offer help. 'I'm still here,' Ingrid said while gently nudging Millie onto the first step. The girl shook, but once encouraged, she took three more steps and accepted the hands which lifted her to the top. Ingrid hung back, ready to catch her if needed, but once they had Millie safely gripped, she climbed each rung at speed.

From the street, the wall of furniture looked sturdy, but as she hugged Millie, the complete structure shook, sending another bolt of fear. It would be the cruellest of fates to fall back onto the street, now they were so close. Their bodies tipped until pairs of hands steadied them, dragging them back from the brink. Millie shrieked, and Ingrid drew her close once more. 'Hush my angel. Look, we can climb down the other side now. Those horrible men can't hurt us now.' Together, they climbed down and backed away. Millie still looked bewildered, so Ingrid stooped and cradled her in her arms once more. 'We're safe now. Come with me and we'll look for your papa.'

Ingrid knew the girl was flagging, but so was she. She rested the girl on the pavement and gripped her hand. The area behind the blockade held fewer people, which allowed quick progress down the road, but before they'd taken a dozen steps, she heard an uproar behind them. The police were immediately behind them, charging the furniture stockade they'd just climbed over.

51

OCTOBER 1936, LONDON

Archie drew to a halt as he watched the police lineup prepare to charge. His jaw dropped at the sight beyond. Before, the mounted police units had broken through a crowd of humans, scattering them like pins, but now they faced something more formidable. He couldn't see how the police could ever progress along Cable Street, and yet horses and men alike stormed forward. While the cavalry covered the flanks, charging along the pavement, others ran on foot, holding the middle ground, each group reaching the wall of furniture in seconds. Immediately, the police set about tearing any furniture they could away from the barrier. The men formed a line, passing each item to a colleague as they disassembled the barrier. The Eastenders weren't about to give up and objects rained down upon the uniforms. Archie watched as one woman from an upstairs window poured the contents of a chamber pot directly on to one unfortunate constable. He looked up, arms raised in protest, and the pot flew down, striking his head and sending him to the ground. *Serves you right, attacking these innocent people*, Archie thought.

Despite siding with the locals, Archie could see the police would soon break through. The defenders couldn't stay on top of the structure any longer, forced now to throw missiles from behind the wall. All this made it easier for the police to pick their way through. 'Damn,' he muttered as a gap appeared and a breech appeared imminent. There was nothing he could do, except to look on in helpless fear. The police poured through the newly formed opening, which quickly widened. After seeing the carnage from the first police assault, he feared the worst and turned his head away.

One thing gave him confidence. No fascist marchers were nearby, ready to fill the void. That at least restored some hope. As his eyes scanned the scene, leaping from one fallen resident to another, his heart sank at the devastation before him. It wasn't just the upturned carts, ruined produce, and shattered windows, it was the human cost. Everywhere he looked, wounded men and women staggered about in a bewildered state, while others lay in chilling stillness.

This should never have happened if Mosley and his thugs hadn't come. A weird calm settled, and Archie realised the riot of anger against the furniture wall had ceased. *Have the police won?* Creeping forward, he cast an eye through the gap. Ahead, police ambled about in a state of confusion. Looking beyond their exhausted and frustrated ranks, Archie saw an unbelievable sight. Beyond the police, the locals had erected a second wall. They'd learnt from the original structure and made this one a lot sturdier. Paving slabs, sturdy iron girders and even the odd railway sleeper knitted together, forming an impenetrable dam.

The uniforms stood, defeat plain on their faces. They'd tried to follow orders, but now, facing an overwhelming blockade and outnumbered at every turn, the police retreated. Buoyed by the sight before him, Archie considered his next steps. Forward through the first barrier wasn't an option, so turning around, he went to help the fallen.

52

OCTOBER 1936, LONDON

'Come on,' Ingrid cried as she pulled Millie's arm, dragging her away from where they'd stood seconds earlier. The feeling of salvation vanished as a familiar battle raged nearby. Ingrid's hands were shaking as she drew Millie close. The noise was incessant, and Ingrid wanted to scream as she sighted a second, stronger obstacle before them. She wanted hope. She needed it for Millie's sake, but what if they couldn't overcome this barrier? Pushing her negative thoughts aside, she bent down and whispered to Millie, 'Look. Here's another climbing castle for us. We'll have some fun getting over this one.'

The second wall loomed. It seemed twice the height of the first and although a line of men stood above, nobody could reach that far down. Their own supporters had trapped them on the wrong side. Ingrid's legs weakened, and she felt her body sag until she glanced at Millie's frightened face. This galvanised her, and she held Millie in a tender hug. No matter what happened, Ingrid would protect this precious little girl at all costs.

The seconds ticked painfully by. Ingrid lost all sense of perspective as she directed her attention to Millie. The small body trembled against hers and it took all of Ingrid's will not to break down completely. The street was quiet – too quiet. *Why aren't the police coming to storm the second wall?* She buried her head against Millie's neck to await the imminent attack.

'You all right, love? Let's get you and the nipper away from here.'

The gruff cockney voice sounded surreal; did she imagine it? She'd had her hopes dashed too many times this afternoon. It seemed unbearable to open her eyes and find no one there. She refused to look up, she wouldn't.

Millie tugged at her arm. 'Ingrid, look.

She opened her eyes. Nothing made sense. Police milled about in an uncertain standoff away from equally stunned locals. No one had the appetite for any further fighting. The vast wall remained intact, so Ingrid and Millie edged away, taking refuge in a nearby haberdashery. The man who'd spoken to her waited until they were safely inside, then he disappeared.

A small woman shuffled forward to greet the pair. The shopkeeper caught sight of Millie and threw her arms wide. '*Shalom*, my little *maudeleh*. I see you peeking back there. Come through to the back with your friend and rest on some cushions while I make some mint tea.'

The woman scuttled away, and Ingrid sank into the cushions with a sigh of relief. She pulled Millie down beside her and tucked her in her arms. The latest crisis was over. Ingrid gazed around the room. Dimly lit, with sun patches filtering through from the adjacent kitchen, she saw rich fabrics and gorgeous colours that were a salve for the eyes after the insanity she'd witnessed outside. For the first time since leaving Yiewsley, she felt safe.

The woman returned, and once they'd all drunk a cup of extra sweet mint tea, Ingrid's thoughts returned to her brother, the rabbi, and Archie. Fear had driven her from the streets to keep Millie away from the warring factions. Now they'd found sanctuary, and feeling fortified after the tea and rest, Ingrid knew what she had to do.

'I apologise for our rudeness, Madam. I don't even know your name, and you've been so kind to us.'

The woman smiled. 'My name is Hannah Blau. I've lived in this street for the last fifteen years with my husband, Isaac.' Tucked behind a curtain lay a door, which Mrs Blau opened to reveal a set of stairs. 'Come, let me show you,' she offered warmly. The group went upstairs, and Mrs Blau lifted a framed photo from the dresser. 'Here he is,' she said.

Ingrid grasped the photo and tilted it downward to include Millie. 'Look Millie, this is Mrs Blau and her husband Isaac.'

'I know him,' Millie offered excitedly. 'He comes to our synagogue.' She paused, a flush rising on her face. 'You've come to our services as well. I remember now.'

With this admission, Ingrid realised this place was a haven for Millie. 'Mrs Blau, where is your husband now?' The fear on the woman's face gave her the answer. Ingrid sighed, and she took the older woman's hand in her own. 'He's out there, isn't he?'

Mrs Blau gave the faintest of nods.

'Please, will you stay here and care for Millie? My brother, the rabbi, and a friend are out there too. I can't take Millie with me.'

The question hung as Millie's young mind processed Ingrid's suggestion, and the little girl surprised everyone with her response.

'Mrs Blau, you aren't a stranger, but I'm really worried about my papa. It's scary outside today. Can I stay with you while my friend Ingrid goes out to look?'

That sealed the arrangement, and Ingrid's heart took a momentary flutter as she knelt in front of Millie. 'I told you once how wise you are. You are also the bravest girl I've ever met. Stay here with Mrs Blau and I will bring your papa back to you.' Then, switching to a conspiratorial tone, she whispered, 'Maybe Mrs Blau could make some more mint tea for you while you wait.' After one more hug, Ingrid descended the stairs and stepped out into the warm autumn air. Earlier, when they moved inside the shop, the battle looked as though it was petering out. She was right. Now instead of a furore of anger and violence, the locals were cheering and singing songs while, in contrast, the police were licking their wounds and preparing to withdraw.

A few minor skirmishes were running their course, but Ingrid figured she could head safely through the thinning crowd, though it wouldn't be easy and as she peered back along Cable Street and through the ruptured barricade, everything looked worse. Despite witnessing the frightening scene ahead, she knew this was just the beginning.

Steeling herself, she pressed on. She passed a police horse on its side and bleeding profusely from a jagged wound. One leg appeared buckled at an unnatural angle, triggering a memory of the fateful day when Stefan had mangled Dieter's arm. Huge, wide brown eyes stared toward her, and Ingrid felt an outpouring of humanity. She recognised the animal's fear, as it looked close to death. She couldn't do anything except move on, but the horse's terrified stare haunted her.

Her progression slowed as more casualties blocked her path and with the increase in bodies, so too, came the painful inspection, forcing her to check all who'd fallen. *Dieter, Archie, where are you?* She wanted to find the rabbi too, for Millie's sake, but her brother and friend came first. Only she couldn't see any of them and with each crippled or unconscious figure, her angst grew. She tried to persuade herself that not finding them was a good thing, that perhaps they weren't on the streets at all.

Had they made safe progress back to the Jewish People's Council? Despite trying to hold on to her positive thoughts, each flittered away, replaced by her darkest fears, at witnessing all the fallen. She even felt sad when encountering the fallen police. They weren't the ones at fault today. No, these poor uniformed pawns had merely been following orders. But they'd encountered a spirited resistance from the Eastenders who'd fought to save their neighbourhood. The leaders were to blame. Ingrid swallowed back the bile. Now was not the time.

As she turned right, heading back onto Leman Street, a sickly feeling crept over her, causing the hairs on her forearms to lift. The barriers in Cable Street had contained the battle, but here no such defences existed and the Eastend people had endured the worst of the police assault. An odd mix of sounds echoed through the street. Ingrid heard wailing, coughs, and groans, along with frequent pleas for help. *How will I ever find the others here?* Her mind asked. She couldn't stop and help these people. In that moment, Ingrid hated herself as she hurried on, ignoring men and women alike as they called out to her, imploring her to stop and help, but she couldn't. Thankfully, others were responding to the cries, bearing stretchers and ready to carry the fallen to nearby ambulances.

By the time Ingrid was halfway along Leman Street, the tiny belief that Dieter and the others had managed an escape grew. She could almost see Gardiner's Corner in the distance and then her heart leapt. She saw Archie's vast outline in the distance and ran towards him. But where were the others? As though Archie had sensed Ingrid's presence, he turned around. His sorrowful eyes locked with hers and before Ingrid registered, the body draped within Archie's arms; she knew a terrible truth.

She ran blindly, tears staining her cheeks. *Maybe's he's just hurt? Nothing more, just unconscious. He'll be* OK *once I get there*, her mind argued. Despite the short distance, her lungs burnt by the time she reached Archie's side. Garbled questions erupted from her, but Archie did not answer. The bloodied rabbi stood behind Archie, but Ingrid was oblivious as she gazed at her brother's lifeless form. 'Is…is he?' She sobbed.

Archie nodded; his face was white with shock.

Ingrid's legs sagged, and an icy numbness swept through her body. *He can't be. No…not after all that's happened. I won't believe it.* Someone held her upright, keeping her from collapsing, just like Archie held her brother. Ingrid gave in, slumping in her saviour's arms. On an already dark day, losing Dieter was incomprehensible. A pain unlike any other seared through her, and Ingrid crumpled in the rabbi's arms and wailed; a primeval, mournful cry that burst unbidden from the depths of her body.

53

OCTOBER 1936, LONDON

At long last Haynes allowed a smile as Mosley rode past, re-igniting the antisemitic chanting. For a while earlier, once the aches in his calves had set in, he feared they wouldn't march at all. His awkward side-long glances up and down the ranks didn't help. They'd turned into a miserable lot and his ability to lead dissolved.

Now, with a new upbeat tone and their commander within sight, they set off. Everyone seemed reinvigorated, but Haynes detected something was amiss. The snakelike marchers were turning about. *How can this be?* He couldn't understand it. He knew London well enough to know that if they continued, they'd soon head west, away from the damned yids. Sure enough, the marchers followed Mosley's newly chosen route, though once it became clear where they were heading, many voices lapsed into a muted hush.

What was the point in marching if they weren't there to crush the Jews or, at the very least, drive fear into the heart of their community? For a second, his loyalty to Mosley wavered before the balance swung back and he decided that somehow, the Jews had to be behind the turnaround. With that irrevocable insight, Haynes wondered how he could make them suffer, and his thoughts returned to Ingrid and her useless brother.

54

January 1937, Yiewsley

Ingrid thought her heart would burst. Some hidden blade had sliced her into quarters. One part held her family, trapped back in Germany. Another; Roy, Florrie, and Archie. The third quarter, she'd saved for Rabbi Cohen, little Millie, and her other Jewish friends. But where the last quarter sat, Dieter's quarter, no light could penetrate. Only blackness remained.

Losing Dieter was her fault. She'd forced Florrie to let them go to the East End; she'd chosen Millie's safety above loyalty to her brother and now, because of her, he lay dead. How could she ever tell her parents and grandmother back in Germany?

The self-imposed pall lasted for days. Ingrid held no appetite for life, not with these burdens fastened to her soul. Even the news that Isaac Blau had returned home safely barely registered. Roy and Florrie tried their best, but in the end all Florrie could say was, 'Let her be.'

Archie tried as well, offering to walk with her in silence before the last of the winter sun disappeared into a darkening horizon. Ingrid refused every offer. Only one thing filled the void, a yearning resentment towards all the fascists. She would make them pay.

Today, as she walked away from her home, along icy streets towards Uxbridge, the bitter chill numbed her bones, giving her a bizarre lift. Where once, she'd felt fearful to walk these streets alone, today she didn't care. They could come at her if they wanted, though one thing had shifted. Before she'd have shrunken, choosing to cower from the threats meted out by all the local fascists. But not today. Not now. The days when Ingrid Stiepermann would buckle were over. Stewing over these thoughts for a couple of months brought Ingrid to a realisation.

Three years earlier, Archie had walked into her life, changing it in ways she could never have foreseen. They'd spent carefree days together, where the world and all its horrors had slipped into the background. Archie's cheeky manner and unusual accent drew her to a strange and happy place. A part of her wished those days could continue, but now, carefree, meant something else entirely. Roy, Florrie and especially Archie all suffered because of her furious melancholy. And there was a risk that, in shutting down, they'd give up on her. Maybe they already had, but nothing would dampen the fury which burnt inside her.

Stopping to lift a brick, she studied its sharp edges while the icy chill crept painfully along her sleeve. Her eyes searched for a target to bombard, but everyone with a brain had left the streets, leaving her standing alone. Within her mind, cowardly Walter, piggy Otto, nasty Klaus, and then the worst. Stefan sat taunting, out of reach from the brick within her hand. Tears pricked her eyes as blood trickled down her palm. Ignoring the pain, Ingrid knelt and, choosing another brick, she pounded the two together. Each strike sent a shuddering pain through her shoulder, but she refused to relent. Each of the boys' images disintegrated before her with every strike, only to reappear and taunt seconds later. The mirage forced her to strike harder and faster, taking the hurt across her body to unbearable levels. Yet still she couldn't stop.

'Ingrid.'

She heard the voice but ignored it. Instead, she focused on the crack appearing in the brick she'd attempted to smash. She wouldn't stop until she'd smashed the object and with it all the ghostly images it represented. The agony in her shoulder barely registered as she stuck down with all her might. Two more strikes should do it. The first hit with all the fury she could muster, and the crack widened. Red dust mingled with the blood across her path, pooling on the frosty floor.

'Ingrid.'

The voice was closer, and a panic set in that someone would come and interrupt her mission to destroy the brick. She had to finish; she wouldn't allow anyone to interfere. Summoning every ounce of strength, her hand swept down in one last strike, only to halt inches above her target. Ingrid lifted her hand slightly, ready to try again, but something wrapped a hand around her fist. She sobbed, with anger for the unbroken brick, for her own shortcomings, and for the injustice of life.

'It's OK,' the voice soothed. 'I understand. Come on, we'll finish this together.'

In her distraught state, she couldn't tell where the voice came from, but whoever they were, they'd transformed from an enemy to a saviour, an angel who lifted her fist in readiness for another assault. Something gripped the brick while tenderly lifting Ingrid's petite hand before lowering it gently across the back of the newcomer's hand, replacing jagged edges with something warm. The next movement felt surreal. The pain faded, and her focus drifted towards a new lightness as her arm lifted upwards, with the support of the stranger.

'Ready?'

With the smallest of nods, the hands rushed down, obliterating the brick, sending dust and shards radiating away from her body. *I've done it*. And with that thought, the hurtful faces of the German boys vanished.

****

Ingrid felt Archie's comforting presence behind her. He gently pulled her upright, away from the pool of rubble, and she buried her head deep into his chest.

'I've been thinking,' Archie said, cradling Ingrid in his arms.

She pulled back, red eyes questioning. 'Go on then. What?'

'Well, it's this country. No, the entire world, really. I'm not one to understand everything but look all around us. Everyone's fleeing.' Settled in the warmth he provided; Ingrid waited for him to continue. 'If I start from the top, then there's Edward. He's our king, well, he was at any rate, but he upped and left. Then there's half our friends in the East End, they're gone. Off to blooming Spain to fight in a war. And you're here, you fled your country. Why's it happening, Ingrid?'

His thoughts caught Ingrid off guard. Archie, strong, dependable, and definitely cheeky, rarely threw deeper questions her way. She wiped her eyes. 'That's not one question, Archie. It's several, and I don't know why all these things are happening. I grew up in a quiet town with mountain air, meadow flowers, and a loving family. We had little, but there was love and beauty. That should be enough for anyone.'

She gripped Archie's hand as a shiver ran through her body. *Why do the Nazis hate her race and others?* The artist in her understood human emotions. She captured them in charcoal often enough. From happy to sad, with shades of anger in between. But this movement, and the emotion it displayed, was entirely different. The movement had harnessed a downcast population, promising retribution. But behind the retribution was something much darker: hatred.

'People are angry, Archie. Some fought and won while we fought and lost, but everyone suffered. Now we have a dangerous mix. A few are standing out, shouting louder than the crowd, persuading people, lots of people, that their way is right and just. Many agree, while others cower, turning a blind eye to the real horrors. As long as people allow these terrible things to happen, then things can only get worse.'

The pair were silent as they digested Ingrid's heavy words.

'So, my darling Ingrid. What do we do?'

Ingrid's eyes flared, not just from Archie's loving sentiment, but from the fire he'd ignited.

'We fight.'

55

MAY 1937, LONDON

'No, not like that.' Babs clucked. 'Blimey, it's lucky we're on this field, otherwise you'd have crashed us by now. Then where would we be? My Alf would have something to say, I can tell ya.'

Ingrid chuckled at her new friend's admonishment. Carefully choosing the correct pedal, she tried to place the Morris Commercial army lorry into gear for the fourth time. The mechanism crunched, before finally accepting Ingrid wouldn't give up, and the vehicle bounced forwards, much to her delight. 'See, I knew I'd get it.' Ingrid's joy was short-lived as she stalled, prompting a howl of disappointment. 'Damn.' Ingrid never swore, and she couldn't ever remember using cuss words back in Germany, though all that had changed when she'd started her first shifts at the factory. Throughout London, newspaper stands showed the coronation of King George VI and Queen Elizabeth, yet Ingrid saw through the façade. A nation in celebration, while Europe and her homeland disintegrated. People needed good news, she knew, but after the temporary blip of happiness, fear and darkness would return. That's why she yearned to wear a uniform. That's why she ran headlong to sign up as soon as she'd convinced Florrie and Roy of her plans. But after all her bluster, she wasn't fighting and, as far as she could tell, stabbing Nazis with a bayonet seemed unlikely.

Only Babs, with her incessant chatter plus a few others, softened her newly found role. And, if she had to learn to drive a lorry then, maybe she could drive herself back to the heart of Germany, where she could run down Stefan and his gang without mercy.

'What are you smirking about?'

Ingrid hadn't meant to let her thoughts carry across her face, but the image of Stefan pleading for forgiveness before disappearing beneath her wheels with a resolute crunch forced an odd smile to her lips. She hadn't told Babs or the others much about her home and she wasn't sure whether she ever would. Archie, Roy, and Florrie knew everything, and for now that was enough. There were questions, of course. And there always would be. Despite the years passing, Ingrid couldn't mask her German heritage.

'I was just thinking about Camila Parkes running out in front, hoping we wouldn't run her down,' she lied.

This time, Babs let out a huge guffaw. 'Well, she's too sharp with us. Can you picture her spindly little legs running this way and that with you driving?'

Ingrid could, but while the mirth helped, she realised she'd need to learn to drive properly first. Then, with luck, she could choose whether to hit Camila Parkes or her German enemies. By the end of the afternoon, she thought she'd got it. Even Babs seemed impressed as all talk of accidentally running down their superior ceased and they focussed on the task in hand. Babs drove the pair back to the compound, much to Ingrid's chagrin. However, her driving had improved, and that was a plus.

'Come on, I'm gasping for a cuppa,' Babs said as they parked just inside the entrance.

'I'll be along in a minute. Put a cup aside for me, will you?' Ingrid knew the brew would stand too long, leaving a bitterness she'd struggle to swallow, but something had caught her attention.

Dashing towards the barrier they'd driven under seconds earlier was Archie. The post had lowered into place, halting his run. Archie's presence unnerved her, as raised voices carried towards her.

'Let me in. I've got to see her.' Archie said, gesticulating at the twiglike Parkes.

'And I've told you. Nobody comes running through here calling the shots without the proper papers. Back off, sonny, until I call you forward.' Parkes' spindly fingers jabbed towards him.

Ingrid rushed toward the pair. 'I'm sorry, Camila. His name is Archie, and he's here to see me. If you'd let me, I can talk with him here and he won't need to come in. We've finished driving for the day, so I'm due a break, anyway.'

Parkes' face voiced her disapproval, but she sighed and shrugged. 'I suppose I could make an exception. Just make it quick, will you, and make sure he stays behind the line?' An awkward pause held before she returned to the compound, allowing Ingrid to approach.

'It's Roy,' Archie exclaimed. 'Come quickly, he's hurt.'

****

Ingrid's throat tightened as she listened to the words tumbling from Archie's mouth. Events beyond her control were happening again and as her mind spiralled towards the worst likely outcome, her head spun. The barrier held her in check, but Archie reached in, steadying her.

'I'm sorry. I shouldn't have blurted everything out like that,' he said. 'He's going to be all right, I'm sure of it.' Ingrid nodded, still in shock. She could feel Parkes' eyes drilling into her back, but for that moment, the woman could take a running jump, and take her rule book with her.

A cough sounded behind her. 'You'll be wanting to go with your chap then.'

Ingrid detached herself from Archie's embrace and turned around.

Parkes' face gave no clue whether she would approve such a request, so Ingrid spoke up. 'May I?'

Parkes nodded, before raising a hand to stop Ingrid's progress. 'Now, I'm bending the rules by letting you hop off without approval, so don't you let me down. I want you back here by first light. You understand me?'

'Of course,' Ingrid stammered, dubious that she could leave straight away.

Before Parkes could change her mind, Ingrid slipped under the barrier, and the pair ran. Archie gripped her hand, leading the way while Ingrid's legs fought to keep pace with his longer stride. She couldn't maintain the pace for long, but as they reached the last building, Archie halted abruptly, causing a minor collision. 'Come on.' He grinned, pointing at a dusty motorcycle. 'Climb aboard. This'll get us back quick-smart.'

Within seconds, they were away, with Ingrid clutching on for dear life as Archie sped across Hammersmith. The Triumph ate up the miles and there was still plenty of daylight when Archie drew to a halt outside Florrie and Roy's home. Ingrid dashed inside.

Where the table used to stand, a bed now occupied the bulk of the living room. Roy lay still while Florrie fussed around.

'Oh, my days. It's you.' Florrie gave Ingrid a tired smile. 'Come on in, child, and I'll get a cuppa made.'

'Uncle Roy, I'm so sorry. What happened?'

Roy shifted his body slightly before issuing a grunt of pain. Florrie held up a hand. 'Now, my darling, you know what the doctor said. You mustn't strain yourself.'

Roy issued another grunt before laying back in the bed. The others withdrew to the kitchen, and Florrie returned to making the drinks.

'It was the cart. Down by the canal. Toppled over, it did. He's been saying for years the path is too steep for Smiler, but with the other bridge too far away, what choice did they have?'

Ingrid's mind pictured the scene clearly. The route wasn't the cause of the accident. No, the problem lay with an overloaded, decrepit cart, unfit for work, and that had the hallmark of one person: Haynes. A familiar sensation of helplessness combined with anger crept over her. Haynes was punishing Uncle Roy because of her. A deep shame within, Ingrid turned away, but

Florrie and Archie quickly blocked her path. 'No, you don't. It's not your fault, Ingrid,' Florrie said, drawing her into a hug.

****

An imperious look on his face, Haynes strode down the street, until the first drops of rain hastened his wobbly stride. The rain intensified, washing away his arrogant façade and forcing him to break into an ungainly trot, waving his walking stick erratically as he went. Soon his breath came in dry rasps, a far cry from the ranks of fit men he'd joined in London seven months earlier, but he was nearing his destination.

His relief at arriving would have shown to anyone passing by, had the rain seen off all watchers. Catching his breath, he paused at the gate. Seeing a motorcycle parked outside Roy's house, Haynes wavered before his natural air of superiority resurfaced and he pushed through to stride along the path. Tapping his cane against the door, he waited an entire three seconds before impatience forced a repeated rat-a-tat-tat.

'All right.' He heard a woman's irritated voice from behind the door. The bolt slid back with a clunk and finally, the door opened.

He shoved forward, eager to escape the deluge. The woman looked shocked, but he hardly cared, and no sooner was he within the tiny hallway. He shook like the old dog he was, scattering droplets of water across the floor. 'Here, take my coat,' he barked.

An icy stare greeted him, colder than the street he'd just left, but Haynes was oblivious. In fact, his mood was buoyant. With the coat seated firmly on his shoulders, he pushed past the woman and into the room. The sight before him swelled his cheerful mood. They'd converted the tiny living room and now a bed dominated the space. Laid out before him, he could see the prone form of Roy Nash. His swift appraisal confirmed his hopes – Roy would not return to work for a while, and that suited him perfectly. While blocking the doorway to prevent Florrie's return, Haynes studied his employee, the one he was about to fire.

'You.'

The predatory eyes fixed in a stare as he spun to the left. He'd expected Ingrid to be home, after all the accident had occurred hours earlier, but it had been weeks since he'd last seen her. He knew she'd gone to work elsewhere, and that irked. No longer was she under his surreptitious gaze. The seed of an idea formed.

Ignoring Ingrid, he returned his attention to Roy. 'Mister Nash, I'm sorry to see you're laid up in bed.' Then, already knowing the answer, he continued. 'When can we expect you back to work?'

'Work. He won't be back at work for months, if ever.' Ingrid fired back. 'You knew the cart was an accident waiting to happen and yet you did nothing. What are you doing here, anyway?'

Haynes had expected her outburst, but Ingrid's fiery response only engorged his desire. Haynes knew the family depended upon Roy's work and he held all the cards. Playing upon her anger, he threw her a contrite response. 'I am sorry. Of course, we should have attended to the state of the cart and if anyone had foreseen the accident, then of course we'd have done all we could to prevent it.'

The woman, Florrie, he recalled, pushed past him and into the room. This time, the chilling stare had gone, replaced with measured words. 'Thank you. It's good you came to check on my husband.'

Haynes caught outrage as it flashed across Ingrid's face. 'Of course,' he said aloud. 'Though it leaves us with a delicate situation. I can't pay any wage if mister Nash can't work. You understand, don't you?'

Mrs Nash's face drained of colour. 'B-but you can't,' she stammered.

Ingrid screamed in anger, but with the bed between them both, Haynes stood his ground. He knew there was nothing they could do, as he wafted one arm in a derisory gesture. And then, he played his ace; the idea formed mere seconds earlier. 'There may be a way I could keep paying your family, though I'm not sure.'

A silence held as the family paused, surprised by the unexpected offer. The older woman spoke up. 'Of course, Mister Haynes, we'll do anything.'

Haynes sniffed. So weak. He despised weakness. 'Since it looks like Mister Nash may not work again, we'll need a replacement.' With Roy unconscious and his wife standing to one side, he moved his calculating eyes onto Ingrid. She would have to give up her dreams to go do his bidding.

56

MAY 1937, YIEWSLEY

'But you can't,' Archie cried once Haynes had left. His body shook until Florrie reached out to calm him.

'I have to. Haynes isn't giving us any choice,' came Ingrid's anguished reply.

'That's not what I mean. You committed yourself to this job. They won't allow you to just walk away; you'll let people down. You heard what she said. I have to deliver you back to the factory in time for breakfast.'

'He's right, you know, and you know it too,' Florrie chipped in. 'Look, you can't work for that nasty man and that's an end.'

'Argh,' Ingrid wailed. 'It's just a job. The factory means nothing. Can't you see I'm trying to help?'

Archie wrapped both arms around her and held her tight before resting his chin upon the top of her head. Despite the sour position Haynes had placed them in; he chuckled inwardly before planting a gentle kiss on Ingrid's forehead. If only she knew just how much she meant to him. One day. Maybe.

Confident she'd come around, he hugged until Ingrid's shakes subsided, and then he knew with absolute certainty he'd sort this out. There was no way he'd ever allow the woman he loved to work for Haynes.

****

The rain finally abated, but as the evening drew on, Ingrid barely spoke. Defeat etched itself painfully across her features until she'd finally relented to everyone's insistence and took herself to bed. Archie stayed over, determined to return Ingrid safely at first light. Florrie was grateful for his presence, that much was obvious, and even Roy woke briefly, though everyone saw his discomfort, hushing him at every opportunity. Eventually, the man of the house settled again, and Archie took his leave.

Upstairs, he paused outside Ingrid's door, suppressing the temptation to walk inside. He could hear her breathing softly just a few feet beyond the wood and he bit down on his lip before moving on. The next room belonged to Florrie and Roy, though it would be a long while before Roy could manage the stairs. He moved to the last door. Passing across the threshold felt wrong. This was Dieter's room, and a guilty shiver ran across his back. Maybe he could have kept his friend from harm. The bedroom looked bare, hardly surprising now Dieter was gone and even the single bed had gone when Florrie took it with Roy using their double downstairs. With threadbare boards and blankets hardly better than rags, Archie settled to lean beneath the window. Shadows danced across the opposite wall and after a while, when the flitting images merged with his own dreams, he nodded off to sleep.

Within a heartbeat, the morning sun rose, and with it, Archie roused from his slumber. His body ached, but he didn't mind. Knowing Ingrid, she'd have a plan, oblivious to the consequences as her determination won out, but Archie could not let that happen. He went downstairs and greeted Florrie. She looked drawn, and he wondered whether she'd slept downstairs to monitor Roy. The sight left him unsettled, but he wouldn't be able to help her, not yet. Spurning any chance of a drink, he gave Florrie a knowing look and returned to rap on Ingrid's door. Five minutes later, after receiving a tirade in German which he could only guess was abuse, Archie mounted his motorbike with Ingrid gripping him from behind. He set them running along the road, keen to rev his engine, despite the early hour. Ingrid could do nothing except hang on as he hurtled along the street, which suited him.

'Go on. Off you pop,' he said when they finally arrived back at the factory gate. Once dismounted, she scrunched her nose in distaste before sidling beyond the barrier. He could see her conflict and even a trace of anger, but before he could discuss anything further, she turned and walked away. Her stubbornness irritated and saddened him. She was angry. He understood that. But here he was, stepping up to fix a problem. *Her* problem. Well, she'd just have to lump it. He'd decided and nothing would interfere, not Ingrid, nor Mister Haynes. Firing the engine once more, he throttled the bike and sped off, heading for the dairy.

Upon arriving, he parked the bike within the main compound. He knew plenty of faces, and he said a brief hello to a few as he cut across the courtyard to the office. He headed for the largest door and marched straight in.

'Morning,' he addressed an older man, who looked up as he came inside. 'I'm looking for Mister Plunkett. Is he about?'

'As I live and breathe. Is that you, young Mister Afford? Blimey, you were barely waist high the last time I clapped eyes on you. What brings you around here this lovely morning?'

Archie beamed a welcome. 'Good morning, Mister Plunkett. I didn't see you skulking in the shadows.'

The foreman roared with laughter. 'Skulking, I think you have the wrong man. Still, it's good to see you. How can I help?'

For the next five minutes, Archie laid out his plan while Doug Plunkett leant against a churn and listened intently. By the end, Plunkett offered just one word. 'All right.'

57

MAY 1937, *BERCHTESGADEN*

Freda Stiepermann peered out through the wooden slats at the stormy weather before turning away in disgust. Outside, the street lay under a bubbling mass of water. Like her mood, the temperature had dropped too.

Abandoning the depressing scene, she stooped to retrieve a cup which had fallen to the floor. 'Oh, Mama.' She sighed as a gentle snore rippled across her mother's lips. The old lady lay slumped in their only comfortable chair in blissful ignorance of everything outside. Freda wished sleep would come for her, too. Then maybe the hunger pangs would lessen, only with sleep also came the fear-filled dreams. It had been over four painful years since they'd taken Gerhard. At first, she remembered the torment of knowing nothing of his whereabouts or his safety. Then, after about six months with no news, she received the first letter. The excitement of that single day, as a flicker of hope shone within the home, soon dwindled. Gerhard's tones offered little in their perfunctory manner. Hardly the letter he'd write under normal circumstances. But, despite this, he was alive and, if the words were to be believed, they were treating him well. When the day of the first letter's arrival ended and Freda placed the paper safely in a drawer, the reflection took hold and she immediately fretted, wondering how long it would be before she heard from her husband again. Over time, more letters arrived, though little optimism flowed across the page. And then, one day which would linger in her memory, Freda saw it. Only by placing several letters side by side did her husband's state become obvious. Where the first couple showed neat handwriting, over time, the content degenerated into a shaky scrawl. Her husband was suffering, despite his brave words.

She wasn't alone at least, and that brought some solace. When awake, Hildegard offered support and everywhere they turned, friends and neighbours shared similar stories, though always in hushed tones. *No, that wasn't right*, she corrected herself. The frightened voices only came from certain quarters, while everywhere else swastika-laden homes broadcast undisguised power.

Hildegard stirred, as though she knew her daughter had thought about her at that very moment. The old woman's eyes sought Freda out in the gloom. 'Is it still raining?'

'Of course, Mama, it's always raining. I can't ever recall floods this bad. Now tell me, how are you feeling after your sleep?' Freda knew the answer, aches and pains which would never ease, but she listened all the same. As her mother listed all her ailments, Freda continued with her jobs. She'd need to venture outside soon as the fire had run low, and she wouldn't be able to make their soup for dinner without it. The walk across to the wood store would be unpleasant, but the task was necessary. Before the light became too dim, she wrapped her shoulders in a shawl and, clutching the scuttle, she marched with purpose towards the door. Bowing her head in readiness against the harsh spring shower which she knew would hit her, Freda tugged the handle and pulled forward.

'Get out of my way, woman.'

Momentarily stunned by the person on her doorstep, Freda retreated before turning to study the strange visitor who'd shouted at her just seconds earlier. She thought the rude caller was a man, though couldn't be sure. He stood underneath the eaves to escape the worst of the downpour. Whoever it was, the tall figure wore a long trench coat and his hunched posture and covered head made identification difficult. As she looked closer, the man thrust a box into Freda's hand before turning to flee.

'Wait,' Freda called while clutching the strange object. The command vanished upon the wind as the figure had hurried off into the distance. She wondered who the courier was, but it didn't matter. Someone had brought a gift, and she wasn't about to wait. She wanted to share with her mother the wonderful surprise. Pushing against the wind, Freda closed the door before walking back to the kitchen.

'I'm glad you're awake, Mama. Look, someone came to the door, and they brought us a parcel. Let's open this together.' Poking the fire caused the embers to glow slightly and Freda settled at the table to unwrap a brown cloth which shrouded the box. Inside lay a wooden oblong. Now she could inspect it properly, her eyes knitted in puzzlement. The tiny casket was only large enough to hold a single shoe. What could it mean? Slowly, she looked for a lid or catch before realising the top would slide away. Suddenly delighted that Freda could reveal the secret contents to her mother, she drew the top back.

With Hildegard looking on, Freda let out a painful gasp. Immediately, one hand went to her mouth, causing the lid to tumble to the floor. It couldn't be, could it? The elation from moments earlier suddenly swept away, only to be replaced with a crippling terror. Freda's body slumped. She couldn't help it. She couldn't know whether the grey powder her eyes had just seen inside the box were the ashen remains of her husband, Gerhard, yet deep down, she feared the worst. As she lay, the pains came. Sharp stabs thrust deep into her gut until a primeval howl erupted. Then She sobbed. She didn't know how long she'd lain there until her mother's calming voice pushed through the paralysis. The only clue came from the failing light as the fire burnt itself out. Eventually, she stood and allowed her mother to hold her in a deep embrace.

Later, despite tears which still flowed, Hildegard and Freda set to relight the fire. Together, they ventured out to gather some logs. The rain had eased, but now in the pitch-darkness, both women worked together to complete the simple task. When they finally closed the latch to secure the wood store, Freda looked longingly, wondering who'd brought the ashes earlier in the day. She wished she'd chased them down the road, eager to learn more, but it was too late now for that, and Freda doubted she'd be able to identify them.

****

Stefan looked out of the window in amusement as the huddled figure approached. He was glad he hadn't gone out in the storm. He waited until the person unlocked the gate before heading to let the character in. The front door was open.

'Did you deliver it?' Otto stood panting on the doorstep, eager to step fully inside.

'Of course. I always do what you tell me to.' Stefan knew that wasn't the case, but this time, at least Otto had behaved properly.

'Did the woman see you?'

'No. I kept my head low. I would not look up in this sodding rain, anyway.'

Stefan would have loved to see Freda when she realised the significance of the box's contents, but it suited him better to have Otto run the errand. After all, he was Stefan's lackey.

'Well done,' Stefan offered as token thanks, before following up with chastisement for the water pooling on the floor. The rebuttal flew over Otto's head and Stefan cursed silently as the oaf nodded in happiness.

'Wait there. Papa will tear into you worse than me if he sees all the water you're leaking everywhere.'

Seconds later, Stefan returned with a pastry, which he thrust into Otto's meaty hand. 'Go on, get out of here before he sees you.'

When the door finally closed, Stefan wiped the pastry grease on a curtain before returning to the window to stare at Otto's disappearing form. Soon he stood alone again, and Stefan allowed himself a wicked smile. It had been a fun idea to send ashes pulled from his own grate to sow seeds of doubt and confusion in the Stiepermann household.

There was a movement behind Stefan as a young woman emerged from the shadows. She went up to Stefan, touched his cheek, and pressed her body against his. 'That was a stroke of genius, my love.'

Stefan took hold of the woman's long plait and yanked her head backwards. She cried out, then nestled even closer to him.

'Of course, it was a stroke of genius,' he agreed, kissing her exposed throat. 'Did you ever doubt me, Christa?' She lifted her mouth to his, but he pushed her away. 'Later, woman. I've got things to do. Get out of here before my father sees you.'

Like an obedient dog, Christa scurried away. His girlfriend, forgotten, Stefan returned to the task at hand. He pulled open a drawer and extracted the letter inside. He carefully cast his eyes across the scribble. This was Gerhard Stiepermann's writing, and Stefan knew any future letters of hope would come directly to him.

58

MAY 1937, YIEWSLEY

Haynes yawned before looking across at Dolly's naked form, which rose and fell in an elegant rhythm as she slept. He loved his secretary's figure, and all she gave him, but that was the problem. Her lithe body and willingness to please should have left him satisfied, but she wasn't Ingrid and that thought festered. While Dolly slept, he thought back to the previous night. She'd excelled this time, resorting to a cunning trick with a mouthful of brandy that still left him aroused. He considered waking Dolly for some fun. *Why wait*, he thought. The girl let out a confused murmur as she felt his press. Ignoring her refusal, he pushed himself on top of her. His attempts were clumsy, taking several attempts before he entered her, and she cried in pain. Her anguish fuelled his desire, and as she bucked against him, it brought him to the brink of climax. And then, with Ingrid's image firmly in his mind, he came. His excitement quickly waned, and he pushed Dolly away. She curled into a ball and cried, but that didn't matter. It was her fault she didn't come. Maybe she should have resisted more.

He turned away from her, wiping sweat against the sheets. He felt Dolly's arm reach across, snagging the rash upon his neck, and he slapped her hand away.

'Don't be like that, Clifford, darling.'

Her plea filled him with revulsion. 'You need to get to work,' he snapped. 'And I want you there before me this time. No need to feed the gossips.'

Before she could respond, Haynes took his leave, his only intent, to wash all smells of their contact away.

****

'Where were you?' Babs asked between stifled yawns.

Ingrid planned a response, one that didn't give too much away. She'd just watched Archie head off on his motorcycle. Now trapped inside the compound, Ingrid grew annoyed, and chatting with Babs would only fuel her bitter outlook. She waved her friend away, knowing she'd only have a brief respite before having to make a hard decision.

Babs saw the look on her face and drew back in surprise. Keen to avoid further conversation, Ingrid turned away and marched towards the darker recesses of the compound. Was Archie right? Was she trapped, signed on to stay in Yiewsley for years to come, with no way out? And if she was, what did that mean for Florrie and Roy? The worry she couldn't help them drew a tear, which she hastily dabbed away before anyone noticed. Ingrid cast her mind back to the fateful day when she'd taken her courage in both hands to present herself at a recruitment drive. She'd had second thoughts on the journey, but she pushed past the fear and continued on. In the end, signing up hadn't gone as expected. A cherub-faced woman in uniform had caught her eye as Ingrid wavered at the entrance to Holland Park, the softness of the woman's features winning her over. As directed, she took a path downwards through a wood, until Ingrid reached a field where a marquee stood. The giant tent looked quintessentially English as union flags fluttered in the wind and the sight reminded Ingrid that she was the foreigner. She pushed herself forward, each step causing the jitters within her stomach to intensify. With self-doubt threatening to overwhelm her, an image of Dieter formed in her mind. Her cheeks flushed in shame. She moved onward, almost in a stumble as the bright sunlight switched to shadow.

She approached a long trestle table with four people sat behind. To the left, a short queue had formed, with three other women busy filling out forms.

'Can I help you?'

The high-pitched voice came from the left, and Ingrid spun, bumping against the speaker, who lurched backwards, sending a cup of tea spiralling through the air before plopping harmlessly on the grass. Ingrid's fingers flew to her mouth as she stood, mortified. 'I…I should go. I'm so sorry.' She bit her lip.

'Not likely,' the woman chided, before offering a chuckle to soften the rebuke. Ingrid stood, confused. 'Come on,' the woman urged. 'Don't stand there with your mouth flapping, pick up my cup and follow me.'

Five minutes later, Ingrid sat nervously nursing a tea of her own. She took a sip, twisting her lips as the deep red liquid flooded her mouth with tannins. Even four years after their arrival, she hadn't adapted to the taste of a powerful brew, and today she lacked the courage to ask for something sweeter.

'Why didn't you say something?' The woman saw her grimace and heaped sugar into Ingrid's cup. 'Now, shall we begin again? My name is Margaret Williams. And what is your name?'

This was the moment Ingrid had been dreading. Her first fear was whether an authority figure would deal with her as a German. The second was far worse. If they accepted her word and reasons for coming to the recruitment, Ingrid had entered the country illegally and, despite assurances from Archie, Florrie and even Rabbi Cohen, the knowledge crippled her with fear. Ingrid studied the woman before her. A middle-aged blonde with shrewd eyes looked back, enquiring. Placing her cup back down, Ingrid took a chance and told her story to the older woman.

'Well,' Margaret replied simply when Ingrid finally paused for breath. With panic once again threatening to overwhelm, Ingrid cast her eyes downward only for Margaret to reach forward and clasp her hand. The warmth returned Ingrid to the moment.

The rest of the day offered a jumble of information which left Ingrid reeling. Ingrid's impulsive desire to join up and fight alongside the British was already in tatters. Without the proper paperwork, Margaret said her superiors wouldn't allow her anywhere near a uniform.

In the end, it took months before the authorities resolved anything and, in a desperate ploy to do something positive, she'd taken a factory job at Waring and Gillow in Hammersmith. Margaret had helped secure the role. From the outside, the building appeared to sell furniture, but once recruited, they'd vetted Ingrid. She learnt a special secret. They were constructing parts which the RAF would use within their planes. It wasn't what she wanted, but for now, until her papers arrived, it would have to do.

With the cold bricks of the factory behind her, Ingrid stood in thought. The happy memory when legitimate papers made her stay official, coupled with confusion when she read the name the authorities had given her; Ingrid Stephens. Apparently, her German surname wouldn't help with integration, they said. Once the surprise had passed, Ingrid accepted the papers meant more. After all, everyone only knew her as Ingrid. Gratitude forced its way to the fore. Gratitude for Roy and Florrie, thanks for Archie and a deep appreciation for those who'd allowed her to remain.

Now, as she looked down at her grey blouse, Ingrid experienced a moment of disillusion. Apart from learning to drive, she remained a world away from any confrontation with Hitler. And even with her newly gained papers, she had to wait for the next recruitment drive before trying to gain a uniform again. Being merely a factory worker didn't suit, and she knew something would have to change, but the thought of working for Haynes made her want to retch.

Whichever way she looked at things, the path remained dour.

****

As planned, Archie marched forward with Doug Plunkett close behind. Together, they burst into Haynes's office with barely a knock.

230

'Good morning,' Archie offered warmly before Haynes could react.

The manager eyed him with cold appraisal. 'Who are you, and what do you want?'

Archie beamed a disarming smile before stepping gently to one side, allowing the smaller Plunkett to enter the room.

'Oh, it's you, Plunkett. What's the meaning of this? You can't just burst into my office unannounced.'

'Shut your noise and listen. I'm sure you know Archie here, despite your blathering. You've lost Roy to injury. Well, Archie here is stepping up as his replacement. And, before you go on with some cobblers, you're going to accept him into your employ without so much as a whimper and fix that damned cart which caused Roy's accident.' Archie stifled a grin as Plunkett dressed Haynes down. 'Of course, you'll also be accepting liability for Roy Nash's injury, and you'll show the company's gratitude by keeping him on the payroll and young Archie here. You're getting a bargain. Roy won't sue the company, Smiler will pull a new, safer cart, and Archie is a strapping lad who'll do the round in no time.'

Haynes's expression hardened. With a slow, deliberate movement, the office manager stood, his chair screeching across the floor. His whole body shaking, he waved his index finger toward the door. 'Get out. Both of you!' He boomed before another man slipped into the office. Haynes's jaw dropped.

'I thought you might object, which is why we spoke with Mister Roper here. Since he owns this wonderful establishment, we thought it best to seek his guidance before coming along to see you.'

Haynes was cornered, and Archie grinned. He knew from Haynes's venomous stare he'd made an enemy but working to support the family while Ingrid remained in the relative safety of north London meant everything to him.

59

JULY 1937, YIEWSLEY

Haynes chewed his thumbnail nervously. Having that bloody Archie Afford step in to work instead of Roy irritated more than it should and with Ingrid away all the time, his ire only intensified. He spat out the nail and returned to his daily ritual neck scratch.

His first move, once owner Jamieson Roper approved the employment change, was to contact Mister Flannigan, the coal merchant. He'd sought Archie's former boss at the coal yard, shelving his distaste for filth in favour of a collaborative approach and, for the first few minutes of their meeting, his hopes rallied. But it wasn't to be. While both felt angered and in full agreement that Archie should return to his coal delivering duties, there was nothing either of them could do.

Not to be undone, Haynes's next move was to contact Cyril and his pair of goons. Their attack to frighten and subdue Ingrid hadn't worked, and now Archie posed a more formidable threat. He remembered his last meeting with the trio days earlier. They'd insisted on payment just to meet him in the first place and then, as one baulked at the request to assault Archie Afford, the others soon folded. *Where were men of violence when he needed them?*

Because of these two setbacks, his mood dropped to a lengthy sulk. Casting his memory back to Mosley and the mini army he'd joined just a year earlier did little to buoy his mood. After the humiliating climb down in October, the whole organisation had suffered a lull in morale. The thoughts made him feel sick, and he returned to chewing the nail. He didn't know how, not yet, anyway, but like the itch he had to scratch daily, he would bring Archie down and then he'd take the person he most desired: *Ingrid*.

60

DECEMBER 1937, *BERCHTESGADEN*

Freda Stiepermann looked downward at a clutch of cobwebs and tutted. She was certain she'd swept that corner, but everywhere she cast her eyes, more dust and dirt revealed. The decaying state of her home was the least of her worries. Today, like all the days before, food was scarce, if you were a Jew. The days when she could walk into town to chatter with *Frau* Huber in the Konditorei were long gone. How she needed their support now, but like so many of her friends, they'd disappeared, leaving no trace. There were rumours, of course, though just being seen talking brought trouble. Those few who shared their views did so only in careful whispers.

The last such conversation had taken place over a month ago, when *Frau* Danielsson brought news of the place known as *Dachau*. The news wasn't good, or welcome. Being told the camp had filled to overflowing filled her throat with bile and since then, nothing could stem her moods downward spiral. She hadn't shared the discovery of Gerhard's ashes with anyone except her mother. *Frau* Danielsson wasn't to know the pain she brought.

A stony hollow persisted and, with little nourishment available, something had to give and as a groan sounded from mama's bedroom, she knew what the next trial would be. Freda's knees creaked like the stairs as she climbed and as she reached the landing, her body spasmed, causing her to clutch the balustrade. She fought back a wave of nausea, and it took several seconds before she felt steady enough to continue. Arriving at her mother's bedroom, she cursed inwardly for not bringing water, but it was too late now. She'd tend to her mother first.

As soon as she stepped through the doorway, she knew something was wrong. Icy tendrils clung to the window, but the cold in Freda's chest was entirely new, one borne of sadness. Where earlier she'd have expected a plume of breath to fill the air above her mother's blanket, now the air was unnaturally still. Her throat constricted as she called her mother's name. Deep within, she understood the groan she'd heard moments before was the last. A tremble rippled down her arm as she reached out to touch her mother's hand. It was still warm. That meant something, didn't it? She stroked the limp palm and hummed a nursery rhyme she'd learnt as a child. She reached the last verse, and Freda risked another glance. Her mother had not moved, her gaze fixed. Freda closed her mother's eyes and wept, her body shaking with grief.

61

APRIL 1938, *BERCHTESGADEN*

Stefan knew a war was coming. In fact, he longed for it. For a start, it meant his father hadn't been home in weeks. Even when Helmut returned to *Berchtesgaden*, Stefan had plenty of opportunities to avoid him. Viktor Lutze had seen to that, leaving Stefan indebted. Three years earlier, the head of the Sturmabteilung had tasked him with rooting out undesirables, a job which sent him on a witch hunt across the whole of southern Germany. He knew he'd changed a lot during that time. Power did that and although grateful, so too came pressure as the new challenges forced him to push his darkest secrets ever deeper.

While he planned his next journey, a dull thump sounded at the door. Otto burst into the room, and Stefan looked up in disgust. As usual, his friend had all the grace of an elephant, with his lumbering gait and a shirt threatening to pop its buttons. Pink skin poked through, leaving Stefan questioning how Otto could ever be part of the master race. Turning away, he scanned his father's bureau, hoping to locate some papers as a ruse to show he was too busy for idle chatter. Otto muttered something unintelligible before disappearing towards the kitchen. Stefan inhaled and counted to five before, as expected, Otto returned with a mouth full of pastry.

'Look at you. You're a slob, dropping crumbs everywhere. You'd better clean up when you've finished stuffing your face.'

Otto spat more food across the floor as he opened his mouth to reply. 'Sorry, but I missed breakfast this morning, as I needed to tell you what's happening.'

Stefan couldn't believe Otto would ever miss a meal, but knowing the quickest way to make him leave would be to humour him, he waved a tired finger towards a seat. 'Come on then, what is it that sent you crashing into my home this morning?'

Otto remained standing, oblivious to Stefan's direction. Instead, he chewed down the last remnants for an infuriating minute before he began. '*Herr* Hitler's done it. Österreich has joined the Fatherland.'

Stefan feigned surprise. He'd expected Austria's inclusion within the Reich, but played along in the hope Otto would finally exhaust himself and leave. 'Who told you?' he asked coolly.

'I heard down at the railway station. The whole town is swarming. Everyone's talking about it. They're really excited. Even our neighbours from across the border have travelled in to celebrate.'

Although Otto's declaration came as no surprise, the news that Austrians were travelling to *Berchtesgaden* to celebrate fuelled his Nazi beliefs. 'This is good. But we knew this would happen. *Herr* Hitler is a wonderful leader and for us to prosper as a nation, we need strength. The Austrians are like us, and together we are stronger. This is only the beginning.' Otto's eyes glistened in dreamy appreciation for Stefan's dialogue, and, for a moment, Stefan almost forgave his subordinate for the intrusion. But he couldn't escape that Otto was a distasteful layabout, and the moment quickly passed. 'You'd best go now. Find Klaus and Walter and share the news.'

Otto looked crestfallen at the dismissal until Stefan suggested Walter's home may have more pastries. Then the hunger returned to the boy's eyes.

The door closed and, once alone, Stefan sighed while pondering whether he could give Otto a new role. One where their paths wouldn't cross.

62

SEPTEMBER 1938, LONDON

Ingrid winced as her lips touched the hot tea, retracting quickly from the scorching heat. 'I don't know how you drink yours so hot.'

Babs grinned as though the sensation of boiling water heading down her throat was a mere tickle. 'Tin guts, my mam always says.'

Placing the mug down before her fingers could succumb to the same fate as her mouth, Ingrid reached across the table for the newspaper. The headline, 'Peace for our Time', caught her attention immediately. 'Is this true, do you think? Has Chamberlain done it?'

Babs shuffled across. 'You know what? I reckon maybe he has. It's there in black and white, ain't it?'

Ingrid hardly dared to believe. But, if true, what did it mean? Could she finally return home to Bavaria? Her eyes scanned the article for further detail.

63

NOVEMBER 1938, PARIS

Herschel Grynszpan leant his body against the corner of Rue de Lille and Rue de Poitiers, trying to look inconspicuous. As he slouched, both arms tucked inward, masking the bulge beneath his jacket. He could feel sweat drenching both flanks, but it didn't matter. As long as nobody interfered, then he knew he would see his mission out.

While he waited, he tuned out all the surrounding hubbub. After two incident free years living in Paris, his world had turned upside down. Only a few days earlier, Herschel received a postcard from his sister, Zbąszyń. She'd witnessed German soldiers drive their father Zindel and mother Rivka onto a train, which disappeared before he could even say goodbye. A few hours of desperate questioning later, she believed he knew the truth. And as he read her theory that the authorities were deporting them back to Poland, a hole opened up in his heart. He'd been born in Germany. They were German citizens, no matter what the new race laws said. Since the terrible news arrived, an acid bile stuck at the back of his throat, no matter how many times he tried to swallow it down. The news led him to a gun shop on Rue du Faubourg St Martin, where he bought a revolver and a box of bullets. Parting with the 235 francs was a means to an end. Nothing else mattered. The journey from his dingy rented studio took little more than half an hour and as he exited the metro at Solférino station, he felt a pang of anxiety, knowing this could be his last day on Earth. But as he emerged into daylight, he steeled himself and headed for his destination.

A figure knocked against him, bringing him out of his stupor. Nobody of consequence, just a clumsy boy who hadn't paid attention. For a second, his heart spiked. Had the boy noticed the weapon within his coat? His eyes bored into the back of the adolescent's head until the figure disappeared from sight. No, the gun remained undetected. Herschel breathed a sigh of relief. His plan would have collapsed before execution had the weapon fallen out. He couldn't relax, but he could focus his attention back to the German Embassy.

Twenty freezing minutes later, two cars drew to a halt halfway down Rue de Lille outside the target building. Six suited men exited the vehicles and headed into the building. Using stationary vehicles as cover, he ducked along the road and took up a crouched position a few metres away from the main entrance. The metal bumper was icy as he rested a hand on it, but the shock helped him focus. The men he'd seen a few seconds earlier were gone, though before he could step forward, a man exited the building and strode briskly down the street. Herschel waited until the man turned the corner, and after the quickest of glances in each direction; he stepped forward, one hand firmly wrapped around the gun. Gripping the brass handle with his free hand, he pushed until he spilled into the embassy. The figures he'd followed were nowhere in sight, though a clerk sat in the foyer. He stumbled onwards, keen to pass further into the building.

A cough sounded behind him. It wouldn't be that easy as the clerk held up a hand in a clear signal to halt.

'I'm here to see his excellency, the ambassador,' Herschel stammered.

'Of course, though you must understand the ambassador is a very busy man and he doesn't see just anyone.'

The inference was obvious. What was he thinking, walking into the German embassy intending to kill the ambassador? He cast his eyes about as a sinking panic threatened to take hold. Then, remembering the line he'd practiced, he rallied. 'I have an important document for the most senior official here. It is sensitive and I can't hand my papers to just anyone.'

The clerk appeared caught in two minds, but after an intolerable wait, he picked up a telephone.

A minute later, a new official arrived and waved Herschel into a nearby office. With no obvious option available, he followed the man, closing the door behind them both. The man from the embassy settled behind a solid oak desk and offered a seat. The name plate read *Ernst vom Rath*, though his position remained unclear.

'You have some information of importance for me?'

Time had run out. Herschel knew that as soon as the door had closed behind him. Of course, he could turn and run, but that wouldn't serve his purpose. Knowing this was the best target he could hope for, and with only the thought of avenging his parents' abduction to Poland, he withdrew the pistol and fired five bullets into the shocked German.

64

NOVEMBER 1938, MUNICH

'Did you hear what happened around Kassel?'

The question threw Stefan. He'd heard of the northern German town, but knew nothing of its significance, or any recent events. He hated looking foolish, but with no option available, he waited for his boss, Viktor Lutze, to tell him.

'They're calling it *Kristallnacht*.'

Stefan considered the name, *the night of broken glass*. Now Lutze's conversation made sense. 'Of course, *Herr* Lutze. I didn't realise that's the town where this began.'

Lutze flared. 'We didn't start this. What happened in Kassel is our response to a murder committed by one of the Jews and, as you'll discover today, this is just the beginning. Let me ask you another question. Do you know about the Beer Hall Putsch?'

This was a topic Stefan was fully conversant with. Although the event had happened fifteen years earlier, when Stefan was only six years old, his father Helmut had told him often enough. He nodded at Lutze. 'Is that why we're travelling to Munich?'

Lutze smiled. 'Yes, it is. I'm glad you understand the significance. The *Führer* may not have overthrown the government then, but now he is our leader, and we will meet him today. Naturally, you will remain silent unless either of us asks you a direct question.'

A thrill of excitement rippled through Stefan. This was beyond his dreams. Lutze was still talking, but Stefan merely nodded dumbly. All his thoughts were a jumble. What would Klaus, Otto, and Walter say when they learnt of his news? Then the image of Christa formed. He knew exactly how she would react. Her desire to share or even take any power he possessed had never been a secret. Confident he could control her, he dragged his thoughts back to the conversation. It seemed his distraction had gone unnoticed as Lutze had moved on to talk of the journey.

Two hours later, Stefan's bubble burst. Yes, he was in Munich and yes, Lutze had placed him in charge of a new squad of troops, but this wasn't the private meeting he'd expected. Instead, hundreds of SS soldiers and officers alike lined up, ready for a huge parade. Stefan took the line with all the rest while Lutze disappeared towards the front. Stefan swallowed his anger. With vast crowds lining the streets, here at least he could shine with the others. He didn't know how long it would be until the march began, but rather than stand idle, he cast a critical eye at those under his command. Most were shorter than him, which suited though one blond-haired individual looked down upon the rest. Keen to mark his authority, he walked down the line, stopping to inspect every person within his squad. Most took his inspection without issue. They knew who Lutze was and his brief introduction was enough to cement Stefan as their leader. Each soldier stood stock still as Stefan took in every detail. All looked immaculate, which boosted Stefan's pride, though it also meant he couldn't stand out as he'd liked. He stopped in front of the tallest soldier. Something about the man didn't sit right. Piercing blue eyes along with a wide smile, which seemed inappropriate given the seriousness of the situation. Stefan's throat became dry, but before he could rally and assert himself, a bugle sounded, and the parade prepared to move off.

In the end, the march was glorious. Far better than any parade he'd ever experienced in *Berchtesgaden*. His troops behaved impeccably, maintaining order and perfect alignment, though Stefan was sure one soldier cast sideways glances toward him more than he should have. But with a throng of cheering supporters on either side, it was possible the tall blond was singling bystanders

243

out for his engaging smile. With the *Buergerbraukeller* visible in the distance, everyone halted. He'd have loved to go into the beer hall and knew the men around him felt the same, but something more important was about to happen.

It took hours and Stefan was footsore and hungry by the time everyone had offered their oaths of allegiance, but despite this, he felt elated. He'd seen the ruling elite, including Hermann Goering and Adolf Hitler himself, albeit in the distance, and their words would echo in his ears for a long time. When the SA Chief of Staff finally found them, Lutze looked both enthusiastic and agitated.

'Ah, Weiss, there you are. Walk with me for a moment. I have news of the utmost importance.'

Stefan immediately snapped his heels together before offering his salute. 'Of course, *Herr* Stabschef.' He could feel the admired eyes of every squad member upon him as he stepped to one side for his private briefing.

'The *Führer* and *Herr* Goebbels agree with me,' Lutze declared with fervour. The statement surprised, but Stefan remained silent. 'Those Jews, with their abhorrent act in Paris, took one of the *Führer*'s personal friends from us, despite the heroic attempts of his personal surgeons. They have declared war upon the Reich. Because of this, we will unleash you and everyone within the SS upon the Jews with our full authority. Tonight, Heinrich Müller of the *Gestapo* will direct all police units in a direct order to support you in the destruction of all Jewish businesses, homes, and especially their synagogues. Fire chiefs will be told they must only attend to fires if they threaten to spread to Aryan properties. Everything else must burn.'

If any doubts remained in Stefan's mind, the next words left no doubt.

'Tonight, take your men and hunt those Jewish scum. Do not distinguish between men, women, or children. You have one task only: to destroy.'

65

November 1938, Yiewsley

A tear formed in the corner of Ingrid's eye as she listened to the crackly news on the wireless. *Peace in our time.* Chamberlain's words seemed oddly hollow if the latest stories were to be believed. On the fourth Wednesday of each month, Ingrid took a day of leave. Normally this meant a trip to see Florrie, Roy and Archie, but today she'd chosen to visit Rabbi Cohen and little Millie. At eight years old, the girl had grown several inches since Ingrid's first visit, but today she was absent: visiting another family for extra study and Ingrid had to make do with just the rabbi for conversation.

Accepting a comforting arm around her shoulder, she let the tears flow. The rabbi was one of the few she could share her vulnerable side with. The weary lines etched across his brow showed he understood. Like her, he had family within Germany, albeit further north on the outskirts of Hamburg. 'I'm sorry,' she said, drying her eyes on the handkerchief offered to her.

'I'd much rather you to shed a tear in preference to holding everything in,' he responded warmly. 'Come, let us light a candle and say a prayer together.'

The peace offered through prayer served its purpose, though the rabbi's message not to worry about events beyond her control hit home. She knew the situation in her homeland was worsening and with her mother, father and grandmother in imminent danger, Ingrid knew she must act, and soon.

66

NOVEMBER 1938, MUNICH

The platoon Stefan led comprised thirty-four men, including himself. Most were older, and as a mere second lieutenant, Stefan knew he was supremely fortunate to be under Lutze's wing, but he fully intended to exploit his master's authority. Tonight, however, he was in command of almost a hundred men, as local police and a small militia of local supporters rallied to the cause.

He'd heard the Jewish population of Munich was close to ten thousand, and he couldn't help wondering how he would fare with just one hundred men, but as they marched towards the Jewish suburbs, onlookers switched to supporters, further swelling the ranks. As they moved through the city, the shouts intensified, and Stefan gleefully struck his baton against some railings. Immediately, others under his command rattled their batons in unison, adding to the din.

They were close to the Jewish neighbourhood now. Behind his men, a column of trucks moved slowly. Inside each one was a chilling secret. Manacles and chains rattled beneath the canvas, ready to imprison anyone who opposed, ready to take dissidents to the camps, though Stefan's orders were simple. Despite the deafening noise, Stefan saw the crossroads before him. He'd already beaten and exiled many, but this was different. Just the sheer scale of everything laid out before him heightened his desire.

Signalling to his men, he divided the group into four. Ahead along *Reichenbachstrasse* stood a synagogue. While three groups attacked Jewish shops along the road, he targeted their place of worship. A huge round window dominated the first floor and, in a show of strength to his men, Stefan hefted a rock which cleaved the glass with ease. A cheer sounded as others followed suit and, within seconds, flaming torches flew through the giant opening. He assumed there were fabrics and wooden benches within because seconds later the insides had erupted into an inferno.

'Barricade the front. Do not let anyone escape the building,' he commanded. While five soldiers worked to follow his orders, he directed the rest to follow him to the rear of the building. Even as they turned the first corner, he heard the screams. Stefan sped onward, with the pounding boots of his supporters sounding in his ears. After leaping over a low picket fence, he saw them through a window. Thirty, maybe forty worshippers, eyes white as they fought to beat away the flames. To the rear, he saw a low arch in the shadows. On closer inspection, he recognised a recessed doorway.

'Here, bring over that cart, and anything else which will burn.' Despite the intense cold, Stefan's hands were slick with sweat as the excitement within him mounted. Within a couple of minutes, the cries from within the synagogue petered out as the occupants brought the fire under control and a strange calm settled around them. There were still shouts from the street and other buildings as soldiers brought the Jews outside for a beating, but at the rear of the synagogue, a silent standoff persisted. Seeing one of his men wielding a hammer, Stefan snatched the tool and set to smashing the cart he'd called for. Others wrenched planks apart with equal gusto. With the rear archway blocked with wood and other detritus, he paused as a face peered out from the shadows inside the synagogue.

'Get back, you filthy Jew.' In a single motion, Stefan swung and released the hammer. It missed the figure by inches as the man ducked back inside, slamming the door in retreat. Not to be undone, Stefan reached forward, taking a torch in an easy swipe. The flambeau drew an orange glow across all the uniformed figures, but before Stefan could become accustomed to the warmth, he threw the flaming baton onto the pile.

Several timbers caught, and he turned away, emitting a primeval roar which the platoon echoed back to him. The roar petered out, but as Stefan moved his men away, the screams from within the synagogue persisted.

67

August / September 1939, London

'Pied Piper tomorrow,' the voice crackled out of the wireless. Rabbi Cohen moved wearily across the lounge and turned the dial. The large box fell silent. Calling Millie, he felt the weight of the world upon his shoulders. His nine-year-old daughter stepped cautiously into the room.

'It's almost time. Tomorrow at dawn.'

Millie's eyes welled up with tears and something deep inside the rabbi's heart broke.

****

'You know why I'm sending you away, my little *bubbale*.'

Millie nodded and clung to her father ever tighter. Around Stepney, Whitechapel and all the way to the river, households poured into the streets. Hundreds of bewildered faces looked about in the chilly morning.

Prising herself away from her father, Millie scanned the crowd. The children looked just like her. Youngsters, some barely out of nappies, stood shaking from the cold, while siblings and neighbours gathered nearby. Other children stood taller than Millie, but apart from size, everyone was equal. Like Millie, the children wore a grey trench coat, with huge buttons and a large label identifying their borough. A few faces were familiar, and that brought solace, though for each she recognised, a dozen more were strangers. Her father's hand gripped hers, but it was little comfort.

They'd be boarding soon. A shrill whistle broke her study, and her small body shook in resigned acceptance.

She leant down to collect her case and gas mask. The handle was an uncomfortable weight in her hand, but seeing other younger children struggling more, she rallied. 'Look, Papa. It's Ruth who comes to worship. She looks scared. Let me go to her. The train will leave soon, and I'd like to ride in the same carriage as her.'

Her father smiled warmly in agreement, and they moved along the platform to the next car, where they met her younger friend. All too soon, the carriage doors slammed shut and Millie pushed down, the fear coursing through her body. She'd cried for half the night, but now, she wanted to show her father and Ruth just how brave she could be. The whistle sounded. This time, the noise barely registered as everyone clamoured goodbyes. There were a few last embraces through the windows, then the train moved away. Within less than a minute, her father was gone, and Millie turned to inspect the crowded compartment.

****

She wasn't sure how long they'd been on the train, though her bones ached, and she knew Ruth felt the same. Miles of fields had passed by, interspersed by the occasional town. But the train didn't stop. Watford, Northampton, Birmingham all came and went. Only the latter, with its urban sprawl, offered any familiarity, but that too fell behind as the train chugged on. Finally, at somewhere called Shrewsbury, they allowed all the passengers to step out onto the platform. It was warm now, at least. A woman shouted, her voice rattling the weary travellers, 'Move through, come on. Don't dally.'

Bunches of children broke off and slowly the crowd thinned, allowing Millie to pull Ruth toward the exit. Once outside, there was an excited swell of chatter as the children looked up at the round towers of a castle looming above them. Placing her case down, Millie wrapped a comforting arm around her friend to show her the sight. The unusual structure caused a cheerful buzz, which grew as the children saw a cluster of trestle tables lined up to one side. The woman's sharp voice called to the children, and Millie and Ruth joined a ragged queue for food. Although thin and curled, the prepared sandwiches tasted delicious. An older boy battered into Millie in a greedy attempt at pocketing more food, before the woman in charge loomed and sent him on his way with a clip across the ear.

The girls sat and ate in a haze of glorious afternoon sunshine. The group stretched along the wide street, a happier place than the awful bench seats which had assaulted their backsides upon the journey. Millie almost forgot why they were there, but she thought of her father, and it took all her will not to show her emotion to Ruth. The other girl appeared happy, so Millie focussed on making sure her friend ate well. It was only when Millie chewed her last mouthful that she detected a change of mood. When they'd left the station with the other children, Millie was aware of the woman who'd bossed them about as well as a few suited men loitering around the edge, but now more adults had arrived, corralling them in. It triggered memories of Cable Street, and her eyes widened at the thought. A hand slipped into hers, reminding her of that fateful day with Ingrid.

'Millie.'

The urgency in Ruth's voice was clear. Millie dragged herself back to the present. Seeing the look of alarm on Ruth's face, her cheeks reddened in shame. 'Come on,' Millie commanded as she struggled to stand. Once erect, with the shorter Ruth standing alongside, Millie inspected the crowd. Although warm, an icy tremble flowed through her, and she was certain the others would see her shake. The more she inspected the group of adults forming the cordon, the more she felt justified in feeling nervous. It was like a market, and the children were the produce. Now her upbringing came back to haunt her. Scriptures, all innocent enough, until she remembered stories of Roman markets as the rich bargained for slaves to rule. She could see it etched into the faces of the adult watchers. Shrewd, calculating. These people were picking the best

251

of the children. A minority looked on with caring empathy, but most of their watchers offered nothing but calculated greed. This wasn't salvation, it was a harvest. Looking down, she pulled Ruth closer, hoping her younger cohort would not detect the threat.

A shout rallied the gathering, and as the bidding began, Millie clung on to her friend. She really needed her papa.

****

It took over an hour. Now the crowd had thinned, and the sun had lost its heat. They'd taken Ruth. Millie didn't know where, though some had returned to the station to head further north. A couple had swept up the younger girl. Maybe that was a good omen. She wasn't sure, and not knowing hurt almost as much as leaving London.

More had come forward, some adults inspecting teeth and fingernails before backing away in disgust. She played with the gas mask in her hands as she waited. She disliked the odd smell of rubber, but out of her depth, she couldn't think of anything better to do with her time. And when the crowd diminished, she settled back upon the ground. With each passing minute, the tension increased. She didn't want to go with them, but equally she didn't want to remain alone, unwanted, unpicked. *What's wrong with me?*

'You'll do.'

The statement, and its delivery, caught Millie off guard. She looked up, unclear whether the speaker would detect her glistening eyes. She pinched them shut, partly in defence against the tears, and partly because the lowering sun prevented her from identifying the speaker.

A hand reached down. Brown, wrinkled, and covered with liver spots. She knew some elderly residents who came to worship, but this was the first time she'd properly met someone so old. Her eyes tracked the arm back to its owner. A wooden cane ran parallel to the hand, which hung down, shaking impatiently. She reached up and gripped the vast paw, which pulled her upward. The gesture, pulling her back to standing, was gentle and kind.

****

It was dark when they arrived, and Millie could barely keep her eyes open. When they'd boarded the train, Millie had asked for their destination. 'You'll see,' came the simple reply. The accent sounded strange. Only Archie spoke with such a rural twang, but before Millie could ponder further, the rocking train sent her into a doze. Whoever her gently spoken guardian was, Mille was too tired to care.

The gentle rocking intensified. 'No. I'm tired,' she murmured before one weary eye snapped wide. 'I'm so…sorry,' she stammered as the cobwebs fell away and she backtracked from her rude response.

'Don't worry, child. You must be exhausted. Come on, let me show you your new home.' As the stranger tugged open the carriage door, cool air swept in, and Millie felt instantly alert. Two minutes later, the gent, walking swiftly for a man his age, led the way, with Millie and her case scuttling along behind. His only concession was to carry her gas mask in its little box, while his other hand clicked his cane along the pavement. Although a few evacuees had followed their route, everyone walked off in different directions as they left the station. She felt envious as cars collected some while they marched off up a hill. The slopes back in London weren't this steep. They passed a strange-looking hotel called The Metropole, where she slowed to gawp.

Her surrogate guardian continued along the road for a few more steps before turning about and raising his cane towards the building.

'It's the wrong way around, you know?' Millie shook her head, confused. 'Our hotel is beautiful. The heart of the town, but this is the rear. What you are looking at is the tradespeople's entrance,' he chuckled. 'The hotel owners thought the road we're walking down would run across the front, but as you can see, someone felt different. Too late now, and I think it looks kind of quaint.'

253

For the first time since she'd started her journey, she felt a glimmer of hope. The feeling spurred her to repeat a question she'd already asked several times. 'Where exactly are we?'

'Of course, how rude of me. My name is Eustace Campbell, and this is my hotel. Welcome, young Millie, to Llandrindod Wells. Welcome to your new home.'

PART TWO

WAR

68

OCTOBER 1939, MUNICH

Stefan smoothed the letter from his father before returning it to his inside pocket. He smiled at the news he'd just read. His former friends had moved from mere cadets in the Hitler youth to fully fledged infantry soldiers, though none had secured his level of authority and prestige. Otto was serving as a cook within a barracks near Stuttgart. The very idea brought humour, as the bungling lump never strayed far from food. Still, Stefan had to admit the boy had been useful in the past. Meanwhile, Walter and Klaus remained in *Berchtesgaden*, though Walter at least had shown sense to join the SS. He couldn't figure what the pair could accomplish there, but as long as they remained away from him, he didn't care. Perhaps they could still be of service by monitoring the power-hungry Christa and her rat of a friend, Gerda.

For now, Munich was far enough away for him to pick up hometown news while sending nothing useful back. Ever since the glorious march where he and his men declared their loyalty to the *Führer*, Stefan had been on a wondrous high. That night, when they gave his platoon free rein to run amok within the Jewish community, left him feeling elated. And he wasn't the only one. All his soldiers took to the rampage with a fervour and commitment, which made him proud and after, alone in his private quarters, he poured a glass of schnapps to celebrate.

A knock sounded, and Stefan's heartbeat quickened. 'Come.' A blond head appeared around the gap in the door. 'Ah, Peter, good to see you. Please come in and close the door.' Peter Klein stood taller than Stefan, but beyond height they were physical equals, though Stefan of course held rank. The man was a true Aryan, which gave him a certain privilege. Normally immaculate, today Peter wore a weary expression. 'What is it, my brother? You look tired. Here, sit.'

'I'm sorry for bothering you so late, but yes, a sleep would do me some good I suppose. I've come here to seek your counsel.'

Stefan stood. 'Of course. You know you can speak freely here. What is it that troubles you? I was just about to have a glass. Would you like one?' he offered, pointing to the schnapps.

Peter nodded. 'Thank you, yes. I wanted to ask about my older sister. She is seeing a Jew against our wishes. I know what must be done, but I want to protect our family from any shameful outcome.'

Stefan brought the drinks over and set them down on the nightstand before returning to the middle of the room. From there, he paced lazily around, until he came up behind Peter, and rested his hands upon the soldier's shoulders.

'Of course. These things are delicate,' he said, kneading the muscles in Peter's neck. His subordinate sighed. 'Good. I see we understand one another. I can protect your family, though you must understand any steps I take to help will leave you indebted to me.' He pressed both hands firmer into the shoulders, widening his caress. Meeting no resistance, he continued, 'Tomorrow, you must give me the details of the Jew scum who threaten your entire family.' He let the inference hang. 'And once I have all the information, I will make sure the abomination disappears and with it all association to your family.'

As Peter attempted to turn his head, he posed the simple question, 'Why tomorrow?'

Stefan ran his fingers ran through the other man's golden hair before returning to the massage. After a few seconds, he gripped Peter's shoulders and turned the man to face him. 'Look at you. You said yourself you're tired and in need of bed. How can you go outside when your uniform looks like this? Your shirt is a mess.'

And then, without warning, Stefan undid the first three buttons of Peter's shirt.

****

Helmut Weiss waited in the shadows for the soldier to leave his son's quarters. He prayed his intuition was wrong, but as a clock chimed another hour, he knew the visitor would stay the night. The thought of their behaviour made him sick, and he considered calling the pair out to answer for their unnatural actions. But knowing he could easily become tarred by association, he stepped away.

Later that evening, he mulled the problem over. He should have noticed his son's tendencies, but with years where their paths rarely crossed, perhaps he wasn't to blame. There had been clues, of course. Apathy, when that local girl, Christa, had thrown herself at his son, when he'd have happily invited her to his bed.

The subordinate would have to go, of course. But better if Stefan moved on first and then Helmut could return to dispose of the other. After wrestling with the issue for a further hour, he concluded nobody could blame him for his son's choices. Maybe his wife, despite being deceased for almost a decade, had influenced their son. Reconciling himself to lay the blame on her, he began writing the first of two letters. Each document would affect the pair. While a new, positive role beckoned for Stefan, his overnight visitor's fate was less certain.

****

Freda looked down at her hands in the dim light offered by fading embers. They shook and no amount of hope could remove the harsh cracked lines which flowed across both roughened palms. She had to go outside before the fire burnt out, but she lacked energy and enthusiasm. Maybe today would be the day she gave up. It should be easier in the winter, with the snow-covered mountains so inhospitable. After all, who would miss her? Years with no news from England left an emptiness as cold as the deepest recesses of the nearby *Saltzbergwerk* mine. She wavered. Was she really considering ending everything?

The slumps were not a fresh experience, only now the pattern had changed. Before, she could brush the odd gloomy day aside, especially when Hildegard was alive, but not now. Now the bleakness of her existence formed a relentless shroud, which stifled all happiness. Her eyes welled as the finality of her situation struck home. She never believed she would give up, yet today all desire to care petered out. Now new thoughts sprang to her mind. Demonic thoughts geared towards her demise. With the last vestiges of will crumbling, tears came to her eyes. Tears flooded her face as she stood. Her fingers shook more now as she gripped the freezing handle and pulled the door open. Icy snow bit into her face, but Freda's eyes were numb and blind to the weather.

'What are you doing? Get back inside, you stupid woman. It's freezing out here.'

The voice barely registered, but then came a slap which brought Freda out of her waking nightmare. Hands gripped her, shaking hard, before pushing her back inside.

'Sit still while I find some blankets and don't move. You looked half dead standing there.'

Freda's lips parted in puzzlement. Darkness combined with brain fog meant she didn't recognise the visitor, but a soft hand reached out to guide her back inside, where she curled upon the hearthrug in a shaky foetal ball. A pair of boots appeared, vanished, and reappeared. Blankets settled across her body. As she lay, warmth spread through her, and fearful the blankets would disappear in some cruel taunt, she closed her eyes against the impending cruelty.

'Here, drink this.'

Freda did not know how long she'd been unconscious, but her side ached from laying upon the floor. She pushed up onto one elbow and her bottom lip dropped in horror as she saw Walter leaning forward to offer a tankard. Her head turned in revulsion, but despite her desire to flee, both legs failed her, and she opted to bury her face in the blankets instead. 'No. What are you doing here?' she cried in a mournful moan.

'I know you hate me, and I deserve every punishment you can imagine, but I came here tonight to say sorry. Here, I've brought you a loaf and a round of cheese.'

She hadn't eaten all day, and the offer of food left her confused. How could she possibly accept after everything he'd done? 'Why?' she croaked.

'I was wrong. We were wrong. I don't expect you to understand, but they force everyone to follow, or they will destroy us. I'm shamed for everything I've done to you and your family. Stefan, Otto, and Klaus, they're not like me. They are monsters. I was a monster too, I know that, and I'm sorry.'

Freda's mind reeled. Earlier in the day, she'd set her heart on ending everything and now her enemy had pulled her back from the brink. Could she trust him? A primitive desire pushed forward. Hunger. Suddenly, she didn't want to walk out and perish in the bleak winter landscape. Maybe this was a test, and she'd take the food only to die in agony from poison. What did it matter? She'd made her peace with the world already that day.

She chanced a peek, but upon seeing Walter's smart uniform, Freda mimicked a tortoise and pulled her head back in.

'Where were you going when I arrived?'

This time, it was Freda's turn to feel ashamed, and she refused to offer an answer.

'Your fire is dying. I'll get some wood. Stay here and I'll be back shortly.'

The door banged behind him. Freda waited before pulling the blanket off her head. Although she lay in her own home, she felt like an intruder. What did Walter's visit mean? Again, she considered whether his visit was merely a ruse designed to bring hope before dashing it once more. But why? Surely if he'd wanted her to suffer, he'd have let her walk into the wilderness. Maybe that was it. Her death could not be too easy. Not if they wanted to milk out her torment. Yes, that was it. Walter was still the devil, just like all the other Nazis. That wouldn't change. The trouble was, his visit brought an unforeseen problem. She'd been ready to bring an end to everything, but now, with Walter's offer of humanity and the first meal she'd had in days, the hunger pangs returned. Tearing into the loaf, she took a bite before drinking deeply from the tankard. Next, she tore into the cheese with equal savagery. With her mouth full, she peered out the window into the gloom and caught a shocking reflection. She was a savage, reduced to eating food with her bare hands. Freda pushed the food away and gave into tears.

She barely registered the door when it banged, signalling Walter's return, but a few minutes later, a warm glow filled the room. The self-loathing at accepting Walter's charity remained, but the novelty of food and a roaring fire tempered her feelings. Still, the questions persisted, but she lacked the energy to ask.

Walter spoke up. 'I have to go soon as they can't see me bringing you a gift, but I hope you'll take better care of yourself. You need to get through this awful war and reunite with your husband.'

Freda's ears pricked. 'What did you say?'

'I said I hope you'll look after yourself and not go walking into a blizzard at night.'

'No, not that. My husband died two years ago. Someone delivered his ashes to me.'

'Who?'

'I don't know. Just some figure on a dark day. They dropped a wooden box and fled,' Freda said, her mind piecing the memory together.

'Whoever that was, they didn't deliver your husband. He is in trouble, but he is very much alive. The last I heard, they were keeping him imprisoned at Camp *Dachau*.'

After Walter left, Freda cried some more, only this time the agony had gone. For the first time in years, she felt the precious emotion of hope.

69

DECEMBER 1939, MUNICH

'What do you mean, transferred?' Stefan could barely contain his outrage at the news Peter had just shared. Peter was one of his soldiers. *I am in command. You go where I tell you.*

He knew he was stretching the truth. There were others higher in the chain of command, but the bitter knowledge only fuelled his ire. Snatching the papers, he read every line twice before returning the document to his visitor.

Poland? What on earth could Peter do within the newly conquered country? And where was Kraków, anyway?

They were alone in his room, somewhere they'd spent many hours together, and this news came as a devastating blow. Certainly not the night of lust he'd planned. As he lowered his voice, his eyes scanned the door. Paranoid thoughts filled his mind. *Had someone spotted them? No, surely not. I've been careful.*

He couldn't fathom how this had happened and worse, now that the decree had come down, what to do about it.

Dissecting the orders brought no answers, and he sank onto the bed. Peter sat beside him. An arm encircled his shoulders, but Stefan threw it off.

'Get away from me,' he barked. 'I need to think.'

Peter's eyes widened at the stinging rebuke, then grew dark with hurt. Stefan didn't care. He wanted to be alone to gather his thoughts.

There would be no lovemaking tonight. As his lover left the room, hurt and bewilderment plain on his face, Stefan realised their relationship was over.

For the first time in over a decade, he felt utterly alone.

70

January 1940, Munich

After an awful month, Stefan tapped the handset impatiently while he waited for the call to collect. He'd already stated his need to speak with *Hauptsturmführer* Alexander Piorkowski. Part of his monthly routine. This was one of the few times he remained patient. Calls were often unreliable, irrespective of the influence he possessed, and he knew Piorkowski was a busy man. A few clicks later, the call connected.

A thin, reedy voice answered the call, triggering Stefan into a quiet sigh. 'Lieutenant Prost,' he said with a politeness he didn't feel. 'Might I speak with the *Commandant*?'

'The *Commandant* is unavailable this morning. I am in charge while he is busy.'

This happened all too often, but Stefan bit down on his anger while he composed his response. Prost was one of the worst the German army held in its ranks. He could cope with sycophants when they held some worth, but all Stefan could see in the second lieutenant was weakness. Unfortunately, he would need to deal with the imbecile. 'Thank you for taking my call. It's *Oberleutnant* Weiss. I'm sure he will take my call.' Although only slightly senior, he hoped it would count.

He was wrong. Before the rebuttal could finish, he slammed the phone into its cradle. While the missed phone call didn't really matter, the arrangement which Stefan had brought to Piorkowski needed careful nurturing. The pair had met briefly a year earlier when Piorkowski was new to the role, and, to Stefan's delight, they'd discovered a mutual interest. While Stefan arranged special privileges for Olga, a housemaid who Piorkowski lusted after, the *Commandant* brought news of Gerhard Stiepermann. They'd given Piorkowski a simple instruction: keep Stiepermann alive, but he had free rein to make the man suffer. When the last reports came in a month earlier, Stefan's eyes had gleamed. Under Piorkowski's guidance, Doctor Sigmund Rascher, assisted by Claus Schilling, was conducting experiments befitting the sub-human occupants of the camp. While Himmler took the plaudits, Stefan consoled himself, knowing they'd adopted some of his own appalling suggestions.

71

FEBRUARY 1940, *DRESDEN*

Hector Lomas watched the procession with interest. He knew the direction that the Germans expected the war to head, though this knowledge was not clear too many. He'd been in place, watching since before the outbreak. It was his job to steal secrets and supply information back to England, and he was bloody good at it. Educated in languages at Oxford, and with a German mother, SIS set their sights on Hector and recruited him.

In some ways, he was an ideal candidate. Unsettled at home, but with talents for language and mathematics, he excelled when presented with puzzles, so working with ciphers came easily. By the summer of nineteen thirty-six, his spy paymasters had smuggled him into Germany where, initially, he sank from view. Masquerading as a teacher who sympathised with the Nazis, he moved seamlessly into German society. His back story of an upbringing in a village outside Trier held enough truth that he could pass with local knowledge. And even though he'd completed his education within England, maternal knowledge passed across to fill any gaps. Today he had a tightrope to walk. *Frau* Umer, a fellow teacher, was showing interest and while a committed, pro-Nazi relationship held value, having someone who could easily stumble upon the suitcase radio he kept beneath three floorboards inside his flat would shatter his façade. He would need to moderate her enthusiasm, though that wouldn't be easy. Playing the disinterested card had become a minefield. He'd seen how easily

266

unjust accusations could cause mayhem with the lives of ordinary people, and he wasn't about to place himself in the firing line. He hoped that by playing it cool and offering little, he could placate the woman. Glancing at his watch, he saw it was almost 7 p.m. He would have to radio in soon.

A few minutes later, the sun dipped beneath the horizon. As the orange glow subsided, Hector stepped away from his flat, lugging the suitcase along the path. There was a curfew, but knowing the risks, he trusted his own guile to navigate *Dresden* alone. Over the previous week, he'd learnt plenty about troop movements. It always amused him how lax the security was within his university. The locals recognised they were well away from any fighting and this lassitude promoted loose tongues which Lomas greased with regular steins of beer. While the pact with the Soviets held, the locals felt safe, and that meant gossip.

After stealing a bicycle from one of his students, he strapped the case behind the saddle and cycled out of the city. Tonight, he would head towards *Stausee Dresdner Heide*. With plenty of hiking paths, he knew that if a radio detection lorry drew too close, he could easily slip away. Before he could get that far, however, he needed to cross the *Elbe*. With several routes available, he opted for the *Loschwitz* bridge, a crossing he'd used many times. Waiting where *Schillerplatz* moved onto *Loschwitzer Brücke* left him exposed, but he couldn't cross until he was certain that nobody was watching.

Everything seemed still. He could even hear the gentle flow of the Elbe a few yards away. Convinced he was alone, he pushed off. The next few seconds were critical. Within *Dresden*, he could take his time and keep to shadows or quieter side streets, but for this part of the journey, lights erected upon the bridge would leave him vulnerable for a few seconds. Finding a rhythm, he pushed the pedals harder and moments later; he was halfway across. A shout to halt broke the silence, followed by the barking of a dog.

Hector's eyes widened in shock. He couldn't just stop. Not while carrying the radio, but equally, what were his options? Perhaps he should throw the suitcase into the river before anyone could catch-up with him. They'd see, of course, and then the inevitable questions would follow. Maybe that was for the best. His feverish mind evaluated his options, eating into valuable seconds. There was another shout, followed swiftly by the sound of an animal running. There was no more time. The opposite bank was only fifty yards away and if he pedalled fast, he might just make it. Cursing the situation he'd placed himself in, he pushed down on the pedals with agonising slowness. Standing in the saddle helped, though above the clicking spokes, a newer, sinister noise emerged. Glancing over his shoulder, he saw the dog gaining, its sides heaving. With the hefty case slowing him, Hector's rasping breath matched those of the chasing animal. Facing the front, he redoubled his efforts. He was almost there. The furthest bank was tantalisingly close and with it, a glimmer of hope that he could pedal to safety.

As Hector swept around the last bend, he felt sharp teeth grip his ankle in a ferocious bite. The bicycle flipped, launching Hector headfirst over the handlebars. He landed hard, and it took several seconds before he could move. Everywhere ached, though the animal had fared little better than him, relinquishing its hold during the crash. He looked across the road at his bike. One wheel completely buckled, forcing him to proceed on foot. He glanced forlornly at the suitcase. His radio and codebook were there, but with many uniforms heading his way, he couldn't hope to escape with the heavy equipment. Pushing his grazed palms against the road, he tried to stand, but his ankle gave way.

A fresh horror entered his thoughts. They would work out he was a spy within seconds. Then what?

72

MARCH 1940, BERLIN

Stefan inspected his shoes. As usual, he'd tasked a lackey to buff them to a mirror gloss, and he had to admit they'd done a good job. That would never do. Taking a cloth, he wiped across the floor until he found the slick mud he needed. Seconds later, both shoes were filthy, and he summoned the servant to come and clean them again. It was a game he enjoyed playing. The junior staff didn't dare to complain, as they knew he would send them to a camp.

A knock sounded, and Stefan turned, ready to mete out the shoeshine task. 'Come in.' The private who entered wasn't the lackey.

'I'm sorry, sir, but there's an important call for you.'

Stefan cursed before sliding his stockinged feet into the dirty shoes and following the soldier. 'Yes,' he announced before shooing the messenger away.

'Weiss. What are you doing, man?'

Stefan snapped to attention, although Viktor Lutze could not possibly see him. Suddenly he felt a self-conscious regret: his shoes were no longer pristine. Shaking off his irrational thoughts, he announced himself and then listened intently to his master's instruction.

When the call ended, Stefan sat in mute contemplation. He didn't understand it. Lutze had instructed him to report to the Reich security office in Berlin. What did the *Reichssichereitshauptamt* want with him? Lutze's order had been both unexpected and explicit. As Stefan considered it, his stomach churned as uncertain thoughts crept in. He liked his work within the SS, though this was merely another part of the same beast. The swagger and prestige, coupled with the state endorsed ruthlessness, fit his character perfectly. Switching roles was an alien concept. Stefan shook himself. His reluctance was moot. Lutze had given his order.

****

Despite his reservations, Stefan had to admit the building which housed the Reich Security headquarters looked magnificent in the autumn sun. Ordinarily, he didn't do pretty, except for the occasional boy, but with his SS uniform looking immaculate, he strode inside the building. To most, the drab grey looked oppressive, but not to Stefan. To him, he saw a mighty edifice and, whether he liked the summons, he would soon find out why they'd decreed his attendance.

'I'm here to see Reinhard Heydrich,' Stefan announced to the receptionist. 'He is expecting me.' While the woman phoned through, he composed his thoughts. It wasn't easy. Stefan felt a flutter of hero worship skitter across his stomach. He knew Heydrich's part in *Kristallnacht,* and this appointment was taking Stefan straight to the top. After a brief delay, a messenger strode up and showed for him to follow. The pair climbed two flights of stairs and swept along a vast corridor before reaching Heydrich's door. The guide retreated, leaving Stefan alone, and for a second, he felt a nervous shiver. After waiting for the corridor to empty, he punched the wall. His grazed knuckles hurt, but he needed pain to distract himself from his own contemptible weakness. After straightening his tie, he knocked twice before turning the handle and marching in.

'Ah, Weiss, you found us.' Lutze nodded. 'Good, good. Tell me, how was your journey?'

Stefan shrugged, reluctant to be drawn into small talk, though if his silence caused insult, Heydrich didn't let it show. 'Why am I here?'

Heydrich placed some papers aside and turned to Stefan with a chuckle. 'Clearly, Lutze hasn't explained. Do you see yourself as a hunter, *Oberleutnant*?'

The question left Stefan wrongfooted, and he took a moment to consider his reply. He knew he loved to hunt, especially all the Jews and other undesirables, but was that what Heydrich was alluding to? Figuring Lutze and Heydrich would have held a frank conversation about him over his own dossier, Stefan nodded.

'Splendid.' Heydrich applauded. He leapt from his chair and offered a handshake. Stefan covered his surprise and shook the man's hand.

'We're not so different, you and us here. We like to hunt too. Only our prey differs. You've shown an obvious ability to hound the Jews, as you should, being an upstanding SS officer. They are, of course, *unerwünscht*, the whole filthy lot of them. Our organisation also seeks certain people, Weiss.' He paused, his eyes searching Stefan's face. 'Do you know who it is that we hunt?'

Stefan knew the answer, but once again, he wondered whether this was a trap. He remained silent.

'Come, come Weiss. Silence will serve you well on some days, but not today. Answer me.'

He plumped for the obvious textbook answer. 'You're the security service, so that must mean you hunt spies and any other enemies of the state.'

'Bravo. Now, I have something important to ask and I want you to take your time before answering me. Do you want to hunt spies and anti-Nazi scum for us?'

The question floored him. He'd expected some singular mission before returning to his SS platoon, but this sounded like a permanent arrangement. 'Of course.' He nodded, to appear nonchalant.

'Excellent. Your father was right to recommend you to me.'

For the second time within a minute, Stefan's mind reeled. My father? 'I...I'm sorry, sir. But I thought Lutze organised my transfer.'

Heydrich's brow furrowed before answering. 'I have plenty of time for Victor, of course, but Lutze had nothing to do with this. In fact, he bitterly objected to your transfer. Fortunately, I have the *Führer*'s ear and my decision carries.'

Stefan digested the news. Immediately, he joined up the dots. Peter hadn't written since leaving the country. Hardly a surprise, given the way they parted, but a frustration. Now, his father had intervened to remove him from a job he loved. He shivered as the pieces fell into place. Whether Heydrich noticed, Stefan was unsure, but believing his father knew his delicate tastes came as a hammer blow.

****

Two hours later, Heydrich and Stefan were striding across some scrub land at the furthest reach of the *großer Müggelsee*. Stefan's stomach churned, but within Heydrich's presence, he had no choice but to comply. In the distance, he spotted a fortified farmhouse with a half-track and complement of soldiers and several Alsatians standing guard. Heels clicked together as each sentry offered a smart salute to Heydrich as the pair entered the building.

As soon as they stepped through the doorway, Stefan saw this was no ordinary farmhouse. Along one wall, he noted an array of wicked looking tools and implements which suggested a sinister purpose. Before he could appraise them further, Heydrich signalled to a guard to unlock a sturdy door at the furthest end of the room. He peered through and, with a nudge of encouragement, descended the steep stairs into the basement. As the door closed behind them, Stefan felt a chill traverse his spine. He wasn't frightened, but the subterranean clinical whitewash reminded him of the frozen Bavarian peaks. A long corridor stretched into the distance, with cells on either side and a desk at the furthest end. All the cell doors were closed, but Stefan could hear at least one occupant, wheezing from within. While two privates remained on guard, an officer stood and marched down to greet them.

'Sir, it is good to see you again,' he offered, along with a smart salute. 'We have continued to question the men as instructed. Your visit today is portentous. I think at least one of the three captured is ready to break. Perhaps if you and your visitor talk to them, you'll tip the balance.'

Tucked in the furthermost shadows lay another, larger room, and Heydrich drew Stefan away from the cells while the other officer scuttled along behind. Here, no whitewash adorned the walls. Instead, brickwork peppered with bullet holes showed a more bloody purpose. Once they were beyond the ears of the inmates, Heydrich spoke.

'As Lieutenant Schwartz explained, we have captured three British spies. The intelligence we've gathered proves beyond doubt that these are enemy agents,' he said, passing a dossier over to Stefan. 'We intend to hang them in due course, but what do you suggest? After all, they could still be of use to us.'

Stefan glanced at the papers before setting his mind to the question. This wasn't the assignment he'd expected, but he would adapt. Detailed code names, activities, dates, and events revealed a damning truth. The English spies were without doubt guilty. He knew he could brutalise the enemy combatants, perhaps yielding information of some worth, but was that the course of action?

'Will you give me free rein to question them all and instigate any punishment I deem necessary?'

Heydrich appeared ruffled by Stefan's request. It bordered on impertinence, but after a pause, the senior officer nodded his approval.

Stefan took a few minutes to study the evidence before calling for the prisoners to be brought forward. Moments later, three degenerate individuals lurched into the room, forming a ragged line. Stefan drew himself upright. It was his time to shine.

'You men, do you accept you are all British spies?' None moved to acknowledge his question, and Stefan's mouth turned upwards in a cruel smile. 'Since you won't speak, I will ask you another question, but first I am going to explain something. You are all spies. Every one of you is guilty. You know this, just as we do.

Now, here is the thing which you all must ask yourselves. Do you want to live?' Stefan watched each of the men for a reaction. The three prisoners remained still, so Stefan used the lull to walk along the line to study the men. With the assurance of armed guards nearby, he could let his natural arrogance rise to the surface. 'Since none of you will answer me, I will explain what will happen. You,' he said, directing his words to the first in line. 'You go by the code name Foxglove. We know you entered our country through *Esbjerg* in Denmark before travelling south to Hamburg, where we observed you, before making an arrest. You British really are. How do you say it? Simpletons, for thinking you could spy within the fatherland, undetected.' He stepped on to the second individual. 'Your code name is Theodore, and you have operated within the Berlin area since the beginning of the year. And you' – he glanced at the last prisoner – 'we've only just captured you, but we know you go by the moniker Mallard.'

Stefan cast his eyes along the line, but the prisoners' downcast eyes offered no insights. He assumed they'd been told all this before, but that didn't matter. Now he would raise the stakes. 'Given everyone in this room knows your guilt, I am going to tell you what will happen now.' Feeling empowered, Stefan played to Heydrich and the other officer. 'You can see along the wall how others fared. Perhaps they were the lucky ones. Facing the firing squad, an almost instant death.' He spun about before continuing his theatrical pacing. 'Two of you will die in this building. The first will receive a noble death in a hail of bullets, but the second won't fare so well. I will see that your death stretches into an eternal torment. You will pray for death, but no one will answer those pleas.' He moved back along the line, aware that he had the attention of everyone in the room. 'So that leaves just one of you who will survive. How, I'm sure you wonder? Come now, you're all intelligent men. One of you will turn traitor to your country and will spy for us. If you do this to our satisfaction, then you will survive.'

Stefan showed to the guards to return the men to their cells. He would give them ten minutes to consider their destiny and if they couldn't decide, then he would choose their fate himself. As he stood in Heydrich's company, Stefan congratulated himself. All he had to do now was assess who would make the best double agent.

****

Hector stood in the middle cell, sandwiched between his two compatriots. His insides churned at the information he'd just received. Perhaps what the German officer had said was true, and a quick death by firing squad was the noble option. The trouble was, he didn't want to die, and he guessed the others didn't want to, either. He tried to gloss over the idea of torture, but the notion overwhelmed him, and soon he could think of nothing else. Tears flowed as his body curled into the foetal position. An agony of seconds passed. He wanted to scream, to beg, but most of all, he wanted to live.

Hector didn't know how much time had passed, but when the keys rattled in the lock, he watched the guard through bleary eyes. Perhaps the delay had given him the strength he needed. He wasn't sure, but when they pulled him to his feet and let him back out with the others, he knew what he must do.

73

MAY 1940, YIEWSLEY

Dolly Fairbanks let out a gurgling cry before pulling the chain. The vomit circled twice before disappearing beyond the U-bend. She was more than a week overdue, and a shuddering realisation cascaded through her thoughts: *Now the damned bastard will have to marry me.*

The secretary wiped her mouth, and with a fitful groan, she climbed to her feet. This was the third bout of sickness that week and with each passing day, all doubts dissolved. Now she knew, and that meant she had Haynes cornered. With other workers around, Dolly bade her time, determined to wait until evening, when she could force Haynes into a long overdue proposal. The day dragged as uncertainty pecked at her confidence. Part of her psyche felt he would do the right thing, and mentally she was already spending his money on a new, lavish lifestyle. But a simple niggle persisted, itching like the rash upon Haynes's neck. She knew his ailment was getting worse, where before it used to cover the space of a few fingers, now the red splotch had spread across his entire neck and down beneath his right shoulder. She was sure he had a lump under there, but during her one attempt at inspection, Haynes came close to violence, and she withdrew. What did it matter if the duffer hid a lump from her? That was his problem, not hers. And, if, she thought with a trace of glee; he fell really ill. Then she'd be more than happy to wear the mantle of a rich widow.

While the clock ticked noisily toward the end of the day, she shook thoughts of rashes and ailments from her head. Even with a minor deformity, his money made a marriage worth pursuing. She could give up this dead-end job for a start. The thought brought a smile until another wave of nausea crashed her down to earth. For a horrific moment, she feared another vomiting fit, where her desk became a canvas for all to see, but with measured contractions in her throat, she fought the urge.

A hooter sounded, signalling the end of the working day, and Dolly steeled herself for the conversation to come. There would be workers still around, of course, there always were, but for this conversation, Dolly wanted privacy. After checking the stairs were empty, she clicked the door shut and turned off the desk lamp to give the impression of emptiness before knocking on Haynes's door. Before he could answer, she walked in, closing the door behind her. A wary smile greeted her. This was often their time together, a place where he could act out his predatory fantasies, but today he looked flustered.

'Not today, Dolly. I have work to do. You head off while I finish here.'

She felt a mix of sourness and panic at the dismissal. This wasn't how she'd practiced the conversation. Instead of complying, she stood stock still until her boss looked up from his desk once more. She knew a wave of anger was coming, but for once, she stood her ground. 'I have to talk to you. Not later, now.' Her voice wavered, though the words were clear.

Haynes dabbed his pen upon a blotter before placing it to one side. Next, with elbows firmly planted upon his desk, he leant forward, and Dolly wondered whether he would reach out across the desk to slap her. It wouldn't be the first time, and she winced at the memory, but her condition demanded a response. Her boss flicked a palm open, allowing her to speak.

'I'm pregnant.'

There, a simple statement. She'd told him. Now all she had to do was follow up with her demands, but her throat was dry, and the words wouldn't come.

Haynes offered a smile, but it held no warmth. Was that a victory she detected in his glinting eyes?

'What is it you want from me? he asked finally.

This was it. Her one opportunity to set out her demands. 'I want you to make an honest woman of me. You've had your fun all these years, and lord, I've let you, but now I've fallen, I expect you to do the right thing and put a ring on my finger. And not a cheap one either. This has to be done properly.'

An ominous silence followed, punctuated only by the sound of harsh breath as her boss's face darkened.

'Get out of my sight and do not set foot on these premises again. You have two choices. You can leave your job quietly and I'll offer you a decent reference so you can start again somewhere well away from here. Or you can put up a fight, and believe me, you don't want to go down that road. I'll have you and your bastard unborn out on the street before the week is out.'

Dolly's mouth parted in shock. It couldn't be. She'd heard his words, but surely Haynes couldn't cast her aside so easily. A fresh wave of nausea swept through her. This time, Dolly did nothing to hold it back.

****

Two days later, Dolly looked at the dairy offices from afar only today, she wasn't alone. Three men stood beside her. The first wore a dark suit enshrouded in a brown full-length coat and matching trilby. The other two wore police uniforms. After the implosion of her world, she'd ran, desperate to get away as everything collapsed around her and that impulsive act served her. Without thinking, she'd scooped up her coat, bag, and contents before fleeing and twenty-four hours later, with tear-encrusted eyes, Dolly examined a bunch of keys with venom in her heart.

Accessing Haynes's office had been easy. She knew the night watchman and his routine and slipped past him in silence. Having the office keys made her task simple and, once inside, she set to work unlocking his desk. She didn't have that key, but the fool hadn't always been careful, and Dolly knew his hiding place. The last part was the hardest. In the darkness, she couldn't find the photographs she desired, so lifted all the papers into a sturdy bag before pushing the drawer closed. Her ears pricked at the watchman passing underneath, but he was soon gone, and she could finish her task. It wasn't until thirty minutes later in the dim lamp glow within her bedsit that she held the photographs she needed. With the war raging in Europe, all antisemitic supporters were now deemed the enemy. She wasn't sure how much damage the photographs would do, but in her hand, she held proof that Haynes was indeed loyal to Sir Oswald Mosley and all his vile kind. Images which Haynes treasured would now count against him.

The first police station she'd visited showed no interest, but undeterred, Dolly bagged her evidence and tried elsewhere. Maybe a provincial station wasn't the best idea, anyway. Her second stop took her into the heart of London and Charing Cross Police Station. At first the desk sergeant appeared uninterested, but just as her hope waned, another man introduced himself as Inspector Tyler, before taking her to one side and pressing for further information.

'You'll find him in there,' Dolly told the men. 'Up the stairs, there is a large outer office, my office,' she stammered before reminding herself he'd sacked her. 'And in the corner, you'll see two rooms. Ignore the first. You'll find him behind the second door.'

'All right, Dolly. Thank you for your help. You stay back and we'll take it from here.'

She waited near the main gate until the men started up the stairs and then she followed. Dolly knew she wasn't popular. After all, she'd acted as an immutable barrier to protect Haynes for several years, but today the dairy employees were in for a rare treat. She waved at Archie and then said hello to Doug Plunkett, a behaviour she'd never done in the past. She wanted them to follow as witnesses to make Haynes's humiliation complete. By the time she reached the stairs, a small, bemused crowd was behind her as the shouting began.

'You can't do this,' Haynes squealed while the two constables showed they clearly could by cuffing his wrists behind his back.

'Look,' the inspector offered calmly, 'you could have come quietly, and we wouldn't need restraints, but given you're kicking off like this, cuffs it is.'

Dolly could barely contain herself. Haynes had used her and now as the realisation hit, walls crumbled and so too her desires. She couldn't believe how warped she'd become under Haynes's control. But no more.

Her boss descended the stairs and walked, head bowed, into the courtyard. Now she saw the real Clifford Haynes, a little man who rendered powerless. Haynes met her eyes for a moment before attempting another pointless struggle. The burly constable reined him in.

'Where are you taking me?' Haynes demanded.

The constable dipped his head to answer. 'My guess, Brixton. They have a nice prison down there and you'll fit right in alongside that scumbag, Mosley.'

The gathered crowd overheard, and the resultant cheer would echo in Dolly's ears for a long time.

74

MAY 1940, *BERCHTESGADEN*

Freda saw Walter approach through the darkness and opened the door before he had time to knock. She silently ushered him inside. Even though the action only took a second, she knew his visit was dangerous for them both.

'Here,' Walter said as he offered his monthly food parcel. It was smaller than the last. Despite herself, she snatched the sack and rifled inside. She took a bite out of a loaf inside before cursing her greed. This food would need to last. Drawing a thick drape across the door, she allowed Walter to walk through to the living room.

'How are you?' she asked. Even now, the question felt strange upon her lips.

'Good.'

He was lying, Freda's maternal instinct knew, but then most people would respond in the same manner. She allowed him to settle before asking, which tore into her every day. 'Have you heard any news about my husband?'

His face dropped, and she had her answer. Her eyes pleaded for something, but only a mumbled *sorry* reached her ears and she felt her body sag. Walter reached over to comfort her, but she shrugged him off. Although he'd turned a corner and now offered her kindness with food and news, she could never be entirely comfortable around the soldier.

'What then?' she asked with a voice tinged with bitterness.

'They're sending me away. I knew this would happen. Otto left months ago, and I haven't heard from Stefan in almost a year. I'm...'

Before he could finish, Freda's bloodshot eyes flared in anger. 'How dare you mention their names in this house.' Shock radiated across Walter's face and, for a second, Freda thought she'd overstepped. Walter still had the power to have her interned like her husband, though she would drag him down too.

No. Nobody would listen to her accusations. He could do whatever he wanted. 'I'm sorry,' she offered meekly. Please don't tell me about them. I'll listen to news about you, my family, and friends, but no others unless it is to protect me. Those others can go to *sheol* for all I care.' She spotted his confused face. 'Hell,' she added.

This time, Walter apologised. 'You have nothing to be sorry for. It is us who are in the wrong, and you are right to feel angry. I shouldn't have mentioned them. Though I daresay you are glad that they're far away, or about to depart.'

'Where are they sending you? When?'

'We're forbidden from saying where, though I believe you won't tell anyone. Belgium, I believe. And my unit will move out in the morning.'

Freda considered the news. Seeing the half empty food sack only magnified her plight. 'So that's it then. I won't see you again,' she said simply. This time, she offered a hug. There was nothing else she could do beyond showing him out and sitting alone while the angst took hold once more.

75

MAY 1940, YIEWSLEY / DUNKIRK

May was dragging. Ingrid hadn't had a day off since Easter and the newspapers had introduced an unfamiliar word to the British vocabulary, *blitzkrieg*. She understood the term *lightning war*, and it filled her with dread. Every day brought terrifying stories as the Nazi war machine swept across the continent. But today would be different, she told herself. Today the sun shone, and she felt a rare moment of brightness. After picking meadow flowers, she set off to see her guardians in the hope she'd also bump into Archie. The gate creaked as she pushed through and walked up the path. A bitter feeling stirred. *Why can't every day be like this?* Before the negative thought could take hold, Florrie's bright face appeared at the window, triggering a yelp of delight, and the door sprang open.

'Ingrid, my darling. Come in. I was just talking about you to Roy. I'm so glad you're here.'

Accepting her aunt's all-encompassing hug, she breathed in the familiar scent of Fairy soap. It was good to be home. Behind Aunt Florrie, tall and proud, stood Roy. Although he didn't offer Ingrid a hug, his face showed delight at her arrival. It was wonderful to see him up and about, but her heart sank when Archie didn't appear.

'He isn't here.' Ingrid's face flashed disappointment. 'I knew you'd be upset. Didn't I just say that earlier? Come on, you'd better sit down.'

With Roy's bed returned upstairs, Ingrid moved across the space and perched at the end of the sofa while her aunt hovered. 'Well, where is he?' She couldn't hide the frustration in her voice.

'He's gone to Ramsgate. Set off on his motorbike late yesterday evening.'

'Ramsgate? Where's that? And what for?' Ingrid's mind leapt to the worst-case scenario. A day earlier, the admiralty had made a plea to the nation on the wireless. Thousands of allied troops desperately needed rescue before the Nazi war machine drove them into the sea. Shallow beaches were hampering the rescue effort, meaning anyone with a seaworthy vessel and a shallow draught could help. A familiar feeling of powerlessness took hold as Ingrid fought for breath.

****

Archie retched for the third time in an hour as the motorboat chugged across the *Channel*. The pitching of the boat, combined with fuel fumes, created the perfect storm for nausea. Adding to his discomfort was the knowledge that Ingrid would be livid. Here he was, actively helping the war effort while she remained in London. In recent months, she'd opened up to him, and he knew how frustrated she felt at the tasks her superiors gave her. *This isn't fighting,* she told him on repeat. His assurances that her efforts were worthwhile fell on deaf ears.

Gazing at the open sea, Archie's confidence faltered. He could swim, though it had been a while since he'd last visited Hillingdon lido, but as England pushed further into their wake, all feelings of bravado waned.

Ahead, he supposed, were the beaches of northern France and Belgium. His geography was fuzzy, but he trusted Harry, the ginger bearded skipper steering the boat. The boat captain had looked doubtful when Archie approached at first light, but one thing had secured his passage. Archie was tall and strong, and where they were going, strength was an asset. A twenty-five-foot boat with a seven-foot beam could not accommodate further passengers.

Swirls of fog and smoke clouded his view as a buzz in the skies overhead mingled with the slap of waves against the hull. After two hours on the water, Archie admitted he was a landlubber. His good cheer on boarding had all but evaporated. However, his memory of leaving Ramsgate harbour sustained him. He'd tried to count how many craft had taken to the water, but with the constant movement from the swell, he soon lost count. It warmed his heart and vindicated his decision. Ahead, in the unknown, lay an army in desperate need.

The first thirty minutes of the journey were full of wonder, but once they'd broken away from the harbour wall, a grim reality replaced Archie's optimism. There was no way he could swim back to shore and with every minute taking him further from land, his nerves intensified. He vainly fixed his eyes on the other boats to distract himself, but to no avail. He ended up gripping a handle in the half open cabin, a move which prompted a knowing twinkle in Harry's seafaring eyes. Archie smiled self-consciously. He could stomach the skippers' wry smiles for the greater good of the rescue.

Glancing out over the bow, Archie's jaw dropped. 'Is that…?'

'Aye.' Harry nodded. 'That's our date with destiny, straight ahead.'

Archie's mind leapt from joyous to stunned to scared in a relentless loop. Compared to the *Daphne*, the warships ahead were behemoths. He'd seen ships moored on the Thames, but nothing had prepared him for this. His young mind craved knowledge, and after a little coaxing, Harry explained that the nearest ship was a British Destroyer. And there were many others, held at anchor. The little ships nudged past as they approached the shallows. Archie didn't feel cowed, despite the surreal situation, until the harsh smell of cordite mixed with salty air drew all his focus. Gunfire erupted all around and with a paper-thin cabin shielding them from the attack, he felt a guilty gratitude that they were one of the smaller boats. Suppressing his flight instinct, Archie held onto the bulkhead and stood firm. If Harry was going to stand exposed while grimly gripping the wheel, then he would, too. Lines of water erupted in tiny fountains nearby as bullets rained down from above. If the rounds came too close, there would be no salvation. Death would likely be swift, though that would offer no comfort for Ingrid, her family, or those they rescued.

Now, with threats all around, Archie looked to the skies, but dark planes soared overhead in constant strafing manoeuvres, while inland explosions assaulted his ears. Dirt and smoke were no strangers to Archie, but he had never known noise like this. Glancing at Harry, he realised the older man was just as overwhelmed. Searching through a gap in the smoke, Archie gasped at the scene before them. Lines of men, some shoulder deep in the water, stretching away from the shoreline. It appeared as though the soldiers' queue went on forever. He knew how cold the water was and pitied the men, while others, further back, stood hopelessly exposed upon the smouldering beach. *How?* his mind screamed, for despite the number of boats surging forward, he could see no easy way to help. Harry too seemed at a loss where best to steer. Some boats held close to the larger ships, attempting to gain instruction, while others surged forward to the beach. Before they could chug forward much further, a yacht swept across their beam, missing their prow by inches. *If the Germans don't sink us...*Archie thought. Harry swore as he wrenched the wheel to the starboard only to heave immediately back to port to avoid another collision. The movement sent Archie lurching across the deck, and he cried out as his arm smashed into a stanchion. A wave of pain radiated up his arm, and he staggered. Harry took a hand off the wheel and steadied him.

Archie shook off the pain and brought his full attention to the scene ahead. He estimated they were about two hundred yards away from the first line of soldiers, but he could already see there was a problem. Just the sheer number of boats buffeting in competition caused chaos but combined with the rolling breakers and sheer desperation of the soldiers queued, progress was difficult. And once a boat had successfully dragged their war-weary troops aboard and turned about, their path to escape lay blocked. More boats steamed in behind while those left behind clung on in agonising hope.

'There.' Archie pointed. Harry wrenched the wheel and veered left. A long outcrop stretched from the land, far into the water, and ideal place for troops to embark. The engine gunned, driving them forward again, drowned out in the noise of battle. Others followed their lead, forcing them to go astern to avoid collision with their compatriots. The tiny plumes of gunfire, which had caught Archie's attention when they joined the battle, had grown significantly. Now thunderous splashes erupted around them, covering the men in spray. Within the melee, a deafening drone caused Archie to look skyward. Where before the planes speckling the sky could have been mistaken for birds in flight, something large and ominous came towards them at a terrifying speed. Archie's heart hammered. They were in the firing line and there was nothing he could do to avoid disaster. He reached an arm around, shielding Harry from the inevitable destruction. The deck shook as a fireball erupted above. With eyes tightly shut, Archie felt a wave of heat sweep past, followed by an enormous splash in the water beside them. Somehow, someone had shot the plane down.

Archie drew a ragged breath as he patted himself down. He turned to check on the skipper. Harry's eyes were confused and grey as two dark stains bloomed across his shirt. Huge metal shards stood embedded in his chest. Archie's throat constricted. He wanted to scream, to beg his life for Harry's, but no words came. He clutched anxiously at Harry, but the man slipped to the deck and, seconds later, only sightless eyes stared back.

Archie looked at the motionless body, his mouth parted in shock. He'd never steered a boat before, much less seen anyone die, but as the wheel twirled listlessly, he crouched to check on the captain. With motion all about and ceaseless noise, Archie searched for a pulse, but the only movement detected came from the sea.

Archie's eyes snapped upwards as the boat juddered sideways. Another boat had hit them broadside. He leapt forward, grabbing the wheel before the vessel could collide with anything else. The wooden rail had splintered, but as far as Archie could tell, the structure held, though if the damage was below the waterline, there would be nothing he could do. Once the two hulls broke apart, Archie did the only thing he could think of. He headed for the pier head he'd seen earlier. Other boats had followed suit, and he turned the wheel in grim determination. The motorboat responded to the turn, though as soon as they were square on to the beach, a large breaker sent the starboard deck on a fearsome arc which sent poor Harry's body slamming into the bulkhead.

Archie corrected and soon the engine powered them along. Although choppy, he worked a system where every few seconds he turned into the oncoming tide. It wasn't pretty, but he was making progress and now a cacophony of shouts and cheers joined the noise. More bullets sprayed the area and the men and Archie alike cowered in fear as the fighter plane passed over.

Archie felt the blood surging through his veins, and it took all his concentration to keep the prow from barging into the concrete ahead. He hit side on, but other than a few extra splinters, the *Daphne* held. Men leaped aboard with no regard for rank or station and within seconds, the new ballast caused them to drop lower in the water. Gunning the engine, he turned the wheel to pull them away. In a blur of figures, he knew several were in the water after falling short as they tried to jump aboard, but there was no room. As it was, the engine whine was reaching a crescendo as they fought to break free from the current. With agonising slowness, they finally turned about and headed for the channel. He looked behind, desperate to see Harry's body was still aboard. He couldn't do anything for his ill-fated friend, but equally, he couldn't leave the man behind. A plethora of dirty, wriggling bodies, most topped with tin hats, blocked his view. He called out to ask if someone could check, but nobody responded to his pleas. As it was, they hemmed him in so much he could barely turn the wheel. Aiming for the nearest destroyer, the boat chugged on a parallel path to the beach, heading toward the harbour, while waves threatened to spill onto the deck. The bombardment continued, and he steered away from a great plume which erupted just off the bow, the water soaking them through. His eyes stung as he forced the boat forward, in the grim hope they could reach the nearest warship. Together with grateful brethren, he had to make this journey count. The vast outline of a destroyer he'd seen earlier blocked his view. Twin smokestacks belched out dark smoke, but along one side, behind the letters *H86*, steps angled diagonally to the waterline. Some of his passengers let out a hopeful roar and the boat sagged on the starboard side. Archie turned the wheel to compensate, but he immediately recognised he'd turned too far, and the boat lurched, spilling two soldiers into the water. The men's cries were barely audible in the chaos, and unsure of what to do, Archie cut the engine. Momentum carried them all forward, but as they slowed, the soldiers cast a rope and drew the swimmers back onboard. The resultant cheer hammered Archie's eardrums, and once he'd confirmed they were safely onboard, he set the boat moving again. Archie felt his confidence lift. He knew how to steer, almost, and operating the engine seemed easy enough, and with a British Destroyer close by, his thoughts turned to what next?

Archie would need to return to bring more soldiers to safety, but how many times before his luck ran out? He'd seen the miles of queuing troops and here he was, taking at best thirty at a time. He tried to work the maths, but with movement, noise, and acrid smoke, he gave up without an answer. There had been no let-up in the strafing from above, and Archie could see no sign that the battle was going their way. They were around a hundred yards from the warship, and Archie focussed. Everything hinged on successfully transferring the men. Only then could he go back for more. Eighty yards now and closing fast. A familiar, dreadful droning sounded above them, and he saw another divebomber. This time, the German aircraft didn't miss his target. He knew the pilot had doomed the destroyer and its crew as he tracked the bomb's release and it took all his strength to veer the *Daphne* away from the impending explosion. Despite being surrounded by carnage, the new gigantic explosion, landing so close, brought them all to stunned silence. Within seconds, the flaming steps plunged into the water as the warship listed and the letters *H86* dipped to the waterline. The men watched in stunned disbelief. Perhaps being close to the harbour would bode well for some, but Archie knew he had others to save. This time he made for open water. Steering between sinking husks as other boats attempted rescue, little by little they drew away from the battle. Archie headed for open water. He wasn't sure how to navigate across the *Channel*, but with the noise of battle fading, he felt sure that within an hour or two, they'd see England.

'Land.'

More cries joined the throng. The boat pitched as soldiers rushed to one side, but Archie kept his focus and powered the craft forward. As the coastline drew closer, he realised he'd brought them too far south. After a slight change, he saw the familiar outline of Ramsgate harbour. They weren't alone either. Other small craft laden to the gunnels followed Archie's lead. A vast crowd cheered their arrival and Archie flexed his aching shoulders as the *Daphne*'s hull scraped the harbour wall. Moments later, his passengers scrambled over the side and onto a wooden pontoon. Amidst cheers of elation, Archie stood exhausted, his hands still clenched at the wheel. He'd done it. He'd saved them, but seeing Harry crumpled like a rag on the deck, his heart broke.

76

JUNE 1940, YIEWSLEY

Ingrid telegraphed the slap when it came, giving Archie time to duck out of reach. He saw she wasn't about to let-up, so as she balled both hands into fists and came at him, he merely tucked her in his arms and held steady until she gave up the fight.

'It's not fair,' she glowered.

'I know you wanted to be part of the rescue, but you're still doing something really important here. You're needed.'

'Needed. They had me working in a soup kitchen. How does that help us win the war and save my family?'

Archie clung on in the hope his hug would calm her mood. She groaned in frustration before reverting to silence. He'd seen her outbursts before, and he knew remaining calm carried an element of risk. Now he recognised the minefield he'd enter if he voiced his thoughts. He had to, though. Losing Harry at Dunkirk had hit him hard, despite only knowing the older man for a few hours. Carrying the boat skipper off the *Daphne* and along the quay was a sobering experience. He had managed the dead weight with ease, but the weight of sorrow was much heavier. While others whooped and shouted around him, he pulled Harry close in death's last embrace, the old man's blood soaking his shirt. Now, holding Ingrid in a similar embrace felt surreal, and he didn't know what to do. He released his hold, but Ingrid caught him by the arm.

'What is it? What's going on, Archie?'

She'd done it again. No one else could make him squirm. As he wilted under her penetrating gaze, he almost wished he were back in the heat of battle. It was no good. He'd have to tell her his plans to join up.

77

NOVEMBER 1940, LONDON

Ingrid let out a rare yelp of happiness as she backed her lorry into the tight bay without help. Babs' cheers from across the compound only enhanced her achievement. Despite her growing proficiency, she remained unsettled in the work she undertook in the factory. It wasn't a feeling of ingratitude, but one of helplessness at everything around her. News of her hometown, family, and friends back in Germany didn't exist, though this was a burden she'd carried for years. But now a new German offensive brought terror from the skies. With London as one of the primary targets, her fear that Roy and Florrie or Rabbi Cohen and their neighbours could easily become casualties was ever present. And knowing there was nothing she could do to protect them ate into her soul. Everyone else understood, and that helped a little as Babs and the others checked in with the residents of Yiewsley, but venturing into the city was fraught with danger and few officers would sanction trips while London burnt.

Beyond the *Luftwaffe* bombs, she also felt a creeping jealousy that Archie was joining an infantry regiment. It shouldn't matter, but it did.

Her one solace came from her ability to drive a lorry, which had improved significantly. Only that week she'd transported loads to Hastings in the south and Birmingham in the midlands. After a sheltered upbringing in the Bavarian Alps, her geographical knowledge of England had exploded. After collecting her usual dockets, she exited the cab and moved towards the canteen before Camila Parkes ushered her over.

'No time for that. There is someone to see you in the office.'

This was unusual and more often meant bad news, but she did as she'd been told and scuttled into the offices. Once inside, she marched forward, but before she could knock, the door to the office swung open. 'Ah, Stephens. Do come in and sit down.'

Despite having the Anglicised surname for over a year, Ingrid still found it odd to hear, but she took the remaining chair as a stranger sat watching her from the other. 'Right, I'll leave you both to it. Be a wonderful chap, Gregson, and let someone know what you plan to do with our girl, will you?' A few seconds later, her colleague had gone, leaving her with the stranger known as Gregson. She waited for his introduction.

'Do you know Brigadier Colin Gubbins?' The man fielded a question out of the blue.

'No.' Ingrid frowned. 'Is there any reason I should?'

'What about the Baker Street Irregulars? Do you know them? I work for pals of theirs.'

'Sorry, who?'

'Who is Winston Churchill?'

The stupid question left her riled. 'Everyone knows Mister Churchill and I can't think of why you'd ask such a thing,' she replied hotly.

'What about Admiral Wilhelm Canaris, Reinhard Heydrich? What do their names mean to you?'

Ingrid paused. Had she heard the name? She wasn't sure, and Gregson's questions were becoming tedious. 'I don't know,' she replied in a flat tone. Gregson's intense gaze softened.

'I'm sorry. You must think I'm extremely rude. Please forgive me and let me start again. My name is Marcus Gregson and I believe you have something I want and perhaps, I may have something you want too. Now, what do you say about a delightful meal, and you allow me the opportunity to explain properly? I've booked us a table.'

Ingrid's brain wrestled with the information, or lack thereof. What was he on about? With rationing, she couldn't perceive any delightful meals. One idea caught though. Her supervisor was allowing this conversation and that had to count for something. This time, she returned the appraisal. Gregson was old enough to be her father, but behind his intelligent eyes, she thought she could see kindness.

'And if I say no, thank you?'

'Then, my dear, I will bid you a good day and I daresay we will never meet again. Though, for a while at least, I promise you that you will wonder. Tell me, are you the lady to seek the what-if's that life throws up from time to time, or are you, I daresay, more restrained? Either way, I'll enjoy that splendid meal I mentioned. With or without you.'

****

The drive from north London took over an hour, and for Ingrid, the journey felt surreal. When they left the office, Gregson had a private word with the manager, and then he led Ingrid outside. A driver opened the doors to an Austin 16 before taking his place at the wheel. Ingrid had never experienced a chauffeur before, though, in honesty, she didn't like it. Not now that she could drive perfectly well herself. But with Gregson, or Marcus as he asked to be called, dictating everything, she lapsed into a watchful repose. They sat in silence mostly, so Ingrid used the time to take in the sights along the route. Shattered, smouldering buildings made her want to weep, but throughout the devastation, she saw wide smiles as ragged people of all ages rallied to rebuild. She didn't understand how they could offer cheer while London burnt, but then what was the alternative? She smiled. Perhaps they were wise after all. They took several detours, avoiding collapsed buildings and a couple of fires that barred their way. While the devastation was shocking and left Ingrid pining for her friends in the East End, one other thing stood out: wealth. She didn't know where within London they'd come to, but some buildings were magnificent.

She'd long since given up on remembering the street names. If Gregson was going to harm her, then there was no way she could retrace her steps. Finally, the car slowed, and Ingrid took note. They'd arrived somewhere called Caxton Street.

The driver scurried around, first opening the door for Gregson before returning to allow Ingrid to step onto the pavement.

'There she is. Isn't she magnificent?'

The question was ambiguous, but following his gesture, Ingrid saw a beautiful red brick building set back from the main road. She had to agree. She looked beyond a short avenue of trees where a white wall and two ornate columns flanked stairs leading inside. Gregson stole a march, forcing Ingrid into a skip to keep up.

When they finally settled inside the dining room, she felt an overwhelming sense of disloyalty. Most homes in *Berchtesgaden* were basic timber builds, but this place oozed wealth. How could she sit in such comfort while others suffered? Despite the opulence of the room, Ingrid felt stifled, and she stood to leave before realising she did not know how to return to the factory. She looked about, wondering whether the driver had remained outside. But it was no use and reluctantly, she sat back down.

'It has that effect on lots of people, my dear. Don't worry. Just take this odd situation for what it is. I will explain to you why I brought you here and then after we've eaten, I will send you onward safely.' Before she could decide a response, her tummy rumbled. 'Well, there you go. If that isn't a signal to eat, then I don't know what is.'

She smiled. Somehow, his jovial attitude was breaking the ice. She ordered a stew but missed the hearty Bavarian dumplings of home. She ate slowly, pushing thoughts of childhood to one side and using the time to listen.

An hour later, they left St Ermin's hotel. Ingrid's stomach churned, but it wasn't the rich food causing her unease. After careful consideration, she'd decided she would leave the aircraft factory behind.

78

February 1941, Surrey

Ingrid found herself in a strange new world. After Gregson had reached out three months earlier, she'd expected to land in Germany as a spy within a matter of days. But the cogs of bureaucracy moved slowly, and little else had happened. She'd said a proper goodbye to Florrie and Roy, though others like Archie remained in the dark. Gregson had forbidden her return to Yiewsley, and with Archie still undertaking basic training, Ingrid felt their absence deeply.

Today, at last, was something new. They'd given her a destination. She didn't know where exactly, only that they'd laid on transport, and an instruction to report to a Captain Roger Wolverton. They collected others along the way, and soon both sideboards at the rear of the lorry were full of passengers. While some chattered excitedly, most remained silent. In the darkness of the lorry interior, Ingrid listened to the voices with growing dread. Had she made the right decision?

By the time they arrived, it was getting dark, and Ingrid climbed down from the lorry with aching limbs. In the dim of twilight, she saw the outline of an imposing manor house. She stretched with the others as a tall man approached.

'Good evening, everyone. My name is Captain Wolverton and I'm in charge. Welcome to phase one. You all know why you are here, so get your gear inside. We'll get started after supper.'

****

After Gregson's swanky introduction to the SIS, food at the manor was basic. Even the canteen behind Roy's depot offered better fare. But everyone was hungry and despite chewing down on biscuits which could break teeth, everyone tucked in. While they ate, most found their voices, but Ingrid's mind sank into a confused muddle.

With the meal finished, everyone filed through to a kitchen where a woman handed out communal tasks. Ingrid accepted a mop and pushed a wheeled bucket to the furthest corner to begin her chore. It was pointless mopping the kitchen floor while twelve others and a cook marched back and forth, but somehow the corner felt more welcoming. Pots and pans clattered, echoing the furore going on inside her head. A room full of strangers prompted the question: *Why am I here?*

The captain returned and after hitting the doorframe twice with a baton; the group became silent. Ingrid turned to listen, though a part of her wanted to run. Fleeing wasn't an option, as she was sure the lorry had already returned to London, so with stomach lurching, she meekly followed the group, the captain leading the way. They gathered in a long room to the side of the main building. Although cold crept through the windows, blankets, and warm rugs combined to make a welcoming atmosphere. Over the following two hours, Ingrid learnt something new, as the captain and two others gave a lecture in map reading. Since the government had removed most road signs throughout the country, this was a useful skill. The exercise left her wondering how the landscape in Germany may have changed.

The lecture finished, and they escorted the group back to their dormitory. Ingrid suppressed a yawn; it had been a long day. The staff gave them free choice of beds with a five-minute warning before lights out. A few had already struck up a quick friendship, and Ingrid felt a twinge of annoyance as she peeled back the bedcovers.

'Are you OK?'

Ingrid spun around. She was tired and wobbly on her feet, and the stranger grabbed her shoulder to steady her.

'Thank you,' she mumbled.

'That's all right. I was concerned. You looked so lost.'

Suddenly, the new stranger took on a new persona, and Ingrid's cheeks flushed. *How can I possibly become a spy when I can't even cope in a room full of strangers? Even this woman saw I'm lost. And she's right.*

The woman wrapped an arm around Ingrid's shoulders. 'We may be strangers, but we're all here for the same reason. My name is Heidi Baker. My family comes from Hamburg. I can't wait to get back to Germany and make an impact.'

79

February 1941, *Dachau*

Gerhard looked about before resting, knowing he could only grab a few seconds of respite. Punishments for slacking within the camp were severe. He withdrew his hands from the wheelbarrow and examined his palms. Lines wracked both hands, deep and scarred. His load for the hour was the same as yesterday. The contorted bodies of four fellow prisoners, stacked with limbs spilling in all directions. Empty. Soulless. Free.

This was the norm. Jews and others, held in terror while the Nazis allowed so-called doctors free rein to experiment. Few survived, though Gerhard had noticed he held some small favour with the guards, which he failed to understand. They still brutalised him, but where other stronger men had succumbed, he remained.

He moved off, pushing the barrow along the uneven path. They were expecting him. No, they were demanding him, and he lacked the luxury of time. Three times cracked slabs and a crooked wheel caused him to veer unsteadily. Each time, it took all his strength to right his load despite the emaciated bodies within the cart. Progress to the furthest reaches of the compound – where dark smoke belched out every waking hour – was slow. But what else did he have to do? His nose twitched, and he silently cursed how accustomed he'd become to the stench of decay. Steadying himself, he approached a ramp which led down to the incinerator. Most days, the barrow would twist and spill halfway down, casting the bodies to the floor, like discarded mannequins from a fine shop. It was difficult to steer the rickety vehicle while guards gathered to mock his movements. He knew he lacked the strength to stop another cascade as two of the four victims fell, each hitting the concrete with dull, empty thuds. Laughter greeted him as he finally arrived at the bottom of the slope. He knew better than to look at the guards. Instead, with head bowed, he rested the barrow and went to retrieve the fallen.

The next task was equally painful. Having dragged the bodies to the incinerator, next he had to open the door, which inevitably scorched his hands as he pulled the handle. Seeing the inferno inside brought a daily stab of bile to his throat. He was literally pushing his friends and fellow inmates into hell, and the urge to throw himself into the pyre was intense. Despite this, Gerhard did what he did every day. He took his mind back to *Berchtesgaden*, to happier, peaceful times, and then, as a robot, he pushed the dead into the burning abyss before turning away to fetch another load.

80

MARCH 1941, INVERNESS

After three intensive weeks undergoing training, the group began an arduous journey to Scotland. Beyond this knowledge, none of the trainees knew their exact destination. Ingrid was unconcerned. Her initial misgivings had transformed into a sense of adventure. The staff in Surrey had a strict regime. Everyone, men and women alike, would run a five-mile country loop before breakfast. Some of the group struggled over the distance, but Ingrid felt freer than she had in years and even found a new worth by helping the stragglers each morning.

So much had changed in those few weeks in south London. On the first morning, everyone experienced their first weapons' training. Holding pistols and sub-machine guns made everything real. The cold metal in her hand, the weight of the weapon, and the report as she fired. For the first time, Ingrid felt like a soldier.

During the transfer to Scotland, Ingrid thought of the group. The continual lessons, physical exercises, and sleep deprivation had forced the group to bond. Some were more outgoing than others. Ingrid remained watchful in the background, while others, like the bright and bubbly Johanna, took charge, warming the room with a considered word here and a risky joke there. Each night, the group collapsed into the deep armchairs at the bar, their tasks complete for the day. They could drink, but their curfew remained. Ingrid measured her drinking, but others took full advantage of the bar. They were a merry bunch, their camaraderie clear. Even Ingrid no longer felt an outsider. She was wise to watch herself as she discovered the following morning.

Johanna's chair was empty at breakfast.

'Where is she?' the women chorused as the cook served up. The cook shrugged and drew a zipper across his lips. Whispers abounded, but as the group finished breakfast, the captain dropped in and enlightened them.

'A few too many drinks.' He sighed and shook his head. While drunk, Johanna had spoken in her sleep, weaving a story that German intelligence would find extremely interesting. Loose lips sink ships, and they quickly gave Johanna her marching orders.

Ingrid dragged her thoughts back to the present. It took two days, with an overnight stopover in Liverpool, before they reached their destination. The entire group was exhausted. The roads had stretched on for miles, the wooden benches in the lorry offering little comfort. Few spoke above the noise of the engine, and those that did joked that they could easily withstand anything the German interrogators could muster after surviving this trip.

Ingrid couldn't find any humour in their words. Any talk of capture was foolish. Beside her, Heidi squeezed her hand. It was a tiny gesture, but Ingrid appreciated it. The closeness made her think of Archie, and she felt a sudden twinge of sorrow. *He'll find someone else. He's sure to. After all, he doesn't know where I am, and I can't exactly tell him.* Although letters were all scrutinised and sometimes censored, she'd written to Archie via Florrie. Those words meant they would never be together and as the darkness closed around her, she wept.

Shrouded within the canvas, the group lost any sense of time. Seconds stretched out for what felt like hours. One man peered through the flap at the rear of the lorry. They had been told not to, but who would notice? Friedrich held his face to the gap for several minutes before declaring they were close to somewhere called High Wycombe. Ingrid had heard the name, and her heart sank. They had so much further still to travel. In the end, everyone settled in for the uncomfortable journey ahead, heads resting against the shoulders of their travelling companions.

The light had changed from dim through to almost umbra by the time they reached their first stop. Two had visited Liverpool before, but this was no tourist layover. A basic meal immediately followed by an uncomfortable bed. Next morning, someone let slip that they were less than halfway to their destination. The driver grinned at them, suggesting the journey was character building, but nobody bought the joke.

On they drove, and Ingrid perceived a change as they continued north. The weather in the London suburbs was crisp, and she'd enjoyed the crunch underfoot during the morning runs. Raised in the mountains, it tickled her to see the others bent over, heaving in voluminous plumes while she ran without issue. Now they were further north, the temperature had dropped to uncomfortable levels, and their threadbare blankets were ineffective. The group huddled together on the bench seats as icy tendrils crept onto any exposed skin.

The air was crisp and clean. It had been nine years since Ingrid had breathed air so fresh and the thought triggered a sad nostalgia. Before the feelings could materialise into something too painful, the pitch of the engine changed, and the lorry slowed.

'Come on, you lot, you're in Scotland now. Out you get. No time for dallying,' a voice shouted as the vehicle halted. The group shook themselves, their stiff bodies protesting as they climbed down from the lorry. White light stung Ingrid's eyes as they formed up in ranks in front of a man wearing three stripes on the arm of his jacket. The driver pulled away, and the group realised their mistake. All the blankets were heading back with the lorry.

The sergeant cleared his throat. 'Come on, lassies. You've got a wee walk ahead of you and if you dinna want to freeze, you'd best be making haste.'

Ingrid suppressed a small smile. While she wore a long woollen skirt and thick blouse, the squat sergeant was wearing a kilt. *He must be freezing*. She glanced down the road behind their leader. In the distance stood a single storey grey building. It looked smaller than the manor they'd left behind, but Ingrid didn't care. It offered shelter.

****

Ingrid awoke to a mighty explosion. The large room in which they were sleeping erupted into chaos. *Were they under attack?* Some of the group sprang for the windows, but Ingrid tiptoed to the door and pried it open. There was no immediate threat, so she pushed the door open and pressed up against the wall. Her first worry was exposure. To the front of the house lay a narrow strip of paving and then grass. She scanned the field before stepping away from the doorway. *Are there enemy soldiers laying hidden, ready to shoot me down?* A few weeks in Surrey hadn't prepared her to deal with this situation. She stood rooted to the spot, wrestling between fight or flight. But where was the threat? The landscape looked barren.

Her thoughts turned to the other trainees. They had gone through so much as a group, she couldn't abandon them. She decided she would have to establish the source of the explosion. She paused, wracking her brain, before realising the sound had come from the far side of the building. That seemed odd. *Why would the enemy attack from just one side? There would have to be a flanking manoeuvre as well*, she thought, glancing in the opposite direction.

As these thoughts flickered through Ingrid's mind, a second explosion sounded. Her instincts kicked in and, breaking into a run, she swept under the dorm window and around the side of the building. If someone was throwing grenades about, she wanted to be on the other side of them. She didn't have a weapon, but she'd go down fighting. Ahead, woodland obscured the path. Ingrid couldn't see anyone, and the feeling of panic returned. *Where were they hiding?* There must be some sign of their presence. She knew what she'd heard. Her head swept back and forth, a clammy sweat beading across her shoulders despite the morning chill.

Behind her, an outburst of Scottish laughter. *What?*

Heidi bolted around the corner of the building, a relieved grin on her face.

'Everything's all right, Ingrid. It's part of our training. See, there's the sergeant who greeted us. We saw him from the window. It's all part of some test. They were blowing up railway sleepers.'

The sergeant appeared, his eyes glinting with humour.

'Fooled you, didn't we, lassie?'

Ingrid dropped her head, hiding hot cheeks. She allowed Heidi to lead her away.

Over breakfast, Ingrid listened to the explanation and with every word she heard, her feelings of foolishness intensified.

'I should've known,' she whispered to Heidi.

Heidi frowned. 'How could you? Don't be silly.'

The comment riled before Ingrid realised her friend was right.

****

The explosions were a daily occurrence, and everyone soon became used to them. On the second day, they experienced demolition up close. After laying the charges as instructed, the group retreated before triggering the blast. In Ingrid's mind, Stefan Weiss lay trussed to the sleeper, pleading for leniency, before the explosion obliterated her enemy. Once the smoke cleared, they allowed everyone forward to witness the devastation. Where sturdy beams had lain, only splinters remained.

Their training continued from daybreak until late in the evening, leaving the group shattered. Inevitably, a split formed, with several weary trainees showing signs they wanted to quit, while others responded to the pressure, developing a never-say-die attitude. Ingrid and Heidi formed a strong bond, though both assumed that their paths would soon separate. The instructors saw the cliques developing, and on the fourth day; they split up the group.

'Stephens, you're in charge of the first team,' Sergeant McDermott barked at Ingrid. A few of the men grumbled before McDermott silenced them with an icy stare. Returning his attention to Ingrid, he handed her a map and compass before selecting another five to accompany her. She cast her eye across her teammates. Not her first choice, but they would do. Heidi and her other favourites were on the second team.

'Where to?' Ingrid asked.

'Away. Anywhere you like. Just you make sure in five hours' time, *all* your team are safe and back here. And don't let the other team track you down. There's half rations tonight and only the best team will get some supper.'

Overnight snowfall dusted the landscape, and Ingrid cursed under her breath. If this was some kind of hunting task, the last thing they needed was to leave a trail. But before she could assess the landscape any further, McDermott reminded her their fifteen-minute head start began a minute ago.

'*Scheisse*,' she muttered before directing her team towards the woods that wrapped around the rear of the property. It was the only choice really, as the frontage looked over marshy scrub, with few opportunities to hide. Multiple paths splayed out and Ingrid immediately chose the one with the least snow. It was an obvious choice, but better than leaving a trail in the snow. Ingrid designated one man as a forward scout, and with the remaining four men and women, the group set off at speed.

Ingrid felt happier once they lost sight of the buildings. She couldn't let-up on their pace, though. They needed to put at least one mile between them and the other team before their time ran out. The rocky terrain was difficult underfoot, but they were making progress, weaving through the uneven undergrowth. The group froze as a trill whistle sounded, signifying starting time for the second group. Ingrid glanced at the group, her face stony. 'That wasn't fifteen minutes.' The hunt was on. They were undertaking commando training, and the Nazis wouldn't play by the rules. 'Come on,' she growled, giving the signal to move out.

They ploughed on through the icy thicket, all pretence of stealth lost. Ingrid felt her lungs burn, and she noticed two within her group were flagging. The path split again, and she signalled to go left. A stream intersected the land, and she plunged into the freezing water. The brook wasn't deep, but the freezing water immediately numbed her ankles. She bit down and struggled forward, but it wasn't long before the youngest, Anna, stumbled and fell with a shriek. Ingrid felt her power slipping away. They may as well have sounded their own whistle. Two of the men scooped up Anna, but it was hopeless. She'd clearly turned an ankle.

What do I do? They couldn't leave Anna alone for capture, but equally they'd slowed to barely a crawl, and this was Ingrid's team, her responsibility. While her mind worked feverishly for an answer, she saw them. Not the other team. That would merely mean a loss of pride. No, it was something far worse.

The wraith, if that's what she'd seen, disappeared and immediately doubt set in. Her heart pounding, Ingrid turned to the others, but the group was oblivious to the danger. There was a panicked fear behind their eyes, but only the fear of failure, nothing more.

Am I seeing things? Time slowed as Ingrid debated their options. Even the gurgling sound of the stream seemed to slow. Suddenly the wraith reappeared, and Ingrid's throat constricted as the being streaked past and locked onto Anna. Before anyone could react, Anna screamed and fell into the water. A thick, scarlet trail merged with the water. Ingrid's mouth parted in shock. None of their training had prepared them for this. Ingrid ploughed into the water. She didn't care that the icy water ran up her thighs and across her abdomen. She didn't care that her team had lost the challenge. What she'd just witnessed was brutal in the extreme.

81

MARCH 1941, *DRESDEN*

Hector walked to the breakfast briefing with Weiss, who'd become his handler. In the five months since he'd convinced the man that he was the best choice to turn traitor, he still hadn't shed the guilt. He didn't owe the other agents anything. They knew the risks. He'd just played a better game by showing he had worth to the Germans, but the treason would never sit well.

The first months were tedious. He had a routine to maintain, only now he had to follow their playbook. The German *Gestapo* officers had kept their part of the bargain. He'd maintained his position at the university and, with their encouragement, begun a tempestuous relationship with *Frau* Umer.

As far as London was concerned, Foxglove and Theodore were still transmitting. Only now his new colleagues within German intelligence saw everything. With an hour to kill before his first class, he watched as Weiss relayed the day's instructions. The German amused him. He wasn't sure why, but there was something about Stefan Weiss which suggested the man was not happy in his role. Hector knew Weiss was cruel, and a shiver traversed his shoulders as he recalled what had happened to Foxglove. He took a sip of his drink, his mouth puckering. It was supposed to be coffee, but beyond the dark colour, it bore no resemblance.

'So, we're agreed then. You will report these minor troop movements which are real, while laying another story that we are moving the 7th Panzer Division south, as you see here on the map. This, of course, is a lie.'

Hector nodded. Although he'd tuned out the first of Weiss's words, he caught up quickly and as far as he could tell; the German man hadn't noticed. He couldn't make any mistakes as a rota of observers would monitor his every communication. Tonight would be different, though. For almost half a year, he'd kept within the exacting guidelines, but tonight he would do the one thing he'd worked towards. He knew the risks, but along with the troop movements, Hector would transmit a hidden duress code. He just had to hope that the Germans would miss his subterfuge.

82

MARCH 1941, INVERNESS

The tin mug of cocoa stung Ingrid's fingertips, but she refused to relinquish her grip. She couldn't believe it. They'd set her up. The bloody British had tricked them. Ingrid along with her team, including the alive and well Anna, sat back in the dining room, wrapped in blankets.

The test was simple. The sneaky bastard instructors had set them up to fail. Before they'd even lined up to be given their challenge, a squad of highly trained commandos was already in place, supported by a couple of snipers. Setting them running and then signalling the whistle, just five minutes into the task, was all about causing panic. While the other team remained indoors, oblivious, they struck. Although it felt real, everything was staged. The combat knives looked authentic enough, but each held a spring-loaded mechanism designed for the subterfuge. Then, with some liberally spilt crimson paint and a swift attack, the entire group succumbed.

'Well, lassies. What have we learnt from this morning's outing?' McDermott asked.

'That you, Sergeant McDermott, are a piece of *scheisse*,' Ingrid shouted.

'Aye, there's that. My momma told me I'm a bastard and worse. I've heard it many a time elsewhere.' He chuckled. 'What else?'

Ingrid felt disgusted. They'd duped them. But despite this, she considered the question. What had she learnt? Like before, when she'd felt a fool for overreacting to the demolition sounds, she discovered a common theme. If the instructors played fair, then their preparation to return to a hostile country would be flawed. 'The Germans won't play nice.' She spoke with authority.

'Bravo, lassie. You can be sure of that. If you're caught spying or disrupting their war effort, then they'll rip your fingernails off in a heartbeat. I know today's been tough on you and I can see for some of you, that's enough, but if yea can withstand these tests, then you might just come out of this alive. Or if you don't, then you'll take a lot of those bastards down with you.'

By the time the cocoa had cooled, so too had Ingrid's ire. She now held a grudging respect for her instructors. She had learnt a valuable lesson about trust.

83

MAY 1941, YIEWSLEY

'Well, you're a sight for sore eyes. Look at you, all handsome standing there in your uniform. If I was a few years younger.' Florrie swooned.

'Oi. I am here, you know.' Roy countered. 'Come inside, lad. You're always welcome here. Florrie, if you can close your mouth for a minute and stop gawping, I'm sure Archie would love a nice cuppa. Isn't that right, sunshine?'

This time, it was Archie's turn to offer a welcoming hug, which Florrie gratefully accepted while Roy offered a handshake. Florrie was right: he looked smart, and he felt it. Gone were the blackened features from his days hauling coal and later running deliveries from a filthy cart. He'd changed during his six months of basic training, but now returning to a place he almost called home was a welcome change. He'd given no warning to his visit. It was a calculated risk, but Florrie and Roy were creatures of habit who rarely strayed from their routine. As his eyes adjusted to the gloom, he scanned more in hope than expectation, but it only took a couple of seconds before he realised Ingrid wasn't there. His face dropped.

'I know. We miss her too.'

The proud feeling he'd had seconds earlier vanished, replaced by an intense feeling of foolishness. *You idiot. She's been silent. She can't possibly want me.* He planted himself down on the sofa; the furniture creaking under his enormous frame. It took a few minutes for the water to boil, and the men maintained an awkward silence until Florrie shuffled back through with the tea.

'Sorry…it's just, you know…I hoped.' Silence again while he tried to gather his thoughts. 'Where is she?'

Roy looked to Florrie to provide the answer. 'She won't tell us. Ingrid said they won't let her say. We get a letter every couple of months, telling us she is safe, but nothing more. Here, there's one she wrote for you.'

Archie set the tea aside and opened the envelope addressed to him.

My dearest Archie,

The months are rolling on, and the war has forced us both apart. I know I rarely spoke of this, but I believe that my mother and grandmother are still alive in Berchtesgaden. I fear for them almost as much as for my father. They took him to one of their camps and every day my thoughts and prayers yearn for their salvation.

You are forging a path to fight for your country and I admire you for that, more than you can ever imagine. I hope you'll understand that I too have to battle for my country. Although England is where I live, Germany is my home and my family needs me. I won't lie. What I'm going to do scares me, though I draw courage from you and your actions. You are my hero.

I'm not working alone. There are others and those who will train me, but that's all I can tell you. This will be the only letter I can send.

And now for the bit which breaks my heart. You are fighting your war and where I am going; I fear I will not return. So, I must do what hurts more than anything else. I beg of you to forget about me. Somewhere, someday, these awful times will pass, but whether we lose or win, survive or die, I cannot ask you to wait for me. You will always be in my heart, but you deserve more than that. What I desire most is for you to find love elsewhere. Please do this one thing for me. Forget about me and find someone else. You deserve happiness and I pray you will find it.

Your loving friend,
Ingrid.

Archie's throat went dry.

The paper fluttered from his fingers to the ground. Florrie and Roy were speaking, but the words were distant and incomprehensible. He stood mechanically and moved towards the door.

Florrie cried out behind him, but he didn't care.

Grabbing his hat, Archie wrestled the front door open and slammed it behind him, leaving Ingrid's letter behind.

84

Hector bit nervously on the tip of his thumb, his arrogant persona a distant memory. While he waited for Stefan to appear as part of their weekly ritual, he wondered how much longer he could continue. Three times now, he'd broadcast a duress code, and each time he knew the risks would increase. *Why haven't you sent someone to get me out of here?* The question played in his mind. Surely, London knew, so why didn't they act? He took a sip of coffee. They'd added chicory, which had slightly improved the taste.

'What are you thinking about?'

Hector's eyes snapped up. 'I'm a little tired, that's all. *Frau* Umer kept me up last night.' He winked, hoping Stefan would accept his half-truth answer. His handler appeared disinterested, but Hector wasn't about to fall into that trap. More than once he'd witnessed Weiss lull someone into a mental place of safety, only for him to snap unexpectedly. He took the initiative. 'What do you need me to send this time?'

Weiss dug into his heavy leather coat for a notebook, which he pushed across the table. The man's writing was appalling and in the dim light of the café, it took all Hector's powers of deduction to decipher the scrawl. He had to get it right. Any blame for errors made while following Stefan Weiss's instructions would rebound.

London understood the dangers of transmission, especially given the Germans' prowess with radio detection technology. That meant that although Hector had a regular schedule to maintain, the reality was different. Sometimes, no matter how much his London paymasters wanted news, they had to wait. This suited the Germans. They were happy to drip feed information, especially as some days they received golden nuggets of information. By the time Hector had read today's notes, he knew today was just such a day. Although murdered by the Nazis and Weiss fully complicit, Hector's former colleagues, Theodore and Foxglove, were fully alive in the eyes of London. With the *Gestapo* in control, they maintained the masquerade. He leant back in the vain hope that by distancing himself from Weiss, he would somehow gain some room to process. They were sending a new agent. A woman.

His heart sank at the plight she would face. He had to do something, but with Weiss and his cronies studying his every move, he did not know what. For now, a silent prayer would have to do.

****

Gerda watched as Christa stepped into the vehicle that would take her up to the *Obersalzberg*. Her friend was leaving, ready to take up a post at Hitler's Berghof. After a brief wave, Gerda turned away and gathered her thoughts.

Christa's words still echoed in her ears. 'They didn't choose me for the post because of my brains, Gerda.' Her friend had rolled her eyes. 'The *Führer*'s thoughts on women are quite clear: *bear children for the Reich* — and I have done that. All that nonsense they told us in the BDM, it's about becoming brood mares, nothing less. But you'll see. I'll make a difference, I always do.'

Gerda followed the *Berchtesgadener Ache* for a while, before peeling away to find a more deserted spot. She came across a remote barn, and the building triggered a memory, buried many years before. Ingrid had shared a secret about this place ten years earlier, she was sure of it.

She hadn't thought about her friend and her brother in years. And now, as the recollection surfaced, Gerda felt conflicted. Ingrid's family were good people. She knew that deep inside her, but there was no room for sentiment regarding Jews in today's German society. And Christa's words about brood mares had only added to her discomfort. What of her plans to study at Frankfurt University? Gerda wasn't ready to live a life of servitude for the Third Reich, no matter what *Herr* Hitler said. Gerda blushed at her fiery thoughts. But they were just that: thoughts, and once she left the barn, she would return to her insignificant life in *Berchtesgaden*, and her ever-growing list of responsibilities with the Belief and Beauty movement, established for the oldest girls of the BDM. They'd forced her into the role, touting it as *voluntary*, but Gerda was the only young woman in the correct age category in *Berchtesgaden*. Besides, they'd already accepted Christa for the more important role of supporting Hitler's housekeeper, Eva Braun.

Gerda felt she was being pushed down an ever-narrowing corridor of destiny, one that involved marrying a good German soldier, and raising a brood of children. Brushing aside a stray tear, Gerda placed her crushed dreams back into the steel box inside her mind, straightened her skirt, and left the barn.

85

AUGUST 1941, INVERNESS

Ingrid's superiors had blocked her request to visit Yiewsley. She understood why, but a painful knot gripped her all the same. Still, no trip home meant she couldn't accidentally bump into Archie. The melancholy thought almost broke her resolve, but she knew she had a bigger calling. She'd faltered with another battle against her paymasters. After seeing the weighty suitcase radio and codebook, she'd pleaded with them to let her sew codes into her clothes rather than commit them to paper, but they wouldn't listen. Stuffy officers told her their systems were perfectly reliable, and her opinion was no longer sought. Fine for them to say, but she was the one risking her life.

With just the dull tapping of rain on the tin roof above, Ingrid looked through her meagre possessions. While not completely proficient at using the radio set, she'd certainly developed her own style, which, according to the listening stations, was a good thing. Made her signals stand out like a fingerprint, apparently. After recruitment through Gregson almost nine months earlier, specialist trainers had come and gone and the group mix had diversified as some dropped out, never to be heard of again. Occasionally someone new entered the group, but always the staff discouraged and sharing of personal information. And now she was alone again. Ingrid guessed she had an hour before they would come for her and move onto the next stage of their program. She wasn't sure what else they could teach her as her mind was full to bursting with codes, strategies, and infiltration methods. She even had new German papers showing she was a nurse called Elsa Keller, living in *Bremen*. When she'd first received the documents, Ingrid failed to hide her disappointment. This was so far north, an alien part of her homeland where she knew nothing and nobody. But that had been a deliberate ploy, and she knew she'd been overly optimistic about spying for the English while also wanting to help her family. Her fingers drummed the table before her, mimicking the rain above as she waited for a break in the tension.

'Ingrid,' a voice screamed.

Ingrid remained unmoved. From now on she was Elsa and calls to Ingrid would go unheeded. A month earlier, they'd orchestrated another test, this time dragging her from bed in the middle of the night. Unknown assailants had taken her, dumped her violently into a vehicle, and driven her for a couple of hours, leaving her hooded and disoriented. Rough hands clawed at her when they'd finally arrived at the mystery destination, pulling her from the transport. There was no respite. Ingrid felt every press as they shoved her onwards until someone called *halt*. A hand took her elbow in an iron grip as they descended a flight of steps. She remembered the icy fear that came from her arrival in the bunker, but this was just the beginning of the process. Questions. Incessant and demanding, with no let-up. She was a liar; they told her. What was she doing in *Bremen*? Who was she spying for? When the barrage finally ended, they removed the hood. Four strangers leered over her as she sat on a tiny stool in the centre of a cell. A bucket of water sat in a corner of the room. Ingrid glanced uneasily at it. She had heard about all the forms of water torture. She remembered the spike of fear when the man forced her head into the bucket. Her hasty breath of air wasn't enough as they continued to hold her head underwater. She couldn't hear the questions and her eyes sprang wide. This was it. The Nazis had found her, and there would be no salvation. Images of all those she loved, her parents, Ōma Hildegard, Dieter, Florrie, Roy, and Archie, stepped through her mind in a sorrowful procession. Finally, her captors relented. They yanked her head upwards, and she spluttered and gasped. Before she could recover, her head plunged into the bucket again.

The torture seemed to go on forever, and by the time they locked her alone in her cell, Ingrid wanted to die. She lacked any sense of time, and her whole body felt wracked with tension. Was she ready to tell her interrogators everything? Her eyes closed, her only defence against the misery. The door to her prison clanged open, and they were upon her again. She lifted her jaw in weary defiance. Could she withstand the next assault?

'We're finished. Well done, Ingrid. You passed.' And that was it. The weight didn't lift immediately, but with time, she came to understand the ordeal and the strength she'd developed.

Ingrid shook off the memory before slowly lifting her eyes towards the door. She waited, careful to display only respectful disinterest. The shouts for Ingrid repeated as her dispassionate gaze lingered upon the doorway. After all she'd been through, they could come to her.

86

AUGUST 1941, *BERCHTESGADEN*

Freda watched as another lorry disappeared along the street, heading north, before slinking back behind the curtain. She knew there would only be two likely loads. Either troops, often poor, bewildered sheep, conditioned to fight for their *Führer*, or worse, her brethren taken to a murderous fate. Before Walter had departed, she'd used his clandestine visits to extract as much information about the German war machine as she could. Only by getting him to spill his guts could she park the history between their families to one side. But, as she knew would happen, both his visits and any news petered out.

Drawing her creaking frame upstairs, she pulled away a floorboard to reveal her letters. A couple from Ingrid, dated years previously and then the ones from her darling Gerhard, before they too dwindled. Her frail fingers traced across the words. Hands almost as translucent as the paper she held. This was her daily ritual. Too fearful to venture into the town, and weary beyond belief, these letters were the only thing keeping her from oblivion.

87

SEPTEMBER 1941, *ESBJERG*

After her briefing, they kept Ingrid in isolation. *For her own protection*, they said. The move was absurd and intensified her feelings of mistrust to all around her. They'd left her with books and maps to study, starting with *Esbjerg* in Denmark. They had a route into Germany they'd used before and were certain it would work this time, too. In a minor concession to her wellbeing, they were feeding her well. *Or perhaps they are fattening the lamb for slaughter*, she thought with a bitter laugh.

Tonight, assuming the weather didn't screw things up again like last time, she would begin her mission. The notion thrilled and terrified with equal measure. *I'm going home.*

****

An hour after they closed the lid down on her, Ingrid wanted to die. Oppressive heat caused sweat to pool at the base of her spine, where it mingled with grease and grime at the bottom of the boat, while the stench of mackerel enveloped her. Within the secret compartment, she had no room to move. No light. Only fear. Only a dull chug sounding from the engines, interspersed with the odd whine and splutter, brought any semblance of existence. Ingrid focussed on the drone. It was all she could do as her body trembled in resonance with the engine.

It had taken almost a day to get there. First, a truck had taken her to a remote beach. She didn't know where, but it was dark when they deposited her on the sand. Then, with only waves for a backdrop, a man rowed her out to a British warship. She knew nothing of either navy, but one thing was clear. This metal behemoth would only take her to another rendezvous somewhere out on the cold, dark *North Sea*. Once onboard, the sailors greeted her with silent mirth. She saw their grins, tucked behind bright eyes and uniforms, but nobody spoke and soon the warship moved off into the blackness. Before long, she could no longer see land anywhere, and the vastness of the open sea only brought more anxiety to tickle her insides. Oh, how she yearned for that openness now. As expected, the last part of her seaward journey comprised a perilous transfer to a fishing boat flying the Danish flag. She knew the irony, months of training, only for her to fall overboard where the solid hull would mash her and the radio to pulp. If the radio wasn't so dammed heavy, she'd have transferred with just a dainty leap, but the bulky case made such a manoeuvre almost impossible. She didn't know where the Danish fishermen had stowed her radio or her second, smaller case. Certainly not within the coffin shaped hole where she lay. All sense of time had gone. At the outset, she tried pairing the throb of the engine with seconds counting by, but that strategy had vanished with the peaks and troughs of the sea.

Suddenly, the engine cut out. *Had she arrived? In which case would they release her soon? Or were they stranded? What would that mean for her?*

'*Papiere!*'

When they'd brought her onboard, she'd only spoken to Hans, the fishing captain, and his grizzly mate, Aksel. There were two others, though they followed their captain's lead in mute compliance. She recognised the new, authoritarian voice as German, and her blood froze. Despite the expectation, Ingrid felt perilous, and her breathing quickened. Starting along her brow, damp beads of sweat meandered downward, stinging her eyes, while one held in a strange dance on the edge of her nostril. She could feel a sneeze building and with the engines and crew silent, only the gentle lapping of the tide would shroud an expulsion.

The shout came a second time, cutting through the night. She guessed Aksel along with the others were complying, but everything seemed to take an age. Craning her neck, Ingrid brushed her nose against the lid, desperate to move the taunting droplet. It worked, though she didn't know when the next tickle would come. Pinching her eyes made no difference, but if they pried open her compartment, she wanted to delay the sight of German soldiers as long as possible. There would be no pity if they discovered her hideaway.

This time, she counted. Working the sound of blood pumping through her veins in a rhythm. It wasn't seconds, but the action served as a distraction from everything above. One hundred turned to four, which turned to six. Each second an agony as the voices upon the deck above refused to die. Did Hans feel as tense as her, knowing he held a stowaway? Perhaps. Now, a new thought. Could she trust Hans and his crew? She dispelled the notion, irritated at the negativity she could ill afford. If the British trusted Hans and his crew, then she must do the same.

Cursing that she'd lost count again, she waited as more sweat trickled across her body. When the boat had pitched across the sea, a gentle breeze drifted through a tiny hole around her ankle. Now, with the engine cut, only heat remained. An ache starting in her calves moved upward as she lay in cramping agony.

'In den Hafen einlaufen.' The command to head into the harbour meant the crew had navigated most of their hurdles. The engines fired just as a sneeze formed and blew out with explosive force. She shook her head desperately to stem a second. Another came and then one more, but it seemed the Germans had gone.

88

SEPTEMBER 1941, *DRESDEN*

What were they thinking? Hector forced his face into a neutral expression as he digested the latest radio transmission. The British seemed oblivious to the duress codes he'd sent, and now he was certain he'd lost his chance. It was just too dangerous to try again. He wanted his country to win the war, but his life was a price too high. He knew Stefan, and the other listeners, understood what he'd heard, and that meant the new spy wouldn't get far once they arrived within the country.

Would they arrest her when she landed in Denmark? Or would they follow until a better chance presented? He couldn't be sure. One thing was certain, however. London believed this new woman spy would link up with Foxglove, and when that time arrived, the Nazis would swoop. He wracked his brain. He didn't owe this new British player anything, though a small protective seed sat as he pondered her gender. Hector had reconciled himself to the demise of the other spies even though witnessing Foxgloves' torture left a mental scar. This newcomer was a woman. *Should have stayed at the kitchen sink*, he mused. Knowing she was coming, he wrestled with the dilemma. Could he help her? Would he help her?

'You want to help her? *Ja?*'

He shrugged, irritated that Weiss had read him so easily. Remaining quiet seemed the best choice as he finished helping to code tonight's message ready for the Germans to send. A dull ache was developing behind Hector's eyes. The pain came each day, often in waves so intense, he could barely stand. His burdens were growing. Tutorials at the university, the passionate demands of *Frau* Umer, merged with the constant pressure of the Nazis. However, it was his British counterparts who caused the biggest disturbance. Coding secret messages and meeting an absurd timetable while masquerading his own identity was one thing, but his head was too small to compute the complexities of Foxglove and Theodore's parallel narratives.

****

Stefan felt sick as he watched Hector squirm. He didn't care for the man, but that wasn't the cause of his discomfort. While distancing himself from Christa, who remained in *Berchtesgaden*, felt good, his other sickly desires remained unsated. Targeting the worst within their society, he'd felt alive. Now constrained within *Gestapo* shackles where everyone watched, he felt a curious empathy for his captive. It was his damned father's fault, all of this.

Stefan's own contacts within the senior ranks of the Reich were of no use to him. What was the point of hearing advanced intel if he remained bound, forced into senseless journeys between *Prinz-Albrecht-Strasse* and the regional *Gestapo* office in *Dresden*? The train journey into *Dresden* that morning allowed him to ponder progress with Barbarossa. While he knew the German forces were laying siege in Leningrad, the show of strength did little to dispel his sour mood. Even his weekly calls to Alexander Piorkowski, the *Commandant* at *Dachau*, failed to lift his spirits. He knew that Gerhard Stiepermann clung to life, but since Walter, Otto, and Klaus had all left his hometown, news of the other Jews was sparse. The absurdity that he could know high-level military secrets while remaining in the dark about the family who'd tormented him all those years before further soured his mood.

At first, when he came to work for the *Gestapo*, he thought his power was absolute. How wrong he'd been. Vast teams of spies and informants reported to him. He should be untouchable, yet the idea was a fallacy. Stefan couldn't identify when the unfamiliar sensation of paranoia had hit. The unease had somehow crept into his psyche as more untrustworthy characters filled his world. As he cast his eye away from Hector to scan the room, he felt his pulse quicken. Surely, the others must sense his weakness. In that moment, he despised himself. His gaze returned to the British spy, and something passed between them. *Recognition? Empathy?* He wasn't sure. There wasn't any attraction. Not from him at least and not like Peter, and he couldn't detect any movement from Hector toward him. But there was something.

Stefan took a moment to compose himself. His mind should focus on the task at hand, controlling Hector to lure out the new, incoming British agent. But all he found was apathy. His genuine desire to return to the looting and torture within the streets remained elusive. He even felt a tingle of jealousy toward Piorkowski. Sure, *Dachau* and the other camps lacked the thrill of hunting Jewish scum as he tore through their neighbourhoods, but having captive victims held some reward. Why must the generals believe his skills were best suited to tracking the few, while thousands of undesirables lay beyond his grasp? He wasn't a bureaucrat and shuffling papers which tracked a small network of British seemed a terrible waste. Despite this, Stefan's normally agile mind could offer no route back to the hunting he so desired. Even a call to his father would prove fruitless, given he'd trapped him in this role. Helmut would do what he always had. Ridicule and chasten his unappreciative son, a pattern so often repeated. And anyway, Stefan had already resolved that his relationship with his father was dead.

Stefan looked across at Hector. Here was someone he could use, and should things go wrong, blame and dispose of. Mental cogs whirred as he mapped out how he could best use the agent to bring about his father's downfall.

For the first time that day, Stefan smiled.

89

September 1941, *Esbjerg*

Ingrid sucked her breath in greedily when they finally drew back the planks, releasing her from her prison. Despite her best intentions, she could no longer hold in her nausea. She apologised profusely, but the crew had clearly seen it all before and took her sickness without comment. A hand reached out, rougher than the planks upon which she'd lain. It didn't matter. As far as Ingrid could tell, the German inspection was over and although the fishing boat was yet to dock, she was close to completing the first part of her mission. Turning her head, she spat, keen to dispel the bitter taste, but the smell and motion left her feeling fragile. In the distance, perhaps a mile away, she saw a narrow channel and the twinkling lights of a small town behind.

'Is that…?'

Several nodded. While discovering *Esbjerg* came as a pleasing sight, it also brought a new level of trepidation. They hadn't told her what would happen next and placing faith in strangers left Ingrid's stomach performing an uneasy dance. Aksel brought out her radio. The man wielded the suitcase as though it weighed little more than a leaf, but she knew different. Hans cut the engine, and the boat slowed, pushing the craft into a gentle, silent glide along the channel.

With the entire crew looking on, the mate nudged her towards the port rail. 'This is where you get off. Keep your arms above your head and walk slowly. Don't force your stride against the current,

329

or you'll fall. Noah will follow you to make sure you get to the beach. He will carry the radio, but you must carry your other case. When you reach the beach, you'll see a narrow track heading away from the town. Take the trail and keep your head down. It's unlikely you'll encounter any Germans, but not impossible. Find the red wooden cottage. Inside you'll meet Oliver. Ask him for some herring. When he offers you *Rugbrød*, decline, saying the last time you ate rye bread, the seeds got stuck in your teeth.'

Ingrid absorbed the instructions without comment. Only a year earlier, her natural curiosity would have forced a jabbering clarification. Now her training brought a new focus. As she eased herself into the icy water, she kept the shock from showing upon her face. Flecks of salty water bounced up, hitting her chin as Ingrid planted both feet in the sand below. The boat moved on, leaving her with just the man called Noah for company. Like the other fishermen, he was a Nordic giant. Immediately, he pushed past, cutting through the water like air and within a dozen steps he stepped onto the beach, away from the churning tide. Planting the suitcase on the sand, he launched back into the water and within half a minute, his friends had pulled him back aboard. Ingrid wasted no time and, although slower, she soon found the shallows. She shivered as her wet hand struggled to grip the suitcase, but on the second attempt, she hefted it and struck out as towards the cottage.

****

Stefan stared into the handset in disbelief. A rage burnt within, and someone would have to pay. His superiors would deem him culpable for this mistake, and that would never do. He'd need another scapegoat. Placing the receiver back in the cradle, he rubbed his chin, feeling an unusual roughness. He was letting his standards slip.

Despite the early hour, Stefan poured a generous measure of schnapps, which he downed in one, welcoming the burn. A second followed, and then he flicked his arm, releasing the glass which exploded upon the far wall. Was his information wrong? Had Hector somehow laid a false trail to allow the new spy's safe arrival? Or were the agents he'd sent to intercept incompetent?

He suspected all the scenarios were plausible, but that didn't help him. Instead, he turned his attention to the two questions which taunted. Had a new female British spy arrived, and if so, where was she?

90

NOVEMBER 1941, EGYPT

Archie stared forlornly at the burning husk of a mark one Crusader tank. Another dozen sat nearby, each destroyed in the last four days. They were better than the Matildas, which came before, but barely. Their two-pound guns made little impact on the heat of battle. Their only value, the agile armoured transport, was everywhere and when you're an infantry soldier like Archie marching through a sea of sand, any barrier to a hail of bullets held value. He'd heard a rumour that the Americans would loan something better, but as a lowly private in the eighth army, he couldn't know for sure.

Before the sun could sink too low in the sky, he opened two tins of bully beef before passing one to his friend Taff. That was one thing Archie liked about their deployment. Taff came from the valleys in south Wales, and Jock from Glasgow. Gordon turned everything into a joke with his scouse humour, while Dennis covered off the northeast with his straight talking. There were others in their platoon, each bringing their own cultural flavour.

He stared downward, queasy despite the hunger pangs that never quite disappeared. The tinned meat pooled and bubbled at the base of the can. Understandable given the intense heat and lack of shade along the Egyptian border. They'd arrived seven months earlier, some place he could barely pronounce, called *Mersa Matruh*, with a frequent breeze that swept inland from the Mediterranean. The Jerries would not allow them any comfort and before long, their unit moved further south, away from any coastal relief. Now, with sweat, sand, and disgusting broiled stew, their only constants, Archie turned his attention back to Ingrid. He cursed his ineptitude when they'd last seen each other. While he didn't fully understand her, he knew in his heart just how much love he yearned to give her. But would that chance ever come around again?

91

NOVEMBER 1941, DENMARK

After leaving the fishing boat in darkness, she'd found her Danish contact and there she'd sheltered for three weeks before moving on. The British had told her there would be a delay before she could head for Germany, but with a stranger for a host, who rarely spoke, the days dragged.

Today, things were about to change, and with Ingrid's natural flair for artistry, she felt buoyed. All around, nature gifted ingredients which helped to alter Ingrid's features until she found the balance she required. She didn't know what had happened to the fishing boat crew, and she didn't ask.

According to her papers, her alter ego, Elsa Keller, was born in 1910 and Ingrid had taken great care to age herself through the make-up. It had taken her hours, but finally, she'd muted her natural beauty. Opting for a dour, insignificant appearance. Even her temporary guardian, Oliver, who had equipped her with clothes to help her silent departure from *Esbjerg*, approved. That's if his indifferent shrug meant what she thought. Her change in appearance was necessary, as the hefty suitcase radio forced her to stow her clothing inside the second, tiny case. That was her constant worry when she rode the train east and then south to the border. How could she explain the inordinate weight of her suitcase? Inevitably, the question arose. Her carriage on the train south had taken hours. She'd have loved to absorb the Danish countryside, but the uncertainty of changes she might discover upon her return home gnawed away. The British had prepared her, of course, and this was her country she was returning to, but neither brought comfort. She knew the small Danish village of *Kruså* sat close to the border with the larger town of *Flensburg*, just a few miles further south, but had little idea how secure the crossing would be. When they'd passed through *Kruså*, the train had slowed and it took a further hour before her, and the other anxious passengers saw much activity. When they finally arrived at the border, Ingrid's heart sank. All passengers were required to leave the train. Steeling herself, she stepped out onto the platform. There were perhaps eighty or more other passengers. Some appeared a little stuffy at the delays, but most showed an air of apprehension. She fell into the latter as her insides churned in empathy.

The passengers, under the order of the German guards, formed three lines along the platform. Ingrid's eyes speared to the front of the queue and immediately she set about sizing up the opposition. Keeping her expression neutral, she picked the middle queue and soon, others stood behind her. Another thirty minutes passed. With fewer than thirty travellers in each queue, the tension rose while the Germans inspected their papers with meticulous precision. Ingrid's forearm ached while she dragged her case along, though not as much as the weight within her abdomen.

'Papers?'

Offering a slight smile, Ingrid presented her documents. A full minute ticked by.

'Where are you travelling to and why?'

'I live in *Bremen*, and I am returning home.'

The guard looked irritated, so Ingrid continued. 'I've come from tending to my sick father, but now I have to go back to St Joseph-Stift hospital where I work as a nurse.'

'Open the case.'

Ingrid heard the order, and knew inspecting luggage was normal, but this was real. This was happening. She'd picked the youngest soldier when she'd adopted her compliant slot within the queue, yet how could she explain the lack of clothes? Replaced instead with radio equipment. Suppressing the panic which threatened to overwhelm, she offered the smaller case for inspection.

'Not that one, the other,' the guard commanded.

Taking a moment, she settled the first case down before hefting the radio onto the table, where she clicked the latches and turned the case.

'What is this?'

She scanned the guard before replying. 'It is hospital equipment. You've heard of X-rays, haven't you?' Ingrid knew she stood upon a tightrope above a wide crevasse. She couldn't belittle the soldier, but equally she had to bamboozle him into believing her equipment was genuine.

'Why?'

The soldier was insufferable with his simplistic questioning, but Ingrid could no more run from the border check than fly to the moon. 'My father, he fell. When we received the call, the hospital in *Kolding* lacked the equipment. I asked if I could take the X-ray machine from my hospital to help.'

The guard reached into the case. She watched as his clumsy hands turned a dial before clicking switches off and on. *For gods' sake, hurry.* Sweat trickled down her spine as she watched his deepening frown.

'Where are your clothes?'

'It was an emergency. The doctors in *Kolding* provided gowns for my stay. Though if you open my other case, you'll see my uniform,' she said coldly. Taking care not to be obvious, Ingrid looked about. The other queues were dwindling. It was the last thing she needed. She had to get the idiot to let her through.

'So, what happened to your father?'

Finally, a crumb of compassion. 'He died,' she replied flatly.

Her response caught the guard cold, and his demeanour immediately changed. 'I...I'm sorry. Here, your papers are excellent. Please, let me carry your case. You can walk through.'

Dabbing her eye upon her sleeve, she accepted and together they walked through. Twenty minutes later, the train was ready to depart, and the juddering locomotive replaced her heartbeat, which had finally settled into a normal rhythm.

92

Rabbi Cohen lifted a block of rubble before tossing it to one side. The work was tiring, only today he'd lost his usual buoyant mood. For months, this had been his daily ritual as friends and neighbours watched in fear as the *Luftwaffe* obliterated the area. Each day, once firefighters had doused scorched buildings and they'd cooled, he'd join vast teams of workers and householders alike, to clear the debris, only for everything to burn around them the following night. It had brought unity and a toughness from repeated nights deep within the shelters that he admired. But at what cost? It had been over a year since he'd heard from Millie and the pain of separation paired with her absence upon her birthday tore into him like a claw. But she could not return.

He cast his weary eyes about. While the building was still standing, his synagogue on Philpot Street looked ready to topple. Nobody could attend a service and for a while, the rabbi himself was homeless. His one solace was that his dear child, Millie, was hundreds of miles away from the danger.

93

December 1941, *Bremen*

Ingrid watched a boat chug down the Weser before approaching the loading dock. She daren't loiter, especially as she had little business being near the pier. The sign to her side read *Getreidenhafen* – Grain Port, and she wondered if that was the true identity of the cargo? She moved away, heading for the safety of a nearby park.

It was early, and with few upon the streets, she made rapid progress to her favoured bench. For once, with dew glistening in the morning sunshine, the tranquillity seemed a world away from Nazi oppression, though along the perimeter, massive swastikas adorned most buildings in a stark reminder. She took the time to relive the previous months. Apart from the border, travelling down from Denmark had gone smoothly. Moreso than she could have ever expected. The authorities had conducted further checks at each station, but within the interior, the checks appeared a formality. Despite this, when she finally exited the *hauptbahnhof* and stepped onto the *Hochstraße Breitenweg* on that chilly October afternoon, she'd crossed the tracks and headed straight for the side space of *Bürgerpark*. This was all part of the briefing the British had given her just days earlier and, once settled at the *Marcusbrunnen* fountain, she took in her surroundings. She'd seen parks during her years in England, but they were an alien concept back in *Berchtesgaden*. Who needed a park when mountain vistas offered a unique level of beauty and freshness? Here, within the centre of

339

Bremen, she acclimatised herself. The wide-open spaces of *Bürgerpark* offered security. Nobody could approach without her detecting them first, and while soldiers and pedestrians alike moved across the paths, no one appeared interested in her. She remained for a further hour. She would move, circling the perimeter, before returning to her first favoured spot. With each pass, she sought familiarity. Were *Gestapo* agents following her? Confident they weren't, she moved on to her next destination.

One man had spooked her. She'd seen him, fifty yards behind her, as she'd crossed underneath the railway. For the short walk underneath the bridge, the December darkness intensified to almost umbra, allowing her follower in his black trench coat and dark hat to remain oppressively within the shadows. She could hear his clipped heels as she moved out into the twilight, and it took all her resolve to keep her eyes from looking backward. Although the constant sound unnerved, she'd seen him watch her when she left the station. Dark piercing eyes, soulless, yet enquiring, sat behind round wireframe glasses. The image triggered an involuntary shudder. Cutting left, she stared at a gigantic statue. The brick elephant, unique and out of place in the park, caused her to halt. She knew her follower would catch-up, and the idea made her want to vomit, but still she stood her ground. She had every right to study the artwork. The stranger came closer. She could hear his approach clearly as both footsteps and a slight wheeze at the man's breathing identified his closeness. Ingrid closed her eyes to offer a silent prayer while simultaneously remembering her new identity. She was Elsa Keller, a trained nurse at the nearby St Joseph-Stift hospital. Someone of value to German society. *Who was this man who'd studied her when she'd left the station? How dare he.*

And then, from the corner of one eye, she saw him. He passed and crucially; he kept moving. She waited. Painful minutes passed as her feet felt cemented to the ground. She'd lost sight of him, but in the failing light, she wondered whether her observer lay secreted within the lengthening shadows.

But that was it. She'd stored his image to memory and failed to see him again when she finally moved. It was dark by the time she found her lodgings just half a mile further north. *Frau* Janke greeted her at the door to a large townhouse. Skeletal thin hands inspected her papers, while tired grey eyes appraised Ingrid. The British had secured the accommodation. Ingrid couldn't fathom how but trusting her new landlady as she'd trusted Oliver in *Esbjerg*, she allowed herself to settle. As in Denmark, the pair had exchanged pass phrases which had sealed the introduction.

After a light supper comprising rye bread and a little curd, the landlady led her upstairs. Her new top-floor room showed no signs of habitation, though other tenants occupied the lower floors. Despite a thick layer of dust coating every surface, it felt perfect. *Frau* Janke introduced herself properly as Asta and the pair set about removing sheets and opening windows to fully air the room. It was cold, but neither seemed to care, and they worked together in companionable silence. Twenty minutes and several sneezes later, they'd cleared the room and Ingrid perched upon the bed while Asta closed both the door and window before settling upon the solitary chair.

'I'm glad you came. I wasn't sure you would.' Ingrid started her reply, before Asta waved a finger to urge silence.

'Tomorrow, when the light returns, we can walk together. Then, once we're outside this stuffy room, you can tell your tale. But for now, you need to rest. However, there's one last task you can help me with before you retire.'

Frau Janke pointed silently toward a metal radiator, which clung to the wall near the corner. The woman stood and ushered Ingrid over to inspect the object. In the dim lamplight, she couldn't see anything amiss, but when the landlady gripped the metal structure and heaved, Ingrid understood. The object was too heavy for one to move alone, but with Ingrid's help, they pulled it forward, revealing a hidden alcove behind. She understood. They would hide the radio suitcase inside. It took their combined efforts, but once hidden, Ingrid felt she could finally relax.

****

Stefan examined the sheaf of papers marked *Top Secret* before returning them to the folder and handing them back to his master. *Nacht und Nebel*. Stefan's brain mulled over the words once again before choking back the bitterness. He should feel delighted. This was what he wanted, a mandate issued down from the high command to abduct and eradicate individuals who threatened his mighty country. Yet, he knew they meant others would carry out this ruling. *Not him*, he thought bitterly.

Stefan looked across to Heydrich and wondered whether the chief of the Reich security office could detect the unsettled mood within the room. Perhaps, he mused. Though if Heydrich saw the thoughts which traversed Stefan Weiss's mind, would he see his subordinate as disloyal? Would he pity him? Or perhaps he'd see where Stefan's talents really lay. His inner musings were moot. Stefan couldn't detect any guidance from his master, nor support or empathy, which suggested, as he feared, he was stuck.

****

'You'll be all right. We've practiced this.'

Despite Asta's reassurances, Ingrid's stomach pinched into a familiar tight ball. She knew her new friend meant well, but if Ingrid followed their plan, the risks were enormous. And, worse, the risks were hers. *Come on. You wanted this, remember?*

After tying her hair up, she stepped out into the morning sunshine. She wasn't ready, but she couldn't waste her time in Germany. She'd walked the route to St Joseph-Stift almost every day since her arrival. Sometimes taking the shortest route, while on other days she walked a laborious circuit, until she'd approached the hospital from every direction. Today, though, she'd step inside. It felt odd, walking in the nurse's uniform. She knew within seconds of donning the outfit; she was in for a long day. Heavy starch bit into her neckline and a crisp rustling sound echoed as she walked along the street. But that wasn't the issue. People watched her as she strode along the street. She hated their eyes upon her, but bottling her anxiety, she pressed on. The walk took ten minutes, though she'd have preferred twenty. And there it was, St Joseph-Stift hospital. Ingrid had the papers, which confirmed her transfer, and she had a job to do, but as she stood, studying the red brick structure, her legs turned to jelly.

'Good morning, *Krankenschwester*. Are you lost?'

Unused to being called a nurse, she spun quickly, and only a swift intervention from the speaker prevented her from sprawling. Whoever he was, he looked gorgeous.

'Was it that obvious? Yes, I am lost. This is my first day.'

'Well, please allow me to offer you some help.' Charm oozed from the stranger, and before Ingrid could protest, he'd tucked an arm through hers and led her into the building. A busy reception area greeted the pair, but once through the main doors, the stranger pulled her to one side. 'Welcome to my hospital.'

Ingrid's mouth parted in surprise. So much for being inconspicuous. This was the last thing she needed. 'Y-your hospital?' she stammered.

The tall man smiled and leant in. 'Well, strictly speaking, no. But I am a leading surgeon here, so I think it is fair that everyone looks up at me.'

Ingrid's mind spun as she digested his introduction. As she spied the exit, she could feel a flush rising to her cheeks, but just as she had at the border patrol, she reminded herself of her mission and assessed the situation. True, she hadn't wanted this attention, but perhaps she could use it to her advantage.

'Do you have an office where we could have a drink and I can show you my letter of introduction?' She couldn't believe how brazen she sounded, but the surgeon's eyes lit up at her request.

'Of course. I'd be delighted to show you somewhere more private.'

Ingrid cringed inwardly. Knowing the encounter could easily backfire, she meekly followed him along a corridor. Now and then, the surgeon looked back and with each inspection, his grin widened. 'It's OK. You'll get used to the smell. Where is it you said you've travelled from?' Before she could answer, he drew to a halt and opened a door and ushered her in. She glanced across at a nameplate before settling into a deep leather chair. It read, *Doktor Degenhardt*. Closing the door and sealing her in, he swept in behind and Ingrid's heart sped up. Had she made a terrible mistake? His arm brushed her shoulder as he circled the desk. As she waited for him to speak again, an anxious itch worked across her body that she was powerless to scratch. His eyes bored into her, and she wondered how many others wilted under his penetrating gaze. She glanced away before remembering the forged letter of introduction.

'Thank you for welcoming me. I didn't expect such a warm greeting. Here…please read this, it explains everything.'

Degenhardt's eyes flickered in irritation. It seemed all he wanted to do was sit and stare, and Ingrid's words had broken the spell. He reached over and pulled the document from her fingers.

'Ah, yes,' he said, setting the letter down on his desk. 'It must have come as a terrible shock. Were you in *Mannheim* when the bombs fell?'

Deciding to play the victim, she nodded. No need to overcomplicate things. According to her planned backstory, she'd just begun her nursing training when a stray British bomber had decimated parts of the city and then, with nowhere to work from and a sick father, further north, the letter spoke of her commitment to the cause.

The room was stifling, further adding to Ingrid's unease. She knew she had to remain composed, but the surgeon's manner was unnerving.

'Come. Take my blood pressure.'

She'd expected this, but suddenly the basic field treatment course she'd undertaken felt woefully inadequate. Ingrid stood up and accepted the equipment with trembling hands.

'Roll up your sleeve, please.' He complied, and she began. His arm was hot, like the room, and as she brushed the hairs, she remembered Archie. How long was it since she'd been this close to a man? The distraction helped as she enshrouded his arm in a sheath. Squeezing a ball, forced air into the mechanism, and the wrap tightened as expected. *I'm doing this wrong. Surely, he can see I'm an imposter*. After checking the dial, she turned a release valve to finish the procedure.

'You're 130 over 80. That's a little high, don't you think?' She didn't know. Was her gamble correct?

Degenhardt chucked. 'You are right. Perhaps this is because of your sudden arrival.'

His humour was distasteful, though she forced a smile. 'So, I can stay then?'

While she waited for an answer, he lit a cigarette, blowing smoke in a cloud above his head. A reptilian appraisal followed, forcing Ingrid to question her reasons for coming to the hospital. She reminded herself that not all men were as sleazy as this one, as Archie reappeared in her thoughts.

The surgeon inhaled once more before stubbing the cigarette out. Next, he pushed a button on his desk and a buzzer sounded. 'I've summoned the matron. She'll show you to your station. Welcome to the hospital, Nurse Keller.' Degenhardt leered at her.

94

January 1942, *Bremen* / Berlin

Doktor Degenhardt looked up from his desk as the director of nursing bustled in without knocking. Before he could admonish her rudeness, she overrode his glare and spoke.

'Where did you say your new nurse is from?' Placing an emphasis on the word *your*.

'I told you. *Mannheim*,' he replied curtly.

'Hmph. I suppose, but she has a low-*Deutsch* accent. I don't understand why a southerner would be here.'

The pair eyed each other carefully. What did it matter if Keller spoke a little differently? He'd accepted the new nurse. Her papers confirmed the transfer, and they were short staffed. He really couldn't see the director of nursing's issue.

'Was that all, or did you have something important to ask?' He really didn't have time for this.

Viper-like eyes burnt before the woman accepted. Her presence was no longer required.

****

In a rare departure from reading endless dossiers which numbed his brain, Stefan returned to the compound beyond *Großer Müggelsee*, where Heydrich had brought him just four months earlier. He needed to escape somewhere quieter. Although he could sate his taste for violence by merely remaining within *Gestapo* headquarters at the stately *Prinz-Albrecht-Strasse* building, this place felt somehow better. Perhaps it was the isolation.

As he approached the building, he considered the *Gestapo* headquarters, with its rows of cells and an army of interrogators. While he understood its terrifying reputation, the place felt congested. He certainly found little comfort stuck within its walls. Today, he hoped things would be different.

The guards allowed him access into the building without issue and as he stepped down the stairs to the cells below; he waited for the thrill to surge, but something didn't feel right. He knew there was just the one prisoner. Two or three would be better, so the others could hear the agony while they themselves would wait in sufferance. Was that why he felt indifferent?

'What is the prisoner's name and why is he here?' he asked the guard in charge of the lower level.

'Says his name is Heinz Janker. He claims he works in a munitions factory, and he says he is innocent of all charges.'

The guard produced a key and unlocked the cell door. Inside lay the fattest man Stefan could ever recall seeing. Even Otto, with his ability to consume pastries, lacked this man's girth. The foetal lumpy mass cowered, and despite the poor lighting, Stefan could see the bruises and welts covered more surface than pink skin.

'Help him up. And get some clothing, or a blanket at least.'

Surprise flickered on the guard's face, though he carried out the order without question and a minute later, three guards had pulled the prisoner to his feet within the tiny space. The obese man could barely walk, so they dragged him out to where Stefan offered a bench. Like a weighted child's toy which refused to roll over, the prisoner sagged and rolled before finally righting himself, though the guards held him in place. A swelling forced one eye shut, but the other eyelid flickered. This was no challenge. The man had submitted already. Disguising his disappointment, Stefan allowed Janker to cower beneath a blanket while they brought food and water.

'I have spoken with my superiors, and we believe you are telling us everything. Once you regain your strength, we will release you and make sure we help you return home safe. In the meantime, I will summon a doctor to attend to your injuries.'

Janker's mouth wobbled. Strands of saliva dripped down as the prisoner tried to form a word of gratitude.

'Keep him warm and do not harm him. I will return shortly.'

Stefan returned upstairs and stepped out into the sunlight. Clearly, the guards didn't know him if they thought he would keep his promise.

A few hours later, Janker lay dead, and Stefan left the guards the challenging task of disposing of the prisoner's body. He felt no remorse for murdering the man. To his mind, someone that huge was harbouring a juicy secret. There was no logic to the thought, but Stefan didn't care. Though he remained unsettled. He'd hoped by saving and then destroying, he would feel alive once more, but as he feared, the excitement flickered out as surely as Janker's eyes. It was all too easy.

By the time he arrived back at *Prinz-Albrecht-Strasse*, the sun had sunk within the sky. He needed a drink, but knowing he had more reports to inspect, he stepped back inside *Gestapo* headquarters.

The pile of dossiers had doubled since the morning, further souring his mood. This would take all night. Perhaps someone above was punishing him for taking time out earlier. Sighing, he flicked through the first two before setting them aside. Someone else could digest the material. While he considered where he could offload the work, his eye caught something of interest. As he drew his gaze across the pages, his eyes went wide, and a smile formed. If the information within the bulletin held true, then his father would be busy and thousands of miles away. The directive specified that Helmut Weiss would join Erwin Rommel's staff as part of the Afrika Korps. Stefan knew little of the African campaign beyond heat and flies, though that was enough. He knew his father would labour in the heat.

Stefan sat the earlier disappointments aside. Now he had a new project, and that meant keeping a close eye on the war raging across the north African continent.

348

95

FEBRUARY 1942, *BREMEN*

Since arriving in *Bremen*, Ingrid had used her radio three times to contact the British, each time from a different location, and never from her new home.

Despite her best attempts, Ingrid bumped the suitcase onto the pavement after descending the steps from her apartment. A dull thud echoed across the empty street, and she shuddered. Part from cold and part from fear of discovery. She glanced about and once satisfied nobody could see her; she set off toward the hospital.

Although a short walk, progress was slow. She preferred to take alternative routes and, wherever possible, shadows were her friend, but not tonight. Just two streets away from her home, a shout rang out.

'Halt. Papers.'

The urge to flee felt immense, but Ingrid knew that beyond the voice, there would be others and likely dogs. She turned and addressed the guard who'd hailed her. 'Good evening. Of course, here, let me show you.' She approached, hoped the shake within her body and voice wasn't obvious.

There were three soldiers holding a cordon, and as she'd surmised, an Alsatian which strained at its leash. 'Why are you out after curfew? And what are you carrying in the case?'

Ingrid was ready for both questions, though that preparation hardly mattered as her insides turned to jelly. 'Of course, I know about the curfew. I wasn't trying to break any rules. As you can see from my papers, I am a nurse at St Joseph-Stift hospital. People don't just need care during the daytime, you know.' She knew the last sentence could overstep, but once the guard had inspected her papers under torchlight, he seemed satisfied.

'Open the case.'

Ingrid's insides gave a jolt, but with no option, she turned the suitcase towards the guard to allow inspection. She immediately saw his frown. 'As you can see, they're uniforms. They get dirtied, and I took them home for cleaning.'

'Surely, the hospital has a laundry,' he countered.

'Of course, but the last time I used their service, my uniform came back pink.'

This brought a chuckle, whereupon the guard closed the case and returned it to Ingrid. 'What is your name, *fraulein* nurse?'

This time, it was Ingrid's turn to laugh. 'You already know that. It's Elsa. Nurse Elsa Keller at your service. And you are?' It was brazen of her to ask, but seeing his face flush, she felt she'd judged the mood correctly.

'My name is Johann. Thank you for asking, but I think, perhaps, you should be on your way. It's best you don't stay out longer than absolutely necessary.'

The other two guards took great humour in Johann's discomfort, so Ingrid took her leave and headed straight for her work.

****

Four hours later, Ingrid had radioed news to the British and received her instructions back. She'd felt sick when she'd used the radio. She always did. Tonight, in almost total darkness, within a boiler house attached to the hospital, she'd called in. It was the middle of the night, so little likelihood that maintenance staff would interrupt, but the possibility of a watchman, or worse a soldier would catch her, left Ingrid feeling wretched. She retraced her steps home, carrying an identical suitcase to the one she'd brought to the hospital earlier.

It was still dark, but this time, rather than keep to the shadows, she sought the three guards she'd seen earlier that evening. It was a risk; she knew.

Ingrid approached the barrier, knowing her home lay just two streets away. She couldn't see Johann, and her bravado faltered. Had she just made a terrible mistake?

A dog growled as she approached. Was this the same Alsatian she'd seen earlier? It hardly mattered. She knew if she didn't recognise the guards, she could be in serious trouble. The familiar instruction to halt and show papers sounded out, and she dug into her pocket, ready for questioning. A new face greeted her, and she paled. She couldn't help it. She knew she'd been foolish. Knowing where the guards had blocked the road, she could have easily found another route. Now she felt frightened. 'Is Johann here?' she asked meekly.

Although busy inspecting Ingrid's papers, the guard appeared impressed she knew one of them. 'Johann. Get over here. This lady is asking for you.' The seconds ticked by, heightening her anxiety, but soon enough, Johann appeared. A wide smile reflected at her.

'Ah, it is my friend, the nurse. Elsa, wasn't it? I didn't expect to see you again. Did you finish early?'

'Yes, that's me. I wish. No, a patient vomited all over my uniform and then another smeared shit down another set while I was trying to clean him. If I don't get this lot back and cleaned, then I'll only have the clothes I'm wearing.'

At the mention of faeces and vomit, both Johann and the other guard recoiled. 'Well, we'd better not keep you then. It sounds like you have a dirty job to attend to and we shouldn't delay you any further.'

Ingrid ducked under the barrier and continued along her route. Five minutes later, within the safety of her apartment and with Asta by her side, the painful constriction within her chest eased. Together, they pushed the suitcase radio she'd been carrying back into its hiding place.

96

***

JULY 1942, *DRESDEN*

Stefan locked the door before returning to study the papers he'd just received. So far, reading the information was no crime. After all, his job required knowledge across the entire span of the Reich. And why wouldn't a loving son show interest in his father's career path? But this was different, and for the first time in almost a year, he felt a surge of excitement. He knew what he planned.

Later that day, he met with Hector as part of their normal routine. As usual, the British spy offered resigned compliance. Stefan passed a sheaf of papers to the agent. It was a calculated gamble. Each piece of information he gave to Hector to transmit contained a grain of truth, merged with a measure of disinformation. Just enough to make the British believe. Only today, Stefan had altered the data to reveal so much more. His clandestine research had revealed a startling truth. For Rommel's *Panzerarmee Afrika*, supplies were low. That left his father vulnerable. His eyes feverishly scanned the documents. Ships carrying essential supplies; manifests, routes, times. He calculated the outcome if the food, water, and other critical materials did not arrive.

Now came the challenge. Stefan didn't understand codes – not in the way Hector and his German analysts did. That meant he had to doctor the information his superiors wanted them to send, and he needed to trust the secrets would transmit as he hoped.

He paused.

Was he about to sell out his own country, just to see his father suffer? It was a pity that German troops would die through his actions, but that was a price he would happily pay to unburden himself from his father.

****

Stefan's heart thundered as he gave the instructions to the transmission team. As usual, Hector keyed the morse code under their supervision. Everything appeared normal, just as it had over fifty times before, but that didn't stifle Stefan's fear of discovery. Twenty minutes later, the message was in the hands of the British. He hadn't just crossed a bridge, he'd destroyed it, and there was no going back.

As Stefan released Hector back into the fake life underneath *Gestapo* scrutiny, he considered the future. It would be weeks, maybe months, before clues surfaced whether his plan had worked. Perhaps he would see out the war, never knowing. His lips curled into a smile. He could live with that. Choosing optimism that his scheme would work, he shrugged and turned his thoughts instead to what he would do once his father was gone.

Alone in his apartment, Stefan stepped into the bedroom and undressed before laying on the bed. His father had sentenced his friend to a fight in another country, but as he closed his eyes, Stefan's only thoughts were of Peter coming home and what they would do together upon his lover's arrival.

97

AUGUST 1942, *BREMEN*

For the first time since the turn of the year, Ingrid felt confident in her nursing duties. She'd integrated herself into the hospital and despite the inevitable wagging of tongues, she'd even dined with *Doktor* Degenhardt, or Manfred, as he asked her to call him. A strange truce had settled between the pair. She knew she was using his influence for protection while he allowed her a greater license within the hospital.

In the first few days, she'd made mistakes. It was to be expected. But nobody died on her watch, and gradually things settled as her skills increased. The other nurses looked overworked and keen to offload their own chores. Ingrid slipped into the breach, and within a few weeks, fledgling friendships formed. Her only fear was for the director of nursing. Ingrid was still an outsider who lacked basic nursing knowledge, and she was keen to keep that a secret. But, beyond carrying out her duties to the best of her ability, and avoiding the woman, there was little else she could do.

Back at the apartment, it was Asta's wisdom and support that made everything easier. Having new clothes and someone to confide in meant Ingrid didn't carry everything on her own shoulders, although the pair were always careful and only spoke of their real purpose when out in wide-open spaces.

But Ingrid was no fool. Her life straddled a tightrope, but she could see no other way around it as she committed to a third dinner date with the surgeon. The thought of dining together caused her stomach to churn. Would he attempt to kiss her? Would she let him? She shuddered at the thought. It wasn't just his tobacco breath that she disliked, or the extra years he held on her; she knew he would take minimal invitation before letting his hands roam. Only this time she could not scream the house down as she had with Haynes, eight years earlier. The thoughts were moot. The surgeon held value, which she hoped outweighed her own discomfort.

Ingrid cast her conflicting thoughts to one side and stepped into the street to begin the walk to *Schütting* on *Marktplatz*. She couldn't help but compare the larger city to *Berchtesgaden*, but she was grateful for the anonymity that a bigger town brought. The Guildhall looked spectacular in the late afternoon, an ideal spot to meet the surgeon. She knew he lived nearby in *Schwachhausen*, and she'd expected that Degenhardt would be there before her.

As Ingrid approached the coffee house, only strangers greeted her. Before settling at a table, Ingrid scanned the scene. *Where is he?* She hated waiting. Her eyes swept up to the clock tower atop *St Petri Dom Bremen* Cathedral. Quarter past the hour. It was unlike the surgeon to be late. Something was wrong, and immediate insecurities wormed into her brain. Squinting her eyes, she returned her stare to the coffeehouse. Most patrons sat inside, where shadows hid their features, but she was certain her date was not among them. Manfred wasn't the sort to skulk in the dark. Standing outside left Ingrid feeling exposed.

Her stomach gurgled loudly, before lapsing into silence. She would have to keep a grip on her nerves. More questions formed in her mind, but before she could plan a course of action, she saw them. A hundred yards away, two men wearing dark, full-length coats striding towards her. She turned away, her mind racing. *Where could she go?* The square was sparsely populated, certainly not a crowd she could disappear into. That left the coffeehouse. The darkness was inviting, but invisible roots anchored her feet to the floor. Now a voice called to her, and she knew she'd dithered too long.

'Keller. Elsa Keller. Your papers, please.'

Cringing inwardly, Ingrid turned to face the men. The strangers had covered the distance at a run and were almost upon her. Realising escape was futile, she pulled out her identity card and offered it up. The tallest snatched the document from her. Ingrid's eyes flashed, but she bit her lip and said nothing, dipping her head in compliance. 'Yes, that's me. How may I help you?'

The pair remained silent, leaving Ingrid acutely aware others were watching her. *Stop staring, this is none of your business.* But the street dwellers merely gawped some more, already apportioning guilt.

'Who were you meeting today?' This time, it was the shorter of the two who spoke.

The question threw her. '*Doktor* Degenhardt,' she stammered.

The pair exchanged a glance, but whatever passed between them, Ingrid couldn't read. 'Come with us,' the man said. A command, not a request.

A tremble shimmied across Ingrid's back. *They know who I am.* She swallowed hard before stepping forward in compliance. Her mind reeled as she wobbled along *Balgebrückstraße* toward the *Weser*. The two men flanked her, though neither seemed interested in restraining her. Her capture pushed questions of the surgeon to one side. Instead, new, more sinister queries plagued her mind. *What did her capture mean? How did they find me? Who betrayed me?*

Her worst fears flooded her senses. As the trio walked, Ingrid considered she might never see her family or Archie again. The pain in Ingrid's stomach intensified, forcing her to stop. 'I'm sorry. May I just take a moment?' She fully expected them to ignore her plea and use force, but they gave her a few seconds. Ingrid remained still while she waited for the pain to subside.

They didn't spare her long. 'Come on. Keep moving.' This time the command came from the taller man, leaving Ingrid bewildered who was in charge. She forced her legs to move. In her heart, she knew no good outcome could come from resisting. The river lay ahead, oddly inviting, though Ingrid pushed away any idea she could swim to safety. Resigned to her fate, she wondered whether she could talk her way to safety, but as the thought occurred to her, a dark saloon pulled up beside the group, and the men ushered her into the rear. She fell inside, tumbling to the floor, when a rough hand pushed her unceremoniously onto the seat. The tall man clambered after her, squashing her in the middle. Her eyes darted about the interior, but it was no good. The other man entered the car on the opposite side, firmly closing the door behind him. There would be no escape.

The car pulled away, and Ingrid squirmed in discomfort as the men crowded her on both sides. Unbidden, the memory of the British fake interrogation struck her like a blow from an anvil. Her eyes closed as she prepared for what was to come.

****

The drive only lasted a few minutes, but the journey felt like the longest Ingrid had ever taken. Nobody spoke, and as they travelled south to a new district, her tension heightened, until finally they arrived outside an imposing four-storey building. The men directed her inside, gripping her by the elbows as they went upstairs. Each footfall upon the stone steps sounded like a death knell. After three flights of stairs, Ingrid felt dizzy, but the men maintained their firm grip on her arms. They proceeded briskly down a dim corridor before stopping at a door halfway along on the left. Ingrid craned her neck to peer through the glass pane. Inside, she saw row upon row of typists. Each finger pressed created clipped taps which assaulted her ears.

'Inside.'

The short man twisted the handle and pointed towards a row of chairs at the far end of the room. Ingrid lifted her head, composing herself as she stepped across the threshold. Twenty pairs of eyes were watching, though the tapping continued without pause. Ingrid skirted a path to the end of the room, settled into a chair and waited.

They left her for over an hour. Ingrid did not know whether this was a ploy, but it worked. Her anxiety had risen to crippling levels. After their initial interest, the typists returned to their work, few giving her any attention. Hands clasped in her lap, Ingrid's eyes darted around the room. She found out there was an office behind her, though the thought of stepping into the unknown filled her with dread. Nobody was coming to save her, and if she vanished into the Nazi war machine, her loved ones would never learn of her fate.

'*Fraulein*. I'm sorry we kept you waiting. It shouldn't take much longer. Some tea perhaps?'

The short man had returned to the room, and his new-found compassion further muddled Ingrid's thoughts. 'Yes, please. Thank you.'

He returned a few minutes later with a china cup, steaming with tea. Ingrid gratefully accepted the warm drink. Her fingers shook, so she rested the saucer on her knees while waiting in contemplation. More minutes passed while she waited for the liquid to cool. She wasn't certain whether she could drink it, anyway. A battle was raging inside her. Too many things she didn't understand fought against the worst potential scenarios. It left her feeling weak. Finally, when the short man returned, his demeanour soured a little. The tea was lukewarm, and she still hadn't taken a sip. Ingrid lifted the cup to her lips and swallowed a mouthful. A bitter tannin taste hit her tongue, but the man appeared mollified. She had trusted him enough to take a sip. As Ingrid took a second mouthful, the door to the inner office opened. The tall man walked through first. She'd expected such, but not the person following in his wake.

A riot of coughing erupted as Ingrid choked the liquid which had entered her lungs, while both cup and saucer smashed on the floor. Standing just a few feet away and glaring like a thunderstorm, stood the director of nursing.

98

AUGUST 1942, EGYPT

Archie gazed out at the Mediterranean Sea and sucked in the cool, salty air. It was the first time in months his company had taken any respite. The men were tired but rejuvenated after their break, and battle hardened for the fight ahead. Earlier in the year, despite heavy losses, they'd brought relief to the port of Tobruk. Archie didn't know exactly what that meant, though he understood the importance of supplies, and so defending a port was a worthy crusade. But now the power had shifted, and Italian and German divisions pushed the British back beyond the Egyptian border until an uneasy stalemate developed.

Two weeks earlier, they'd received a morale boost when General Montgomery had toured their camp. Archie dwarfed the man as he inspected the group on parade, but the field marshal stopped in front of Archie to enquire how he thought the war effort was going. 'I think we're doing well, sir,' he'd responded.

Montgomery had beamed up at him. 'That's the spirit. Our mandate from the Prime Minister is to destroy the Axis forces in North Africa...It can be done, and it will be done.'

Now there was a man Archie could fight for. And Mister Churchill, of course.

Today, they had an additional reason to cheer. Along the distant horizon sat a German ship. Thick smoke belched into the sky as the vessel listed to starboard. Moments later, it had vanished into the sea. Archie heard later that the allies had sunk dozens of enemy ships in the Mediterranean that week.

Fifty miles away, Montgomery and his senior staff received intelligence that agreed with Archie's optimism. The war was swinging in their favour.

99

AUGUST 1942, *BREMEN*

Ingrid finally brought her breathing under control. She'd destroyed the cup and saucer, and a pool of tea lay at her feet, but it was nothing compared to her epiphany: *the director of nursing. That's who betrayed me. Why?*

Her superior had left the room, which left Ingrid feeling torn. If she hadn't choked, perhaps she could have launched at the woman. The thought came too late. A typist interrupted her work and scuttled over to clear away the mess. Dismayed, Ingrid wanted to cry.

'Come inside, please.' The tall man beckoned to her from the office.

She stepped into the room and took the seat offered to her. Part of her wanted to hurl herself through the window. A quick death. Anything to escape this nightmare. Instead, she sat quietly, clasping her hands in silent prayer. The tall man took up position behind a large desk, while the shorter man remained standing.

'Thank you for attending today. Tell me, what do you know of *Doktor* Degenhardt?' the tall man asked.

Ingrid shook her head. Had she heard right? 'He's the senior surgeon at the hospital. But I'm sure you'd be aware of a man of such standing in the community.' The words came easily. A light had come on in her head. *They don't want me. It's Manfred they're after.* A new shake rippled through her, only this time she felt some level of control.

'Have you attended surgery with *Doktor* Degenhardt?'

This one was easy. She'd witnessed surgery three times in her tenure, so she quickly shared the details.

Next, they asked what happened when people died from their injuries. Ingrid paused. She knew about the record store, but had to choose her words carefully. Part of the role the British had given her was to unearth secrets, and she was well aware of how many clandestine hours she'd spent rifling through hospital records. The fear returned. Had the director of nursing seen her down there? It was a fear she refused to dwell on. Her thoughts focussed squarely on the surgeon, she nodded. 'Yes, I know he spent time down there. Most days, in fact. Why?'

It was risky to pose questions back, but she needed to steer the conversation to safer ground.

'We believe *Doktor* Degenhardt did not conduct himself appropriately.'

The ambiguous answer helped little, but at least they'd admitted the surgeon was the wrongdoer. Ingrid thought about how Manfred spoke toward her, especially when they were alone. Yes, he showed signs of a philanderer, but was that all this meant? Was he some kind of sexual predator? She studied her questioner before deciding to question him further. 'Did he assault someone?' Then, in a minor act of self-preservation, Ingrid threw the surgeon to the wolves. 'He always was attentive.' She hoped they would catch the nuance.

'No. We know his reputation with the ladies. We have no interest in that.'

The statement left Ingrid flummoxed. 'What then? What has he done? Why have you brought me here?' The pitch in her voice had raised, but Ingrid couldn't help it. They'd kept her here for hours, leaving her frightened and thinking the worst, when she was merely a witness.

'I think we can tell her our suspicions, Jürgen. After all, the director of nursing and other staff members agree with our findings.'

The tall man considered his colleague's request. 'Very well,' he agreed, before focusing on Ingrid once more. 'You said that *Doktor* Degenhardt spent a great deal of time looking through the records, especially when patients have died. Do you agree?' Ingrid nodded. 'Why do you think he did this?'

Ingrid scoured her memory, searching for a plausible explanation. It couldn't be mere diligence on the surgeon's part. No, he'd spent far too long searching. The answer, or part of it, at least, seemed obvious. Degenhardt had done the same things she'd done. Was that it? Was he a spy? If so, who for and could she denounce him? The director of nursing and others had worked it out, so following their path seemed the safest route. 'Now that I've taken the time to think about this, I feel sure he spent too long looking through all the records. And that's not all. He had a case. Took it with him everywhere, including when he inspected the records. He could easily change or steal information and nobody would question his authority.'

Gleaming eyes shone across the desk and Ingrid was confident she'd worked out part of the puzzle. If he had indeed taken patient records, then Ingrid remained in the dark as to the reason, but her words appeared to cement his guilt. She waited.

More questions came, with little offered back to her, but with each word spoken, Ingrid's belief that she was safe, despite sitting within the lions' den, grew. Thirty minutes later, and this time unaccompanied, Ingrid walked back towards her apartment. She felt physically and emotionally exhausted and failed to notice the pair of eyes watching her from the shadows as she entered the building.

****

Ingrid didn't return to the hospital until the following day, but when she did, *Doktor* Degenhardt was nowhere to be seen. She didn't know what to expect, though it felt as though all eyes were upon her. Glancing left, she saw the corridor which led to the records store. She snapped her head away before anyone could question her stare. While the surgeon's disappearance remained a mystery, the previous day's questioning had come as a blow. Ingrid knew any future time spent scanning records would come under intense scrutiny.

Her walk slowed as she approached the ward. The director of nursing would be there, fussing and ordering, as usual. But would there be anything new in her treatment of Ingrid after their recent encounter?

'What are you standing there for? Come on. The bedpans won't change themselves.'

Ingrid leapt as though stung. Meekly, she swung into action. The next hours flew by, leaving no time to dwell upon the director of nursing.

Later that afternoon, Ingrid heard a voice behind her. 'Elsa. A moment, please.'

The command came from the director of nursing, and Ingrid cringed before setting a pile of blankets to one side and following. The older woman led them to her office, where she sat behind a small desk. 'Close the door and take a seat, will you?' Ingrid lowered herself onto the chair and crossed her legs before burying both palms deep between her thighs. 'No need to be nervous. We're all here together, though I suppose you're feeling a little shocked after yesterday's questioning.' Although a pleasant surprise, Ingrid wasn't about to accept a sudden switch from the woman, so she merely nodded. 'Now that we've unearthed *Doktor* Degenhardt's treachery, is there anything else you'd like to know?'

Ingrid gulped. 'What is it exactly that he did? They only hinted at something terrible yesterday.'

The director of nursing pulled her glasses off her face and gave them a polish before replacing them on her nose. Ingrid thought she detected a tiny smirk. *What did that look mean?*

'I'm surprised the other nurses haven't told you. They're awful for gossip, though not all of them went through the questioning that we did. Mind you, they know there'd be trouble if they spoke out. *Doktor* Degenhardt is a traitor to you, me, and everything the Fatherland stands for.' The older woman looked clearly agitated, and Ingrid's mood softened. She leant forward and offered a hand. 'Oh, that's kind,' the director of nursing said as she gripped Ingrid's fingers. She lowered her voice, her eyes flashing. 'He was helping them, those *Unerwähnbares.*'

Ingrid's whole body stiffened. She didn't understand the details, but it sounded like they had caught the surgeon helping Jews. A brain fog descended, shrouding the remaining conversation, and when the director of nursing finally pulled her hand away, Ingrid felt an inner rage. She stood, bowed her head and made to leave. 'Thank you for sharing this terrible news,' she said. As Ingrid left, she turned and did the unthinkable, raising her arm in a *Sieg Heil* before leaving the room.

100

SEPTEMBER 1942, *BREMEN*

The shock revelation that Doctor Degenhardt had helped Jews to escape from Nazi persecution churned Ingrid's stomach, and once she'd escaped the confines of the director's office, she found a quiet corner in the hospital to gather her thoughts. If only she'd discovered this knowledge sooner. She wiped away a stray tear, gathered herself, and returned to her duties.

Later that evening, she walked along the bank of the Weser with Asta. Her friend reminded Ingrid that she couldn't have done anything to prevent his capture, while earnestly adding that she, too, had to be more careful. Her guardian had a point, and Ingrid steeled her resolve to do more.

Today, however, Ingrid had a mission. Technically, she'd had the mission for the entire year, but today was the first time she could actively take part in one critical element, and it filled her with nervous excitement. Usually, when she transmitted to the British, she felt her information held little value. Records of the recently deceased, for instance. Certainly, no troop deployments or names and locations of the ruling elite. But one question had lain dormant since her arrival and today she hoped to unearth a truth.

It was early and deserted streets greeted her when she left the apartment. As always, she scoped the surrounding area before making any movement. Empty roads weren't ideal. It meant she stood out on any encounter, but she had a long journey and with just one day off from the hospital, an early start was essential. The walk to *Bremen Hauptbahnhof* went smoothly. She had to pass through a guard check, but she'd acclimatised to such inspections and without her suitcase radio, she passed through easily. Despite the information on the timetable, she had an hour to wait before the locomotive departed for Hamburg. Time she could ill afford. But despite the delay, the journey felt liberating. Yes, she saw soldiers and yes; she passed endless buildings, each sporting swastikas, but in between lay jewels of scenery, which lifted her heart. The carriage held twenty others. Twenty strangers. Some spoke, others sat in silence like Ingrid. She didn't mind. This was her first outing since returning to her homeland.

For the journey, Ingrid had worn her nursing uniform. It was a gamble. Someone people may remember, weighted against others who would show support for a critical worker. Together with the outfit, Ingrid clutched a small bag. Asta had given her the large purse as a gift, but delight turned to outrage when she discovered the blade hidden inside. They'd argued briefly before the fear that someone would see quelled the discussion. But Asta remained firm and in the end, Ingrid relented, though with every checkpoint, the object weighed heavily in her hands.

Upon arrival in Hamburg, Ingrid stepped out of the station and looked out onto an unfamiliar landscape. The city was busy, and she felt her resolve slipping, but she had to try. Turning right along, *Glockengießerwall* led her to *Lake Binnenalster*. Here at least was a landmark she could follow, though by the time she'd walked around the edge and then across *Planten un Blomen* park, she felt drained from the morning heat. Here, things would become trickier. She knew she must cross the railway, but beyond there, she would have to ask a stranger for directions. The city centre crowds had thinned, but she still had plenty of people to choose from. Ingrid waited until a young woman appeared across the street. Guessing her age at close to twenty, and pushing a large, unwieldy pram, Ingrid set off to intercept. 'Good morning. Are you all right? You look like you're struggling a little.'

The young woman smiled. 'Thank you. It's kind of you to notice. One wheel sticks, and then I give it a kick. Little Georgi seems to like the bouncing, though.'

Ingrid leant in. 'Oh, he's just gorgeous. How old is he?'

'Just six months. He cries throughout the night, but I can't get cross with him when his teeth hurt. At least I have my mama with me.'

'Perhaps I can help. I think we're going the same way, though I'm a little lost. Can you direct me to *Rappstraße*?'

The woman frowned before returning to a smile. 'Yes, I think I know where that is. It's a few streets away from where we live, but not too far. Come on then, let's walk together.' The girl introduced herself as Lina, and while they walked, Ingrid allowed her to chatter on. She understood. Motherhood had left the woman isolated, and it suited Ingrid to listen rather than give out free information. Fifteen minutes later, they parted company, and Ingrid was alone once more. She knew her task was to meet another spy. One known as Foxglove and she'd given her approach serious thought, but now she stood in the neighbourhood, doubts set in. Ingrid had received instruction from the British, so it seemed fair that Foxglove would expect her arrival, but what if he thought she was with the *Gestapo*, or worse, they'd captured him like the surgeon? At first, the idea of Foxglove's capture seemed absurd, but then she reminded herself that the British remained uncertain. They needed confirmation. Was their man still an active spy?

She waited on the street corner. Although the road ahead lay empty, rows of darkened windows above could hide a multitude of onlookers. The situation did not differ from her first meeting with Asta. A stranger, then pass phrases exchanged and everything worked out. Surely this was just the same?

Familiar taunts circled in her mind. She knew what she had to do, but her legs refused to move. *Come on you, idiot. You can't stay here.* It took two minutes before her sensible brain won out. Standing still looked obvious and unnatural.

Ingrid stepped forward and once she'd located the house she wanted, she approached and knocked on the door. After what seemed like an eternity, the lock rattled and once the door stood open, a dishevelled man peered out. 'Yes?' he asked testily.

The stranger looked too old to be her contact, and Ingrid immediately feared she had the wrong house. She would ask her questions, then return to *Bremen*. 'I'm sorry to disturb you. The hospital asked me to deliver some medicine.' She paused theatrically to consult a scrap of paper before continuing. 'Yes. Here is it. I need to pass this to someone called Robert Kramer. Is that you?' Before she could properly study his reaction, the man summoned her into the building. So far, this wasn't going as Ingrid hoped, but she moved into the home and waited in the hallway. The door closed, darkening the space, and then her heart spiked as the man bolted the door behind her.

'Why are you really here?' he demanded.

The initial welcome evaporated, and Ingrid considered her position. She had to remain calm, but her insides were in a state of turmoil. 'I told you. I'm here to deliver some pills. All I know is the hospital sent me. They said that Mister Kramer has a heart condition. I need to give these tablets to him. Here, I can show you if you'd like.'

'Heart pills? That's odd, it's my stomach which causes the problem.'

Relief flooded across Ingrid as she accepted his correct response. The man smiled and led her towards a kitchen at the rear of the house. She looked out on a small garden behind. The high fence meant privacy.

'I wasn't sure you'd come.'

'I wasn't sure either,' Ingrid replied. 'It isn't easy, you know. What we do. How long have you been here, working for them?' Robert pressed a finger to his lips before unlocking the rear door and leading her outside. She understood and followed.

'Please, take a seat while I make us some tea, and then we can talk.'

Ingrid chose a bench bathed in sunshine and she felt her mood lift. She'd done it again. Success. She'd found the right person and could report the good news back to the British that their agent was operating safely. While she waited, a warm glow of pride settled.

Soon the nostalgic whistle of a kettle coming to the boil sounded and Ingrid tore herself away from her reverie. She looked back through the doorway into the house. Where was Robert? She couldn't see him, so stepped toward the kitchen. As she reached the interior, she heard voices, followed by a click. She only caught one sentence, but the words filled her veins with ice. *She's here.*

Ingrid returned to the bench, where she clutched her bag nervously.

'Here you go, fresh tea. Just as I promised.'

Planting a fake smile, Ingrid grabbed the cup and in one swift moment, she swept her arm in an arc, flinging the hot liquid back towards its maker. The makeshift slingshot hit its mark, and a howl erupted, allowing her to dip her left hand into the bag. Quick as a viper, the man pretending to be Robert leapt forward and grabbed her wrist in an iron grip.

'You bitch.' he hissed.

He was hurting her now, and that galvanised Ingrid. She thought she'd found the right man, but his call to someone else, combined with the searing pain in her wrist, fuelled a single belief. He must work for the *Gestapo* and if so, then others would come. She tugged her arm to break the hold. The action was fruitless, as he clung on even tighter. Ingrid could do nothing except watch her antagonist, and her chance came swiftly. With scalding tea dripping into her attacker's eyes, she watched as his concentration broke. This time, it was her turn to dive to one side. He pulled her backward just as her right hand gripped the purse. Knowing she couldn't open the bag one handed, she opted for her best alternative. Ingrid gouged the metal clasps into his tea-stained eye and, as the howl returned, his grip slackened. Before he could rally any resistance, Ingrid opened the purse and gripped the hilt. The British had trained her how to perform a silent kill, but that was a practice theory and only once before had she stabbed out in anger. This time, her wild slash barely scratched, though now a gaping hole showed through his jacket. She stabbed two more times and her second attempt struck home. Fake Robert grunted before dropping to his knees. Ingrid felt nothing as she pushed him away, and her attacker dropped to the ground. She didn't know whether she'd killed him, only that she had to get away, and quickly.

Stepping away from the prone body, she returned to the kitchen, where she washed his blood from her hands. She'd been lucky. After a brief inspection, her uniform appeared untouched. Ingrid cast her eyes about the room, wondering whether she could learn anything from the man. She heard a groan and her training kicked in. If she'd had the luxury of time, then perhaps she could have questioned him, but no, that held too much risk. It was time to go. She had to leave the city as quickly as possible. If others arrived, then a hunt for a nurse would begin.

Her return journey to Hamburg *Hauptbahnhof* went without incident, though all Ingrid's senses were on full alert. She hadn't checked on the man before leaving. Perhaps she should have, but what then? Killing him in cold blood made her as bad as them. As she inspected the timetable, she feared the worst. Even now, he could have called for help, or a rescuer appear. The more she thought about it, the more she worried. Ingrid considered the evidence. He'd called someone. So, someone would come, and quickly. And that meant trouble for her. Seeing she had half an hour to wait, Ingrid went to buy a ticket for Berlin. She didn't need it, as her return ticket to *Bremen* was valid, but she needed to be seen heading elsewhere. Next, she waited near to the platform for trains to the capital. The wait was torturous. Banks of soldiers occupied most of the space, while select others took on the ominous guise of the *Gestapo*. She knew her uniform singled her out, but with the summer warmth and no opportunity to change, Ingrid had little choice. Her eyes scanned the exits. She'd entered the station for her return journey after passing through a simple security check, but now she felt trapped. Ingrid cursed. Perhaps, like Esslingen years earlier, she should have sought a quieter station. More soldiers entered the station, rendering the idea moot. The clock ticked down, and she wondered if anyone was watching her. *Of course, they're watching you, you idiot.* Ingrid continued to wait. The bustling commuters made counting the soldiers impossible, so in frustration she returned her gaze to the clock. The hands had barely moved, and she turned away in disgust. After waiting near a stairwell, she climbed to an upper level, desperate to gain a vantage point. At last, something of use. She had ten minutes to spare before the Berlin train departed and a further five for her train to *Bremen*. A porter stood with a trolley, laden with luggage and, importantly, a full-length coat, ready to load. The owner had to be close by, but Ingrid didn't care. She needed to alter her appearance. Next, she scoured the platform for some kind of distraction.

With nothing obvious coming to mind, Ingrid opted for the simplest solution. With only a few minutes before departure, she descended the stairs, marched towards the porter, and with a hefty shove of her shoulder, toppled a suitcase to the floor. The porter turned away and, in that moment, she snatched the coat, wrapping it quickly into a tight bundle. Next, Ingrid made a play of apologising and helping secure the fallen luggage before boarding the train for Berlin. She didn't have long, so she rushed to the rear compartments, taking a paused between carriages. In that small gap, few could see her drape the coat across her shoulders. With head down, she silently moved away and boarded the train to *Bremen*.

The next five minutes were excruciating. The porter finally calmed down, only for a passenger to tear into them because of a lost overcoat. More soldiers entered the station. Ingrid watched with head bowed as an officer grabbed a station official. *They're going to find me. It's just a matter of time.*

A whistle blew and the Berlin train pulled away. What she saw next produced a small smile. Someone had apparently informed the officer that a nurse had boarded the Berlin train as he reacted with a wild shout and gesticulation. His men charged down the platform, but it was too late.

The Berlin train had left the station.

Two more minutes until departure. Would they think to halt her train?

Probably, she thought. Her wary eyes monitored the officer, who seemed apoplectic in rage.

By the time her train began its slow movement out of the station, she saw he'd headed for a telephone.

Perhaps he was calling someone senior to explain his failings, or maybe his call went ahead to Berlin. It didn't matter. For the first time that day, Ingrid dared to breathe normally.

101

Two days later, and despite the calming routine of working at St Joseph-Stift hospital, Ingrid was still looking over her shoulder. She cursed her stupidity.

'You weren't stupid,' Asta told her testily while out for their morning walk. 'And anyway, what if you were? It's done now. You had good reasons for hiding in plain sight like that. You weren't about to know the man you met was *Gestapo*.'

Ingrid knew she couldn't have foretold the events in Hamburg. She'd been exceptionally lucky to escape, but she had, and that left a critical task to complete.

'Have you worked out when?'

'No. I need to use the radio soon. We've got to tell the British that Foxglove is dead or captured. I just don't know where is safest. Someone almost caught me the last time I used the hospital.'

'I could transmit the message.'

Ingrid felt her heart swell as she considered the offer. Could she ask her friend to take the risk? The answer came back quickly.

No.

'Thank you, *meine freundin*, but no. It has to be me. Oh, don't look at me like that. You don't know the codes like me, so I have to send the message.'

****

375

'What do you mean, a British agent stabbed one of your men and you let them get away?'

Stefan saw no reason to hold back his vitriol. For the rest of the call, he screamed down the line as outrage at their incompetence fuelled his words. The conversation took twice as long, but he didn't care that they needed to repeat the tale. Stefan didn't even ask about the *Gestapo* stooge's fate. What did it matter to him if the enemy stabbed him in the incident?

People got hurt all the time. What mattered was someone was out there, helping the British, and he did not know where to begin the hunt. But that wasn't the only concern. Soon the British would know, and if Heydrich discovered, then Stefan could easily see himself dangling from a streetlamp by piano wire. He shuddered at the thought, determined to avoid the worst.

102

OCTOBER 1942, LONDON

Marcus Gregson yawned before returning to study the news just in. After rubbing his eyes and blinking repeatedly, he stood and rushed out of the door.

'Damn it, I have to see him.'

The secretary offered a granite stare before politely refusing. Evidently, she'd seen this kind of approach before. With the door ahead sealed and the unhelpful woman barring the way like Cerberus, he chose a seat. Half an hour later, with nails chewed to a shorter length, he finally gained entry.

'It's Foxglove, sir.'

His boss peered over a sheaf of paper and pressed his glasses back upon his nose before Gregson continued. But he knew he had his master's attention. Ten minutes later, they'd accepted the news they'd lost an agent and turned their attention toward damage limitation. When he finally left, Gregson wondered, like his boss, just what state were Theodore and Mallard in? He hated to admit it, but both he and his boss were fearing the worst.

****

Gregson paced the room while he waited. He had other things to do, but he needed answers first.

Twenty-four hours had passed since the initial meeting with his superior triggered the queries, and his frustration that everything was taking so long had already bubbled over. One unlucky secretary entered the office with no news. He'd balled her out, until, reduced to tears, the woman fled. He should have felt guilt, but this was bigger than just one woman.

'Here you are, sir. That should be everything.'

'It had better be,' he replied while accepting an armful of files which he carefully placed upon his desk. The next job took a further four hours, but this wasn't a task he daren't delegate. When he finally finished reviewing, he took a further hour to double check his summary notes. Now he felt certain, but the truth left him dismayed. *How did they miss this?* Taking the pages he needed, Gregson secured the rest and set off to see his boss again.

'Go on then. Tell me the worst.'

Gregson cleared his throat. 'We're certain we've lost Theodore, and we believe Mallard is in the hands of the Nazis.'

'How long?'

'A year and a half. Perhaps longer.'

Gregson jumped as his boss slammed his fist against the wood. 'Eighteen months. What the blazes do you mean, over a year? That's impossible.'

'No, sir, it isn't. If you care to look over the sample transmissions I brought with me, you'll see the repeated use of distress codes. Hector tried to tell us. Three times, but nobody here spotted it.' This time Gregson felt more sure-footed. It wasn't his fault that an analyst had made the errors. Still, he could understand the wrath bubbling from the opposite side of the desk. For a moment, Gregson felt a pang of guilt for laying into the secretary earlier. Would he receive the same treatment?

The expected tempest didn't come. Instead, his superior sighed before reaching across for the data. 'Churchill's going to have our balls in a vice when he hears about this.' Gregson nodded, though remained silent. 'Damn it.' His boss shook his head. 'I hoped you were wrong, but it seems not. Well?'

'Well?' Gregson repeated back.

'Yes. Now we know what happened. What are you planning to do about the situation?'

The inference that this was on him landed, and Gregson cursed. He'd devoted so much time to validating the news that he hadn't considered a response. 'Well, let's look at the good news.' He caught the eye roll but continued. 'The first news is we still have Elsa Keller. She's active and unknown to the Germans. It's because of her we discovered the collapse of our network. Then there is Mallard. He may still be exploitable. After all, he's tried to warn us. We were just too ignorant.'

'Yes, about Mallard. When exactly did we receive his first duress code?'

Gregson scanned his notes. He sent his duress code three times with the first happening in March 1941. He mumbled the answer shamefully. 'And the last?'

'September. Same year.' That made sense. Hector could hardly send the same code over and over. The Germans weren't that stupid. While his boss scowled, Gregson looked for further evidence that Hector remained loyal to the British. On the surface, it looked as though they could count upon the agent. Somehow, and right under the noses of the Nazis, he'd transmitted valuable intelligence. The German shipping losses within the Mediterranean validated that idea. In appearance, it seemed Hector deserved a medal. He couldn't fathom any reason the Germans would let golden intel like that through.

While this was good news, both could see Hector's clock was running out. The likelihood that their *Dresden* spy would ever live to collect an award seemed bleak.

103

OCTOBER 1942, BERLIN / *BERCHTESGADEN*

Starting with Hamburg, Stefan cast his eyes down an enormous list. *How could there be so many nurses within the one city?* He set the pages to one side and looked at the next city along the railway line, Berlin. The witnesses said she'd boarded the train to the capital, but was their information reliable? Even if she had, his target could have easily disappeared at a provincial station along the way. If that had happened, or the nurse persona was fake, they'd never find her. But he had to try. The second pile ran to a dozen pages, with many more entries than Hamburg. With two further listings yet unstudied, his task appeared hopeless. As his eyes flitted across the data, he pondered delegation before discarding the idea. No. Whoever she was, she'd escaped because of other's incompetence, and he wouldn't allow that to happen again.

Four hours later, he'd barely made a dent. With his resolve wavering, he took a break. The coffee tasted too bitter against his palette. Although disgusting, the beverage cleared his senses. Resigning himself to continuing the hunt, there was a brief tap at the door and in walked Christa. Stefan's jaw dropped.

The interruption came just as he appraised the *Bremen* records. Further down the page lay the undiscovered name: *Elsa Keller*.

****

Gerda looked nervously at her hometown, *Berchtesgaden*. The streets remained quiet, but the silence was deceptive. Her town was like any other in Germany, crammed full of conspirators, each ready to sell any indiscretion to the *Gestapo*. Being in the League of German Maidens could only protect her so much. And with a curfew in place, her decision to go was perilous.

She'd waited all week for this opportunity, and now the sun had disappeared for the day. Donning her mother's cloak and with hood up, she stepped quietly away from her home. She hated clandestine behaviour, but it was a necessity and anyway, as the years had rolled on, she hated herself for all the neglect she'd shown. Tonight, she would take the first step toward putting that right.

Moving through the shadows, the usual ten-minute journey downhill took her over twenty. A few times, she had to stop as dogs barked or people moved about the town, but finally she arrived. Upon seeing the familiar house, Gerda's hand flew to her mouth. Even in the poor light, she detected dilapidation. No lights came from within and for the umpteenth time, Gerda questioned her visit. Blackout curtains, she hoped. She gently tapped her knuckle against the doorframe before retreating to the shadows.

Immediately, she felt foolish. What was she thinking, approaching the front of the house? Nothing stirred, though, and Gerda resigned herself to trying the door at the rear. Edging around the house was easy, though the unkempt garden held dangers. A bramble caught her ankle, and she winced as a thorn sliced into her calf. But she remained silent and found the back door. This time she didn't dally. Turning the handle, she pushed forward and stepped through the opening. Gerda's hand shot to her mouth as the pungent smell assailed her nostrils, and she stumbled. She couldn't tell in the dark what she'd collided with, but something hit a flagstone with a resounding crash. Adjusting her stance to prevent a fall, she waited for someone to come. Where was Freda? Had the neighbours heard the noise, and would they come?

Now fear overcame her. Why hadn't she come earlier? Her inner loathing surfaced and driven by her own self-recriminations,

Gerda moved cautiously through the house. Walls felt frozen to her touch as she used the surfaces as a guide within the gloom. *Freda must be upstairs*, she thought. Clutching the banister tightly, Gerda trod on the first step upward. The stairs creaked, but she'd made enough noise already. This time, she called out softly to Freda. No response. However, with each step, the putrid smell intensified. Several strides and four soft calls later, Gerda reached the upper landing, and she knew something was terribly wrong. Deep down, she'd known as soon as she'd entered the property, but her mind had stubbornly refused to admit it. Now, the impossible stench caused her to halt. She wanted to retch, to run away. Instead, she stood, one hand clutching the rail as her body shook. The air reeked of death and Gerda knew within her heart the worst. A tear trickled down one cheek as she wrestled with her emotions. Staying on the landing was torture. She should go downstairs. There, perhaps she could find a candle and return to view the scene properly. An absurd idea. Gerda knew that if she returned to the ground floor, she would flee the building and never return. Her whole body trembled, but she pressed on. Finding a window, she drew back a curtain. The ambient light improved, and she could see a door at the end of the hallway. As though drawn along on a silent conveyor, Gerda moved towards the room. Her breathing became difficult, but she had to know. After shuffling the full-length of the hall, she didn't need to enter the room to know. With insects buzzing around Freda's bedroom and the stench of death overwhelming her, Gerda's stomach could resist no more and she vomited violently across the landing. Freda Stiepermann had departed her world.

****

Stefan didn't get many visitors to his office in *Prinz-Albrecht-Strasse*. He preferred it that way. So, Christa's unexpected arrival threw him completely.

'What are you doing...?' he blustered.

She smiled demurely. He remembered that look, often a precursor to a strike, and his body stiffened.

'Oh, don't be like that,' Christa purred while reaching down to stroke his arm. 'Don't you remember how we used to be?'

He knew exactly what she meant, but while youthful kisses and more had meant something to her, he'd known from the outset where his desires lay. 'That was a long time ago, and we haven't seen each other in years.' Stefan paused. Why was this woman from his past here?

'But it was good. Wasn't it? I remember when you made a woman of me.' She flicked a devilish smile.

Stefan had only ever shared intimacy with two women, Christa and Ingrid. One forced, the other consensual. And he knew which one he'd enjoyed and would do again, should the chance arise. Now, however, he felt uncertain.

'Of course. You made a man of me too,' he lied.

'Good. I thought perhaps tonight we could...'

How had she done this? He was squirming. 'I'm sorry, but as you can see, I'm very busy,' he said, directing his palm to the papers. Christa's eyes flickered, though she said nothing. Her look left him unsettled. 'Why exactly are you here?' He hoped his bluntness would unsettle her.

Christa's face looked smug. 'I'm here with the *Führer*. I came to see you while he's having a meeting with Heydrich. Reinhard is quite charming, you know.'

'Hitler's here?' Stefan's jaw locked in surprise, and it took a few seconds before he could process her statement. He suddenly felt very queasy. 'Of course,' he stammered. 'How is the *Führer*?'

He could see his attempt at deflective small talk wouldn't work, so he changed tack. 'Perhaps these papers can wait. Would you mind if I placed them somewhere safe and then perhaps we could go somewhere more private?'

Christa stepped forward with authority. Before he could protest, she'd shoved him back against his desk, scattering the papers everywhere. The fear that she was close to Hitler forced Stefan to comply.

104

OCTOBER 1942, EGYPT

With a previous career working for a coal merchant, Archie was no stranger to grime, but even he couldn't recall ever feeling this dirty. The others in his platoon looked equally grim. Despite this, he persevered by scrubbing each digit across his calloused hands.

'Don't be daft. You'll only get them pretty fingers grubby again. Here, have a fag instead.'

Archie grinned before waving his friend away. How many times did he need to tell Taff that he couldn't abide cigarettes? Accepting his fingers would remain blackened for a while longer, he stuck one into his ear to stem the ringing noise, which had lasted for well over a month. It did not surprise him when, apart from retrieving a small, waxy residue, there was little improvement. After the weeks of bombardment, the silence was eerie, so Gordon took out his harmonica to lift the mood. Soon, Archie and several others were singing along to 'It's a Long Way to Tipperary', and for a moment, they felt a world away from the horrors of war.

Even the dreaded bully beef tasted better when they sang like this, but they all knew this was merely a shroud to what was to come. While their sergeant shouted orders at an impossible volume, their captain offered a calmer perspective. Often Archie and the others just did as they were told, with little understanding, but today they'd received a speech designed to rally and inspire. Their captain was only recently posted in and a little wet behind the ears. Archie struggled to connect with the man, but today their leader appeared truthful as he outlined their part in the upcoming battle. Archie was too young to understand the horrors of the Great War, but he imagined his predecessors behaving similarly before climbing out of a trench. Some soldiers were frightened, and Archie reckoned the newly minted captain would be too. Archie felt empathy, but chose not to focus on the future. Instead, he kept his strength up by pausing his singing to dip a spoon into the molten stew.

He'd learnt a lot in his time in the desert. Archie understood they had the Mediterranean Sea to the north and a mire of quicksand known as the Qattara Depression to the south, and that these two natural barriers were the reason Rommel hadn't overrun their army. But, if the captain was to be believed, they were in for another tough fight. He remembered the first battle at *El Alamein* and shuddered. Fingers crossed, this one would be an easier fight. Finding a bit of shade, Archie placed his pack down behind his head and closed his eyes. Sleep came quickly, but all too soon, his eyes snapped open at the sound of a deafening artillery barrage. It was growing dark, and as he shook away the cobwebs, he saw the others readying themselves. Immediately, he stood and sought his mine detector.

They had more soldiers, more tanks, more everything. Or so they'd been told. But without a way to pass through the minefields to get to the enemy, such strength was useless. Archie knew he and the others had an important part to play and that day, after the artillery had done its work, he would do his.

105

Ingrid awaited instructions from the British with trepidation. She knew the agent Foxglove was dead or captured, and it seemed likely Theodore and Mallard had met a similar fate. It was a timely reminder that what she was doing was incredibly dangerous. Her escape from the Berlin *Hauptbahnhof* brought chills every time she thought of it. She supposed the *Gestapo* could easily search the region for a nurse fitting her description. But what would she do if the British sent her on another mission to locate the other two spies? Her stomach churned at the idea, although staying in *Bremen* didn't seem wise either.

These were weights she carried daily, despite Asta's attempts at lessening Ingrid's burden. Her guardian was wonderful, but she couldn't fill the void that *Berchtesgaden* and Yiewsley had left in her heart. Folding the sheets in the laundry room, she wiped away her tears on the warm material before straightening her uniform and returning to the ward.

'Are you all right, Elsa? You look like you've been crying.'

The voice came from Mia, one of the other junior nurses, and Ingrid smiled as the girl had always come across as genuine. 'Yes, I'm fine, thank you. I felt a little sad we couldn't save *Herr* Becker. He was a nice man.'

Mia nodded acceptance before passing on down the corridor, leaving Ingrid glad that the woman had accepted her lie without question. Friendships were rare within the hospital. And after she'd almost become close to the surgeon before his capture, Ingrid kept most at arm's length. Mia was an exception. Not exactly a friend, but hardly an enemy, either. The rest of the day went smoothly, though Ingrid could feel the director of nursing's scrutiny at every turn.

Her shift ran on late and by the end of the night, she felt exhausted. She stepped onto the street, unable to stifle an enormous yawn. Great frosty plumes caught in the muted lamplight as she exhaled. At least the chill brought some sharpness to her senses, though she shivered as she began the walk home. She met with the usual soldiers at the checkpoint, but despite the curfew, they all knew one another and she passed without incident. Five minutes later, Ingrid reached home. She heard the bolt slide back and smiled in relief as Asta opened the door. As usual, her friend had done more than required, as Ingrid discovered a plate of cold meat sitting on her bed. She tucked into the platter with relish before drawing the shutters and collapsing into bed.

Outside, alone in the shadows, Mia stared up at Ingrid's window with intense interest.

106

JANUARY 1943, BERLIN

Stefan found his thoughts returning to that night. Christa had called. He hated himself for submitting to her demands. Since then, there had been three conversations between them, though Stefan hoped to end her recent interest. His grumpy mood persisted as he considered how to break free of her control. But with her close to Hitler's circle, he knew any threat directed at her must not leave a trail back to him.

His meandering thoughts led him to wonder whether he could repeat a second leak to the British. The idea appealed. If only he could guarantee they'd act on his intelligence and somehow liquidate the dreadful woman. But with Christa's closeness to the *Führer*, he felt powerless, especially when he worshipped his leader and all the ideals the man stood for. Unless he could silence Christa and her alone, he would not act.

He'd like to use Hector as a disposable patsy to rid himself of her, but with no coherent plan forming, he shelved the daydream. Instead, he continued to split his focus, monitoring the mountain of daily reports while returning to the hunt for the mysterious nurse. Christa's unsettling intervention had spooked Stefan so much that he'd neglected his search for the British spy. Another reason to despise the woman. By the time he'd finally gathered the papers she'd scattered about his office, he'd gained fresh worries. But today he would renew his search with vigour. He'd already reversed his earlier decision. There were too many names to wade through, and every time he requested detailed information about each individual, the pile of papers grew like Jack's proverbial beanstalk. Although he'd experienced failure at the hands of others too many times, he knew how ruthless his *Gestapo* colleagues could be. He would just have to trust the process.

But first, before he could pick sheafs of nursing profiles to delegate to others, he had his tiresome daily tasks to perform. Others who looked on at such data did so with selfless interest towards the Nazi war machine. Their country, its ideals and survival were paramount. Not Stefan. His ideals were entirely self-centred. If the news wasn't about Peter, Christa, his father, or a small clutch of others, then he lacked the empathy to care. Even Hitler's decrees failed to make an impact. His superiors were wasting his talents and with the bile he reserved for the Jews shackled, the emotion turned towards others around him.

Taking care not to jumble up the masses of paperwork, he returned to the daily bulletins when one caught his eye. Stefan snatched up the report with a mixture of excitement and elation. He'd already heard the British had been victorious at El Alamein. Such losses were inevitable, and he knew his leak had probably tipped the balance, but here was news, which made it all seem worthwhile. The list ran longer than his inventory of nurses, but one name stood out. *Obertleutnant* Helmut Weiss – MISSING IN ACTION.

At last, Stefan thought. *I'm free of him.*

****

Christa's thoughts bounced from anger to sorrow before returning to anger again, as they had for several days. There, in anger, the mood stayed. Earlier that evening, she'd re-read a letter dated February 1940 from Stefan's father, Helmut Weiss. When she'd first read the words, almost three years earlier, she'd baulked at the loathsome ideas he presented. And for years she'd pushed the idea of Stefan's immorality to the darkest reaches of her mind. Her disgust toward Helmut had not wavered until recently. With the war raging, Christa had settled into her work and almost forgot. But while Stefan had left *Berchtesgaden*, she had returned, and memories of him and their brief time together were everywhere. And then, a dream transfer to Hitler's *Obersalzberg* beckoned. Despite the proximity to Hitler and his inner circle, Christa found the plum posting an ideal antidote to Stefan's intrusive memories. Until one day, when she heard of the *Führer's* intention to visit Heydrich in Berlin.

Her meeting with Stefan three months earlier had lacked any spark, though she'd refused to admit it. *She was beautiful. Wasn't she? That was why she'd got the job at the Obersalzberg. She was the epitome of a young German woman. Why didn't Stefan want her then?*

Deep down, she knew, but admitting it meant acknowledging the contents of Helmut's letter. Bitterness filled her. She accepted her own stupidity for holding out so long for passion, which would never come. Walter left her unsatisfied, although she supposed they had produced a beautiful child for the Reich.

The direction of her thoughts altered as she reminded herself that she was not the one at fault. Stefan was the deviant. Christa considered the dilemma. The *Führer* valued Heydrich, and, by extension, Stefan Weiss. And while she'd secured a visit to Berlin to see her former lover, Christa lacked enough influence to damage Stefan directly. That meant she would target Stefan's lover, Peter Klein. She knew from Helmut's letter that he'd transferred the abomination to Krakow years earlier. Christa had no way of knowing whether their relationship had died, but she knew she must try to remove Peter Klein from existence. Even the thought of his demise eased her personal pain.

A week earlier, she'd typed up a letter requesting a status report on the man. The military wheels turned slowly, and she used the delay to scour military reports for a suitable hellish place to send Stefan's lover. She settled on the Donets Campaign. Now, if she could just locate Peter Klein, she felt sure she could organise a transfer, sending him into some of the worst fighting on the Eastern front. There was more work to do, but a smile of satisfaction crept across Christa's face.

107

Hector was no fool. He knew his time was running out. The problem was, he couldn't fathom what to do about it. On the surface, his work at the university, along with intense nights spent with *Frau* Umer, suggested no end to his situation. But Stefan's behaviour worried him. And, despite the German's best attempts to hide the truth, Hector still guessed that things weren't going well within the mighty German war machine. The authorities didn't share the truth, of course. Not with him, or even the German public, whose blinkered lives were driven through government propaganda. The clock chimed, reminding Hector of his appointment. He wanted to turn and run, but without papers and on every *Gestapo* watch list, he knew he'd be lucky to make it out of the city. That left compliance, and with it, a bitter taste. He shook his head and tried to refocus. All he could do was watch and hope an opportunity would come his way.

****

'You don't have to go, you know. It's too dangerous.'

Ingrid agreed with Asta's assessment of the situation, but what choice did she have? The British knew about Foxglove, but doubts persisted with Theodore and Mallard. And her paymasters demanded answers.

Before Ingrid had returned to Germany, she'd reconciled her plans. She couldn't return to *Berchtesgaden* and offer a permanent sanctuary to her family if they remained in the village. No, that plan was impossible while the Nazis remained in power. And that meant she had to supply these answers to her British counterparts. She touched Asta's arm and offered a comforting smile. 'You know my time here is ending. I can never thank you enough, but I have to follow this task. And anyway, staying here is no less dangerous, particularly if the *Gestapo* are still looking for a nurse in the region. By staying here, I could bring them to your doorstep.' Ingrid pulled her hands away as tears welled. Through the blur, she could see Asta's struggles mirrored her own.

When they finally returned to the apartment, Asta looked doleful before entering the building alone, while Ingrid continued along her walk. She returned an hour later to gather her things. Asta had washed her face, but the sallow lines across her face remained. The woman assisted Ingrid's packing but remained silent. And when the time to leave came, Asta stepped away to leave Ingrid on the threshold alone. She'd left her nurse's uniform behind. Onward, Elsa Keller would vanish and Ingrid would start again under a new moniker.

There would be questions starting with the hospital, of course. And likely the authorities may throw Asta under a microscope, but she couldn't fight that battle. One thing was critical. Asta did not know where Ingrid's destination was. If pressed, her friend would probably think she'd gone to Berlin, but her goal lay further afield. Bottling her regret, Ingrid pulled her two cases to the front door. Placing down the suitcase radio, she turned the handle and stepped outside.

The walk towards *Bremen Hauptbahnhof* took around twenty painful minutes. She'd lived in the city for fifteen months. Enough time for people to get to know her. The British had trained her in evasion, but today, all that knowledge meant nothing if she ran into the wrong person. So far, she'd been lucky, but as she turned along *Bahnhofplatz*, her heart sank. There were too many soldiers loitering near to the station entrance. It seemed too big a risk, so she continued on toward the *Weser*.

Just as she loved the mountains back in *Berchtesgaden*, the Weser was another place close to her heart. Maybe that was because of Asta. There would be no more walks beside the gentle flow of the river. Ingrid rested on a rail, her emotions threatening to overcome her. She needed time, somewhere quiet where she could wait, before approaching the station in the hope the soldiers had moved on. Ingrid knew that may not happen, and she'd have a stark choice. Return to the apartment and resume her nursing, or pray they let her through. She let her eyes take in the view, in a desperate ploy to be elsewhere. Somewhere safe.

'Elsa. It's a lovely afternoon. Is this where you usually come when you have a day off?'

Ingrid's body snapped taut. As her head turned to answer the speaker, her eyes went wide.

'Oh, hello, Mia. Yes, despite the sludgy colour, I like to come down to the river sometimes. What are you doing here?'

Her friend looked about to answer when Ingrid saw the girl falter. 'Why are you here with suitcases?'

Ingrid's heart sank, as she had no answer.

****

A lump lodged itself within Ingrid's throat as she struggled for an answer, while Mia looked on with a peculiar expression.

'Sorry,' Ingrid said finally. 'I'm delivering the cases. Do you know Asta who runs my apartment building? She has a new tenant coming in and she asked me to go to the station and collect their luggage. I don't know when they're due, or why they couldn't carry their own bags, but Asta does so much for me I could hardly say no.' Ingrid immediately saw the flaw in her statement, they were by the river not *Bürgerpark*, so she rushed on. 'As today is my day off, I wanted to come down to the river and relax. Otherwise, I'd be stuck in my room, when what I really wanted was some air.

So, here I am. I'll take the bags over to Asta soon. What about you? What brings you down here today?'

'I'm like you. I like to come down and watch the water passing by. After the chaos of the hospital, I like the calm.'

Ingrid doubted her words. She often came to this spot, and she'd never seen Mia anywhere along the bank. So why was the other nurse here, today of all days? Given Ingrid had only arrived a few minutes earlier, she wondered whether Mia had seen her walk down to the Weser. *She must have been watching me.* The thought left Ingrid unsettled. She leant against the rail, outwardly calm, but her mind racing. She wanted to leave. Either go back to the station or to the apartment. Anywhere really, as she sought to avoid Mia's stare. *She doesn't believe my story.*

Was this uncomfortable for Mia, too? The girl was always friendly and even today her nursing colleague showed no outward threat, but...*No. Come on, Ingrid. You're being ridiculous.*

Mia rested on the railing beside her. 'Do you mind if I wait with you a while?'

'Of course, it's nice to have your company,' Ingrid lied.

Having the junior nurse stay was a burden Ingrid could do without, however the girl's attention shifted to the river and before long the pair were giggling as some ducklings swam in circles while their mother tried to keep the brood together. After twenty minutes had passed, Ingrid felt she'd given Mia enough attention, and it was time to leave.

After bidding goodbye, she set off, certain Mia's eyes were burning into her back. A few streets later, she neared the station. This time, there were fewer soldiers guarding the entrance, but Ingrid kept straight on. The lure towards the railway was strong, but if Mia was watching, then she had to stick to her story and head back to the apartment. She knew one person who'd be happy to see her, at least.

And she was right. Asta let out a little scream of delight upon Ingrid's return, though inside, Ingrid remained frustrated. This was a setback and once she'd lured Mia out of the way, or uncovered the young nurse's motives, then Ingrid could move away from *Bremen* for good.

****

It had taken Stefan several weeks to come to this point, too long, but finally, he had some information he could act on. Some delays were down to Christa's interference, while another setback came when the *Gestapo* stooge bled out before he could properly brief them on his attacker. But he'd persisted. His team had questioned a hundred or more commuters from Hamburg station and the surrounding area, and over time, a pattern emerged. If the intel was correct, then the nurse who'd fled aboard a train to Berlin had done so merely as a lure. He smiled, approving of her misdirection.

And, once they'd made that leap, their attention shifted to where she'd arrived *from* and whether she would return to the same location. He couldn't be certain she would return home, of course, or even that the spy was a nurse at all. But now Stefan was confident she'd travelled in from *Bremen*. And that was where he would focus his attention next.

Stefan had four days before he needed to check on Hector in *Dresden*. Enough time to begin the witch hunt. He considered announcing a visit to the *Bremen* office before deciding against it. No. He wanted to see firsthand, without warning, whether his *Gestapo* colleagues in the west were up to the task. With that decision made, he placed a call to find out the next train's departure time. He fully intended to be onboard.

****

Asta swept Ingrid into a tearful hug when she returned to the apartment. Her friend's genuine surprise and joy both gladdened and dismayed, as Ingrid knew her reprise would not last long. She had a creeping suspicion that Mia was watching the apartment. If only she knew why. She also didn't know whether she could talk freely within the building, so, after safely stowing the radio in their hideaway, the pair stepped out into the sunshine.

Ingrid scanned the area before setting off, her mind a jumble of thoughts. Today was her day off, and her preferred day to depart the city. Otherwise, leaving after a nursing shift could lead to further complications. She could feign sickness, of course. Yes, that was it. Mia was bound to be working on the ward tomorrow, and if Asta passed a message to the director of nursing, then Ingrid could slip quietly away. At first, the plan appeared flawless, but then doubts crept in. She'd leave Asta right in the firing line as soon as they discovered Ingrid wasn't bedridden.

She voiced her concerns to Asta, and they agreed on a compromise. Ingrid would write a letter to say she was unwell and Asta would provide a clandestine delivery. Then, if asked, the older woman would deny any knowledge of Ingrid's departure. The move still left her friend in danger, but at least Ingrid had armed her with plausible answers.

****

Four hours later, with Ingrid resting before her early start the following day, Stefan stepped off the train in *Bremen*.

108

February 1943, *Bremen*

Early the next morning, Asta woke Ingrid with good news. 'You're certain you saw her?' Ingrid asked.

Asta nodded. 'I made sure the director of nursing was busy before slipping into her office and leaving the note. Then, just as I snuck out, I saw that Mia woman. Just as you described. She's tied up with her duties for a while yet. So, if you're going to leave, you'd best do it now.'

The lump in Ingrid's throat returned. Their parting today seemed so much harder, and she questioned whether she should remain in *Bremen*. What did it matter if she upset the British by ignoring their orders?

'You were right, you know,' Asta admitted. Ingrid's brow furrowed, but her friend continued. 'Yesterday, after you'd left. I cried until my eyes were raw, then I took myself off to bed. That's where I thought everything through.' She nodded in understanding. 'Go. Everything you told me about why you're leaving makes sense. It's too dangerous for you to remain.'

Ingrid swallowed, and then after a brief hug, she stepped through the door and onto the street. She chose not to look back, focussing instead on the journey ahead. First, she adjusted her gait to allow for the heavier case containing the radio. She would never overcome her fear of exposure. All she could do was control her response to those fears. And today it would take every ounce of courage.

Despite knowing that Mia was being kept busy at the hospital, Ingrid felt eyes upon her at every turn. She dipped her gaze to focus on the road ahead, before catching herself. *Stand tall, don't be furtive.* She straightened up and strode forward with purpose. Better. She was close to the station now. Just one more turn. She almost managed a smile. And then, as she reached the turning, she saw him, and her world imploded. An agonising pain erupted through her belly. Ingrid clutched the brickwork to steady herself before chancing a second look. She choked back the bile rising in her throat. Stefan, here in *Bremen*. How? Her breath tightened in her chest as she backed away, her eyes locked on her nemesis until she'd rounded the corner and drawn herself out of sight. All composure evaporated as Ingrid considered her next move. Her leaden feet refused her simple command to move. So, she did the only thing she could. She waited, pressed tight against the wall as though the structure would somehow camouflage her from her enemy.

There was a tight band of pressure across Ingrid's forehead, and she rested her head against the bricks. She was unaware of how much time had passed since she'd caught sight of Stefan, or even where he'd gone. Perhaps this was an evil twist of fate life had thrown. Was he standing mere meters away, ready for her to walk straight into him? Ready to snare her in a trap she'd never break free from? She looked down at both hands. They were shaking, but if she gripped both cases tightly, the tremors lessened. She was terrified, but she leant forward until she could see around the corner.

Nothing. Just the normal passing of pedestrian life. She waited. Her breathing still came in rasps, but there was nothing she could do about the tightness in her chest. She had to decide. Stay or flee? Asta's words from earlier lifted Ingrid into action. Stay, and Stefan would eventually arrive on Asta's doorstep. Ingrid could not bear the thought of her friend's capture at his hands.

With a supreme effort, Ingrid took a deep breath and stepped away from the safety of the wall. She struck an assured walk towards the station entrance. Stefan could leap out at any moment, but she filled her mind with a calm resignation. If that was her fate, then so be it.

By the time she reached the guard checkpoint, a fresh fear surfaced. She'd lived her the first part of her life as Ingrid Stiepermann. Then the British changed her surname to Stephens to help her integrate. Next, she'd turned against the Nazis to spy under the guise of Elsa Keller. And now, in order to comply with the British once more, she would have to assume yet another identity. As soon as she passed her papers to the guard blocking the entrance, she would be Mila Koch, a seamstress originating from Cologne.

Taking a deep breath, she stepped forward to discover her fate.

****

Stefan felt vindicated when he arrived at *Gestapo* headquarters in *Bremen*. The first soldier he met appeared slouched against the doorframe in an awful lack of professionalism. He barked an order and the man almost collapsed in surprise as Stefan swept past. For the next hour, after identifying himself, he talked to the senior staff before returning to the station. He and four others would visit the hospital soon, but first he wanted to familiarise himself with the area. The usual questions persisted. Was the mystery nurse in *Bremen*? If so, where did she live?

Unfortunately, the guards allocated to audit every passenger seemed inadequate, and Stefan made a mental note. It was no wonder British spies could operate with impunity. There would be consequences for this lax behaviour.

His new colleagues leading the way, the group moved into the hospital. They entered the building straight into a medical maelstrom. Doctors, nurses, and even some patients were rushing about, and none showed any desire to stop and talk. Stefan held his composure with difficulty. He wanted to scream until everyone in the corridor stopped and bade him attention, but the herd was too great, and he bit back his temper. He glanced at the *Gestapo* officers, though they seemed next to useless, entirely at a loss as to their next move. With no idea where to go, Stefan stormed down the corridor, determined to find someone in charge.

It took him almost fifteen minutes, and it was only through luck that one of his officers recognised the director of nursing. The woman protested, claiming she they needed her elsewhere, until one of Stefan's men grabbed her by the arm. With a nod of his head, his officer squeezed harder, and the director of nursing cried out in pain. Forcing themselves into the woman's office, Stefan's rage bubbled over, and he shouted at the woman to sit.

'Now,' Stefan said, taking up residence behind the nurse's desk, 'perhaps you can offer me some courtesy, or should I instruct my men to take you somewhere more private?'

There was a flicker of fear behind the woman's eyes. *Good.* 'We believe one of your nurses is a spy,' he continued. 'I require a list of all the nursing staff who have worked here over the last two years.'

'Of course' – the woman swallowed – 'naturally, I will help, but you must understand it will take me a day to get this information. There are others here I will need to consult with.'

Stefan consulted his watch. 'You have one hour. We will wait here. I expect refreshments to be served to my men. And if you do not bring me the information I require, you will come with us for further questioning.'

The woman's jaw dropped, and as she bolted out of the door, Stefan wondered if she would return in time. With all the others present, the office felt cramped, so he instructed the four to seek any records they could find while he remained alone. He doubted the answers lay within the director of nursing's office, but he would use the time to ransack the woman's files all the same.

Fifty minutes later, the director of nursing returned. She was out of breath and puffing, but her face turned ashen as she took in the papers strewn across the floor. 'Here,' she said. 'It's everything we have.' She passed several files across to him.

'And the refreshments?' *So much for a woman of authority*, he thought as she faltered under his stern gaze. 'Make sure you return with more than just tea. You've kept me waiting long enough. And then, I want you to bring me all your nurses. I will interview everyone.'

It didn't take Stefan long to realise the director of nursing's office was too small for his needs. His patience snapped, and he boomed to the first nurse waiting in line. 'Get the director of nursing back.'

Two minutes later, the director of nursing reappeared. 'Well? What do you want? I've done everything you asked.'

Stefan looked down his nose at the woman. While he admired her spirit, he would not tolerate insolence. He splayed his palms before continuing. 'As you can see, we lack the room to conduct our investigation.'

'That's hardly our fault.'

'True, but it means we must make alternative arrangements. I am sure it will hearten you to hear that I am leaving with my men, however I must insist I take you and all your nurses with me for interrogation.'

The director of nursing's jaw dropped. 'You can't do that. We're in a hospital. We have patients. People will die if we get up and leave.'

Stefan's eyes gleamed. What were a few more deaths, as long as he found the truth he desired? He paused as he considered telling her to hurry, as any deaths would be upon her. But then he relented. 'Of course. I am not a monster. Separate the staff into two groups. We will take half your staff with us now, leaving the rest to cover. That should suffice. And then we'll return later.' He checked his watch. 'In, say, six hours, when everyone will swap over. Unless, of course, any staff reveal guilt at helping the enemy.' Delight spread across his face as the senior nurse opened her mouth, then shut it, admitting defeat. 'Now, which nurses will you choose, and would you like to accompany the initial batch?'

'We're not cattle.'

Stefan shrugged. To him, they were.

In the end, he'd divided the nursing staff alphabetically, which left the director of nursing to follow later. Outside, rain had fallen, but Stefan used his men to corral the nursing staff into an orderly line before setting off along the walk to *Gestapo* headquarters. They had close to a mile to cover, and most would arrive wet and cold. Stefan found the heavy raindrops invigorating. He didn't care for the hospital workers' comfort. Perhaps after their soggy escapade, tongues would loosen as they hoped to return to the warmth and safety of the hospital.

When they arrived, most were shivering, and with around forty women to interview, Stefan realised even the *Gestapo* offices would struggle to accommodate so many people. His men ushered the sodden women inside before leading them into a corridor to wait.

'Wait here until you are called,' he commanded before gesturing to the first shrivelled figure to accompany him through to the office beyond a typing pool.

By the time he'd interviewed five, he felt he was getting nowhere, and yet he couldn't countenance failure, or trust others to complete this task, so he persevered. 'What is your name?' he asked the latest girl.

'Mia. Mia Becker,' she replied meekly.

As he continued through his questions, he kept a keen eye on her movement. The girl kept biting down on her thumbnail. Was she hiding something? He thought they all held secrets, and that fuelled his desire to dig deeper. 'Have you ever travelled to Hamburg by train?'

A twitch. 'No. Never.'

'You don't sound certain. I'll ask you again.' The resulting squeak further convinced Stefan of her guilt. 'What is it you're hiding? He demanded. This time, before she could answer, he reached across the desk and twisted her arm.

'Stop. Please. You're hurting me.'

'Then tell me. When did you travel to Hamburg?'

'I didn't. It wasn't me.'

'Who then?'

The young nurse wept as he gripped her wrist even tighter. Seeing her waver, Stefan reached over with his other hand, and grabbed a fountain pen off its blotter. His thumb flicked the lid off, and in a swift movement, he speared the nib into the nurse's palm. The girl screamed, her face turning white. Stefan stood up, pressing down hard. The pen had sunk deep into her skin and blood mingled with ink. As the girl looked to pass out, he reduced the pressure on her hand.

'Elsa. Elsa Keller.' The nurse gasped, wrapping a handkerchief around her bloodied hand. 'She travelled. I followed her to the station and I'm sure she travelled, like you said.'

Stefan's ears pricked up. 'Who is she? When was this?'

The nurse was dissolving into tears. A multitude of questions peppered Stefan's mind, but he saw the girl was weak. He marched to the door, flung it open, and ordered the *Gestapo* lackeys to locate this mystery woman's file. *She must be the one.*

He returned to his seat, fierce eyes on the cowering girl. 'My officers are finding the staff record. While we wait, I want you to tell me everything you know about your friend who travelled to Hamburg.'

Thirty minutes later, Stefan placed the staff record to one side. His mind was reeling. *How?* He'd questioned the young nurse and then, once the paper records had arrived, he'd allowed the sobbing woman to leave. Already an uneasy picture was forming, but as he scanned the documents before him, there was no denying it. Ten years had passed since he'd detained Gerhard Stiepermann, while Ingrid and her loathsome brother had evaded capture. *The Stiepermann Jew, a British spy.* He stared at the evidence in utter disbelief.

****

'She's worked here for fifteen months. You had the woman in for questioning, you stupid fucks. How could you let her go?' Stefan's tirade continued for several minutes, but none of the *Bremen Gestapo* could offer mitigation.

It was his third day in *Bremen*. Another day with little sleep. He was supposed to return to *Dresden* for his regular meeting with Hector, but these latest revelations had taken precedence. Someone else would need to deal with the British spy. He returned to the unearthed puzzle pieces, wondering how he could scratch the itch that Ingrid's involvement caused. Nobody knew how Ingrid had re-entered the country, though Stefan had an idea. He remembered whispers of an agent, coming in through Denmark, before the scent went cold. It mattered not, but he'd loved to have caught her at the border crossing all those months ago. He wrestled with the simple question: where was she now? Again, he had no answer, and that she'd slipped through his grasp tormented him. He had to find her.

After pausing for a drink, Stefan decided two people must have the answers, Mia, the young nurse, and a woman named Asta who'd sheltered Ingrid during her time in *Bremen*. One phone call later, he allowed his eyes to close. Soon the pair would be within the building, and neither would leave until they'd given him all the information he required.

****

Ingrid was reliving similar memories. A decade earlier, she'd slept outside near Esslingen with poor Dieter as they fled from the Nazis, and here she was again, doing the same. Only this time, she was alone and with no intention of leaving the country. Although fraught with danger, taking a circuitous route via Hanover, Kassel, and *Leipzig* seemed her best option. At last, *Dresden* appeared within her reach.

Each night, she'd risked everything by seeking deserted buildings for shelter. On her first night, she was lucky. She wasn't sure whether bombs caused the damage to her shelter, but it was empty of others and had half a ceiling at least. It was bitterly cold, and Ingrid had little to nourish her. The hope that the British and other allies would prevail gave her resolve, paired with the deepest desire that one day she would reunite with her parents. How she yearned for her parents and *Ōma*. For now, she could only see one way to weather the current storm. Find Mallard and use his network for some respite. Even that seemed a fool's errand. The first British agent, Foxglove, was dead. It seemed likely that the

British had lost the others, too. During her second overnight layover, she had plenty of time to think through all the information the British had provided. It wasn't much. Like Hamburg, they'd given her an address. They'd also described Mallard, and she was aware of his connection to *Dresden* university. She hoped it would be enough.

As she walked to the next station, the usual fears pecked and assaulted her. Seeing Stefan again had opened old wounds. Walking through stations on previous occasions, even on the rare occasion when forced to carry the radio, she'd done so with enough confidence to see her through. Now, she had only doubts. Ingrid knew she'd been lucky thus far. Three times German officers had offered to carry a case and each time she'd feigned that the one containing clothing was the heavier, but such luck could not hold. At the last station, the guards behaved differently toward her. Ingrid's dishevelled appearance paired with a musty smell saw to that. Vagrants were an automatic target for many and she was sliding too quickly toward that state. If Hector couldn't offer a haven, then she didn't know what she would do.

First, she had the hurdle of accommodation within *Leipzig* to overcome. Another strange city, and another late afternoon arrival. Her bones ached as she stepped off the train and pulled her cases along the platform. Already the air felt chilly and, knowing the station would feel warmer than the streets outside, fuelled Ingrid's discomfort. She wanted to stop. Give up. Abandon the radio and walk away to find a new and safer world. But seeing the usual guards around the entrance and perimeter meant such dreams were foolish. Instead, she straightened her hair and rubbed her hands for warmth before continuing on. That night was the coldest of her life. Alone in a damp and desolate cellar, she wrapped her arms around her shoulders, but her teeth chattered and she lost feeling in her fingers. Sleep refused to come and by the morning, she faced an uncomfortable truth. She was too tired to carry both suitcases up the steps to ground level.

Once she'd stepped out into the grey morning, Ingrid's mood improved without the burden of the radio. Suddenly, she could move freely without risk of discovery. She'd stowed the radio safely in the deserted cellar. Knowing she could return to *Leipzig* at any time and collect the radio lifted a weight from her shoulders. The sun had barely risen and a fine drizzle dampened the quiet streets, but Ingrid gazed at the city in a new light. She had time, and for once she failed to see enquiring eyes as she lugged two suitcases along the street. Thirty minutes later, she ran numb fingers across her mouth as the aroma of baking reached her nostrils. Discovering a *konditorei* returned her to childhood, and she took a moment to lean against a wall before venturing in.

A warming pastry later, her mood had lifted, and she set off to find a train to *Dresden*. For once, she believed everything was going to be OK.

109

MARCH 1943, *DRESDEN*

Hector lay back on *Frau* Umer's bed. A sheen of sweat coated his skin, and he dipped his mouth to kiss his partner's shoulder. He wanted to take a shower before returning home, instead he held the woman close. It was part of his act. She took everything he gave, but he held little desire towards her. His motive was simple. Hector didn't believe she held any affiliation with the *Gestapo*, so his time with the woman was purely a release from their scrutiny.

He caressed her warm body for a few more minutes, then swung his legs out of bed. 'I have to go.'

'You work too hard.' She pouted. 'Can't you stay longer?'

He could, but he made his excuses and left. Outside, the icy chill clung to the sweat on his neck, and he shivered. With hands plunged deep into his pockets, he strode on, scanning the street as usual. One figure had a familiar stance. *Gestapo*. Seeing the watcher, he deliberately changed direction to see the man head on, and he chuckled as his tail turned away. This happened frequently, though by heading home, Hector hoped they would leave him alone. After all, they knew where he lived. His counter surveillance continued and for a while he was alone, but as he approached his street, he sensed a new pair of eyes. A woman was watching the road. She wasn't walking, or even pretending to read something, so her stagnant pose raised a flag. With barely a change of stride, he switched left down a side street. The woman was probably innocent and certainly not interested in him, but she'd piqued Hector's interest.

After checking his surroundings and seeing his street deserted, he stole a glance around the corner. He took his time studying her. The woman was tapping her feet against the pavement – understandable in these temperatures, but it could easily be a demonstration of anxiety. Hector felt secure in his position. She hadn't looked toward him and even if she did, he could easily duck out of sight. With this advantage, he took his time to pick apart her appearance. Thin, but this was wartime and food was scarce. Haggard, again, expected. All he had were his instincts, and this woman was definitely waiting and watching. But for who?

As the cold penetrated his exposed skin, a part of him considered walking past and continuing on home. So what if she was there to spy on him? He would merely keep to his routine. Go home, shower, and meet with Stefan for his weekly briefing. His training kicked in. He always behaved within the *Gestapo* boundaries. His life depended upon it. But here was a newcomer, acting strangely. And Hector had to know.

Within a few minutes, he'd figured out an alternate route to approach his home. His adrenalin surged at the prospect of the hunt. He wasn't sure whether he was the hunter or the hunted, but for the first time in months, he felt alive. Before his key had turned in the lock, he'd seen her and his instincts appeared correct. She wasn't just watching: she was watching him. And he felt certain she saw him now. He turned his head away. Knowing her interest focused on him only fuelled his intent. If she was working for the *Gestapo*, then he would simply confront the woman. If not, then he needed an explanation.

Behind his flat lay a connecting alley and within seconds he'd exited the building and was sprinting flat out. He skidded around the corner and sped on. Hector's eyes focussed on one thing. He would fly up to the woman and question her directly, giving her no time to react. He rounded the last corner. The woman was gone. *Damn*, he cursed inwardly, before realising what had happened. She'd only gone to knock on his door. With the element of surprise diminished, he jogged towards the apartment before coming up behind her. Up close, he caught a musty smell, and his brow furrowed at her shabby appearance. She hadn't seen his approach, and that suited Hector. Out on the street a scene helped nobody, but here, on his doorstep, with his front door unlocked, he held the upper hand. He coughed, and she spun. Her eyes were wide, but before she could react, he surged forward and knocked her inside, before kicking the door shut.

'Who are you?'

Head bowed, she remained silent. Hector made a snap decision. His instincts said this woman wasn't *Gestapo*. He wasn't about to share information about himself willingly, but she had answers. He raised a hand, ready to land a strike he hoped he wouldn't need.

'Stop,' she cowered. 'Your name is Mallard. Isn't it?'

Her words threw up more questions than answers, but he lowered his arm.

'Who are you?'

'You don't know me, so my name isn't important. But I know both you and I are in danger.'

He didn't doubt that, but before she could continue, he reminded himself that the *Gestapo* could easily listen in. Hector couldn't trust the stranger. Not yet, at least. But as his heart rate settled, he realised this wasn't the place for introductions. Hector stepped away and beckoned for her to follow. She had a slight build, so he was confident he held the upper hand. Just a few minutes after he'd sprinted along the alley, he found himself back outside. This time, he had a stranger in tow.

Hector looked left and right before turning to face the newcomer. In a lightning move, the girl grabbed his wrist and twisted. Hector felt a jolt of pain, and then his body somersaulted before the joint could snap. The paving had no give and the hard landing emptied his lungs. *What? How did she do that?*

'I'm sorry,' the woman apologised. 'I can't give you my name, but if you'll listen, then maybe we can be friends.'

411

Hector could feel a lump forming across the back of his skull. But after the way she'd laid him out, he listened, even if her offer of friendship seemed ludicrous.

****

After sharing more knowledge, Hector saw his fears allayed. Ingrid knew his code name was Mallard, but that proved nothing. Then slowly she'd convinced him with other seeds of knowledge which could only have come from England.

'You can't stay here,' he said to her. 'You know that. They're watching.'

'I know I can't. But now I've found you, I don't know what to do. I've got to tell the British you're alive and, of course, the Nazis killed Theodore like they murdered Foxglove. After that I don't know.'

'But you said you don't have a radio anymore. Or were you lying about that?'

The woman's face flushed. 'I have a radio – *had* a radio. It's hidden. Before I came to *Dresden*. I can go back for it, but I'll have to be careful.'

Hector doubted her claims. If someone stumbled across her equipment, they would lie in wait for her return. It would be impossible to get close. They'd chatted for almost an hour and Hector knew he'd need to forego his shower prior to his meeting with Stefan. He considered his options. Everything seesawed between survival and his original mission to help the British. He hadn't shared his destination and he couldn't, but time was running out for him to decide. The time had come to choose a side. Continue to help the Germans and hope to live, or help the stranger who'd landed on his doorstep and hope this shortened the war for the allies.

****

When Hector left, Ingrid felt a mixture of terror and elation. She'd found him, she was sure of it. The description fitted, as did his answers. They'd lost Theodore, yet somehow Hector was thriving as a British agent. She marvelled at the ingenuity he'd shown to operate under their noses. Although she'd only left *Bremen* and her haven under Asta's wing a few days earlier, it felt as though her world had descended into anarchy. She didn't like to admit it, but she'd struggled during the journey. Evading the crowds empathised her sense of isolation, while blending in with the greater population teased her paranoia to greater heights.

Wary that someone could listen, Ingrid crept, cat like, around the flat. Hector said she could eat, and she took full advantage. Only when she'd eaten the bread did she hold a guilty pause. Refuelled, she hid within the shadows to spy on the street outside. The exit to the alley behind lay close by, but Ingrid was no fool. If they came for her, then there would be no escape. As she leant against the soft fabric of the curtains, her eyelids dropped and seconds later she'd fallen into a deep sleep.

****

Three hours later, Hector returned to his apartment. As expected, the interior was dark, a direct reflection of his mood. Stefan hadn't appeared for the briefing, and no explanation had been forthcoming. They wouldn't tell him, he knew that, but Hector took this as a sign all the same. He knew he could have outed the new British spy to gain kudos with his oppressors, but if their leader wasn't there, then that was on them, not him. Instead, he'd behaved as normal. Under their supervision, he'd transmitted the usual run-of-the-mill intel to the British. Believable snippets intermingled with subversion. He hated this. Losing Allied lives because of the information he sent. Did that make him a coward, a turncoat, or a survivor? He lit a lamp and looked about. There she was, slumped in the bay window. He cringed, knowing that anyone who came to the door would surely see her, though at the same time he felt a wave of compassion for the young woman. Hector was tired, so if her story was true, then her exhaustion must match his tenfold. He drew the curtain before draping a blanket across the woman's shoulders. Then, reluctant to leave her alone, he fetched a second blanket and settled on the couch.

One night. That's all he could allow. Then he would have to move her on. But still the nag persisted as he questioned his loyalties. After a few hours of self-recrimination, he moved his attention to another topic. He'd accepted she could stay, and he would help the woman. But not here. The British sergeant who'd trained him years ago had often said, *you don't shit on your own doorstep*. That left only two choices, and neither were palatable. Hide her within the university buildings, or, perhaps worse, convince *Frau* Umer to hide her. The second idea seemed ludicrous, and yet the more he picked each option apart, this seemed the better. The academic buildings offered uncertainty. Hector couldn't stay there all the hours and when he stepped away, what would she do? To the tune of the newcomers' gentle snoring, he wondered how his lover would react. Damn, he cursed again. He knew exactly how this would play out and unless he kept *Frau* Umer under control, then everything would turn sour quickly.

****

'Good morning.' He spoke to the spy in hushed tones before tapping a finger across his lips. He hid a yawn behind his hand. It had been a long night. 'It seems we need to trust one another. Hopefully, by now you realise I have brought no one back with me. Otherwise, you'd be in a cell by now. But you must understand, last night was a one off. I can't let you stay here much longer.' She nodded. 'Of course, if you want to stay in *Dresden*, you'll need my help. I have to go out now, but I should return within a few hours.' Hector left before the woman could protest.

****

'You're back. I didn't expect you.' *Frau* Umer's delight was obvious and for a moment Hector thought she'd rip his clothes off in the hallway. Although his plan included keeping her onside, intimacy wasn't on the agenda. In fact, he hadn't a clue how to proceed. The

414

next words from his lips surprised even him.

'Do everything I say.'

'What?' *Frau* Umer gave him a bemused look. 'Stop it, Hector. I don't understand.'

He gripped her wrists and pulled the confused woman into the lounge before sitting her down. 'The *Gestapo* is after you. And, unless you follow my instructions to the letter, they will take you away to one of their camps and nobody will ever hear from you again.' None of this was true, though he banked the very idea would stir terror within her. And seeing the fright within her eyes, he pulled her close. 'It's okay. We're both scared, but I'm here to protect you. You just need to do as I say.'

'What? How?'

Hector sighed. He'd hoped to keep the truth from her, but there was no choice. 'They believe you are working for the British. *Gestapo* agents are watching you, waiting for you to slip up, and then they'll take you in.'

Umer's whole body shook. 'That's ridiculous. I'm a loyal German, they know that.'

The tremor in her voice betrayed her, and Hector placed his damning ace. 'But you have been helping the British.'

She was slow and shrieked another confused question. He pulled her close, hoping she would join the dots herself, but when she didn't, he whispered in her ear. 'I am a British spy and the *Gestapo* know you've been helping me. If you don't do exactly as I ask, then they will torture you.' He pulled away and studied her frightened eyes. 'Do you understand?'

Frau Umer dipped her head in bewildered compliance.

****

He left it two days before introducing Mila Koch to *Frau* Umer. That wasn't her real name, merely the persona her papers identified, but just as she had secrets, so too did Hector. He hated the risk his newcomer had burdened him with. Hector used the delay to cement his control over his lover before bringing the two together.

In the meantime, he'd behaved as normal. Attending classes and cheekily waving whenever he saw someone spying on his movements. Each day, he allocated more time to Umer. Sometimes he took her to bed to normalise the situation, while on other occasions he programmed her. Hector geared every word he presented to the woman with finesse until he felt certain she'd sunk so deep into the conspiracy that helping him was her only salvation.

He'd never really understood women, and bringing two volatile females together carried an inherent risk. Hector's brain wished he could turn the clock back and force his British ally to hide within the university. He'd burnt that bridge, however, as soon as he'd coerced Umer into cooperation, and it was too late now to change his plan. Hector had told Umer that nothing would change. That together they would continue on as lovers, spending hours pleasuring one another. Only now, after introducing a new house guest into the equation, she saw the error of his ways. And then the darkest of thoughts crept in. Either Umer would support their endeavour or reach her expiration date. At least with another British spy watching her movement, the chance of controlling the woman increased.

The door closed and within seconds Hector realised he'd made a terrible mistake as the two women squared off, each offering nothing but malevolent stares. Now, events forced him to take a side. *Frau* Umer's pleading eyes struck a nerve, and against his better judgement, he lashed out at her. He immediately regretted his actions, but it was too late, as the woman lay unconscious on the floor.

'I...I'm sorry,' he stuttered, though it was unclear if he was talking to Umer or Mila Koch. 'Help me tie her up.' This time, the instruction was implicit. Despite Hector's indifference toward his lover, he had intended no harm. Control, yes, but seeing her crumpled form filled him with sadness and a dilemma. Striking Umer down, although unintended, meant they were in terrible danger. The door where Umer would shelter his guest had irrevocably slammed shut.

The pair bound and gagged her in silence. Hector thought it unlikely the *Gestapo* were listening, but he could never be sure. His mood was souring by the moment. What had he done? And what to do next?

****

Ingrid understood why Hector had tied Umer up, but the action complicated matters for them. They carried the unconscious woman down to a cellar. After resting Umer's limp form on some sacks, she turned to face the other British agent. 'Well, that was unexpected.'

'Sorry,' he repeated.

'You don't understand women, do you?'

'No,' he admitted, palms spread wide.

Ingrid looked about the cellar and shivered. The dingy area reminded her of her recent sleeping quarters after fleeing *Bremen*, and she needed to leave. 'Come on, those knots should hold. We'll go upstairs and decide what to do.'

****

Hector held his head in his hands. *What have I done?* He couldn't believe the rashness of his actions. But it was done. That *Frau* Umer could take this woman in and provide shelter had gone up in flames. As he thought through all the events of the week, his mood mellowed. He wanted to escape from Stefan's control. He was loyal to the British. Wasn't he? Maybe this was an opportunity. He would tell the new girl everything.

****

Ingrid sipped at some tea and allowed Hector to speak. She already knew some of his story, but what she heard next unravelled her world. The cruel deaths of Foxglove and Theodore. His survival under *Gestapo* licence. And then one name entered the conversation: *Stefan Weiss,* and Ingrid felt the teacup slip from her fingers. Her throat constricted as she fought an overwhelming desire to run. Twice within a few days, her nemesis had surfaced, and this time, the evil man was working with Hector. The explosion as her cup hit the stone floor, sending scorching tea across her calves, failed to penetrate the woollen state of her head. Hector was talking again, but none of the words made any sense, and this time Ingrid dipped her head to cry.

The room was silent as the pair struggled for composure. A hand pressed into hers, and Ingrid accepted the gesture. She looked into Hector's eyes and saw a combination of confusion, empathy, and concern. This time, after asking a few more questions, to make absolutely certain about Stefan, Ingrid revealed her true identity and her connection with the evil man. She couldn't explain her honesty, but something about her meeting with Hector suggested an alternate path where, allied together, they just might bring Stefan down.

110

Stefan berated himself for not returning to *Dresden* for his weekly supervision with Hector. Heydrich had already queried his absence from the daily routine in Berlin. But he refused to tear himself away from the office in *Bremen*, where he desperately pursued the truth about Ingrid Stiepermann.

He'd broken the young nurse, Mia, quickly. After allowing medical care to tend to the girl's injured hand, he reverted to his nasty persona. Her face crumbled when she realised the torture would continue, prompting a sinister smile on Stefan's face. He despised her weakness as she'd begged for release. In the end, he believed the girl. Mia was innocent, guilty only of a girl's crush on Ingrid. She was unaware she'd worshipped a British spy, and the revelation caused further heartache for the girl.

That left the landlady, and Stefan could not find out if the woman's stoic resistance meant she knew nothing, or if she hid a cause to die for. This was the one time when he'd reluctantly delegated. The days in *Bremen* had left him exhausted. At least he had the indulgence of a bed each night, while his colleagues ensured his prisoner remained awake. Another few days, and she'd break.

****

'Do you still have your old papers, the ones you used in *Bremen*?'

419

Ingrid thought briefly before nodding. And after checking a hidden compartment within her case, she pulled the identity papers she'd used for over a year.

'Good,' he said as he handed *Frau* Umer's identity card to Ingrid. 'There are things I need to collect if we're to stand any chance of getting away. It will take me roughly an hour. See if you can switch your photo over while I'm gone and keep your other identity papers spare. We'll need them later.'

Leaving Ingrid to work on her task, Hector hurried into the street. He'd made this his city, and he made rapid progress before sneaking into his flat via the alley at the rear. Within a few minutes, he'd gathered basic provisions and exited from the front. They were probably watching and on this occasion that suited him, so he made no attempt at discretion as he strode toward the university. His move was purely for show and upon arrival at his work, he delivered a sick note excusing *Frau* Umer from work before slipping away.

'It's me,' he announced to Ingrid upon his return. The girl's face paled before a tight smile of recognition formed. 'How are your papers looking?' He examined the forged paperwork. 'You're quite good at this, aren't you? Here, I've got another one for you to work on.'

As Ingrid worked, Hector paced the room. 'We have to leave soon, but before you say no, I'm going to the cellar to feed Umer.' He caught a momentary flash of anger, which Ingrid quickly masked. 'I know, I know,' he said, hands raised in supplication. 'But she hasn't harmed either of us. She's not a Nazi. I can't leave her to starve, and neither can you. We don't kill innocents.' He saw a flicker of agreement and continued. 'As soon as Stefan realises I've gone, he'll tear this place apart and will find her. But I have to give her a meal before we leave.' Hector didn't wait for approval before stepping down into the cellar.

Five minutes later, he returned to inspect Ingrid's handiwork.

'I gave her food and double checked she can't escape.' Ingrid's face adopted a sour pucker, so he changed tack. 'Are you nearly done?' She returned the papers to him, and his eyebrows lifted in surprise. 'Impressive.'

'What about Stefan?' Ingrid asked. 'When is your next transmission due?'

'Wednesday. That gives us four days, though they're bound to check in on me before then. I see people watching me on most days.' She nodded, and they silently gathered their things together.

****

'You have a car?' Surprise and delight crept into Ingrid's voice.

'Not mine. It belongs to the university. But I've forged *Frau* Umer's name on the paperwork, so, if we're lucky, they won't miss it, or her, for a few days.'

The sight of a car came as a relief. Ingrid knew *Gestapo* informants lay throughout the city and with Hector's identity at the top of most watch lists, avoiding the railway offered hope.

Together, they loaded the Volkswagen type 1. It felt odd to leave *Frau* Umer restrained in the basement, but taking her would create further problems. 'Which road do we take?' she asked as Hector climbed into the driver's seat. Ingrid suppressed her irritation. She wanted to drive, and it annoyed her to cede control again.

'I'd like to head north and follow the Elbe,' he answered, reversing the car out of its spot. 'But there are sure to be roadblocks. They'll block the main road west too, so I think we should keep on the quieter roads.'

Hector nursed the spluttering car through a cautious weave of the inner suburbs, with Ingrid crouching low every time they saw a uniform. Progress was slow, but Hector knew the city and where roadblocks were likeliest, so she acquiesced to his lead. Eventually, the city gave way to open fields and, after adopting a new zigzag route, they were on their way to *Leipzig*. Ingrid dared to hope. If their plan stood any chance, then they needed to retrieve her radio, and that meant they must act fast. Both knew her hastily doctored identity papers wouldn't pass detailed scrutiny.

It was early afternoon, and three times they had to navigate roadside checks. Each time, Ingrid watched Hector remain calm while fear pricked her insides. She drew strength from his manner, though his calm demeanour left her amazed. *How's he doing this? He looks in charge.* Adopting yet another identity was part of it. Ingrid's suitcase contained papers for Elsa Keller and Mila Koch, and they'd even brought *Frau* Umer's identification along. So far, the questions had been cursory, but someone would dig deeper before too long. *You're getting soft. You let your guard down, became settled in* Bremen. *What were you thinking?*

The voices in her head were right, but she'd fled and now she faced a problem. She cringed as Hector asked for directions as they arrived within the city boundaries of *Leipzig*. Nothing was familiar, and she twisted about, hoping to see a landmark she would recognise. She'd only spent a few hours in the city before fleeing to *Dresden.*

'Look, I'm not sure,' she admitted to Hector. 'I only stayed one night, hidden in the shadows. You can't expect me to take us straight to the radio. It's stupid for us to quarrel.' She knew she was right and stuck to her argument. Hector pulled the car to a halt in a deserted street, and they stared each other down in silence. *He should be grateful. I've helped him escape* Dresden. *He isn't a* Gestapo *puppet anymore.* Her inner anger continued to boil.

'I'm sorry.' Hector broke the stony silence.

His apology caught her out. Ingrid hadn't expelled all her anger yet, but here he was, accepting his part in their situation. Ingrid sighed, thumping her leg.

'I'm sorry too.' It seemed absurd they hadn't foreseen this issue during their hours in the car together, but now they'd accepted *Leipzig* wasn't so easy to navigate. 'Come on,' she encouraged. 'I'm hungry and we only have a few hours before dark. We need to find our way around before then. I suggest we start by finding the railway station since that's where I came in last time.'

Having parked the car, somewhere they both hoped was safe, they'd struck out on foot. Sometimes they walked together, holding hands, portraying a couple. At other times, they walked as individuals, but were always within sight of the other. Ingrid took the lead. It felt odd to hold Hector's hand. The act was a ploy, but memories of Archie flooded back, a hammer blow of regret. She was unsure how long she'd be able to sustain the charade with Hector.

Her feet hurt when they finally stumbled across the *Marktplatz*, but finally, an element of familiarity. 'I think it's this way,' she pointed down a narrow street. Thirty minutes of walking, pausing, and evading, passed before she spotted the building. 'Wait here,' she commanded. AS Hector observed from a distance, she crept forward to inspect her hideaway. Her stomach churned as the enormity of her next steps hit home. Venturing into the cellar lair left her horribly exposed. What if someone had found the radio? She'd be walking into a trap. She glanced to the windows above, blank eyes shrouding who knew what danger. *Come on, pull yourself together. You've done this before. Today's no different. Nobody is watching.*

But she couldn't convince herself, and her churning stomach persisted. Ahead lay a set of steps. Dark brickwork disappearing into the abyss. She faltered, clutching the wall, holding back a wave of nausea. A coughing fit ensued and then, catching her heel, her body spun out of control. Time slowed. Ingrid sensed she would fall, and sadness overcame her. *What a waste. Failure at the last hurdle*. At the last minute, she regained control of her body, snapping upright as her arm snatched at the railing. Her shoulder hurt, but from behind, she heard Hector's assurance that he would retrieve the radio while she waited outside.

Ingrid retreated to the shadows, hiding tears of gratitude. Hector descended the stairs, and she counted in her head as the seconds ticked past. To calm herself, she remembered key events which had brought her to this place. And then, as her resolution returned, she followed Hector into the cellar. Her eyes adjusted quickly to the gloom, and spotting her friend's familiar figure rooting about renewed her strength. He'd lit two candles, and their tiny flames dispelled her fears.

'I thought you were waiting outside.' Hector looked up as she approached.

'I know, but it felt odd, leaving you to do my dirty work. Anyway, I can see you're struggling to find the radio. You men,' she joked, before marching to the opposite corner where she began to unstack a pile of boxes. 'There,' she said, revealing the suitcase. Relief flooding her, Ingrid sank onto a sturdy box to rest. Hector shrugged and settled upon a crate across the room, and after a minute of fumbling, he brought out some bread. 'What next?' she asked once he'd eaten a few mouthfuls.

Again, an infuriating shrug. Clearly, Hector was a man of few words. Ingrid set her mind to the problems. They needed somewhere safe. For tonight, the cellar might do. It felt warmer today, but what then? Next came the British. Together with Hector, they had a radio. The equipment needed checking, but perhaps once they established contact, their allies could help. It was worth a shot, and a car parked within the city gave them a mobility that could keep them ahead of German detection. A glimmer of hope formed. Not enough to light the path ahead, but a start. While she pondered, another thought formed. A familiar yearning: home.

'Hector. I need to go back to *Berchtesgaden*. Will you help me?'

Her friend stood and brought the bread across. 'Of course, but don't you think that will be dangerous?'

'More than staying here?'

'We can't stay here,' he replied flatly. 'It won't take them long, perhaps a day or two, and then they will come looking for me. Well, *us*, as soon as they find *Frau* Umer. We need to move on, and soon. And you shouldn't go back to your hometown.'

'But…'

'No. Listen to me,' he commanded. 'We have an hour, maybe two, before the light goes. We should bring the car closer, ready to drive away early tomorrow. No sense in lugging the radio further than we have to. Tonight, we will rest. Then we can contact the British and then, maybe, I should go on to *Berchtesgaden*.'

The conversation hadn't reached a satisfactory conclusion, but after chewing a couple of mouthfuls of bread, Hector reached to pull Ingrid forward. She reluctantly gripped his hand and stood, though her mind was a muddle. She'd hoped for support for her to return home, not for him to seize the task himself. Short term, his suggestion of retrieving the car made sense at least, so they returned the radio to its hiding place before stepping into the sunshine. Could she allow Hector to go to *Berchtesgaden* instead of her?

111

MARCH 1943, *DRESDEN*

Stefan returned the receiver to its cradle before holding his head in his hands. He deserved Heydrich's wrath. Events had gone from bad to worse with a trail of ineptitude which led straight to his door. He poured a shot of schnapps and stared at the translucent liquid. When no answers came, he threw the glass against the wall. The resounding shatter brought nothing and no one except a festering bile in Stefan's belly. If he was honest, Ingrid was the problem, not Heydrich. Stefan's personal feud meant nothing against losing the ability to feed fake intel across the North Sea.

He'd interviewed Hector's lover, *Frau* Umer. She seemed innocent. The report of her kidnapping stated there was no physical way she could have secured the tight knots binding her. The woman had soiled her clothes too, further showing her status as a victim. Umer's statement described another woman: Ingrid. She'd found Hector, that caught Stefan out, but the more pressing concern was where they'd gone to. And so far, beyond a stolen Volkswagen, he had little clue. His agents were out, questioning every soldier at every roadblock, but so far nothing.

Stefan reached for the telephone to call Alexander Piorkowski, before remembering the *Hauptsturmführer* wasn't in charge at *Dachau* anymore. The monthly calls to the former *Commandant* had petered out almost a year earlier, but Stefan desperately wanted to know the status of one inmate. Checking his facts, he saw the new

Commandant was indeed his namesake. He hoped it would help as he placed the call.

It took several minutes and two disconnections before a simmering Stefan heard his call answered and even then the operator within the camp seemed reluctant to connect him to the *Commandant*. The camp official changed his tune once Stefan dropped the name, Heydrich.

'*Obersturmbannführer* Weiss? It's *Oberleutnant* Stefan Weiss calling on behalf of Richard Heydrich. Thank you for taking my call. I'll come straight to the point, as I am sure you have important duties to attend to. You may know our office has a special interest in one of your guests. At our request, your predecessor, Piorkowski, took special care with Gerhard Stiepermann. Are you aware of this arrangement?'

'I am.'

'May I ask, is this arrangement still in place?'

Stefan heard a non-committal grunt, and he wondered whether his question was impertinent, but finally the *Commandant* replied in the affirmative.

'I understand. The reason I am calling you today is to rescind this arrangement. From now on I hope you will use your authority so this man receives *sonderbehandlung*. And, if you'll excuse my impertinence, I would consider it a personal favour, if your staff could update me once you've liquidated this problem.'

'Of course. I will take care of this matter personally.'

The line clicked dead and with it, Stefan's mood lifted. The bitch may have slipped through his fingers, but knowing her father wouldn't see another dawn helped to ease the pain.

112

APRIL 1943, LONDON

Marcus Gregson couldn't believe the report he'd just read, but he hoped the news was accurate. Naturally, he followed protocol and sought verification, though if the latest news was true, then his office had missed months of German counterintelligence. He respected most of his colleagues, the long hours they worked paired with innovative minds, but they'd completely missed this intelligence. And that oversight called everything into question. Straightening his tie, he stepped along the corridor to inform his boss.

'Sir. It's as we feared. Foxglove and Theodore are both dead.'

He received a curt nod of understanding. 'And the others?'

Gregson consulted his notes. 'The Keller woman is alive, though she had to leave *Bremen* and she's using the second set of papers we provided. She goes under the name Mila Koch now.

'What about Hector?'

Never sure how his boss would react, Gregson braced himself to reveal the remaining truth. 'He's alive too. With the woman, apparently. It's amazing he's still in the game after all the business with the duress codes he sent.'

'Come on, man, get to the point. Where are they? What's going on?'

Gregson sighed. 'Where, they don't say. Our best guess is they're in central Germany somewhere, certainly not *Dresden* anymore. Though they are requesting our help.'

'Damn it. That's a ridiculous request. Getting into France is one thing, and that's bloody risky, but Germany, when we don't even know where they are?' He shook his head. 'They're on their own – they'll have to make their own luck. What else can you tell me?'

There wasn't much. Only that for now the pair were alive and mobile and would attempt to broadcast again soon. But in terms of intel, nothing. While Gregson was relieved the pair were free, for the moment, intel was a tradable commodity and without it, the worth of the two agents diminished.

113

May 1943, North Africa

Archie looked on in awe at the sight before him. Tens of thousands of German and Italian soldiers lined up, conquered. The wireless bulletin had mentioned over two hundred thousand. He'd never seen so many people in the one place. The scene felt surreal, as it was clear none were fighting back. Instead, the disarmed men hung their heads: grimy, dispirited, broken. Only a tall wire fence separated them from the enemy. Taff and others in his unit jeered, but Archie remained silent. Both sides had lost friends to the heat of battle, but he couldn't find it within himself to blame the foot soldiers. The scene filled Archie with a mixture of pity and envy.

For the men beyond the fence, the war was over. And, for a few lucky others stationed to guard the surrendered masses, it appeared they, too, could finally rest. But not so Archie. He had new orders and after the briefest of rests, his battalion would soon ship out to the next battle.

114

AUGUST 1943, *BERCHTESGADEN*

Gerda looked across the mountain vista in disbelief. The rolling hills and mountains were the same, but she gained no solace from the view. Her German world felt like a corrupt illusion, a poisonous veneer beneath the surface. She was lucky, in some ways. Deep down, she could acknowledge that. Others were fighting, dying, and most were suffering. She, at least, had the mountains.

Walking along the bank of the *Berchtesgadener Ache* did little to placate her mood. Instead, intrusive memories bombarded her senses. Ingrid, Dieter and, of course, the rest of the poor Stiepermann family. All gone. Then there was Christa and her departure to work with the elite at Hitler's *Berghof*. The bile rose in Gerda's throat at the thought of her former friend. Christa was never someone she would mourn for.

It was dawn, and Gerda didn't have long. She'd need to return home and from there, change into her uniform before heading into town to stand in front of others in a ridiculous display of national unity. She despised her meetings but knew she must attend. While life in Bavaria was indeed simpler than other parts of the country, she navigated a minefield every day. Her twenty-sixth birthday was approaching and although she kept quiet, others knew. The authorities who issued her papers knew. A constant hum echoed every time she attended. *Why wasn't she pregnant yet? She had a duty. She'll be a shrivelled prune if she doesn't start soon.* Others had fallen, and with each pregnancy announcement came joyous celebration. One of her former school friends had four children already. Gerda's insides squirmed at the thought.

The trouble was, beyond the beauty of her hometown, Gerda had no interest in German politics. She had a brain and a love of science, and this life wasn't her choice. So far, she'd accepted her fate. She knew any resistance would cause harm to her family. The League of German Maidens had been as Christa had originally forecast: fitness and general wellbeing. Gerda had expected to leave the group five years earlier, but someone in authority had prevented that choice. Instead, they'd steered her into leadership in the Faith and Beauty society for older girls.

Today, however, all this would change. It had taken months of cajoling her mother and further badgering toward multiple professors at Goethe University in Frankfurt before she'd finally found a sponsor. In a few weeks' time, her life would start afresh as she began a course in applied physics. At last, she could follow her dream path.

Gerda tore herself away from the river. It was time. She could see other younger interns skipping in merriment along the street. Each, proud to wear the uniform. It wouldn't do to be late.

'Good morning, *Frau* Lange. Are you ready to put the girls through their paces?' Gerda asked with forced pleasantry upon her arrival. At some point this morning, Gerda would need to tell the woman she was leaving, and the thought of that left her terrified.

Her superior drew her to one side before replying. 'Today, things are going to be different.'

A trickle of fear ran down Gerda's spine. 'H-how so?'

'The *Führer* has graced us with splendid news. A new programme which will soon roll out across the country. In his wisdom, he had chosen us to be the first to adopt the additional measures.'

Gerda's eyes went wide, and she spluttered a response. 'Additional measures?'

'Yes. Aren't you excited? You're going to lead a new section of *Herr* Hitler's army. And, once you've set everything up here, they want you to set up other units across the country.'

The words *Hitler's Army* shocked Gerda. 'What exactly are you saying?'

Frau Lange offered a bemused expression before reaching across and patting her hand. 'I don't know why they didn't do this sooner, but the girls are going to receive weapons' training. At last, we're arming up, ready to fight.'

Gerda felt a creeping sickness envelop her. If this was true and they demanded her to lead other groups around the country, how could she leave to study in Frankfurt? Once again, the crush of helplessness overwhelmed her.

115

SEPTEMBER 1943, FRANKFURT

Ingrid and Hector had only used the radio three times since departing *Leipzig*. Once within the city and a further two times as they headed further southwest into the country's interior. But it had been weeks since their last transmission. Both Hector and Ingrid had agreed to lie low for a while, and with no support from the British, the pair felt a sense of betrayal. Ingrid suffered the worst of the burden. For now, the Germans did not know the name Mila Koch, whereas they knew Hector's identity. The trusty Volkswagen had served them well, however. But the time had come to abandon the car, and after bringing them three hundred miles to the southern outskirts of Frankfurt, they left the vehicle parked in a narrow suburban street.

Hector had brought money from *Dresden*, but it wouldn't last forever, and sourcing food fell upon Ingrid. She had no choice but to join the queues for food. A necessary task, yet one which Ingrid feared. At *Bremen* hospital, they'd provided regular meals. The queues were often lengthy, meaning forced conversations with elderly spinsters all hunting for gossip. She would smile and keep her story simple while showing an interest in them, but she could spot fakers digging for dirt a mile off. And they were everywhere.

In the end, and out of necessity, the pair discussed parting company. It made sense, though Hector bucked against the idea. With the *Gestapo* hunting them both and only Ingrid having some freedom of movement, he reluctantly ceded. That forced a choice.

While Ingrid looked for work within the city, he could hide or leave. She'd grown accustomed to his presence, so sending him away was unpalatable, yet staying together seemed too risky.

'I spoke with someone today who can offer me lodgings and food in return for fixing up her house.' Ingrid said.

'You mean repairs?' Hector arched an eyebrow. 'That kind of thing?'

'No silly. I'm no builder. Repairing clothes, bedding, curtains. That sort of stuff. She said once I'm done in her house she has friends who I could work for to pay my way.'

'And you believe her? This stranger.'

'I don't think I have a choice. We can't stay in barns and cellars forever.' Ingrid watched as Hector's face frowned in calculation. A few months earlier she'd felt drawn to *Berchtesgaden*, but with all the running away to escape the *Gestapo*, she'd shelved the idea. And with Hector offering to go in her place, it felt the right time. 'You could do something for me. Do you remember, you offered to go to *Berchtesgaden* for me? Did you mean it?'

'Of course,' Hector replied while placing his hand in hers. This time, Ingrid didn't feel the need to pull away. His offer was sincere, with no strings attached.

Later that day, Ingrid returned to their hideaway. She'd made her arrangements and accepted the job. Hector would leave with the radio. It was possible that they would never meet again. After passing her new address over, Ingrid offered Hector a lingering embrace, though there was no happiness in the gesture. Ingrid yearned for answers, and she hoped Hector would bring them, but accepting the need to put down roots and recharge, she hastened away.

116

OCTOBER 1943, FRANKFURT

Ingrid yawned before pulling the blanket tighter around her torso. It was late, yet despite this, she didn't worry. Her new employer had welcomed Ingrid into her home like a lost daughter. And as for work, she'd barely done any. While Ingrid rested, her mind counted out the weeks since her arrival. *Has it really been five weeks?* The shocking statistic brought another realisation: her new-found work arrangement was making her soft. With that thought, she threw off the bedclothes and stood up. It still felt odd to experience this luxury amid war, but Ingrid also acknowledged the house's opulence was a far cry from the bare floorboards she'd known as a youth.

A few minutes later, after a quick wash, Ingrid dressed and hurried into the kitchen. A fresh breakfast and a warm smile greeted her. 'You shouldn't have,' she exclaimed.

'It's no trouble, and anyway, I thought you could help me later. I have a friend who wants some clothes repairing. Perhaps we could do this together.'

'Of course,' Ingrid agreed before enjoying the tart taste of a mouthful of *sauerkraut*. After she'd eaten, the pair stepped out onto *Metzstraße*. 'Does your friend live in *Bockenheim*?' Ingrid queried.

'Yes. She's like me. Lives alone. It isn't far.'

The journey took barely ten minutes and with a warm sun on her back and the comforting shield of her new patron alongside,

Ingrid felt unusually safe, despite being taken to meet someone new.

'Here we are.' Ingrid looked up a set of stone steps to the front door. The new house, while a template of the one she'd just left, looked even more opulent. 'Come on. She's expecting us.'

Ingrid closed her gawping mouth and followed meekly along, as though her landlady was the Pied Piper. After introductions, the new homeowner appeared completely at ease with Ingrid's appearance, and Ingrid sighed in relief.

The day turned into an absolute delight and Ingrid listened with interest as the women conversed about life before the war. With soft fabrics to darn and a complete absence of hatred, their words soothed. The hours passed swiftly, though it was only when their host lit a lamp that Ingrid acknowledged the approaching nightfall.

'We should go.'

'So soon. That's a shame. Could I persuade you both to stay longer? I have some meat for dinner.'

Ingrid watched with interest as conflict washed across her landlady's face. Would it matter if they stayed another hour?

'We'd love to, but the curfew.'

'Of course. Though you're both welcome to stay. No need to go back until tomorrow morning.'

Ingrid smiled. It seemed odd that her landlady sought her permission, but with the temptation of stomach-filling meat and the bond the two ladies shared, she nodded her approval.

'That settles it then.'

The cured meat was delicious, and Ingrid felt vindicated by their extended stay. Despite her sedentary part in the day, she felt tired a few hours later as everyone looked set to retire. When her head finally hit the softest of pillows, Ingrid melted into a deep, dreamless sleep.

A deafening crash snapped her awake, and Ingrid leaped from her bed. *Where am I?* More explosions sounded, adding to Ingrid's confused state. The building shook, forcing her to grip the bed frame to steady herself. She remembered the two ladies. Something was terribly wrong, and it was up to her to help them. She couldn't do anything in the gloom, so using the bed as a guide, she padded across the room and pulled back the curtains. The inferno which greeted her eyes brought instant horror and, for a moment, she froze in disbelief. Another blast shook both her and the building, prompting action. Under an orange glow, she quickly dressed and once both feet were inside her shoes; she stepped onto the landing.

Where are the others? After such a relaxing day within the unfamiliar mansion, Ingrid couldn't recall which bedrooms held sleepers.

The landing swept off in both directions and in a snap decision, Ingrid tore off to the right. Three doors lay along her path before a shadowy set of stairs moved upward. The first two doors imploded as Ingrid burst through.

Empty.

The next door held fast and after a few seconds of furious pounding, she abandoned her pursuit and took to the stairs instead. Two steps up, a fireball erupted on the floor above, and Ingrid threw her body downward. She landed heavily, losing vital seconds before she regained her feet. An intense wave of heat forced her back to where she'd come. A new, perilous thought intruded. This wasn't just about saving the women. Escaping the building at all seemed unlikely.

An ominous plume of thick smoke belched out from the stairwell, spurring Ingrid along the landing. A sting hit her eyes and as she ran, fire crackled above. Her legs felt like clay as she lumbered along, and each time she barged against a door, pain radiated the length of her arm. On the third try, she swept into a bedroom and a new pain caught in her throat. Only the dress identified the crumpled mess on the floor as the homeowner. Tongues of flame licked the still form, and Ingrid knew the lady was beyond salvation. That left her landlady. Ingrid sprinted on towards the next bedroom. Again, the door gave easily and this time she found the woman.

'Come on,' Ingrid shrieked, though with the building close to collapse, her cries went unanswered. She lost valuable seconds crossing the room to grip her friend's arm. Ingrid raised her voice again as she pulled hard. Slowly, bewilderment faded, replaced with recognition, and together they rushed toward the doorway, but their momentum halted. The staircase down to the ground floor had gone, and with it, Ingrid's hopes for their survival. With no time for niceties, she shoved the woman back inside and slammed the door.

Ingrid groaned as the realisation hit her: the fire had them trapped. Her frantic eyes zipped around the room. If they were to get out alive, then it would be up to her. 'Sit here,' she commanded while pushing the woman onto the bed. Next, she returned to the window. Outside, other buildings were aflame, with some close to collapse. More explosions thundered, one after the other. With each eruption, the room shook, shaking plaster from the ceiling. The vast bedroom held a dresser, a chair, a single wardrobe, and a double bed. Suppressing her skittish thoughts, Ingrid looked back toward the door to the landing and the sight of the heat-curled paint spurred her on. Ignoring the woman, she snatched up the wooden chair and smashed the window. Freezing air swept in, but the relief to her stinging eyes was only momentary.

As though the fire could sense their attempted escape, oxygen sucked underneath the door, feeding the inferno to new intensity. Shards of glass and splintered wood still blocked their path. forcing Ingrid to redouble her efforts. Once clear, she leant out and took in her surroundings. The view wasn't promising. The neighbouring houses and those opposite were all aflame. Turning her gaze downward, smoke obscured the view. Leaping into the unknown held little appeal. She saw the stone steps which had brought her into the building earlier that day. They were further along, but other obstacles offered a frightening threat. Near to the road lay a cast iron rail topped with decorative filigrees. And further on, within the darkness, lay stone steps leading to the cellar. The women might survive a drop of twelve feet, but not if the fall was twenty. A crack in the ceiling appeared and, with the building tearing itself apart, Ingrid tore into action. Blankets, cushions, clothes, bedding, and even the curtains hurtled into the darkness below. They had one shot at this. She returned to the bed and pulled the woman to her feet. The woman was in shock and sagged against her. Ignoring the pain in her shoulder, she dragged the landlady to the window.

'Come on. We have to jump.' No reaction. Ingrid slapped her patron twice before seeing a flicker of recognition. After the tiniest of nods, she coaxed her friend to the ledge. They would jump together. If the fates decided this was their time, then so be it. After a few seconds to adjust her position, she held her landlady's hand as their four legs dangled into space.

As Ingrid coiled for the jump, a further explosion erupted. The building lurched, and Ingrid fell. A second later, her ankle hit something solid, and a wave of pain ran up her leg. The rest of her body crumpled, finding some cushioning from the bedding she'd thrown out.

Her landlady was nowhere to be seen. Dirty, confused and in agony, Ingrid half crawled along to the entrance and from there out onto the street. *Where are you?* Her mind screamed, but there was no movement at all. A second later, the building imploded and Ingrid knew no answers would come. Unable to stand, she lay in the road and wept.

****

'Name?'

Ingrid's eyes fluttered open. 'Where am I?'

'Don't worry, child, you're safe. You are in what's left of the hospital. I'm a nurse here. The director of nursing is tasking us with identifying everyone who came in last night.'

'Last night. What happened?' Ingrid could have guessed, but she needed to hear it.

'Bombs. Hundreds of planes dropped them. Thousands within the city are dead.' The nurse passed a hand over her brow.

Oh, the irony. Ingrid had escaped the *Gestapo* only for the British to bomb her city refuge. She didn't know whether to laugh or cry. Tightening her diaphragm to keep her expression sombre brought pain, so she tried another tack. 'I escaped from a house with an older woman. Is she here?' Ingrid knew the answer, but the woman's sad shake of the head brought fresh tears. Guilt wracked at Ingrid's senses. *If only I'd gripped her tighter.*

The nurse patted her hand, though the gesture brought little comfort. 'I'll leave you for now, as I can see you're upset. We can speak further when I come around later.'

It took Ingrid a few minutes before her nerves steadied and she could assess the ward. Here, at least, was some familiarity. Next, she practiced her cover story, over and over. If the hospital provided any pain relief, she couldn't let slip the wrong name. Reassured, she turned her gaze to inspect her injuries. Her ribs hurt, and she saw some deep scratches across both arms, but her mouth dropped open at the swathe of bandages encircling her ankle. That brought the previous night's fall into sharp focus and the tears fell again. What was she to do? An odd thought occurred to her. Either she was homeless and forced to accept charity to survive, or, if by some miracle her adopted home was standing, she might have just inherited a home.

117

DECEMBER 1943, FRANKFURT

Gerda called the girls to a sudden halt. Seeing the university buildings in the distance left her feeling both seething and sorrowful. She was supposed to go there, studying, not leading a group of silly girls.

'Come along,' she commanded. Behind her, twenty-four hapless teens trailed in ignorance of their leader's discomfort. To them, this was an outing, something to garner excitement, and if Gerda paused, then it merely provided an opportunity for chatter. Disgusted, she turned away before picking up her pace and leading her troop toward *Grüneburg* Park. Her first backward glance identified four stragglers, and she screamed an order to maintain orderliness. It wasn't like her and she hated the outburst, though the girls fell meekly into line.

Stepping through the trees, she felt a satisfying crunch as she marched across the grass. Reluctantly, she drew to a halt again. This time, she needed to gather her bearings. Ahead, somewhere, lay a temporary barracks, where they'd tasked her to deliver the BDM girls. Instead of spying pristine white frost and the odd statue, residents had built and erected a small market.

Gerda's mood soured as a clutch of gleeful giggles filled the air. She lacked the will to scold the girls again. Accepting that leadership didn't suit her, Gerda waved them past.

'Just ten minutes, then meet me back here.' The girls sprinted off, though Gerda found little to excite within the meagre

Christmas stalls. Instead, she turned to pace the perimeter, hoping to spot the barracks. So far, Frankfurt had impressed her. She loved the buildings and once again she felt anger well up inside at the injustice which had stolen her education. Her mother had been next to useless when Gerda explained her dilemma. So much for supporting her quest to better herself. As soon as the authorities summoned Gerda to the cause, her path became set in stone.

Twenty minutes had passed and, although cold, Gerda forgave the girls for their merriment, though they really had to leave. Hoping she knew the way, Gerda led them to the far side of the park.

****

Ingrid's face was as white as the frost. At first, she wasn't sure. Years had passed, but after using the traders as cover to sneak closer, she spied her former friend. Pain and anguish crashed through her body, and with her ankle not fully healed, she rested against a stall. She recognised the uniform, and a sickly pall wormed down her throat. For a moment, she couldn't breathe until a sympathetic trader offered her a mouthful of mulled wine.

'Thank you,' she said after taking a few sips. But by the time she'd steadied herself, her childhood friend had vanished. After a few months of relative stability, Gerda's sudden appearance threw Ingrid's world into chaos. Questions bombarded her. *Did she see me? What do I do if she did? Is she a Nazi? She must be. She's wearing a uniform. No. Surely not. Not my Gerda.*

Suddenly, Ingrid felt lost. As she cast her gaze around the market, more young women, each wearing smart BDM uniforms, stood out like a beacon. They were everywhere, but all too young. None were Gerda.

Conflict raged. Should she get away before being seen, or investigate and discover the truth? Seeing all the uniformed girls made up Ingrid's mind. She couldn't stay. For a few months, she'd found a haven. Somewhere to recharge until Hector could bring news. Apart from him, nobody knew her address in Frankfurt. She couldn't risk discovery. What she had with Gerda, a lifetime ago, had died the day her friend had chosen the uniform. Decision made, she turned to head home.

'Hello, Ingrid. I thought it was you.'

Ingrid staggered; her mouth open in disbelief. Gerda was standing just six feet away, and the warmest smile crumbled the chasm of years between them.

'I...Sorry, I just didn't expect to see you.'

'I'm as surprised as you. You caught my eye as we were leaving the park, a spark of familiarity. As soon as I realised it was you, I had to run back.' Her eyes were wide with curiosity. 'Listen, I have to go, but now that I've worked out where to take the girls, I could come back in a few minutes. Please say you'll wait for me. I promise I won't be gone long.'

Ingrid nodded mutely. She didn't know what to think and, as her friend returned to the younger girls, a storm of questions froze her in place.

****

Ingrid's body shook with equal measures of cold and shock. The jolt of seeing Gerda refused to subside. She retreated beyond a line of trees, acutely aware of how furtive her actions looked. Each glance beyond the nearest trunk back toward the market further fuelled her anxiety. She glanced at her watch. Ten minutes had passed. *Why hadn't Gerda returned? Should she stay or flee?*

She'd experienced a similar response when she almost stumbled across Stefan in *Bremen*. However, this time was different. Ingrid hated Stefan with every fibre of her being, but despite the uniform Gerda wore, Ingrid still felt an odd loyalty to her childhood friend.

To remain waiting seemed an impossible risk, she argued. She'd grown accustomed to solitude. The last couple of months spent rattling around in an empty house had seen to that. She only had herself to trust. And when she went out, she hid behind her adopted identity. But Gerda knew her true identity and could out her in a heartbeat. Oh, how she wished for the sound counsel of Hector in this moment, or Archie's powerful, protecting arms. Ingrid had neither.

****

Gerda was out of breath when she finally caught up to the girls. They had already formed up, and she automatically performed a headcount. Twenty-four girls present, thank goodness. For the first time in months, Gerda ignored the girls' incessant chatter. A curious elation swept through her. Thankfully, the group was oblivious to their leader's improved mood. Gerda wasn't ready to advertise her friend's sudden appearance, though her mind churned with a hundred questions.

Calling the girls to attention, the group marched towards the botanical garden. Off to the left was an enormous field, where close to a hundred uniformed soldiers scurried about like well-organised ants. Relieved they'd reached their destination; she directed the girls towards a large tent by the side of the field.

Gerda stood the girls at ease and went in search of the officer in charge. No one appeared keen to take charge of the girls, and Gerda's mood deteriorated. Her brief was to deliver the girls here, nothing more. She approached the senior officer and showed to the waiting group of girls. Finally, she could hand them over to someone else's care and get back to Ingrid. She lifted her arm in a *Sieg Heil* and turned to leave.

'Where are you going?' he asked.

Gerda frowned. *Wasn't it obvious?* 'I thought you were looking after them now.'

'I hardly think so. These women are *your* charge, not mine. The day I have women under my command is the day I die,' he sneered. 'You're their leader. So, lead.'

A reply lodged in Gerda's throat, and for a second, she struggled to breathe. She had to go. Ingrid wouldn't wait forever. Her pleading eyes sought the exit before dipping in resignation.

The minutes ticked by, and Ingrid's anxiety increased. Was the *Gestapo* surrounding the park while she stood idle? She had no way of knowing, but the real possibility ate away at her, leaving her rigid. She shouldn't be here. The winter light was fading, and still she remained in place. A trader stoked nuts, roasting on a brazier nearby, and Ingrid's stomach rumbled with hunger.

'*Fraulein.*'

The male voice sounded muffled, but Ingrid shook herself and looked around. It was the man who had offered her mulled wine earlier in the day. Perhaps it was a sign. She smiled, but her jaw locked, frozen from the cold. Perhaps the seller deemed her a simpleton for her muted response? He shrugged in puzzlement and turned away. It was enough to break Ingrid's stupor. She stretched and quickly left the park. The walk home took much longer than usual, and it was almost completely dark when she fumbled at her door. Her small fist jabbed her key towards the lock and missed. She placed the other hand on top and guided the key home. Stumbling inside, her shoulder glanced against the doorframe, and she collapsed on the floor. With the door still ajar, Ingrid's slight frame shook with a curious mixture of relief and disappointment.

****

Gerda's emotions fluxed between grief and hatred. Surrounded by soldiers and the girls under her command, she couldn't ever remember feeling so alone and frustrated. For three days, they'd held her at the barracks, with no clear end – or further orders – in sight.

Before venturing to Frankfurt, she'd been aware of their expectations, but her chance meeting with Ingrid completely altered her focus. Stuck inside her own head, Gerda operated on autopilot, providing only the smallest guidance to the girls. Some had noticed, she was sure of it, but thankfully the girls were more restrained in the barracks' environment. Naturally, Ingrid was gone. But was she still in the city? Even if the bloody soldiers relented and released her, an hour or two wouldn't allow her to search the entire area.

They were heading home soon, anyway. She was reluctant to return to her mother and her constant Nazi doctrine. So where did that leave her? *Berchtesgaden* was her home. It always had been, but the prospect of return left a bitter taste in her mouth. They had her trapped, ensnared within the institution. Yet somehow, her childhood friend had discovered freedom that remained elusive to Gerda. At least it seemed that way. Their chance meeting was too brief to make an accurate assessment. She pushed aside the jealous thoughts forming in her head and focussed on her own life. How could she escape as Ingrid had done? The League of German Maidens be damned.

Gerda lacked a coherent plan, but something would come, she was certain. She'd lost too many years to the German war machine. Her return home was inevitable, but the war would not last forever. And if providence favoured, then somehow, she would meet her friend again.

****

The day after seeing Gerda, Ingrid awoke to a splitting headache. She'd dragged herself to bed fully clothed, but cold and dehydration had resulted in a band of pressure across her forehead. She rubbed her face, wiping crusts of sleep from her eyes.

The house was empty, as it had been for weeks, but the desolate atmosphere of the house weighed on Ingrid. Nobody would call, and after Gerda had failed to keep her promise, Ingrid questioned her own existence. She needed to know what had become of her family. The itch she couldn't scratch festered. As she lay, considering her existence, the hours passed by, interspersed with occasional slumber. Eventually, her parched throat reminded her of the need for food and drink, and Ingrid dragged herself from the bed.

Stirring her tea, she conceded her chance with Gerda had passed. And with no news from Hector, her desire for answers burnt ever more harshly than before. Acknowledging her need to regain some strength, Ingrid ate a morsel of bread and then rested. But the desire to return to *Berchtesgaden* wouldn't diminish. What use was a huge townhouse if she spent all her time alone? If Hector didn't return soon with some news, then she would travel home herself.

118

Hector's breathing laboured as he climbed into the hayloft. Hefting the bulky radio up the wooden ladder took all his strength. The building was exactly as Ingrid had described. Outside the town, away from prying eyes, with the river flowing close by. Safety, for the moment, at least. As he rested, he took in his surroundings. The fields offered a good view of anyone approaching, though if it came to a foot race, the river restricted his movement. Next, he examined the lower floor, remembering a tale Ingrid had told of fighting off Stefan with a pitchfork. He'd have loved to have seen that. What would have become of them if she'd killed Stefan all those years ago?

His journey down to *Berchtesgaden* had taken months and was not without incident. A single man carrying a suitcase through war-torn Germany would always stand out. Keeping his wits about him, he moved about constantly, a shadow in the shadows. Each day was a drain, but there was no choice. Scouting remote railway stations offered his most successful avenue to move through the country. But eyes were watching. He was a stranger, and not to be trusted.

Carrying known identity papers was perhaps his greatest issue, and one which he tackled early in his journey. Finding a beer hall within the Frankfurt city limits was easy enough, though, to use the building he'd need to stow the radio before entering. He only took a minute to assess the venue before returning outside to wait in the shadows. There were several patrons who seemed viable targets. The bitter night wore on and the sound of polka music drifted outside as he kept vigil. He had a rough idea how many were in the beer hall, but not when they would leave, or even if someone suitable would show. All he had on his side was surprise and sobriety.

His target appeared just before midnight, by which time Hector could barely feel his feet. A minor disability, as the solitary drunk before him seemed oblivious. The man wore an infantry uniform. Home on leave, Hector supposed. He called out to the man, asking for a cigarette. The stranger turned just as Hector launched. His punch hit the man squarely in the guts, and the figure folded up like the accordion playing inside. Hector experienced a moment of regret as he dragged the soldier into an alley. He didn't know the man, or how badly he'd hurt him, but he needed a uniform and fresh identity papers, so this was necessary. A few minutes later, he left his victim and fled the area.

He repeated the act another four times as he meandered south through the country. Once he'd botched the attack as his punch failed to drop his victim. Only the speed in his legs – and his intended victim's drunkenness – saved him. The event left him exhilarated but frightened, but somehow, he'd escaped. One problem remained. Each time he'd stolen identity papers, he would go to ground and use his basic skills to transfer his own photo across. The task wasn't sustainable. With each new facsimile, his own photo curled at the edges, making the fake documentation even more obvious. It wouldn't take much for someone in authority to question their authenticity. Hector needed a new set of documents, and soon.

For now, he had three goals: stay alive, report back to Ingrid news of her family and help the Allies win the war. Begrudgingly, he acknowledged he needed the British. He could see things from their perspective. Unless he showed worth, then both he and Ingrid were disposable. Acceptable casualties should the worst happen. He shuddered at the thought. It didn't do to dwell on *Gestapo* torture.

He'd used the radio just once during his journey, though he had little to report. Certainly not enough for the British to deem him useful. Life on the run. Skulking in the shadows made things hard. Back at *Dresden* university, he could talk openly with people, people who saw him as a friend. Their walls came down, making it easy to glean valuable information, which he'd eagerly transmitted home. But now, he had to hide and watch. One thing was obvious. For years, he'd watch Germany grow stronger under Hitler's leadership. It flexed its military might with gigantic rallies, but those days had come and gone. It was heartening how much the German leaders had overreached. With so many Germans committed to the cause, few adults remained. This hampered his movement as he watched on as the ever-younger recruits answered the call to join up. These weren't men. They were boys. Finally, an admission of weakness, a glimmer of hope. Germany couldn't hope to win the war with mere children.

Today, however, he would attempt to keep his promise to Ingrid, and that required some special planning. He knew how to find Ingrid's family home and the names of her mother and grandma, but turning up unannounced was fraught with danger. He also knew the names and addresses of a couple of others. People he should avoid. But even with addresses committed to memory, navigating the strange town wouldn't be easy. He would wait. The straw in the hayloft offered a small measure of comfort, and he'd killed a couple of rats earlier. He descended the ladder and set about clearing enough space to light a small fire. Roasted vermin weren't his favourite dinner, but along with fresh water from the river, the meal would keep him alive.

Later, after the darkness returned, he ventured across the empty field, navigating towards Ingrid's home. Wearing a stolen uniform helped as he walked through the outskirts of town with an air of confidence. But he didn't want any encounter. Tonight, he wanted to find her family and then use their hospitality before returning to Frankfurt. But when he arrived, his heart sank as he stared upon a derelict home. He took a minute to confirm the address. There was no doubt this was Ingrid's home.

Before leaving Frankfurt, Ingrid had told him they'd arrested her father years earlier. So it came as little surprise that he wasn't there. The empty property chilled more than the outside temperature. He'd heard the whispers. Few were reckless enough to speak outright, but everyone knew people had disappeared. He'd borne witness himself, as university staff and students vanished overnight.

He'd come a long way for Ingrid, so he would make absolutely certain before moving on, but deep down, he knew there would be no answers tonight. After looking about, Hector battled through weeds towards the rear of the property. In the dim light, it was difficult to move quietly, but he waded through the long grass and soon he located a door. The handle felt like a shard of ice as he gripped and drew the handle downwards. He pulled, but beyond a rattle within the frame, the door did not move.

'Who are you?'

Hector froze. It was a woman's voice. Close, though too far away for an immediate strike. He cursed at being seen. At the worst of times, his mind drew a blank. He'd changed his identity so many times in the previous weeks, suddenly he wondered who he was today, and a ridiculous panic caught in his throat. He had to regroup fast and somehow regain the initiative.

'I should ask you the same.' He challenged. The riposte was weak.

'My name is Gerda Müller. I live in this town and have done all my life, so I ask you again. Who are you and why are you breaking into my friend's house?'

Hector's mind reeled as he recognised the name. He broke down her questions in his mind. She'd said, *my friend's house*. That was a positive. And her command, while it showed authority, her voice was also quiet. Was she scared to be seen, too? He only had seconds to muster his thoughts before she sounded the alarm. Ingrid had warned him about Gerda, and he thought back to his friend's exact words before he'd travelled south. One thought struck. Although Ingrid had spoken about her childhood friend, her observations seemed conflicted. A childhood friend. Someone

452

Ingrid loved. And yet, someone who'd willingly joined the League of German Maidens. *Who was the real Gerda?*

Hector took an enormous gamble. He wasn't about to identify himself, but he would get the woman talking, which would allow him to close the gap. 'I met Ingrid. She asked for news about her family.'

'Was that in Frankfurt?'

The question floored him. Nobody else knew Ingrid was living there. How could this woman know? Did she work for the *Gestapo*? Had she followed him here? He paused, desperate for a rational answer to come. Hector moved away from the door, keeping his arms away from his body while stepping back into the garden. There, in the middle distance, he saw her, perhaps ten yards away. Ingrid had described her former friends, Gerda and Christa, but with the distance and poor light, there was no way Hector could identify the stranger.

'I'm coming closer,' he called out, 'so I can see you before I answer. But you needn't worry. I'm no threat.' He knew the statement could prove false. If the woman threatened him, he would have few qualms about silencing her. But only if she acted against him first. She stood stock still as he drew nearer. He could see her now, though only in silhouette.

'That's close enough. Now answer my question about Ingrid.'

Hector halted. The pair held common ground, Ingrid. So that's where the conversation would lead. 'Yes, I met your friend in Frankfurt some months ago. Perhaps, since we don't know one another, you could share how *you* know her.'

In a surprising move, the woman stepped closer, allowing Hector to see her features. 'Tell me, is Ingrid well? What happened to her? I saw her, but only for a few seconds before I had to leave.' Emotion crept into the woman's voice. 'I'm sorry. We don't know one another, but I hope you'll believe me when I say I miss my friend.'

The woman appeared earnest, though Hector wasn't about to trust. But he would try to get her to trust him. 'I don't know all of your friend's story,' he said, deliberately steering the focus away from himself. 'I know she left *Berchtesgaden* eleven years ago with her brother and father, but a man, I believe you both know, detained Mister Stiepermann.'

There. Surprise and dismay flashed across her face. That helped make his mind up. If she was a Nazi, she'd have known about Gerhard Stiepermann's detention. 'I'm sorry. I thought you knew.'

'He never came back.' She brushed away a tear. And suddenly, for both of them, the entire world felt a little heavier.

It was a rash move, but Hector didn't think too much about it. He closed the gap and swept the woman into a hug. The embrace was brief, and they broke apart, both surprised at his boldness. Hands raised before him in a conciliatory gesture, Hector said, 'Look. It's freezing. I came here expecting to find Ingrid's family. What happened?'

The sorrow he'd seen earlier returned as Gerda pushed past him. She stepped up to the backdoor and deftly lifted the handle. A small jiggle later and the door opened. Bemused that she'd opened the door so easily and taken the initiative, Hector followed her inside.

Gerda had clearly been there before, and as the woman lit a pair of candles, he realised the room had received recent care. He accepted a flickering wick and watched as she brushed a solitary cobweb to one side before sitting at a table. The rest of the room appeared clean. Not wanting to be seen, he pulled the door closed and with curtains drawn; he sat down opposite her. Now he could study her properly. Of course, Gerda could do the same, but at least they were alone and unlikely to be disturbed.

Before he could take everything in, he spotted her nose pinch.

'Euch. You smell.'

As ice breakers went, it took the cake. Though within the confines of the room and away from the fresh outside air, Hector had to agree. He'd spent too long hiding in hedgerows, and his hygiene had taken a back seat. Snatching his hand, she pulled him to standing and let him upstairs. Echoes of *Frau* Umer hit with every step. Surely, she wasn't that forward...

He needn't have worried. Although the water she drew was icy, Gerda helped lather his beard before helping to shave him clean. 'There, much better. I'll wait for you downstairs while you finish bathing.'

Bemused, Hector didn't know when he'd get another bath, but as he sank back into the water, he smiled. Gerda was right, he stank.

****

Stefan read the battle reports and feared the worst. Army recruitment numbers were down, borders were shrinking, and everywhere the news looked bleak. His own *Gestapo* agents were ruthlessly effective, but there were threats everywhere. For every stone his men lifted, more abhorrent insects poured out.

If they were to turn the war around, they would need a massive change in direction. As always, he kept his inner thoughts private. In a rare departure from his devotion to the cause, he allowed anger to simmer in the direction the senior leaders had led them. With the allies pushing up from the south and the Russians repelling the earlier German gains, Stefan assumed the worst. It was unlikely he would ever see Peter again. He'd already dealt with his father for meddling in his life. Now, he would turn his attention to Christa.

Stefan picked up a tiny capsule and spun it within his fingers. He knew exactly what would happen if someone ingested the lethal cyanide. Already, Stefan's mind fantasised about Christa's death. She would need to know, of course. That he, Stefan, was the one to bring about her demise.

It wouldn't be easy, and Stefan, though senior enough to have some freedoms, couldn't just poison the woman then leave, unannounced. There had to be an excuse.

He put the tiresome papers to one side and focused. It took most of the day, but when he finally returned to the documents, he discovered an opportunity. There were risks and too many uncertainties, but with luck, he could eliminate one enemy while furthering his career.

119

MARCH 1944, *BERCHTESGADEN*

Hector sat within a deserted copse of trees and thought, as he did every day, back to his chance encounter with Gerda. The meeting brought happiness but also restless discontent. Recounting their conversation, he was sure he'd only offered token information. Nothing substantial. Yes, he'd confirmed Ingrid lived in Frankfurt, though he refused to divulge where. He'd also skilfully danced away from his own story, focussing instead upon Gerda and Ingrid's upbringing. That had been easy. Once the pair had decided that neither offered a threat, Gerda had opened up. And with her honesty came a certain poignancy, and a vulnerability that struck Hector to the core.

They'd sat together, listening to one another, hands outstretched across the kitchen table. The surrealism of the situation was both bizarre and interesting. Their fingers touched, then withdrew, as each felt the magnetism between them. Their common bonds of grief, struggle, and yes, even Ingrid, had drawn them together. It felt inevitable. Had he seduced her, or she him? He wasn't sure, but as they shared a gentle kiss, Hector knew his life, and Gerda's, had inexplicably changed. The pair had parted soon after as the house was frigid, but that one kiss stayed with Hector. He hadn't planned for this at all, but his thoughts inevitably strayed to Gerda as he lay in bed first thing in the morning and last thing at night.

While sitting upon a clump of leaves, Hector mulled the encounter over again. How did one kiss offer more intensity than every encounter he'd shared with the insatiable *Frau* Umer? He didn't know, but the thought scared and excited him with equal measure. Then, as usual, the doubts proliferated. *This is ridiculous. I can't fall in love with someone after just one kiss. And what about her? Surely, she can't feel the same.* Next, his training cut in, voicing several unwanted summations: *You don't know the woman and can't trust her. Come on, man. Pull it together. You have a job to do. Otherwise, the war may never end, or worse, the Germans will win.*

The points were valid, but the arguments failed to remove his smile at reliving the memory. He'd felt a tear when he'd left that night to return to his secret hideaway within the barn, and he hoped Gerda felt the same. But the pair had agreed. He would return to Frankfurt to find Ingrid. He'd accepted that. His fellow spy deserved to know the fate befallen her family and, with Gerda constrained by her role within the BDM, Hector would serve as a messenger.

He'd taken a different route on this occasion, choosing to head towards Nuremberg before proceeding north-west. It made sense. He didn't want to leave an obvious trail, and the more of Germany he could see, the greater the chance he could stumble across valuable intel which he could supply to the British. There was an inevitable downside to this plan. When he'd lived in *Dresden*, he'd gained confidence through knowledge of the local landscape. Now, however, his erratic path left him open to capture with little likelihood he could plot a safe escape route.

Today he would make another push which should return him to Frankfurt and, with luck, the sanctuary of Ingrid's home. He was sick of eating foraged leaves and within a few hours, the lure of Ingrid's sweet tea drew him on.

****

Ingrid sat at the kitchen table and chewed her fingernails. It was a new habit, something she'd begun at Christmas, but it helped pass the time. What was the value of a safe home if all she had was solitude? Her mother would despise the state of her nails, but she wasn't there, and the absence triggered another nibble. She should find some charcoal and return to her art, as that usually calmed. What was the point, with no audience?

The stupor melded with self-recrimination as Ingrid's mood spiralled downward. Outside, rain pelted against the window. The sound normally soothed her, and she could watch the rivulets running down the glass and lose herself for hours. Today the downpour held no interest. Instead, the weather merely reiterated her desire to flush herself away.

Ingrid tore herself from the sight of the street below. Feeling both empty and disgusted, she thumped the wall repeatedly until the pain became too great. *No. Enough*, her mind commanded. Without considering her actions, she grabbed her coat and ran out into the storm. It was stupid to go ill prepared, but determination overrode common sense. She was heading to the station, intent on finding a train south. She'd waited too long. Ingrid was heading home.

120

Archie thought North Africa had been a bad enough experience, but nothing prepared him for Italy. Sure, the climate was tolerable compared to the incessant heat and diving overnight temperatures. But that was the only advantage as sure as he could tell.

In Africa, they fought, dug in, retreated, and fought again. Here, the art of war was different. The Germans were different. Along with many of his comrades, Archie had assumed the mass German surrender on the African continent and Italy's earlier capitulation would bring easier times. He was wrong. To an outsider, it may have seemed the war was turning in favour of the Allies, but not to Archie. While physically strong, his eternal good humour and mental strength had taken a battering. It wasn't just the glacial pace of progress through the country which bothered him. It was the sights he'd seen which ate at his psyche.

The troops had become accustomed to death. They'd seen enough of it. The enemy's actions portrayed an army in flight, and this should have heightened his mood. But now the enemy didn't shoot to kill. Their aim was to inflict injury. The enemy had laid traps everywhere. Not just mines. He'd had his fill of them, but at least he had his trusty mine detector, even if it was Polish. To be fair, until today he'd never met a Pole, but he'd heard they'd suffered terribly under Nazi occupation. It was hard to alter old habits, and Archie admitted he still liked things to be British. He

460

could trust a British invention, and trust in a war situation was imperative.

He ate his breakfast and revisited the events of the previous evening. The Poles arrived overnight, bolstering their numbers, according to his sergeant. Archie's mood had lifted with the news. They had as much right to fight as any of them, and the increase in numbers was certainly welcome. Archie's platoon was currently in limbo, awaiting fresh orders. He held little desire to return to the demanding mountain terrain. His corporal had shared a story that Allied artillery strikes had decimated a mountaintop abbey, only for the Germans to flood in and fight, using the newly formed ruins as cover. Archie didn't know what to believe. There were always conflicting stories, but one thing was clear: the Italian hills were a death-trap.

'Afford.' A voice broke into Archie's thoughts. "Get a move on, lad. Don't you know there's a war on?'

'Yes, Corporal,' Archie responded, smiling sadly at the poor attempt at humour. He'd heard it too many times to instil mirth.

The corporal assembled the men near the command tent, where a topographical map showed the latest battle positions. Archie frowned. They rarely included the lower ranks in these briefings, and when they did, he'd expect the captain, or at least the lieutenant, to take charge. As expected, their captain appeared a couple of minutes later with a newcomer in tow. Archie's eyes swept across the unknown figure. He recognised the red shield emblem on the shoulder, but the other badge left him bemused. A half human, half fish, warrior, wielding a sabre above its head. Putting two and two together, Archie realised these were the 2nd Polish Corps. His eyes moved onto the newcomer's rank. Three stars above two thick wavy lines. Did that make the newcomer a colonel or someone more senior? He supposed it didn't really matter. What mattered was that this was a world war. It drew everyone in, and they were all willing to fight together for a common cause.

'Listen up, men,' the captain broke in on his thoughts. 'This is General Stanisław Kopański. While we've been having all the fun

461

coming up from Naples, our Polish comrades have fought some tough battles across the country. I'm sure those who aren't asleep have heard of San Angelo. If you haven't, then trust me, the San Angelo veterans are battle hardened. Tomorrow, their forces and ours will combine as we punch through the German lines before heading on to Rome.'

Archie had heard such speeches before. He knew the British were the equal of the newcomers, but his captain was merely being polite to the general. He wasn't afraid, but he couldn't help casting his eyes about, wondering who would see another sunset. After three failed attempts to breach the German line already, he knew the costs of advancement.

****

In battle, the Poles were exactly as Archie had hoped: tenacious and fearless. They found a way forward, worming their way through the forbidding terrain to change the angle and create an opportunity for retaliation. The British fought hard too, but in the heat of battle, uniforms became muddied, and confusion reigned. Archie admitted a begrudging respect for the German position. Dug in, high, and difficult to approach. Blasted ruins, a legacy of the repeated allied bombardment. It did them no favours. Just another hole for the Jerries to fire from.

A crack split the air, followed by an agonising cry. Someone close had fallen. All thoughts of advancement vanished as Archie sought the attacker. The victim was groaning. A good sign, Archie thought as he squirmed between some boulders. A bullet ricocheted just inches above his head, and he jerked backwards. Archie cleared the flurry of thoughts in his mind as he attempted to get eyes on the enemy. They were still high, and he stood little chance of identifying the sniper. Glancing behind him, he saw more of the combined force pushing forward. Perhaps they would draw the shooter away, but the pitiful cry from just a few yards away meant Archie couldn't wait. Attaching his water canister to the end of his rifle, he thrust it forward, beyond the safety of the rocks.

Another crack and the bottle exploded. *Sod it.* Losing it was a nuisance, but it gave him a good sign of the shooter's position. Searching his webbing, he discovered he had two grenades. He pulled the pin on one and lobbed it up the hill. He was far enough away to watch the missile deflect off a rock and moments later; it exploded harmlessly. *Damn. That was a waste.* He'd need to get closer. He listened out for his comrades. Spread across the valley, so many exposed. He could do little for them, but the man who'd fallen close by needed saving.

Archie threw himself down and edged backwards. To one side, he saw thick clumps of the bushes the locals called Macchia. Good to hide in, but no defence against a bullet. He had to hope the sniper wouldn't see him enter the thicket. More gunshots sounded further along the valley, and Archie took his chance. Within moments, he hid in the thicket, encountering a painful new enemy: *thorns.* Under other circumstances, he'd have howled as blood seeped from the back of his hands. Other thorns penetrated the rough material of his uniform and into his back. Another spurt of gunfire, and Archie took a deep breath and began the slow, painful crawl toward the fallen soldier. Progress was excruciating, but the new vantage allowed a better appraisal of the German entrenchment. Glancing over his shoulder, he saw the boulders where he'd lain earlier. There was a patina of bullet holes across the rocks, a deadly reminder that the enemy was uncomfortably close. He crawled forward. The moans were a little louder. Now he saw it, the red emblem from the day before. It mattered not whether this was a Pole or someone from his own regiment. It was someone who needed saving.

Only a few yards lay between him, and the other soldier, but it was open terrain. Archie manoeuvred himself around for a better view. The Polish soldier looked in a bad way. Blood covered his tunic, and his helmet was gone. But the man continued to groan, and that spurred Archie on. This could be his last action on earth, but he was saving another man.

Pained and tortured eyes met his as he lay alongside the soldier, followed by dull recognition. Archie gave him a relieved smile, knowing the universal language would offer hope, though inside he knew they were stuck. He was strong enough to lift the soldier and carry him to safety, but how far would he get under a hail of bullets? As if the Germans had heard his thought, more strafing kicked up dust just yards away. Waiting wasn't an option; the poor soul would bleed out.

He couldn't drag him through the thorny thicket. He could stomach more scratches, but it would be too much for the wounded soldier. There was nothing for it. Archie would have to fireman carry the soldier to safety. He just had to hope he could dodge the barrage of bullets while bearing his charge. Steeling himself, the artillery cover he'd prayed for didn't eventuate. Opting for a tiny distraction instead, Archie pulled the pin on the remaining grenade and hurled it towards some boulders about ten yards away. The explosion reverberated around the valley.

Archie didn't wait. Shouldering his weapon, he bent down and scooped up the soldier like he was a mannequin. Head down, he ran. Zigzagging between the bushes, only a few more yards to the safety of his own line. Save the man, then return to the fight. His chest was heaving, but these two thoughts centred him as he ran. He wove a path through the rocks, retracing his steps down into the valley. Bullets whizzed around him, and the man's blood had saturated his shirt, but none of this mattered. A few more steps and he'd be out of range.

His heart lifted, and the hint of a smile was forming on Archie's face when a projectile pierced his left bicep. He didn't feel the pain, or even register the strike. But the ferocity of the hit sent his already moving body into a cartwheel. Both men fell heavily, Archie softening the Pole's fall. It took valuable seconds before Archie's breathing could subside and then the pain hit. A white-hot spear through his upper arm, a pain unlike any he'd experienced. Gritting his teeth, he rolled over. His left arm was useless, but using his right, he found he could prop himself up to assess the area. The shooting had stopped – for now. *Come on, Archie. You didn't come this far to come this far and no further.* The profound thought spurred him on. It took him three attempts to stand and pull the Pole upright and progress was slow. But absurdly, like a marionette with half its strings cut, he tucked the Pole's arm across his shoulders and limped forward, conscious of the drag on his left side.

There was a sudden explosion of shouts. Archie couldn't understand what they were saying. Was he walking towards his own lines or circling back toward the enemy? He was no longer sure. Their lumbering three-legged race continued, and the pain in Archie's shoulder grew. Now, as they slowed, Archie could feel a sense of urgency. His strength was waning, something he'd never encountered in the past. The voices sounded again. They were foreign, and Archie's disquiet grew. Surely, he hadn't delivered the Pole to the enemy? The belief slowed his progress and, without meaning to, he sank onto one knee. *You bloody idiot*, his mind said. *What are you doing?* The scene slowed around him. Perhaps the Germans would spot the two injured men and finish them. Perhaps he died today, but Archie knew he'd done all he could. He sank to the ground and closed his eyes.

121

MARCH 1944, FRANKFURT

Hector called out to Ingrid, but it was too late. The noise of the storm drowned out his cries. He tracked her run until she disappeared around the corner, and then he cursed under his breath. With the cumbersome radio, there was no way he could catch her, so instead he headed for the front door of the house. That, at least, remained unlocked, and he stepped inside, shaking droplets across the floor. He considered his next course of action. Safely stow the case while Ingrid ran further away, or ditch it in the hallway before sprinting after her? He opted for a middle ground. The cloakroom offered only basic security, but it would have to do, and he tore off into the stinging rain. At the intersection, he skidded to a halt. *Where are you going?* Wherever it was, he'd lost sight of his friend, and that bothered him. It was unlike Ingrid to run off. She wasn't carrying anything, and he didn't think it was just the weather which sped her on. Something was wrong.

He paused before choosing a direction, determined to get it right. Heading east made little sense, not where bombs had landed a few months earlier. She hadn't turned about, as far as Hector could tell, so that left two choices. Unless, of course, she was running away from someone? The possibility unnerved him, and he looked around to make sure nobody had followed his run. But the streets behind were devoid of people. *Only a fool would venture out in this weather*, he thought. *A fool, or a soldier on duty.* The sickening thought spurred him into action.

Ingrid knew the station wasn't far away and yet despite spending six months in the city, the torrential downpour left her disorientated. The shells of ruined buildings only added to her confusion. Her eyes stung and she could barely see. Spotting an awning, she dived underneath. Whoever owned the shop had shown sense, with thick shutters drawn behind the glass. Ingrid caught her reflection and blanched. What was she thinking, running out unprepared into a storm? Standing still hardly helped as the pause allowed her to feel every wet tendril tickling her skin. Along the street, someone approached. A man, she guessed from the clothing and gait, though they stooped to avoid the worst of the deluge. Ingrid saw the figure and felt her body contract. Whoever it was, they reminded her of the *Gestapo* officers who'd come for her as she'd waited for her date in *Schütting*. It didn't matter there was only one of them – someone was coming for her. She turned inward towards the building. A foolish decision as she could no longer see, but perhaps they would pass by, leaving her unnoticed.

'*Fraülein.*' Reluctantly, Ingrid turned to face the speaker. 'Ah, you heard me. It's hard to hear anything above this rain. Do you mind if I take shelter with you for a few minutes?'

To refuse would seem churlish, so Ingrid wordlessly nodded. This was the last thing she needed. Whether to turn tail and return home or push on to the station was still in debate, but not until the rain cleared and the stranger left her alone.

'Why are you out in such terrible weather?'

It was hardly an inappropriate question, but Ingrid's suspicions resurfaced, convincing her that this man was digging and, therefore, a threat. 'I was halfway home when the rain became too heavy.' *That's it, Ingrid. Offer him nothing.*

'Of course. And where is home?'

Her heart sank. These were reasonable questions and in an alternative reality where Naziism had failed to prosper, she'd feel flattered that a stranger cared. But not here. Not now. She pointed in the vague direction of home.

'I have another mile to walk,' she lied.

'You should not be out here alone. I think, perhaps, when the weather eases, I should escort you home. For your own safety.'

And there it was. To Ingrid's mind, the stranger had left a tell, confirming her worst fears. 'I...I'm sure I'll be fine,' she stammered.

'Nonsense.' The man shook his head. 'I will escort you...unless, of course, you'd prefer me to deliver you somewhere else?' Before Ingrid could compute the stranger's words, he took her wrist in a brutal grip. '*Fraülein*. I don't know who you are, or why you are out here, but I am not the sort of man to take no for an answer. Now, since we must wait out this rain, you can show me your papers.'

Ingrid tried to pull her arm away, but the grip was too strong. Fear gave way to anger, and she flared. 'If you could just let go, I'll show you my identity card. There's no need for roughness.' The man's grip slackened, though didn't entirely release. Ingrid moved to comply while her mind searched for an escape. She had to take a chance. In a snap decision, she lifted her right foot and slammed it down in a calculated move. Her heel dug into the stranger's shin before stamping on his instep. As the man howled, she spun inwards, and seeing his exposed throat, she threw a well-timed chop just below his Adam's apple. He dropped immediately, eyes bulging as his arms flailed to clear his airway. Ingrid lifted her foot a second time. She daren't leave the man conscious before escaping, but new hands gripped her waist, pulling her away. Whoever her new, unknown attacker was, they were strong as they lifted her away from the man on the ground.

'Stop.'

She kicked wildly, but her assailant was too strong. The pair swung around, and she found herself at the mercy of the rain once more. Another shout. Familiar, yet in her rage, distant. Her attacker planted her onto the pavement before stepping away. She coiled her body, ready to spring back into the fight.

And then the recognition hit as strongly as any blow could, and Ingrid's mouth parted in shock as her assailant's features swam into view. Hector.

'I thought you may need my help,' he said, 'though it looks like you were doing just fine without me.' Her friend reached down and pulled Ingrid to her feet. 'Come on, let's find out who he is.'

The stranger lay motionless as Ingrid approached. Was this man simply a predator, or worse, *Gestapo*? She had to know. 'Help me turn him over,' she said. White fearful eyes greeted their inspection. The grey pallor and bruising to his throat suggested Ingrid had crushed his larynx. The man only had moments to live. Ingrid's training kicked in and she searched his pockets. Her fingers touched the cold metal of a pistol grip, proving her instincts correct. With Hector helping, they stripped the agent of his Walther PPK and his identity papers. The man was *Gestapo*.

'Take the arms, I'll get the legs.' The rain was still falling as they half-dragged, half-carried the man further down the street to a townhouse with street access via stairs to a cellar below. They heaved the body down the stone steps and spun away. Ingrid wasn't sure whether the man was alive or dead, but it was clear he was in no state to pursue them.

An hour later, Ingrid wrapped her hands around the warm tea Hector had brewed. She shuddered at her foolishness but swaddled in a double layer of blankets. She listened, crestfallen, as Hector described his visit to *Berchtesgaden*.

At the outset of the day, Ingrid had felt desperate for answers and optimistic about a family reunion. With Hector's news, she sank into a deep state of self-recrimination. If only she hadn't left her home and fled to England. Her mother and Ōma were dead. Dieter was dead. Her father lost to the Nazi machine. The news of Gerda was too little, too late, and made no impact.

As Ingrid dug her sobbing head into the blankets, she had only one thought: *all this was her fault.*

122

JUNE 1944, FRANKFURT

'Do you think Gerda's one of us?' It was a question Ingrid had posed to Hector many times over recent months, and she knew his answer would be consistent and affirmative. If true, then it meant they needed her. With ambivalence from the British and a desire to do something about the Nazi regime, they needed allies. But trust was not something easily gifted.

The pair had toyed with leaving Frankfurt three months earlier. The death of the *Gestapo* agent would lead to reprisals, but it was hard to leave the comfort of the house, and with diminishing options, they stayed. It seemed a sensible option: keep quiet and wait out the storm.

Hector kept out of sight, along with the radio, which they'd temporarily bricked up within the darkest recesses of the cellar. They both realised the futility of operating the equipment if there was no intel to share.

Visitors inevitably came knocking. But Ingrid had planned for their visit, leaving her prepared. The soldiers routinely worked their way along streets, asking residents a stock series of questions. Ingrid presented legitimate papers and with nobody to dispute her fabricated inheritance, they soon moved on.

She had dodged another bullet, but the knowledge didn't bring a sense of comfort.

They were in limbo again, but Ingrid had achieved one thing of value during their hiatus. She'd used her skills as an artist to create fresh papers for them both. In theory, should Hector decide to travel again, movement would be easier.

Ingrid sipped thoughtfully on her tea. She and Hector agreed Gerda held value, though neither knew how to use this to their advantage.

123

JULY 1944, *BERCHTESGADEN*

Gerda's eyes rested on the beautiful vista of the Bavarian Alps. The year had been a strange one. News filtered down to their town, always buoyant, but the propaganda failed to fool her. She wasn't alone. More and more people were waking up to the fact the war was going badly. Only the iron will of the authorities prevented dissenters from voicing their fears. But that only reinforced Gerda's privately held opinion. Many were expressing shock at their nation's heavy losses, and there were whispers of horrific treatment at the camps. Gerda still wore a uniform, although she was far too old for any role in the League of German Maidens besides a token leadership role. Most of the girls had learnt to stay well clear of the *old maid*, as they referred to her. She was supposed to be married, a mother. But none of that had happened. Gerda knew she was an oddity in an increasingly odd world.

Wearing a uniform was akin to wearing a mask; but her chance meeting with Ingrid and the appearance of Hector had flicked the switch. And, as the mask dissolved, Gerda saw clearly. From the rubble of insight, a new stoic robustness was forming. Indifference toward the Nazi regime felt like a weight lifted, although she was careful to keep up appearances.

'Gerda.' The excited shout came from behind, and as Gerda spun, Christa barrelled into her with an all-encompassing hug. 'Oh, it's so good to see you. It seems like years since we were together.'

Gerda rested her head on Christa's shoulder, carefully substituting her dismay for joy. 'Look at you, Christa.' She forced a wide smile. 'I can't believe it. I thought I'd never see you again after you began your job at the *Obersalzberg*. Tell me. What is it like being so close to the *Führer*?'

Christa's face became smug. 'Oh, it's the best. And I don't just spend my time here. Sometimes I visit the *Kehlsteinhaus*' – she waved across the valley to the teahouse high atop a hill – 'and then there are the longer trips to Nuremberg and Berlin. It's allowed me to see the country in ways I couldn't have dreamed of.'

'Then you must tell me all about it. But first, how long are you home for?'

Christa shrugged. 'Not long. But there's time enough for us to eat and drink and enjoy this wonderful summer together.'

****

The morning passed swiftly, and Gerda noticed that while she gave Christa her full attention, her friend failed to show more than a cursory interest in her life. Perhaps that was justified. After all, Gerda had accomplished little since their childhood, and what she had done had come under sufferance. While Christa, *the wonderful Christa*, had gone from strength to strength. There were some startling revelations as Christa gleefully revealed Walter had fathered her child as part of the Lebensborn program seven years earlier.

'You're a mother?'

'It was necessary for the good of the country. Walter was pretty, but oh, so weak.' Christa's full lips curled in distaste.

'But what of the child? Where are they now?'

Gerda read one expression on her friend's face: no sadness, just apathy. Beyond knowing she'd borne a boy, Christa didn't know or care. She hadn't even given the child a name. Gerda found this lack of feeling horrifying, and she wondered whether it showed, but Christa had already moved on. 'I'm convinced of it, Gerda,' she repeated. 'Knowing the *Führer* the way *I* do, it was my commitment to the cause that brought me into the inner sanctum.'

Without missing a beat, Christa shared further exploits. It seemed she'd been everywhere and seen everyone. A far cry from Gerda's life. Despite the gloating, Gerda fuelled her friend's ego, encouraging her to tell more. Besides, it deflected any interest in her own life.

'What did you say?' Gerda shook her head in annoyance that she'd tuned out Christa's words.

'*Kummersdorf*. There's an artillery range there.'

'But why?'

'Weren't you listening? It's the new rocket they're building. It'll destroy the Allies, leaving us victorious. I'm going to the demonstration launch next month.'

'That sounds exciting,' Gerda lied. Truth be told, she could not trust the Nazis with any superior technology. But her friend was clearly proud of the new weaponry, and as Gerda feigned interest, Christa boastfully revealed details about her upcoming trip.

By the time the pair parted, Gerda felt compelled to act. Her loyalties to the Fatherland were both entrenched and wrong. Ordinary Germans, good people, were suffering horribly under the new regime and that was before she lifted the stone to reveal other atrocities. Uncertain whether the Allies were as bad, she was in two minds as to her course of action.

As Gerda lay awake that night, her normally agile mind wrestled with the new-found intelligence. She'd learnt so much from Christa. Not just about the rockets, but also news of an Allied invasion of France. The British, Americans, and all the other nations were coming, and unless Germany unleashed the rockets, it seemed there was no hope for her country.

It was clear the war hung in the balance and, although fearful of defeat, Gerda couldn't countenance the use of another killing machine. She had to do something. Only what?

124

AUGUST 1944, BERLIN

Stefan appeared smug as he gazed along the line of senior German officers. Most appeared immaculate. There was even talk that the *Führer* would visit. That would be a real coup. Stefan had no right to attend, but after months of reading reports about the work carried out here, he knew today's presentation held hope. And that meant he needed to secure entry at all costs. In the end, he'd felt a fool as he'd practically begged to be included, but it was worth it. He was here now.

Within the tightly secured compound, he saw a simple sign – *Aggreat 4*. Although he lacked the understanding for the science, Stefan had scoured enough papers to realise the potential these new weapons offered. And this looked big. Not just the physicality, more the threat.

Even the weather held favour. Midsummer sunshine warmed the assembled crowd as they waited patiently. He took the time to study the others. Plenty of familiar faces stood in line. Standing in a suit, Goebbels stood out against the uniforms. That was good. Stefan intended to buttonhole the propaganda minister. He hoped to persuade the man to adopt a new name for the programme: *Vergeltungswaffe Zwei*. Vengeance seemed a far more fitting title than just V2.

Casting his eyes further back, his eyes widened with a mixture of dismay and excitement. Christa was here, though, further back with the junior ranks. He saw annoyance cross her face as she

475

caught his stare. *Yes, dear Christa, I'm the senior one here.* However, her presence was good news. As part of Hitler's entourage, her appearance suggested the *Führer* may be close by.

Stefan watched in awe as the scientists wheeled out a huge contraption. Mounted above, lay a gigantic rocket. He'd read the articles, but the sheer scale of the weapon was incredible. Judging by the quickly muffled *oohs* and *ahs*, others standing in line thought the same.

Stefan's attendance today was for two main reasons. He wanted obvious proof the Germans held the means to turn the war around, and he could not deny the majesty of such a weapon. Bearing witness, while a privilege, was the simple part of his plan. He subconsciously patted his jacket pocket. The cyanide capsule was secure in its depths. Did he dare use it on Christa, should the opportunity arise? He could rid himself of the despicable woman once and for all, but equally, they could catch him out, and the penalty for killing a member of Hitler's staff would be swift and brutal.

He bade his time as the demonstration continued. The buzz within the attendees was infectious. After a gigantic roar and a dark smoke trail that disappeared to the heavens, everyone agreed on the significance of such a weapon and the devastation it could wreak against their enemy.

The demonstration over, the group retired to a hangar where the lower ranks laid refreshments out. The senior staff filed off to a stage at one end, though Stefan found himself forced to remain on the main floor.

'Impressive, wasn't it?'

Recognising Christa's voice, he turned, forcing a smile. 'Hello, Christa dear,' he said, air-kissing the woman's cheeks. 'I didn't realise you were coming to see this demonstration of German engineering superiority.' Naturally, this was a blatant lie.

'Dear Stefan. You should know I go wherever *Herr* Hitler goes.' Although a jibe, there was playfulness in her tone.

Stefan let his smile linger before spying the lunch spread across the nearby tables. His brain considered the capsule, and he edged toward the food. 'Hungry?' he asked, keen to be the one to offer Christa some sustenance.

'Always,' she responded. 'Did you mean food or something else?'

Playing along with Christa's flirtation, Stefan grasped her hand and led her toward the tables. His calm mind had one simple goal: palm the cyanide into Christa's food and then move away before she could take a bite. He twisted his body a few degrees. Not much, but enough to release the pill, ready for him to secrete. He was ready. All he had to do now was deposit the poison and get away. The only downside, he couldn't stay to watch. He couldn't run, either, as that would be a giveaway, but he couldn't stand close to the woman. He felt his blood coursing through his veins as he steeled himself to commit the deed. As he withdrew the capsule, he paused and placed it back in his pocket.

The *Führer* had just entered the building and taken centre stage.

****

Gerda peeked out from behind a clump of thick bushes and shuddered. What was she thinking? She had no business being here and if they caught her, then consequences were unthinkable. The authorities had granted her three days' leave to attend to a sick aunt in Berlin. But that was just the start of her lies. With no family member, ill or otherwise, living in the capital, her excuse was wafer thin. She'd even lied to her mother before taking an overnight train north, arriving in the metropolis for breakfast. And there, within Berlin, she could have halted. Instead, she took another train south, this time heading to *Luckenwalde*. She'd have preferred to exit the train earlier at Trebbin, but security looked tight, and she moved on to the next stop.

The decision did her no favours. Not only was she further away from her target, but now she had *Sperenberg Airfield* and its associated security barring her path. As she sat on a divot of dried mud, she wondered why she'd bothered. Her answer came only moments later. An unnatural whine carried across the fields, and

Gerda stood to identify the source. Her eyes on the sky, her mouth parted in shock. A rocket, travelling at supernatural speed, going higher and higher, until it appeared to pierce the sky and disappear.

Gerda's legs buckled, and she collapsed on the earth. Some would view the enormous rocket with admiration and wonder, but to Gerda, it heralded an apocalypse. She'd seen enough. Somehow, she had to find Hector. He would know what to do.

125

SEPTEMBER 1944, *BERCHTESGADEN* / BERLIN

A cruel mantra was playing out in Gerda's head: *You're a worthless fraud*. She had spent the last few weeks dithering, and the intel she'd garnered from Christa remained a secret. She was desperate to find Hector, and, she hoped, Ingrid too. But no knowledge beyond an approximation of the Frankfurt area left her stymied. With each passing day, she asked herself how much further the German military machine would push this new weapon while she stood idle. How many innocents would lose their lives?

She'd asked her superiors if they'd allow another journey to Frankfurt, but they declined, offering training for girls in Potsdam instead. Then, when she rejected their appeasement, they came down hard on her, and Gerda realised the trip to seek Hector or Ingrid was bordering on the impossible.

Taking a different tack, she'd pleaded for a few days' leave. Again, they refused. That left her with two options: stay home or travel to Potsdam. While Potsdam brought her much closer to the weapons testing facility, Gerda lacked any influence and opted to remain in her hometown. But as she sat, the stewing continued. The likelihood that Hector would return seemed remote.

One thing lifted her mood: her pact with Hector. After their brief liaison, they'd agreed to dates and times when she would return to the Stiepermann house. It seemed absurd she should take the risk and venture out to the home on a schedule. Someone will notice. But she owed the family, and she yearned for Hector's return. Tonight, she would return, and with just an hour to go, her stomach turned over in excitement.

The time dragged, but the mantel clock finally chimed the hour. Gerda eased herself out of the bedroom and descended the stairs. The house was silent as she pulled on a coat.

'Where do you think you are going?'

With a sinking feeling, Gerda turned to face her mother. She thought fast. 'I'm off to see Sabine Schwartz, Mama.' She kept her voice neutral. 'As you know, her sister is growing up and wants to join the Maidens. They asked me to go along as an authority and explain how things have changed since we first joined.'

'Well, that will have to wait. I made fresh soup, and it won't keep. Come. Eat your food like a good girl and then, once you've helped tidy away, perhaps you can go.'

Why are you treating me like a child? Gerda's mind screamed. She hated her lack of backbone, but she couldn't risk upsetting her mother. She buttoned her lip and joined her mother in the kitchen.

****

Hector jiggled the back door as quietly as he could, but it wouldn't budge. He remembered how Gerda had made it look easy and tried again, without success. His defeat told him that Gerda wasn't inside, otherwise she would have greeted him. He would wait as long as he could, but in his heart, he feared she wouldn't show, and that bothered him. Another month would pass before their next scheduled meeting, too long to remain hidden within the town. And, if she didn't show, what did it mean? Was he the only one who had felt a connection? Time had eroded his certainty, and now he sat conflicted. But the visit wasn't just for him. Ingrid, too, yearned for news, and he was afraid of letting her down.

He glanced at his watch. He decided he would wait another half an hour, then he would have to leave. Impatience and anxiety overwhelmed, overtaking the numbness within his thighs as he waited on the cold step. His self-imposed time limit passed, and he wearily accepted Gerda was not coming. He stamped his feet and turned as Gerda swept through the gate and kept coming, meeting him head on. She ran into his arms and pressed her lips to his, and he knew everything would be all right.

'I thought you weren't coming,' he admitted, touching a hand to her cheek.

'It was Mama,' Gerda explained. 'She insisted I needed feeding. In the end, I had to lie to get away.'

Within the dim light, he saw a spot of soup on her upper lip, and he kissed it away. 'There,' he whispered, 'now you're even more beautiful.'

Gerda blushed, then took his hand and led him back to the house. One swift movement, and she had the door open again.

'How did you do that?' he asked in amazement.

'I told you I have a knack.' She grinned; her eyes sparkling.

'That you do,' he said, pulling her against him. They would need to exchange information, but there were more pressing needs.

****

'What did she say?' Ingrid demanded as Hector came up the front path to the house. He had left her a week ago. She hated time alone, rattling about in a vast, empty house, and news was always scarce. There was a note of reproach in her voice, but she didn't care.

'Hold on.' Hector held up his hands. 'I'm barely in the door. Let's have a cup of tea and I'll tell you everything.'

As they sat at the kitchen table, Hector shared Gerda's news about the V2 rockets. They immediately agreed that they'd have to tell the Allies. But another admission bothered Ingrid more; Hector had shared their Frankfurt address, and this seemed an unnecessary – and dangerous – divulgence. And now Hector was saying Gerda would head for *Potsdam* to get closer to the *Kummersdorf* artillery range.

Ingrid's hands flew to her mouth. Poor Gerda lacked the training to spy against her own country.

****

'Have Gruppe Nord launched the rockets?' Stefan barked to a subordinate. 'How many?'

'Over one thousand, *Herr Sturmbannführer*. They launched just minutes ago.'

Stefan's lips curled into a smile. Both at hearing his new rank repeated back to him and at the volume of rockets about to hit London. He'd followed the rocket programme with interest, but this was the first large-scale assault.

After asking for an update once they'd hit, he sat back, eyes narrowed, his hands forming a steeple. This was exactly the news he wanted to hear.

126

SEPTEMBER 1944, OXFORDSHIRE

Gregson could barely contain his excitement. They'd finally received news from Hector and Ingrid. The elation faded before becoming tinged with dismay. His team was already aware of the German rocket programme, but the news validated critical details and bore grave concern.

The British and the Allies as a whole were stoic – the Blitz had proven that, but the V2 rockets had the potential for massive casualties. But by some minor miracle, their two agents were still alive. Their intel had value, and that meant Gregson would have to act on this information.

He organised a car which would take him fifty miles to south Oxfordshire. He hated driving and with a short day, he'd likely have to stay over, but this couldn't wait. The journey took longer than expected, but when the sign for RAF Benson appeared, Gregson breathed, the tension releasing from his shoulders.

They were expecting him, so after undergoing the usual security checks; they brought him to see the Officer of the Day, a Flight Lieutenant who appeared familiar to Gregson. The pair shook hands, but both were well aware of the ensuing dance between Intelligence and the Air Force. Gregson would request some reconnaissance sorties, putting the pilots' lives in danger. So, like all before him, he had to plead his case. However, Gregson was an old hand at this dance and thought ahead, gaining preliminary approval from higher up the chain of command.

'Thank you for seeing me.'

'Always a pleasure,' the officer replied, giving nothing away.

'Can you get the aerial intel we need?'

'Get it? We've already got it, old chap.'

Gregson followed the officer to an adjacent hut where a vast table dominated the room. Photographs littered the space with a curious piece of equipment sitting at one end. It looked like a set of eyeglasses, mounted to look vertically down. Gregson recognised the stereoscope, though he'd never used one before.

'Go on,' the officer prompted. 'Take a gander. You have the clearance.'

Gregson dipped his head over the device, and whistled in surprise Flat, indistinct photographs came to life as buildings lifted off the table, giving them a real, three-dimensional appearance. 'Impressive, though you know the target I'd like to inspect.'

For the next hour, they pored over hundreds of photographs. Although the Germans had gone to great lengths to camouflage their true intent, there were some signs they couldn't hide. Twin scorch marks across the earth told a tale, and the men agreed they'd found the rocket launch site.

A new uniform burst into the room. 'Sir, you'd better look at this.'

The officer frowned. 'Can it wait, Sergeant?'

'Not really, Sir. It's London. The Germans have launched a gigantic wave of rockets on the city.'

Gregson's face paled. This was no longer just a threat on paper. Now, more than ever, he needed Hector and Ingrid's intel to help defeat this new menace.

127

SEPTEMBER 1944, BERLIN

The British had come through at last, though the news was bittersweet. They'd supplied Hector and Ingrid with contacts, who, with luck, could help them in their efforts. Naturally, there was a price involved. It was wartime, and there was always a price.

For now, the pair would have to split, with Ingrid making the rendezvous with one such ally, while Hector would return to *Berchtesgaden* to meet with Gerda. Hector had left at first light, and it would be Ingrid's turn in the morning. She'd have preferred to reunite with her friend in *Berchtesgaden*, but Hector's enthusiasm for the task won out. There was something between the pair, Ingrid could tell. She smiled. Despite being a trained spy, Hector failed to keep his feelings toward Gerda hidden. While happy for the pair, their blossoming relationship cast a spotlight on the relationship-sized hole in her own life. Drawing a pillow to her chest, she closed her eyes and dreamed of Archie.

****

Gerda felt a sense of unease as she read Christa's letter. Her friend gave information freely, with barely a prompt from Gerda. Perhaps it was Christa's lack of diligence causing her disquiet. Gerda wanted news and Christa delivered, but was anyone else reading the letters her friend sent? Still, anyone reading the note could clearly see where any fault lay. Christa was a blabbermouth, freely sharing information to elevate her own position.

Today Gerda was taking a break from Potsdam and the BDM girls to travel into the city. Berlin was vast, and she'd have preferred to stay away, but Christa's invitation was too good an opportunity to miss. With time to spare, she walked a path beneath the neoclassical Brandenburg Gate.

The columns gleamed golden in the Autumn light, and Gerda took shelter in their shadows, away from prying eyes. While she waited, she studied the people passing by. Most, like her, wore one uniform or another, which added a layer of invisibility. Despite bombing attacks which had hit the city, nobody appeared bothered. Such outward nonchalance seemed absurd to Gerda. A clock chimed the hour, and Gerda shook herself. She walked along Pariser Platz to the Aldon Hotel, her meeting place with Christa.

The building was opulent, and Gerda privately hoped Christa would foot the bill. Her friend had specified the venue, so could hardly complain. A doorman admitted her into a large atrium, and then a concierge took over. 'You are Miss Gerda?' he enquired with a charming smile. 'Come, your friend is waiting for you in the lounge. Follow me.'

As usual, Christa rose from her chair with an excited squeal before summarily dismissing the concierge. The man withdrew, a scowl on his face. Clearly, he was not used to being dismissed by a woman. The old friends embraced, and over lunch, the women repeated the same old pattern; Gerda would listen, while Christa would boast and unwittingly let secrets slip. It took all Gerda's powers of concentration to keep up with events while playing the sycophant, but she played the role admirably.

'So, why did you choose this hotel to meet me?' Gerda asked.

Christa's face flushed as she leant in. 'Don't tell anyone,' she whispered. 'But *Herr* Hitler doesn't like this hotel. He's only ever visited once. I worship our leader, but sometimes being at the pinnacle, I need some breathing space.'

Gerda bit back a smile, before assuring her friend she'd keep her confidence. Although a small secret, it amused Gerda that Christa felt the need to escape. That didn't make her an ally, however. The next topic was slightly more sensitive. Gerda could ask about the demonstration at *Kummersdorf*, but beyond chit chat, she daren't push it too far. She needn't have worried. While Gerda had sat in the thicket to see the rocket testing from afar, Christa told the inside story. She'd even seen Stefan.

'I haven't seen him in years,' Gerda admitted. 'What's he like these days?'

'He hasn't changed. Full of himself and out for power.'

Like you then, Gerda thought.

Christa prattled on and by the time their lunch meeting ended, Gerda had learnt some intriguing details about Stefan and his role within the Nazi machine.

****

'Are you certain Stefan will be there?'

Ingrid, Hector, and Gerda had met in a small house near the League of German Maidens camp in Potsdam. The Nazi leadership had handed down a new directive. They would conscript the older girls to reinforce frontier fortifications. Gerda saw this as further proof that the regime was crumbling, but she kept her mouth firmly shut as she delivered the girls to the citizen militia for training. From there, she'd ducked away to rendezvous with Ingrid and Hector.

Ingrid's contacts had updated her on the Allies' progress across the continent. Finland and the Soviet Union had recently agreed on a ceasefire, and just yesterday, Ingrid heard that the British Second Army had captured Brussels. There was a suggestion that an extraction could occur, but she and Hector would need to be near Berlin. Hector had reconnoitred an abandoned farmhouse that was convenient for all parties, and the group had met in the late afternoon.

Gerda had brought them up to date with Christa's latest divulgence as they ate a simple meal. She drained the soup from her spoon and turned to answer Ingrid's question. 'I think so. Christa's meeting him in November. From what she said, he practically begged her to attend.'

Ingrid took the empty bowl from her friend and washed the dishes in the sink. By the time she returned, Hector had covered the table with a map. 'Are you sure that's what she said?' Ingrid frowned as her eyes spied the open wilderness to the west of Berlin. Grunewald Forest bordered by the wide Havel waterway seemed a curious meeting spot.

Gerda shrugged. 'She said, "Grunewald Forest".'

A black rectangle marked the farmhouse with two smaller dots off to the west. Ingrid measured the distance to the closest alternative structure. It looked like the neighbouring buildings were almost a mile away. Was that a good thing, or would they be walking into a trap?

They spent the next hour discussing their options, but in the end, they all agreed. Their presence at the farmhouse was an absolute necessity.

128

NOVEMBER 1944, BERLIN

In the distance, Stefan spied Grunewald Tower. It was an imposing edifice against the dark backdrop of trees. Stefan wondered whether anyone stood guard. He cursed, wishing this had crossed his mind earlier. It was highly likely soldiers stationed on the viewing platform would have an excellent vantage point across the Havel. *It's too late now*, he thought. He clung to the hope that Christa would follow his instructions and come.

While he'd forgotten to check for guards, he had been more circumspect toward his current destination. *Saubucht* was, as expected, deserted. Stefan sighed as he approached on the motorcycle. Once he killed the engine on his *Zündapp* KS 750, the only noises that reached his ears came from woodland creatures. That suited him. A fox wouldn't retell his involvement.

The tower lay half a mile away, and while the trees prevented noise from carrying, he couldn't be certain whether they'd hear his bike. The river was close too, though it seemed highly unlikely anyone would come ashore to investigate a solitary motorbike.

Stefan estimated he had an hour before Christa's arrival. That suited him, and he wheeled the bike around the picket fence before tucking it behind an outhouse. There he set the bike along one wall. It would take him a few seconds to pull the vehicle back onto the path, but he wanted to leave little evidence of his arrival.

Next, after checking the outhouse and finding it deserted, he walked the perimeter of the main building. Satisfied he was alone, he moved inside. The large two-storey house suited his needs perfectly. Remote enough, at the end of a maze of tracks, but solid enough to mask his clandestine purpose. He pulled out a chair and, for the first time that day, relaxed and turned his attention towards Christa. *Will she come?*

He believed she would, but the woman had never been reliable. If she didn't, then he'd only lost a few hours from his day, although it would leave a bitter taste if she continued to walk the earth. No, he corrected himself. She will come. He'd dangled a carrot, suggesting he had information she'd find valuable. A blatant lie, but one which preyed upon the woman's craving for power.

He imagined her arrival. The initial enthusiasm, then horror as he forced the cyanide capsule down her throat, or, failing that, a bullet from his Walther. And with dozens of paths to choose from paired with a thick forest to hide a body, he'd finally be free of her interference.

Minutes ticked by and Stefan revisited all possibilities as he sat waiting. Would she come alone? He expected she would, but the 'what-if' persisted before he laughingly dismissed the idea. Christa wasn't the type. She was too self-assured to predict any peril within their meeting. Or too naïve, Stefan smiled.

****

'Can I come with you?' Gerda asked Christa.

Her friend's eyes narrowed as she considered the request. 'I don't think you should,' she shook her head. 'Stefan wouldn't like it. Besides, there are things I need to hear which are just for my ears.'

'Of course, I understand,' Gerda said, even though she didn't. 'But Grunewald. Why there? It's so remote. What if he attacks you?'

'Some things are better done in secret. You needn't worry. I know things about him which would curl your ears,' she chuckled. 'And anyway, I have this,' she said.

Gerda's eyes widened as Christa revealed a sharp dagger. Granted, it was a weapon, but Christa would need to be at her best to overpower a strong SS officer. 'Well, if you must go alone, tell me exactly where you're going and how long you think you'll be. If you're not back in a few hours, I'll come looking for you.'

Christa rolled her eyes before nodding and relaying the details.

As Christa left for her rendezvous, Gerda dashed into the street. She didn't have long, and Ingrid and Hector needed this latest intelligence.

****

Ordinarily, Christa hated driving, especially within the city streets. She preferred to be driven and had grown accustomed to this luxury while working at the *Obersalzberg*. But today, as the trees whipped past, she felt elated. The bumpy track remained dry and with branches whipping past at the side of the borrowed BMW 319 cabriolet, she thought about seeing Stefan again and smiled. She enjoyed the sense of control she felt when meeting Stefan. Ever since she'd learnt his dirty secret, she'd considered him a toy. Someone to use when it suited.

Still, his request to meet today had piqued her interest. It was usually her calling the shots. *Perhaps he wants my help to locate his depraved lover.* After all, he didn't know she'd sent Peter to the Russian front. She wouldn't offer that form of help. But offering in return for something useful held no threat. What could Stefan do if she failed to help? Her attention drifted as she thought of the likely information Stefan would offer, and then a branch whipped across her hand on the wheel, drawing blood. The car twisted into an arc before she threw the wheel in the opposite direction.

Damn.

The cut dripped blood onto her skirt, but Christa barely slowed. Instead, she dangled her hand out to one side in contempt toward the onrushing foliage. She reached a fork in the trail, and without slowing, she swung the car left, enjoying the thrill as the vehicle shifted beneath her. With only another mile to go, she pushed the car harder, intent on confronting Stefan.

****

Ingrid and Hector pedaled furiously, with Gerda trailing further back. It had taken them half an hour to get this far, and Ingrid knew she couldn't go on without a rest. Breathless, she signalled to Hector, and together they waited for Gerda to catch-up. Suddenly, their mission seemed ludicrous. *Stefan will be long gone if we ever find the place.* Irritated, she pushed her negative thoughts down.

Once Gerda arrived, Ingrid said, 'I'm sure we're close, but these paths are so similar.' The trio listened intently, but beyond the nuthatches and other birds chirping in the trees, they heard nothing untoward.

'Do we split up?' Gerda asked.

'No.' Ingrid shook her head. 'Stefan's too dangerous. He's not stupid. If we seize him, we must be together.' Taking a deep breath, she pushed off along the trail.

****

Stefan felt his body tense as his ears caught the growl of a vehicle approaching at speed. *Is it her?* He remained in the shadows until the car came into view. The clouds of dust cleared, and a rush of excitement ran through Stefan. His smile was cruel as he advanced to the door.

'Christa, I'm so glad you came. Quickly, come inside.'

The pair exchanged insincere cheek pecks as she crossed the threshold. She was barely inside before she spun towards him. 'Well? What is it you have to tell me?'

She was all about business. *What a shame*, he thought. He wanted to savour her death, but so be it. 'I have everything you need upstairs. Follow me.'

He expected reticence, but Christa obligingly followed him. Part of him felt disappointed. *A lamb to the slaughter.* Where was her fight? He wanted to see terror in her eyes before ending her. *Silly me, I haven't attacked her yet. The stupid woman doesn't know.* The cruel smile returned.

'Sit,' he commanded when they entered the master bedroom.

'I'll stand. Now tell me. Why am I here?'

****

Christa looked on in anger as Stefan failed to answer her question. His only offering was a strange grimace. *Stupid fool, he has nothing to give.* She turned to one side and considered the dagger sheathed against her thigh. Could she threaten him? Her hand tracked down to her skirt, revealing a tiny bulge against her leg. No. The man was a degenerate, but she wasn't sure whether she could bring herself to stab him. Her hand lifted, and she lifted her eyes to Stefan's face.

'Well, this was nice,' she said, her voice rich with sarcasm. 'You're wasting my—'

The punch to her gut came without warning, and Christa crumpled to the floor. She couldn't breathe. Her abdomen was on fire, and she curled into a ball, incomprehension etched across her face. The question wasn't why had he hit her, it was why had she been so stupid to not foresee he could? From dismissing Gerda as an unwanted chaperone to her high-risk drive through the forest, Christa had considered herself invulnerable. Now all she felt was agony as her breaths came in quick gasps. She could barely move and with no clue to where Stefan stood, she rolled and crawled out onto the landing. Her mind told her there was something she could do to fight back. If only she could remember. One arm reached the doorframe. A jack boot swept in from the left and connected with her palm, and she screamed in agony.

'You think you're better than me?' Stefan roared. He gripped her hair and pulling her face around towards him.

Christa saw the insanity in his eyes and swallowed. 'What do you want?' she whispered.

'Look at me, you bitch. You think what I do is disgusting, but you're the corrupt one. Sticking your nose in, before twisting the knife. It's all about manipulation with you. So how do you feel now? Now *I'm* the one in control.'

Her mind went into overload. Why hadn't she foreseen this? *He's a fucking Gestapo officer.* 'Please, Stefan…I'm your friend.'

Stefan laughed. 'Don't try that on me.' The grip on her hair tightened, then her head rushed forwards as he slammed her face against the wall. Her head spun, and she struggled to orientate. She remained silent, hoping he'd keep talking, buying some time. Christa forced herself to focus through the pain.

'You bitch. We were never friends. I want my face to be the last thing you see.'

His words were another punch to the gut. Stefan meant to kill her. He held her hair tight again, forcing her to look as his fingers dug into a pocket. Her addled brain struggled to comprehend his actions, and then she saw the capsule in his hand.

'No.' She groaned, pulling back but powerless to remove herself from Stefan's grasp. This wasn't happening. Her arms flailed, but Stefan swatted them aside with a delighted smile. Her hand dropped to her thighs, and through the fog of pain, she remembered the dagger. Without breaking eye contact, her fingers slid towards the hem of her skirt. She couldn't signal her intent. Her fingers inched slowly upwards.

Just a bit more, release the clasp, stab Stefan and it'll all be over. Her eyes flickered with pain and concentration. *Come on, seize the weapon. Do it.* The simple eye flick was all she needed. She gripped the handle and swung the knife in an arc. The blade connected with Stefan's hand, triggering a surprised scream as the cyanide capsule flew off across the floor. His hand swung back in a slap, and Christa's head snapped to one side. Another blow landed, then another. Blood merged with her tears, and all strength deserted her. She slumped on the floor and cried. Not from the pain, but from the knowledge that nobody would come.

****

Ingrid pushed Hector to one side, silencing him with a stare. If

Stefan was here, she wanted to be the first to confront him. Memories of the day she'd fought him off with a pitchfork fuelled her ire. With blood pumping furiously, she turned the handle and silently pushed the door open. As the group entered the hallway, they knew something was terribly wrong on the floor above. Gripping the Walther she'd stolen months earlier, Ingrid tested the first step. It bowed slightly under her weight, and she adjusted her position toward the outside of each step before moving upwards. The ominous thumping from above continued. Each bang, triggering a pause. At the sound of the scream, Ingrid threw caution and bounded up the remaining steps.

The legs of a female twitched on the landing floorboards. Christa, Ingrid assumed, though the doorframe obscured her upper body. She barrelled into the bedroom, colliding with a man and sending them both sprawling. The collision forced her to land awkwardly, sending a jolt of pain through her elbow, but she wasn't about to let Stefan recover. She rolled, wincing as her supporting arm dug into the floor, and then she rose and faced her enemy.

'You.' There was a look of shock on Stefan's face, but something more: fear.

With Hector and Gerda were near, Ingrid retrieved her pistol and levelled it at her nemesis. She nodded and Hector swept forward, unleashing a vicious punch, which sent Stefan sprawling. Then, under Ingrid's watchful gaze, he disarmed the Nazi.

She'd waited a lifetime for this moment, and now it was here. All thoughts of learning secrets of the German rocket program dissolved, as the desire for retribution flooded Ingrid's body. She remembered the last time she'd seen him in *Bremen*, and her utter paralysis and fear. Now Stefan showed panic and disbelief at their sudden appearance. With Hector holding Stefan's Walther, she cut her eyes away. Gerda had helped Christa up, supporting the woman from behind. The girl looked in a bad way, with one eye swollen almost to closing, her breathing ragged.

There was an unmistakable pause as Christa recognised her saviours. Then she emitted a gurgling sound as she pointed across the room. Ingrid tracked the finger and immediately understood. A pill, standing proud against the floorboard.

A multitude of thoughts crossed Ingrid's mind. Then she reached a decision. 'Hold him,' she barked to Hector.

Stefan struggled against Hector's grip before a pistol whip to the head forced compliance.

Ingrid picked up the cyanide and smiled as Stefan registered her plan. They had the untouchable Nazi man ensnared in a net of no escaping, reduced to a whimpering animal. She stepped in front of him, taunting him, waving the pill across his eyeline. As the capsule danced across her fingers, Ingrid heard Christa's voice from behind.

'Let it be me.'

With a mixture of regret and relief, Ingrid nodded. Supported by Gerda, Christa lurched across the floor. Stefan's body erupted in a frenzy; legs and arms lashing out, but with four standing over him, the man succumbed. Hector held his head back as Christa forced the pill into his mouth. Then, together, they pinched Stefan's nose while clamping hands across his lips.

Ingrid considered looking away. But this man had inflicted so much pain on her family, and if she could gain any honour from the moment, it was by witnessing Stefan's demise. She knelt on the floor with the others and held the monster down until his movements subsided. She gazed across the body at Hector, who gave a brief nod of confirmation.

No one spoke. Ingrid, Hector, and Gerda stood up, leaving Christa slumped against the body of Stefan. Ingrid looked at her face. Battered, broken, and ultimately confused. Christa hated the Jews, yet one had saved her.

The trio left Christa in the upstairs room, retrieved their bikes, and pedalled back into the city.

129

DECEMBER 1944, YIEWSLEY

Archie pushed at the creaking gate and wondered what kind of welcome he'd receive. Years had passed since he'd stepped along this path, but it was like coming home.

He pushed at the door handle and stepped across the threshold. Florrie was there, standing in the kitchen, and upon seeing him, her eyes lit up. She rushed across the room, hands covered in flour, and swept him into a hug. He gave an involuntary grunt at the welcome.

She pulled away, catching the grimace on his face. 'What? she said. 'What's wrong?'

'It's all right. Just hurts a bit, still. Where the bullet hit, and like.'

'Oh, my days. I'm so sorry. I…' Archie saw the shock on her face and held out his good arm to steady her.

'Easy now,' he said as he drew a chair and lowered her onto it. 'I'll be fine, just as long as nobody pokes or prods. Though I don't suppose Mister Flannigan will have me lugging coal for a while.'

Allowing Florrie time to recover, the pair chatted, bringing each other up to date. Archie's old boss and indeed the entire coal merchant enterprise were no more. Obliterated in a *Luftwaffe* bombing raid two years earlier. The dairy was still standing, although Florrie couldn't say what had happened to the staff. Archie learnt they'd coughed up for a new cart for Roy when he returned to work. It was clear Florrie hated the demands of the round, placed upon Roy, but money was short.

'Roy will be home soon, and you can tell us about your adventures.'

Archie smiled. Glad to be accepted, though reluctant to recount the horrors he'd seen. They stayed in the kitchen, as the only warm room in the house, and recognising Archie's hunger, Florrie returned to her baking.

'Don't ask what's gone into this.' She grinned as Archie took a mouthful of cake. The cake at first had a chalky texture. The next mouthful was slimy with the taste of stewed vegetables, while another chunk seemed the opposite, almost gritty in texture. But it was food, and Archie woofed the remaining piece and smiled. 'We've lived on a diet of tinned beef and little else, so this, whatever this is, it goes down a treat.'

The light was fading when Roy returned. Archie noticed that despite the new cart, the round was becoming too much for his adoptive uncle. Before the war, he'd have finished by mid-afternoon. He hugged Roy at an angle to avoid any press against his wound, before Florrie yanked her husband away.

'Get off him, you old sod. Can't you see he's carrying an injury?'

Roy stepped back, bewildered at Florrie's forceful intervention, before Archie moved to calm the situation. 'It's all right, it's all right. He can't see with me wearing a full-length coat, can he?' He quickly winked at Florrie, and said, 'How about a pot of tea?' Florrie took his hint and set about making a drink.

The older couple insisted Archie stay overnight. It was the first time in years he'd felt safe. Even his evacuation from Italy by hospital ship had been fraught with danger. They were beyond Gibraltar before he'd regained consciousness, though he'd heard hair-raising tales of their exit from Italy. The best news was that the Polish soldier he'd rescued had survived. Archie didn't feel so bad about abandoning his mates after that. He'd saved a man's life, and getting shot was a small price to pay.

The following morning, Archie declined Florrie's offer of a single egg for breakfast, knowing she may not see another for a while. Instead, he took another slice of cake before setting off. Overnight the confection had dried a little, which took the edge off the steeped vegetables. It would keep him going for a few hours.

Officially, they hadn't demobbed Archie, and there was a risk they could throw him back into the fray, but for now, he had free rein to recuperate. Once he'd completed the walk to West Drayton station, he knew things would be different. His uniform made sure of that. Strangers shook his hand and patted his shoulders, in blissful ignorance of the bullet wound only a few inches away. He didn't mind. It was in stark contrast to the horror of war, and their friendliness warmed his heart.

The train took an age to arrive. Archie thought back to another train ride, years ago, with Dieter and Ingrid. Today wasn't about Ingrid, as it seemed he'd lost her to the war machine. But a memorial visit to pay respects to Dieter's memory, along with a visit to Rabbi Cohen, seemed appropriate.

Eventually, the train reached Aldgate, and Archie exited the station. He felt momentarily disoriented. He recognised the streets and the tramlines which ran across his path, but the neighbourhood took on an alien landscape. Whitechapel had taken an absolute battering. He was glad to have fought against the people who'd done this, but his heart fell as he saw ruin after crumbling ruin. And yet, despite the devastation, East End workers offered stoic cheer. As Archie approached Rabbi Cohen's home, his disquiet grew. The side streets stood deserted and when he reached Philpott Street, he realised his worst fears. The German bombers had obliterated the synagogue.

Archie sank to his knees. He should have foreseen this. *Where is he? Where is the rabbi?* He was oblivious to the cold, but as rain fell, Archie felt a hand on his shoulders.

'Come on, lad. You can't stay down there. You'll catch a chill.'

He shook his head, knowing the strange woman meant well, but with her help, he regained his feet. 'Do you know what happened to the rabbi?'

499

The pair stood under a shop awning and chatted until it became clear the frail lady was suffering from the cold.

Archie walked back to Aldgate station and by the time he arrived, he'd developed a new resolve. He had no clue where they'd evacuated little Millie, but with her father lost, Archie was determined to find her and bring her home.

130

APRIL 1945, BERLIN

Christa bit down on her lip as she followed the others. They hadn't said what would happen, though she feared the worst. The huge metal door she'd just passed through clanged shut, sealing them in. She'd been to the Reich Chancellery building before, but this was her first visit to the *Führerbunker*. From outside, the monolith was nondescript, with only a small cone-shaped turret marking it out from other buildings.

They moved downward through a tunnel under the guidance of flickering bulbs. She knew most who were there: Hitler, Eva Braun, Otto Günsche, Hitler's personal adjutant, and further ahead, Josef Goebbels, and his family. Now, more than ever, she yearned for the fresh air and open spaces of Bavaria.

Hitler had been here since the beginning of the year, leaving Christa to wonder why he'd summoned her now. There was a rumour he'd married a day earlier, though their current actions hardly felt like a celebration. At the bottom of the stairs, Günsche led Hitler, Braun, and Christa into a small anti-room. Another metal door closed behind them. Barring a solitary desk and chair, the room lacked any furnishings.

The *Führer* whispered some instructions which Christa failed to hear. Her mouth dry with anticipation, she watched Hitler step forward and grasp Eva by the shoulder. Christa was used to the man's strong physical presence, but she now noticed his haggard looks and shaking hands. Leading his new bride to the chair, Hitler settled her down before offering a small parcel wrapped in a handkerchief. Braun unwrapped the gift and then, to Christa's horror, the woman calmly swallowed the pill. Christa held back the scream forming in her throat. As Braun's breathing became more laboured, Hitler placed a delicate kiss on his wife's brow before doing the unthinkable. Her leader drew his Walther, set the pistol to his temple, and pulled the trigger.

Christa's legs slipped from beneath her.

'Komm, Christa. Komm.'

The order barely registered until someone shook her violently, forcing her to focus. *Herr* Hitler was dead. His face a mask, Günsche called the remaining troops to action. Two stretchers appeared, and within seconds, Christa gripped a corner, ready to lift. It took just five minutes to get Hitler and Braun out of the bunker. Christa worked on autopilot, oblivious to the blood seeping into her blouse. The *Führer*'s arm slumped over the side of the stretcher, and she mechanically moved it back into place. It was still warm.

The group laid the pair down on the grass. Christa watched, numb, as they bought fuel canisters forward and poured across the corpses. Even as the flames engulfed the pair, Christa couldn't comprehend what had happened. Günsche pulled her away from the flames. Her arms flailed as she sought answers. 'What now?' she cried.

Günsche pointed about. 'Russians, Americans, the English...take your pick.'

Christa stared back at him. The fairy tale was over; the spell broken. She was utterly alone, and there was no escape.

131

APRIL 1949, *DACHAU*

They'd waited until the spring thaw before travelling. Ingrid stepped off the bus and stared at the coils of barbed wire atop the outer perimeter fence before standing to one side to allow Archie and Millie to pass. The bus pulled away, leaving the trio to look on as their transport bounced away along the rutted track.

Ingrid's face pinched with emotion as examined the camp. She'd heard the stories. Emaciated bodies, tortured souls, crushed beyond recognition. Her father lay out there. And that was why they'd come.

Regret overwhelmed her. She should have done more. Perhaps if she'd jumped off the train in Munich with her brother and overcome Stefan and his guards, things would have turned out differently. It was a delusion, but there was a vicious joy in revisiting it.

She was also beset with guilt that they'd brought Millie along, but Ingrid had admitted defeat early on. At nearly twenty, their adoptive daughter had flatly refused to remain behind, and had even paid her share of the passage. The trio linked hands and walked down the road toward the gates.

Before he succumbed to lung cancer, Gregson had greased the wheels to allow their visit. Ingrid remained anxious about admittance, and she hoped his paperwork would gain entry. In a rare moment of honesty, Gregson had shared other details, too. After the Allied liberation, there were reprisals. Ingrid listened with little emotion. The camp guards had committed unspeakable acts. She would sleep well, knowing that they would suffer as much as her father. But there was a lingering sadness that she couldn't unleash her wrath at the SS officers held interned at the end of the war. The camp victims and the imprisoned German SS officers, now mere ghosts, absent or unreachable.

Spring had not touched the camp. The ground was bare, the bloodied landscape tainted in shame. Ingrid slowed her pace. The camp was no longer the site of vile atrocities, though it remained occupied. Now guards kept vigil over a poor, displaced population. Germans, Czechs, and others from the east. Hounded from their lands by an encroaching Russian army.

So much suffering, so much grief. Ingrid remained lost in thought until Millie spoke up.

'We can do this. And then, once we've made our peace, you can take us to your old home in *Berchtesgaden*. I know it hurts, but we're here with you. Every step of the way.'

Her adopted daughter's words warmed Ingrid's heart. She swept the younger woman into an embrace. 'You're right,' she said 'We can do this. There are brighter days ahead, and let's not forget about Gerda and Hector's wedding.'

Ingrid stepped up to the *Dachau* guard post. It was time to leave the past in the past. She glanced up at Archie and saw the love in his eyes. Her heart fluttered as he took her hand in his. As one, the trio entered the camp.

It was over. Time for a new beginning.

The End

ACKNOWLEDGEMENTS AND ADDITIONAL NOTES

FROM ALISTAIR

I would like to take this opportunity to offer my personal thanks to a few people who have helped get this book written. My greatest gratitude falls to two amazing people, one in the UK with me and the other across the opposite side of the world. At home, thank you to my wife, Claire, whose unwavering support gives me the freedom to write. And overseas to my fantastic co-author, Kim Rigby. These are two of the kindest people you could ever wish to know.

With this project, and everything she does, Kim's patience, intelligence and creativity shine out from her pages and bring a lot of much-needed balance to this story. She also has an expert eye for detail.

Thanks also to my wonderful beta readers: Luke Afford, Dawn Ilsley, Megan Ilsley, DeeAnn Magboul, and Dawn Angels. Your feedback and support are invaluable.

FROM KIM

Alistair and I 'met' via a Facebook writing group some years ago, and I admired his work from afar – literally, as I live in Australia, while Alistair lives in the UK.

We discussed the possibility of collaborating, and I realised I could bring my knowledge of German history to the table. In addition, I have had the privilege of visiting various parts of Germany, including Ingrid's beautiful hometown of *Berchtesgaden*.

I am immensely grateful to have taken this journey with Alistair, who, as a published author, has masterfully guided us through the process. His skill as a thriller writer is self-evident in every action scene in this story.

On a personal level, Alistair's kindness and encouragement have seen me through many dark days over the past year.

FROM BOTH

While *The Girl from Berchtesgaden* is a work of fiction, there is plenty of truth in the story. We hope we transported you to a new world with characters you'll remember.

Roy and Florrie Nash, and even Smiler the horse really existed, living in Yiewsley, albeit post war. Archie Afford was a wonderful, super cheeky chappie, taken too young. The real Archie left us at just two years old, sadly losing his battle with leukaemia. With family permission, we've included his name in this novel as a tribute to what could have happened had Archie survived into adulthood. Archie lives on in our hearts and in the pages of this novel, we hope we have done his memory justice.

Other characters like Ingrid, Gerda, Christa, Stefan, and Hector are purely fictitious, although many such conflicted characters lived through the war, interacting with real-world figures from history.

And lastly, our thanks go to you, the reader.

You are a critical part of this cyclic process. We write, you read and then, with luck, we all enjoy and go again.

We hope you loved this novel as much as we enjoyed writing it. And if you did, then please show your support by leaving a review and telling friends. As independent authors, support like this means the world.

Thank you for coming with us on this journey.

Alistair & Kim x

Printed in Great Britain
by Amazon

62914336R00296